Critics and Authors praise
THE OTHER END OF TIME

"Award-winning veteran writer-editor Pohl takes a hoary science fiction cliché—alien abduction—and turns it on its head.

"An impeccably crafted, absorbing, and enjoyable reworking of mostly familiar material that, while satisfyingly self-contained, seems perfectly poised for sequels."

—*Kirkus Reviews*

"Frederik Pohl hasn't been named a Grand Master for nothing. *The Other End of Time* is a nonstop intellectual treat—the thinking person's *Independence Day*."

—Greg Bear

"If you read science fiction in search of wonder or read anything for sheer suspense, read Frederik Pohl's *The Other End of Time*! The characters are very human humans and a wild mix of aliens. Their story of the eschaton held me to the final page. It strikes me as the ultimate adventure possible in our universe."

—Jack Williamson

"The story is conceived and executed with Pohl's usual acumen."

—*Publishers Weekly*

BOOKS BY FREDERIK POHL

*denotes a Tor Book

FREDERIK
POHL
THE
OTHER END OF TIME

TOR®

A TOM DOHERTY ASSOCIATES BOOK
NEW YORK

This is a work of fiction. All the characters and events portrayed in this book are either products of the author's imagination or are used fictitiously.

THE OTHER END OF TIME

Copyright © 1996 by Frederik Pohl

All rights reserved, including the right to reproduce this book, or portions thereof, in any form.

Cover art by John Harris

Edited by James Frenkel

A Tor Book
Published by Tom Doherty Associates, Inc.
175 Fifth Avenue
New York, NY 10010

Tor Books on the World Wide Web:
http://www.tor.com

Tor® is a registered trademark of Tom Doherty Associates, Inc.

ISBN: 0-812-53519-7
Library of Congress Card Catalog Number: 96-8297

First edition: October 1996
First mass market edition: July 1997

Printed in the United States of America

0 9 8 7 6 5 4 3 2 1

THE
OTHER END OF TIME

BEFORE

WHEN THE FIRST MESSAGE FROM SPACE ARRIVED ON EARTH, five people who were on their way to the eschaton were busy at their own affairs. For one, Dr. Pat Adcock was having a really bad day with her accountant in New York. For another, Commander (or, actually, by then already ex-Commander) Jimmy Peng-tsu Lin was on the lanai of his mother's estate on Maui, glumly running up his mother's telephone bill with fruitless begging calls to every influential person he knew. Major General Martín Delasquez had just been given his second star by the high governor of the sovereign state of Florida. *Doctorat-nauk* (emeritus) Rosaleen Artzybachova was discontentedly trying to make the time pass with chess-by-fax games against a variety of opponents from her boring retirement dacha outside of Kiev. And Dan Dannerman was holed up in a seedy pension in Linz, Province of Austria. He was hiding from the *Bundes Kriminalamt* with a woman named Ilse, who was by profession an enforcer for the terrorist Free Bavaria Bund, more commonly referred to as the Mad King Ludwigs. (Dannerman himself was a mere courier in the same group.) Most of these five people had not even met each other yet. Pat Adcock, being an astronomer by profession, might conceivably have had some rough idea of how the message would affect all their lives—though even she couldn't have known just how, or how very much. None of the others could have had a clue.

All the same, all five of them were, in varying degrees, startled, thrilled or frightened by the message, because nearly everybody in the world was. What would you expect?

It was a major historical event. It was definitely the very first time that the patient astronomers who tended the SETI telescopes, or for that matter anybody else, had received an authentic, guaranteed alien message from an extraterrestrial source.

Of course, that left a lot of large questions. Not even the few dogged hangers-on in the nearly extinct SETI program had been able to interpret what the message said, either, except for a few fragments. The dits and dahs of the radio signal were not Morse code. They were certainly not in English, either—were not, in fact, in any recognizable language of any variety; unless pictures are considered to be a language of sorts. When the signals had been painstakingly massaged by some of the world's biggest and fastest computers, which they naturally were very quickly, it turned out that at least one chunk of the message wasn't in words at all. It was in pictures. When the bits were properly arranged, what they displayed was an animated diagram.

In their hideout on the Bonnerstrasse, Dannerman and his girl watched it over and over on their wall screen, Dannerman with curiosity, Ilse with only cursory attention. She was one of the very few who didn't give a hoot in hell what the stars had to say. Even her cursory interest didn't last, since whatever this bit of drek from space was meant to convey, she declared, it certainly had nothing whatever to do with the unswerving determination of the Mad King Ludwigs to free Bavaria from the cruel Prussian grip—to which liberation at any cost, she reminded him, they had both agreed to dedicate their lives.

As a matter of fact, the diagram really wasn't much to look at. That didn't keep the channels from repeating it endlessly, usually with some voice-over commentary provided by somebody who possessed several scientific degrees and a passion for seeing himself on TV. The commentaries varied, but the diagram was always the same. First the screen was dark, except for one tiny brilliant spot in the middle of it. Then an explosion sent a myriad smaller, less bright spots flying in all directions. The expansion slowed, followed by a general contraction as all the specks slowly, then more rapidly, fell back to the center of the screen. Then the central bright spot reappeared . . . and then the commentators took over.

"Unquestionably there is much more to the message," one said—this one an elderly *Herr Doktor* from the astronomy department of the University of Vienna, "but we cannot decipher the remainder as yet. That is a great pity, since as you see the diagram by itself is quite uninformative in the absence of the rest of the message. This segment, by itself, is no more than perhaps five per cent of the total transmission, merely the first few seconds. We have not been able to decode the rest. Still, I believe I can interpret what that fragment is intended to show. It is nothing less than a description of the history of our universe, compressing to a few seconds a process which in fact will require many tens of billions of years. The model begins by showing the tiny and—I must confess, even to those of us who have given our lives to the subject—the quite incomprehensible quantal-realm object that preceded the birth of the universe. Then the object explodes, in what is called the Big Bang, and the universe as we know it begins. It expands—as we actually do see the universe doing now, when we measure the red-shifts with our telescopes. Finally it contracts again in what the Americans call the 'Big Crunch.' "

"Big Crunch! What nonsense. Come to bed now," Ilse said crossly. "You have seen all that a hundred times at least, Walter."

"You don't have to call me by my party name here," Dannerman said absently, watching the screen. The *Herr Doktor* had begun talking about Stephen Hawking's theory of repetitive universes, just as he had the last three times Dannerman had watched that particular interview.

"Do not tell me what to do. You are a dilettante," she said severely, "or you would not say a thing like that. It is basic doctrine, which you have not adequately studied: There is no security ever unless there is security always."

"I suppose so," he said, his attention still on the screen. He switched channels until he found the diagram on another newscast.

"You are impossible," she told him. "At least turn down that totally useless sound. I am going to sleep."

"Fine," he said, but he did as she asked. He didn't look away from the wall screen, however, in spite of the fact that he was beginning to be as tired of the damn thing as she. What Dannerman wanted was something different. He wanted her to go to sleep without him; and when at last her gentle, ladylike snores assured him that that had happened he moved silently to the door, collecting his down jacket on the way, and slipped out.

He wasn't gone long, but when he came back Ilse was sitting on the edge of the bed, arms crossed, wide awake, greeting him with a glare. She was quite a pretty woman most of the time, but, in this mood, not. "Where were you?" she demanded.

He said apologetically, "I just wanted some fresh air."

"Fresh air? In Linz?"

"Well, a change of scene, anyway. And, all right, I stopped in the *bierstube* for a drink. What do you want from me, Ilse—I mean, Brunnhilde? I get tired of being jailed twenty-four hours a day in this dump."

"Dump! Your words show your class origins, Walter. In any case, what I want from you is proper dedication to our cause. Also, if you were seen you would become far more tired, because in five minutes they would have you in a real jail."

"Hell, uh, Brunnhilde. The Bay-Kahs aren't looking for us in Austria, are they? Anyway, that was part of the reason I went out. I wanted to see if anybody was watching the pension. Nobody is."

"And how would you know if they were, dilettante? Security is my task, not yours, Walter. Did you telephone anyone?"

"Why would I go outside to telephone?" he asked reasonably. It wasn't a lie; Dan Dannerman preferred not to lie when a simple deception would do.

"So." She studied him for a moment; then, "All the same," she said, softening slightly, "you are not entirely wrong. I too would like to leave this place. It is in Bavaria that we are needed, not here."

"We'll be there soon," he said, trying to make her feel better. The funny part was that he did want her to feel better. All right, the woman was a criminal terrorist, a known killer with blood on her hands, but he had to admit to himself that he was—almost—fond of her anyway. He had noticed that about himself before. He often came to like the people he put in prison, though that didn't keep him from putting them there anyway.

He reached for the control for the wall screen, and Ilse

moaned. "Oh, my God, you are not going to turn that on again? It is not of any importance to us."

"It's just interesting," he said apologetically.

"Interesting! We have no room in our lives for what is only 'interesting'! Walter, Walter. Sometimes I think you are not a true revolutionary at all."

Of course, she did not know then just how right she was about that, and by the time she found out much had happened. For one thing, the second message from space had arrived. That was the one that showed the furry, Hallowe'en-grinning scarecrow creature with the twelve sharp talons on each fist crushing the Big Crunch in his paw, and, one after another, the seven other aliens, picture-in-picture like little cameos surrounding a central figure, that went with it.

No one knew quite what to make of it, though there were plenty of speculations. In their nightclub routines the world's standup comics had a wonderful time with this brand-new material. It was one of them who christened the seven peripheral aliens the "Seven Dwarfs," and another who claimed that the whole message was either an alien political broadcast or part of some ET children's horror animation film, inadvertently transmitted to all the billions of nonpaying viewers on Earth. The more easily frightened scientists—plus every buck-hustling guru of every bizarre religious cult in the world—thought it was more likely to be some kind of a warning.

They didn't know just how astonishingly right they were, either.

For all of the persons involved, by that time a great deal had changed in their personal lives as well. Dan Dannerman, having finished his assignment with the Mad King Ludwigs, was busily infiltrating a dope ring in New York City. And Ilse, glumly marching around the exercise yard of the maximum-security prison at Darmstadt, was cursing the day she'd ever met the man.

CHAPTER ONE

Dan

When Jim Daniel Dannerman heard the WHEEP-*wawp* of the police sirens, he was on the way from his family lawyer's office to his cousin's observatory to beg for a job. The sirens gave him a moment's confusion, so that for the blink of an eye he could not remember which one he was going to see, the autocratic career woman who was the head of the Dannerman Astrophysical Observatory or the five-year-old girl who had peed her pants in the tree house on his uncle's estate. He was also already en route to the eschaton, though, to be sure, with a weary long way still to go. He didn't know that was true yet, of course. He had never heard of the eschaton then, and after the first moment he didn't pay much attention to the sirens, either. City people didn't. Cop chases were a normal part of the urban acoustic environment, and anyway Dannerman was busy accessing information that might come in handy on his new assignment. He had been listening to the specs of the Starcophagus, the abandoned astronomical satellite that had suddenly seemed to become important to the Bureau, when the shriek of the stop-all-traffic alarm drowned everything else out. Every light turned red, and he was thrown forward as the taxi driver slammed on the brakes.

Every other vehicle at that intersection was doing the same thing, because the ugly stop-all enforcer spikes were already thrusting up out of the roadway. In the front of the cab his driver cursed and pounded the wheel. "Goddam cops! Goddam spikes! Listen, they blow one more set of tires on me and I swear to God I'm gonna get rid of this crappy little peashooter I been carrying and get me a *real* gun. And then I'm gonna take that gun and—"

Dannerman stopped listening before she got to the ways in which she was going to take the city's police system on single-handed. He was watching the drama being played out at the intersection. The car that was being pursued had tried to make it through the intersection in spite of the spikes, and naturally every tire had been stabbed flat; the three youths inside had spilled out and tried to get away on foot, dodging among the jam of stalled vehicles. They weren't going to make it, though. Police were coming at them on foot from all directions. The running cops were weighed down by radio, sting-stick, crowd-control tear-gas gun, assault gun and body armor, but there were too many of them for the criminals. The police had the kids well surrounded. Dannerman watched the fugitives being captured with mild professional interest—after all, he was in the law-enforcement business himself, sort of.

His driver perked up a little. "Looks like they got 'em. Listen, mister, I'm sorry about the delay, but they'll have the spikes down again any minute now—"

Dannerman said, "No problem. I've got time before my appointment."

It didn't placate her. "Sure, you've got time, but what about me? I'm stuck trying to make a goddam living in this goddam town—"

The thing was, she had one of those Seven Stupid Alien figures hanging from her rearview mirror and it was singing out of its picochip the whole time she was talking, a shrill obbligato behind her hoarse complaints. That wasn't particularly odd. There were pictures of the aliens all over the place. On the kids being arrested, belly-down on the pavement: the backs of their jackets displayed little cartoon figures of the alien they called

Sneezy—gang colors, those were; but even his lawyer's secretary had had a coffee mug in the shape of another on her desk. The taxi driver's singing good-luck piece was the fat one named Sleepy, for its half-closed eyes—well, there were three of the eyes, actually, on a head that was maned like a lion's. It wasn't much like the ancient Disney original, but then neither were the secretary's Doc or the gangbangers' Sneezy.

It was an odd thing, when you thought about it, that the hideous space aliens had become children's toys and everybody's knickknacks. Colonel Hilda had had an explanation for it. It was like the dinosaurs of a generation or two earlier, she told him on the phone: something so horrible and dangerous that people had to translate it into something cuddly, because otherwise it was too frightening. Then she had gone on to tell him that the space message might, or might not, be relevant to his new assignment, but it wasn't his job to ask questions about it, it was his job only to close out his assignment to the Carpezzios' drug ring and get cracking on the new job.

It wasn't the first time she'd explained all that to him, either, because that was the way it was in the NBI.

That, of course, Dannerman didn't need to be told. After thirteen years in the National Bureau of Investigation, he knew the drill.

The funny thing was that Dannerman had never set out to be a spook. When the college freshman Jim Daniel Dannerman signed up for the Police Reserve Officers Training Corps he was nineteen years old, and the last thing in his mind was the choice of a career. What he was after was a couple of easy credit hours, while he went about the business of preparing himself for a career in live theater. He hadn't read the fine print. All the way through his undergraduate program and even in graduate school it had meant nothing but a couple of hours a week in his reserve uniform, plus a few weekends; By the time he did read it—very carefully, this time—it was his last day of graduate school, and he had just received his orders to report for active duty.

By then, of course, it was a lot too late to change his mind. But it hadn't been a bad life. When you worked for the Bureau you went to interesting places and you got to meet a lot of interesting people. The downside was that sometimes you had a pretty good chance of getting killed by some of those interesting people, but so far he'd been lucky about that.

The other downside was that when you had to go under cover there was always the problem of remembering all the lies about who you were and where you'd been all your life. That was one of the things that made the new assignment look pretty good. As the colonel had explained, the only identity he had to assume was his own. Indeed, the fact that he was a sort of relative of the person under investigation was what made him the best choice for the job.

Dannerman snapped off the portable and leaned back, closing his eyes. He hardly noticed when the traffic jam began to dissolve, because he was working out just what he wanted to say in the interview with his cousin. There wasn't much doubt that he would get the job he was going to apply for—the lawyer had all but promised that. Dannerman was pretty sure the old man meant it, if only because he had a little bit of a guilty conscience over Dannerman's lost inheritance. But it would be embarrassing if he was turned down. He was surprised when the taxi stopped. "Here you are, mister," the driver said, friendlier now when tipping time was near. She pulled the slip with the ten-o'clock fare update out of the meter and handed it to him, peering over his shoulder at the plaque over the building door. "Hey. What's this T. Cuthbert Dannerman Astrophysical Observatory business? I thought telescopes were, you know, like on the top of a mountain someplace."

Dannerman glanced at the midtown skyscraper that housed

the observatory and grinned at the woman. "Actually," he said as he paid the bill, "until this morning, so did I."

Time was, indeed, when astronomers shared the night with the bats and the burglars, huddling their freezing buns in drafty domes on the tops of snow-clad mountains. If they wanted to peer far into space, they had no choice. That was where the telescopes were. That was time past. In time present the camera had made the all-night vigils unnecessary. The spread of electronic communication and control exempted the astronomers from having even to show up anywhere near their telescopes—and the best of the world's telescopes, or at least the ones of that kind that were still working, weren't where they were easy to visit anyway. Like the Starcophagus, they were in orbit. But wherever the data came from, they arrived—processed, enhanced, computerized, digitalized—at an observatory comfortably located in some civilized place.

Uncle Cubby's final gift to the world of astronomy occupied the top floors of the building, but of course there were turnstiles and guards between the street door and the elevators. Dannerman presented himself at the lobby desk and announced his name. That drew interest from the guard. "You a relative?" he asked.

"Nephew," Dannerman admitted. "Mr. Dixler made an appointment for me to see Dr. Adcock."

"Yes, sir," the guard said, suddenly deferential. "I'll have to ask you to wait over there until someone can show you to Dr. Adcock's office. It'll just be a moment."

It wasn't just a moment, though. Dannerman hadn't expected that it would be. The observatory's private elevator doors opened and closed a dozen times before a large, sullen man came out and lumbered over to the holding pen. He was not deferential at all. "You the guy from Dixler, J. D. Dannerman? Show me some ID." He didn't offer to shake hands. When he had checked the card he passed Dannerman through the turnstiles and into an elevator, and only then introduced himself. "I'm Mick Jarvas, Dr. Adcock's personal assistant. Give me your gun."

Dannerman took his twenty-shot from his shoulder holster and passed it over. "Do I get a receipt?"

The man looked at the weapon with contempt. "I'll remember where I got it, don't worry. Who's this Dixler?"

"Family lawyer."

"Huh. Okay. Wait here. Janice'll tell you when you can go in." That ended the conversation, and Dannerman was left to sit in the waiting room. It didn't bother him. It gave him a chance to see what a modern astrophysical observatory was like. This one wasn't like the mountaintop domes he remembered from his childhood. It was full of people glimpsed down corridors, elderly men talking to young dark-skinned women in saris, groups drinking Cokes or herbal tea out of the machines, a couple of people sharing the waiting room with him and improving their waiting time by talking business on their pocket phones. What interested him most was the big liquid-crystal screen behind the receptionist's desk. It was showing a great pearly mural that he recognized as a picture of a galaxy, some galaxy or other; switched to a picture of what he took to be an exploding star; switched again to a huge photograph of an orbiting observatory. He had no trouble recognizing that. It was the one he had been studying on the way over; it was also, he was aware, the gift that had eaten up half of Uncle Cubby's fortune before he died. The observatory was Starlab—sometime uncharitably called Starcophagus, for the dead astronomer who was still orbiting inside it. Starlab was the ancient, biggest and best—but unfortunately no longer operational—astronomical orbiter of them all.

Dan Dannerman's only previous experience of an astronomical facility had been when he was four years old and his father had taken him to visit Uncle Cubby in the old optical observatory in Arizona. Starlab was quite different, and all the engineering specs he'd been able to dig out of the databank didn't make it real for him. Getting up, he strolled over to the reception desk and cleared his throat. "Janice? I mean, I don't know your last name—"

"Janice is good enough," she said agreeably. "And you're Mr. Dannerman."

"Dan. I noticed you were showing the Starcophagus on the wall a minute ago—" She had begun shaking her head. "Is something wrong?"

"Dr. Adcock doesn't like us ever to use that word here. It's the Dannerman Astrophysical Starlab. Mostly we just call it Starlab."

"Thanks," he said, meaning it; it was a useful bit of information for someone who was about to ask the boss for a favor.

"It used to be the Dannerman Orbiting Astrolab," she went on, looking him over, "but Dr. Adcock changed that. Because of, you know, the initials."

"Oh, right," he said, nodding. "DOA. I see what you mean. I guess nobody wants to be reminded about the dead guy up there. Anyway, I was wondering if you could fill me in a little bit. I understand, uh, Dr. Adcock's trying to get a mission flown to reactivate it."

"There's talk," she admitted cautiously.

"Well, when's that going to happen, do you know?"

"No idea," she said cheerfully. "You'd have to ask Dr. Adcock about that—wait a minute." She paused, squinting as she listened to the voice in her earpiece, and paid no further attention to him.

He went back and sat down. Evidently he was to be kept waiting for a while, as was appropriate for someone who wanted to ask a favor. He didn't mind. It was what he had expected from a cousin-by-marriage he hadn't seen for years, and wouldn't be seeing now if the Bureau had not taken a sudden and serious interest in just what the woman was up to.

CHAPTER TWO

Pat

Dr. Pat Adcock's morning was pure hell—crises in the money problem and the Starlab problem, not to mention all the usual flurry of regular observatory problems—but she took the long way from the bursar's office to Rosaleen Artzybachova's anyhow. That way passed by the reception room, and that let her get a quick look at her waiting cousin Dan.

She let him wait. She was impatient to hear what Rosaleen had to tell her about Starlab's instrumentation. Then the bursar had had no good news for her, and she needed to do a little thinking about that. She needed, too, to think about whether she wanted to go out of her way, at this particularly hectic time, to find some kind of spot on the staff for her job-seeking cousin. It was not a good time to be adding to the payroll. On the other hand—

On the other hand, family was family, and Pat wasn't displeased to have one of her few remaining relatives ask for a favor. Especially when the relative was Dan Dannerman. So she rushed through her meeting with Rosaleen Artzybachova, door closed and electronics off; the woman might be old but she was still sharp, and she was doing a good job of tracing the history of all the additions and retrofits Starlab had suffered in its observing career. "And there's nothing that would account for the radiation?" Pat demanded. "You're sure?"

The old lady looked up at her thoughtfully. "Are you getting enough exercise?" she asked. "You look like you could use some fresh air. Yes, I'm sure."

"Thanks," Pat said, not answering her question. But when she got back to her own office the first thing she did, even before she closed the door, was to study herself in the wall mirror. It wasn't really exercise she needed, she told herself. It was rest. A good night's sleep, for a start, and no worries. But what were the chances of that?

While Pat's office door was open the walls were displaying a selection of the major current projects of the observatory: the Lesser Magellanic Cloud, with its new gamma-ray bursters; the huge mass of neutral gas in Capricorn that Warren Krepps was investigating; and, just for the sake of prettiness, some particularly nice shots of nearby objects like Saturn, Phobos and the Moon. Those weren't really high-priority projects. The Dannerman Observatory didn't do much planetary astronomy, but the pictures were the kind of thing that impressed possible donors when, after leading them through the grand tour of the observatory, Pat took them into her office for the glass of wine and the kill.

When Pat closed her privacy door the display changed. Then what the walls showed was Starlab, and, on either side of it, like a portrait gallery, the images of the aliens from the space message. Pat didn't look at the freaks as she settled herself at her desk. She didn't need to; but she wanted them there, to remind her.

Time for Cousin Dan? She decided not; it wouldn't hurt him to sit a while longer, and there was still the business of the observatory to run. It took more than science to keep an enterprise like the Dannerman Observatory going.

After her name Patrice Dannerman Bly Metcalf Adcock was entitled to put the initials B.S., M.A., Ph.D., D.H.L. and Sc.D. Considering that she was still a young woman, not very much more than thirty (and looking younger still when she got enough sleep), that was quite a lot. To be sure, the last two degrees were honorary, being the kind of thing you got from small and hungry universities when you happened to be the head of an institution that might offer useful fellowships to underemployed faculty members, but she had truly earned all the rest.

The trouble was, they weren't enough. Why hadn't someone told her to slip a couple of economics and business-management classes in among the cosmologies and the histories of science? Her skills at reading a spectrogram were all very well, but what she really needed to understand was a spreadsheet.

And this morning, like most mornings, the problems were mostly money. Kit Papathanassiou was requesting twenty hours of observing time on the big Keck telescopes in Hawaii. Pat knew that Papathanassiou would make good use of the time, but the Kecks were a big-ticket item; she cut it to five hours. Gwen Morisaki wanted to hire another postdoc to help out with the Cepheid census in NGC 3821; but that job only amounted to counting, after all, and why did you need a doctoral degree for that? Cousin Dan? Probably not, Pat thought, and decided to offer Gwen an undergraduate intern from one of the local schools. That wouldn't save much money. You could hardly hire anybody for less than the average postdoc would gladly accept, but a dollar saved, plus its cost-of-living adjustment, was a dollar plus COLA earned. This month's communications bills were higher than ever; Pat reluctantly came to the conclusion that it was time for her to get on everybody's back again about keeping the phone bills down. She didn't look forward to it. Hassling the staff to watch pennies was not what she had earned all those degrees for. Maybe, if things got better—the way she dreamed they might, if the Starlab thing worked out . . .

But it was all taking so *long*.

That was a big disappointment. Pat had hoped that once the judge decreed that the feds were obliged to honor the contract

Uncle Cubby had made with them—had to provide a Clipper spacecraft to take a repair mission to Starlab and, what's more, had to pay for putting the old spacecraft into working order— why, then, the whole thing should have been automatic. It wasn't. The feds and the Floridians were dragging their feet. Somehow somebody somewhere in their bureaucracies had begun to suspect that she knew something they didn't.

Well, she did. And it was none of their damn business.

She leaned back and studied the pictures on the wall. Not the Starlab itself. She didn't need to look at that again; with Rosaleen Artzybachova's help she had already memorized every centimeter of that. What she was looking at was the freak show from the space messages. There were eight of the aliens, starting with the universe-crushing scarecrow, and every one of them was ugly. One looked like Pat's idea of a golem, huge bipedal body with some arms like elephant limbs and some like limp spaghetti, and the bearded head with its glaring eyes; that was the one the comics called "Doc." Another—the "Grumpy"— looked a little like a sea horse with legs; a third, the "Dopey," had a whiskered kitten's head on a chicken's body; another might have been a huge-eyed lemur if it weren't for its own extra pairs of limbs, and she couldn't recall what nonsensical name it had been given.

Pat closed her eyes and sighed. She wished, as half the world wished, that she knew why the unidentified transmitter of these unpleasing pictures had wanted humans to see them. What were these creatures? Not a zoo; these were not animals; most of them wore clothing, some carried artifacts of one kind or another—some that looked unpleasantly like weapons.

Of course, the fact that they had weapons didn't mean they were killers. Everybody carried weapons. Pat kept one on her person whenever she left her office or her home—not counting whatever additional firepower her bodyguard carried—and she certainly wasn't intending to shoot anybody. Unless, of course, she absolutely had to.

Which raised the question of under what circumstances the freaks might think they absolutely had to; but she didn't want to think about that. Pat Adcock had considered the possibility that some of those alien creatures might be hanging around somewhere in Earth orbit, where the mission to Starlab might encounter them, and decided that the odds were strongly against. There wasn't any reason to reconsider that question now—most likely.

She opened her eyes and looked at her watch.

Actually, she had kept Cousin Dan waiting long enough. She pushed the button that transformed her desk screen to a mirror, checked her hair and her face—yes, still not bad, in spite of what Rosaleen had said—then sighed, pushed the control that unlocked her door and restored her wall display to the one she was willing to let the world see and called the receptionist. "My cousin still out there, Janice? All right, then send him on in."

CHAPTER THREE

Dan

When Dannerman entered his cousin's office they didn't kiss. Nor did they shake hands, and she didn't even look up at him. Her attention was on her desk screen, displaying the resumé he had given Mr. Dixler to send over. "Says here you've got a Ph.D.—but it's in English literature, for Christ's sake? What the hell does Dixler think we're going to do with an English major here? Do you know anything at all about astronomy?"

"Not a thing," he said cheerfully, studying her: blue eyes, rusty brown hair, yes, that was the cousin he remembered, though now physically well matured. She was wearing a white lab coat, but it hung open. Under it was a one-piece skorts outfit, thermally dilated to adjust to room temperatures. She kept her office warm, so a lot of Pat Adcock showed through the mesh. At thirty-something she was almost as good-looking as pretty little Patty D. Bly had been when they were children; two marriages and a career had just made her taller and even more sure of herself. "I just happen to need a job pretty badly," he added.

She finally looked up to regard him thoughtfully, then smiled. "Anyway, hello. It's been a long time, Dan-Dan."

"It's just Dan now that I've grown up, Cousin Pat."

"And it's just *Doctor* Adcock if you're going to work here," she reminded him, a touch of steel peeking through the velvet. "I don't know about hiring you, though, Dan. It says here you got your doctorate at Harvard and your dissertation was called 'Between Two Worlds: Freud and Marx in the Plays of Elmer Rice.' Who the hell was he?"

"Early-twentieth-century American playwright. Very seminal for Broadway theater. Some people called him the American Pirandello."

"Huh." She studied his face. "Are you still stagestruck?"

"Not really. Oh, there's a little theater group in Brooklyn I help out now and then—"

"Christ."

"It wouldn't interfere with my work," he promised.

She gave him an unconvinced look, but changed the subject. "So Dixler wants me to give you a job here. I was surprised when he called; I thought you weren't speaking to him."

Dannerman shifted uncomfortably. "You mean about Uncle Cubby's estate. Well, I wasn't, but I thought the least he could do was put in a word for me with you."

She was gazing at the screen again. "What happened to the job you had with, it says here, Victor Carpezzio and Sons, Importers of Foods and Fragrances?"

"Personal problems. I didn't get along with the Carpezzios."

"And you've had—" She paused to count up. "Jesus, Dan, you've had four other jobs in the past few years. Are you going to quit here too because you don't like somebody?" He didn't answer that. "And you've been dicking around with little theater groups all over the place, not just in Brooklyn. I thought you were the kind of guy who went for the macho kind of thing."

"There's enough macho in the world already, Pat."

"Hum," she said again. Then, "All right, our mutual uncle gave a lot of money to found this observatory, that's a fact. But it doesn't mean we have to support the whole damn family."

"Of course not."

"If we decided to take a chance and we did give you a job for Uncle Cubby's sake, don't expect it would be anything big. You'd be getting minimum wage, daily COLA, no fringe benefits. This is a *scientific* establishment. We're all highly trained people. You just don't have the skills for anything better than scutwork."

"I understand, Dr. Adcock."

That made her laugh. "Oh, hell, Dan, I guess Pat's good enough. Considering we've known each other since we were in diapers. You don't bear any grudges, do you? About the money, I mean?" He shook his head. "I mean, you got as much as I did under Uncle Cubby's will."

"Not exactly."

"Well, you would have if you'd been around when the will was probated. Then the whole thing wouldn't't've been eaten up by inflation by the time you collected it and you wouldn't be looking for a scutwork job now, would you? What were you doing in Europe anyway?"

"I guess you'd call it postdoctoral research," he said, coming reasonably close to an honest answer. The statement was technically true, at least; he really had had his doctorate by then and what he had been doing in Europe surely was research of a kind.

"And maybe there was a girl?"

"You could say a woman was involved," he admitted, again skirting the truth—Ilse was indeed female, and so was the colonel. "I guess I made a mistake, not keeping in touch."

"I guess you did. All right, I don't see why we shouldn't do old Dixler a favor—and you too, of course. We'll find you something to do. Go down to Security and get your badge and passes from Mick Jarvas. You can start tomorrow—but remember, you get no medical benefits, no tenure. You'll be a temp, hired on a week-to-week basis, and how long you stay depends on you. Or, actually, it will depend on me, because I'm the director here. Is that going to give you a problem?"

"No problem."

"It better not be a problem. I don't mix family loyalty and

science. We've got a lot to do here right now, trying to get Starlab back on line and all. I don't want you thinking that the fact that we played together when we were babies is going to get you any special privileges."

Dannerman grinned, thinking about the kinds of games they'd played. "You're the boss, Pat," he said. But of course she'd been the boss then, too.

As soon as he was out of the building he paused before the window of a betting parlor to lift his commset to his lips and make his call. He didn't give a name. He didn't have to. All he said was, "Mission accomplished. I got the job."

"That's nice," the voice on the other end said chattily. "Congratulations. You've still got one thing to do with the other guys, though."

"I know. I'll phone it in when I get home."

"Make sure you do, Danno. Talk to you later."

On the subway ride home Dannerman pretended to watch the news on his communicator—the hot new story was that the President's press secretary had been kidnapped—but he wasn't paying it much attention. He was content with the day's work. To be sure, he didn't know exactly why he was going to work for his cousin, but he was reasonably sure he would be told in time. What he had to take care of with the Carpezzios wouldn't take long. And of course the eschaton, that ultimate transcendence, had never yet even crossed his mind.

CHAPTER FOUR

Dan

The process of getting photographed and fingerprinted for the job had made Dannerman late leaving the observatory. It got even later; he got caught in the rush hour and the subways were running even slower than usual because of a bomb scare at the Seventy-second Street station. That meant the trains weren't allowed to stop there until the security police finished checking out whatever suspicious object was worrying them, so Dan Dannerman had to travel an extra stop north and make his way back on foot through the jammed sidewalk vendors along Broadway. The peddlers did their best to slow him down—"Hey, mon, here we have got tomorrow's top collectibles, get them today while the price is right!"—but Dannerman was interested only in food just then. By the time he'd picked up some groceries for his dinner and got home, all the other tenants had finished their meals. He had the condo's kitchen to himself.

He dumped his purchases on the kitchen table and began to cut up the vegetables for his stir-fry. While he was waiting for the rice to steam he tried to get some news on his landlady's old screen. All the stories looked very familiar. The only additions to the ones he'd heard on the subway were that a new serial killer seemed to be at large in the city, two senators were under indictment for embezzlement, the heavyweight boxing champion of the world had announced his plans to enter the priesthood, the President had received a ransom demand for his kidnapped press secretary and the time for the free-fire zone that the Law'n'Order Enforcers had announced for the Wall Street area had just expired, with only seven persons wounded. Nothing very interesting. Nothing about the possible bomb in the subway, even on the local menu; but then the services hardly bothered reporting that sort of thing anymore.

Stirring up the fry didn't take more than five minutes, but Rita Gammidge must have smelled it cooking from her room. "Evening, Danny," she said, appearing at the door as Dannerman was ladling it into his plate. "Um. Do I smell chorro sausages in there?"

Rita Gammidge was his landlady. Tiny, old, white-haired, quick and inquisitive, she owned the duplex condo where Dan rented his room—well, his half a room, if you went by the original layout. The condo was a valuable piece of property, originally eight big rooms and three baths; but Dannerman knew that the condo was also about the only thing Rita had saved out of what must once have been a considerable fortune before she, and a lot of others, were wiped out in the Big Devaluation. Dannerman did what was expected of him. "Join me," he invited. "There's plenty for two."

She hesitated. "If you're sure—?"

"I'm sure." There was. There always was; the rents Rita collected were barely enough to keep her ahead of the taxes and the maintenance charges, and so he made a point of cooking enough for both of them. He knew that the other thing she wanted from him was his day's rent, so they settled that before they began to eat.

"The good news," she said, ringing up her deposit, "is today's inflation adjustment was only two per cent."

He nodded, and remembered to tell her, "There's other good news. I've got a new job."

"Well, wonderful! Calls for a drink—let me supply the beer." She had unlocked the fridge and brought out a bottle from her private stock—one half-liter bottle for the two of them to share—before she thought to ask, "What was wrong with the job in import-export?"

"No future," he said. As was usual with most of the things he told people about himself, the statement was true enough; whatever future there had been with the importers had vanished when the colonel ordered him to drop it and try to hook on with his cousin. "The place I'm working for now is an astronomical observatory."

"Oh, boy! What, do you think there's money in looking for Martians?"

"There aren't any Martians, Rita, and anyway that isn't what we do." He explained to her, from his small and very recently acquired store of astronomical knowledge, that the Dannerman Observatory spent its time analyzing data about distant gas clouds and quasars, trying to puzzle out the origins of the universe. Then he had to explain why the observatory was called "Dannerman."

Rita approved of that. "It's good to have family, these days," she said, chewing wistfully. "You're close, you and your cousin?"

"Not really. She's not a blood relative. She was Uncle Cubby's wife's sister's daughter, and I was his younger brother's son."

"Even so," she said vaguely, and then commented: "You could have put a little more sausage in the fry."

"Nobody's making you eat it."

She didn't take offense. She didn't even seem to notice what he'd said. She went on dreamily, "We used to eat really well while Jonathan was alive—truffles, guinea hen, steaks you could cut with a fork. Oh, and roast beef, and rack of lamb, and three or four different wines at almost every meal. Dan, do you know we used to have as many as twenty-four at dinner some nights? We'd eat in the main dining hall—that's where the Rosenkrantzes and the Blairs live now—and we had the butler and the maids to hand everything around. If anybody wanted seconds, why, they could have as much as they wanted. There was plenty, and we didn't even mind when the servants took the leftovers home. And then, if the weather was nice, we'd go out on the terrace for coffee and brandy afterward."

"I don't have any coffee," Dannerman said, to keep her from getting her hopes up.

"Neither do I," she said, swallowing the last of her beer. "Thanks for dinner. I'll clean up—and, Dan? It's nice about your cousin, but this city's no place for a young man like you. You ought to get out of it while you can."

"And go where?" he asked. She didn't have any answer for that. She didn't even try.

Before Dannerman unlocked the door to his own room he checked the telltales. They were clear. No one had entered while he was out; his stock of collectibles was still intact, and so were the more important items concealed among them. He locked the door behind him and began his evening chores.

After Rita finished partitioning the condo for lodgers, her original eight rooms had become fourteen. Dan Dannerman had a windowless chamber that had once been a kind of dressing room to the condo's master bedroom, now occupied by the Halverson family of four. His part got the huge marble fireplace, but it was the Halversons who got the direct entrance to the bath; when Dan wanted to use it he had to go down the hall.

All in all, Dannerman would gladly have traded with the Halversons. He couldn't use the fireplace, because of pollution regulations, so it was just an annoyance that took up wall space he could have used for his personal stock of inflation hedges.

Those were the goods that people with jobs bought from the pitiful sidewalk vendors, the fixed-income people or the no-income people who were reduced to selling off their possessions to stay alive. It didn't matter what you bought. With daily inflation running at two or three per cent, sometimes more, anything you bought was bound to be worth more than you paid for it if you just held it for a while. It was part of Dannerman's cover to be just like everybody else who had a little spare cash, but not enough to put it into the good inflation hedges like option futures. He spent his surplus on collectibles as fast as he could. In Dannerman's personal store he had glass paperweights, small items of furniture—all he had room for in the tiny chamber—a Barbie doll from the 1988 issue in nearly mint condition, old flatscreen computers, bits of costume jewelry, CDs, optical disks and even magnetic tapes of music of all kinds. Of course, the stock in his room didn't represent all of his *real* capital, but since he couldn't admit what his real capital was he couldn't draw on it; the Bureau would hand it over to him, fully inflated with whatever the then-current cost-of-living adjustment might be, when he retired. Meanwhile, in times of unemployment Dannerman, too, had had to protect his cover by setting up a booth along Broadway and selling off goods.

He checked his watch and noted that it was time to take care of his last bit of business with the Carpezzios. He dialed the number, let it ring once; dialed again for two rings; then dialed again and waited for an answer. "Nobody's here but me," said the voice of their main shooter and watchman, Gene Martin.

"Shit," Dannerman said. He wasn't particularly disappointed, and not at all surprised—he had timed it for when none of the bosses would be in—but that was just the way you started most sentences around Carpezzio & Sons Flavors and Fragrances. "So take a message. I can't come in, I have to go to the dentist, but tell Wally he'll have to do the meet tonight himself."

"He'll be pissed," sighed Martin. "You got a toothache?"

"No, I just like to go to the dentist. See you later." And he would see him later, Dannerman thought, but not until it was time to testify at their arraignment, and they wouldn't be very sociable then.

That taken care of, he had chores to do. From behind a print-book set of *Lee's Lieutenants*—not a very good investment, really, but one of these days he intended actually to read the books—he pulled out his rods and cloths, turned on his room screen and switched his pocket phone over to the screen to check the day's messages while he cleaned his guns.

The messages were almost all junk, of course. That was what he expected; his pocket phone was set to record everything that came in as voicemail except for the ones from Hilda. He reminded himself to add calls from the observatory to the priority list, now that he had a job, and set himself to review the day's garbage accumulation. People wanted to cast his horoscope or sell him weapons. A men's-clothing store was inviting him to a private advance sale of the season's newest sportswear and impact-resistant undergarments. A real-estate office had forced-sale condos in Uptown to offer. A couple of news services urged him to subscribe; a finance company offered to lend him money at just one per cent over the COLA; in short, the usual. There were just two real calls. One was from the theater group in Brooklyn, and, although the caller didn't give a name, he recognized the voice: Anita Berman. The other was from the lawyer, Mr. Dixler. Both wanted him to return their calls, but he thought for a moment and decided against it. Dixler could wait. And Anita Berman—

Well, Anita was a separate problem, and Dannerman wasn't quite ready to deal with it. Thoughtfully he left the phone live, while he began cleaning his twenty-shot, considering the case of Anita Berman. She was a sweet lady, there was no doubt of that. She liked him very well, and that was for sure, too. But Hilda thought she was a security risk, and now with the new job Hilda was bound to think Anita was excess baggage.

That was going to be a pain, he thought, and then remembered that he still had homework to do. He put the cleaning materials back, coded the room screen for library access and, automatically wiping the sales messages as they came in in their little window at the corner of the screen, cued in the search he had begun in the taxi for data on *astronomy, orbital instruments*.

It took him only a moment to access once more the entries for the Dannerman Observatory's wholly owned satellite, Starlab.

There was a lot about Starlab that Dannerman had no need to retrieve from the databanks, because he clearly remembered when it had been launched. He had been only nine at the time, but his mother had taken him to Uncle Cubby's grand compound on the Jersey shore for the launch party. The whole family was there to watch the launch on television, Cousin Pat and her parents included, as well as a dozen famous astronomers and politicians, but while the astronomers and the politicians were thoroughly enjoying the party, Dannerman's mother had been a lot less thrilled. It was Uncle Cubby's fortune that paid for the satellite, as it was also Uncle Cubby's fortune that endowed the Dannerman Astrophysical Observatory a little later; and, while Starlab and the observatory were undoubtedly great contributions to astronomical science, what they represented to Uncle Cubby's heirs was a considerable depletion of the remaining fortunes they might someday expect to inherit.

Still, there was no doubt that Starlab had done great things for astronomy in its time. When it was built there was still money around to spend on pure science. It was designed to house a few actual living astronomers for weeks at a time as they took their spectra and their shift measurements. That part had been abandoned early, when it became too expensive to ship human beings up to orbit; the last of the visiting astronomers

had died up there, and was still there. No one had been willing
to spend the money to reclaim his body. But Starlab's instruments had gone on working for more than twenty years—

Until, three years earlier, they stopped. Just stopped. The
transmissions ceased in the middle of a Cepheid count, and the
satellite did not respond to commands from its surface con-
trollers.

Dannerman put the screen on hold and got up to get a beer
of his own from his private cooler. It all seemed pretty straight-
forward: satellites went out of commission every day, and the
money to fix them got scarcer. Why was this one particularly
interesting?

He meditated over that for a moment, sipping the beer and
wiping the new messages as they arrived—until one came in,
voice only but definitely the voice of a female, that said flirta-
tiously, "Hey, Danno! I hear you got a new job. Give me a call
and let's see if we want to celebrate."

There wasn't any name on that one, either, but there didn't
need to be. No one called him by the code name "Danno" but
Colonel Hilda Morrisey.

A call from the colonel was not
one he could answer on the open lines. Dannerman pulled
down an old flatscreen converter from its place on his shelf and
jacked it into his modem. Then he dialed the number he knew
by heart. His screen instantly showed a bewildering fractal pattern of wedges and wriggling lines, until he cut in the 300-digit-
prime synchronized-chaos decoder.

Then Colonel Hilda Morrisey was looking out at him, plump,
dark, bright-eyed—just like always.

"Evening, Colonel honey," he said.

She didn't acknowledge the greeting. She didn't waste time

on congratulating him on getting the job, either. "All right," she said, "cut the crap. Have you done your homework?"

"I sure have, Colonel honey, all you gave me, anyway. Starlab went out a few years ago so the observatory applied for a repair mission to fix it. Naturally nothing happened. The red tape—"

"Don't tell me about the red tape."

"Anyway, the application wasn't moving. There's no public support for space missions. Let's see, I think the latest polls show about seventy-four percent opposed to spending another dollar on it anywhere. How much of that is Bureau dirty tricks, do you suppose?"

"Never mind."

"Anyway, now, all of a sudden, my cousin Pat got hot. She took the government to court, and she won, but it still don't move. So now she's doing a lot of wheeling and dealing on her own."

"And spending serious money, right. Okay, look. I had hoped to have background checks for you on the people you'll be working with but, right now, with this President's press secretary thing, it's hard to get any action out of Washington. So far it looks like two of them are dirty—not counting your cousin. One's a bruiser named Mick Jarvas—"

"I've met the man."

"He's a doper; that might be useful. He used to be a professional kick-boxer, now he's your cousin's bodyguard; he stays with her wherever she goes, so he knows what she does outside the office. The other one's a Chink named Jimmy Peng-tsu Lin. He's an astronaut, or was until the People's Republic privatized its space program and he went freelance. He got in some political trouble in the People's Republic, too, but I don't know exactly what yet. That's all I've got so far. Any questions?"

"Matter of fact I do have one, Hilda. Mind if I ask how the Carpezzio case is going?"

"You're not on the Carpezzio case anymore, Dannerman. That's just a routine drug bust and we'll handle that."

"You shouldn't do it yet," he said, as he'd said before—knowing that it was useless. "If you'd just wait two weeks till the major guys from Winnipeg and Saginaw get in—"

"Can't do it. You're needed on this one."

"But you'll just be getting low-level dummies—"

"Danno," she sighed, "are you empathizing again? You damn near blew the Mad King Ludwig operation because you didn't want to get your girlfriend Ilse in trouble."

"She wasn't my girlfriend," he protested. "Exactly. I just thought she was basically a decent human being." And, for that matter, the Carpezzios weren't that awful, either; sure, they sold drugs, but they were loyal to their people and he was going to miss some of those all-night parties in the loft with its constant aroma of room freshener and oregano that they hoped would keep any stray police dog from detecting the more interesting scents from their merchandise.

"Your kind heart does you credit, but forget it. What you're on now is a number-one priority from the director himself. Don't screw around with anything else, you hear? Check it out; see what you can get. And I want you to report in every night about this time."

"You're not making it easy for me. Do you want to tell me what I'm looking for, exactly?"

"No."

"Come on, Colonel! How the hell can I do my job?"

She hesitated. "You might see if you can find out anything about gamma-ray emissions from the Starlab," she said reluctantly.

"Gamma rays?"

"That's what I said. Don't use that term unless someone else uses it first."

"Aw, Colonel, you don't give me much to go on."

"I give you all I can. Tell you what, I'll see if they want to give me permission to tell you more. Now, get some sleep. You want to be fresh and pretty for your cousin tomorrow—and that reminds me, have you ditched that actress from Brooklyn yet? Well, do it. Your cousin likes men, and we want you concentrating on making her like you."

CHAPTER FIVE

Dan

With Starlab out of action the Dannerman Astrophysical Observatory didn't have a telescope of its own anymore; what it had was people. A lot of people. More than a hundred full-time scientific and clerical people worked there, with another twenty or thirty visiting astronomers, postdocs and slave-labor graduate students on and off the premises. That was good, for Dannerman's purposes; tradecraft said that the first thing you did in a new assignment was to let yourself be seen by as many people as possible so that they would get used to you, think of you as part of the furniture and accordingly pay no attention to you. On his first day in the new job he covered all the floors the observatory occupied, and was pleased to be generally ignored.

Most of the staff had no time to chat with a new low-ranking employee, at least until they discovered he happened to be a Dannerman. Then they became more cordial, but were still busy. If the observatory didn't have any instruments of its own, it did have shared-time arrangements with ground-based and radio telescopes in New Mexico and Hawaii and the Canary Islands, not to mention neutrino instruments in Canada and Italy and even odder observatories everywhere in the world. The scientists made their observations, and then they, and all the other specialists at Dannerman, massaged, enhanced and interpreted the data and added it to the general store of human knowledge.

Of course, Dan Dannerman wasn't qualified for any of that. If you didn't count Janice DuPage, the receptionist who doubled as payroll manager, or old Walt Lowenfeld, who ran the stockroom, Dannerman was pretty nearly the least professionally qualified human being on the payroll of the observatory. He hadn't been granted the dignity of a title, but if he had it would have been "office boy." Exploring the observatory was made easy for him, because his work took him everywhere. It included carrying things from the stockroom to the people who needed them, making coffee, killing, for Janice DuPage, a wasp that had somehow made it into the reception room, fetching doughnuts from the shop in the lobby for Harry Chesweiler, the senior planetary astronomer on the staff . . . taking messages, in fractured English, from the Greek friends of Christo Papathanassiou, the quantum cosmologist from the island of Cyprus . . . getting Cousin Pat's jewelry out of the safe for her when she was going out socially . . . bringing tea with a measured twenty cc of clover-blossom honey, no more and no less, for old Rosaleen Artzybachova, well past ninety and still spry but crotchety, as she pored over her instrument schematics. What he did, in short, was whatever they told him to do. "They" could be anybody, because he took orders from any of the fifteen or twenty principal astronomers and physicists and computer nerds and mathematicians who made up the major science staff of the observatory, and from any of their assistants as well. But he especially took orders from Cousin Pat Adcock, because she was the one who ran it all.

Cousin Pat wasn't a bad boss, as bosses went. She wasn't really a good boss, either, though. She seemed to have little patience and no interest in whether any of her employees might have lives of their own. She snapped her orders out—not only to her low-man-on-the-totem-pole cousin but even to people like Pete Schneyman, the mathematician-astrophysicist who, it was said, was high on the list for some future Nobel laurel (and had been everybody's logical best bet for becoming the next director until Pat Adcock came along) and to old, honored Ros aleen Artzybachova. Maybe part of the reason for the impatience, Dannerman thought, was that everybody knew that the only reason Cousin Pat was the director was Uncle Cubby's money. But she seemed tense and preoccupied most of the time. Janice DuPage whispered that Pat hadn't always been like that and probably one reason was that, having gone through two husbands, she didn't currently have even a steady boyfriend. "Maybe so," Dannerman told the receptionist. "But she was a bossy little kid, too."

He didn't believe that was the explanation, anyway. There had to be something else, something most probably to do with the Starlab; or else what was he doing there?

What he was doing there, of course, was following Colonel Hilda Morrisey's orders. As ordered, he kept his eyes and ears open, and if he didn't find much that interested her in his nightly reports it wasn't for lack of trying. It wasn't because the people he worked with weren't willing to talk, either. They were a sociable lot—particularly with somebody who, however lowly his present status, was a definite relative of their great benefactor. "But all they want to talk about is their jobs, Colonel," he complained to her on the coded line. "Dr. Schneyman kept me after work for an hour talking about stuff like something he called isospin and how proton-rich nuclei were created in novae and neutron stars."

"Screw that stuff, Danno. That's not what you're there for. What about the gamma-ray item?"

"Nobody brought it up, so I didn't either. You told me—"

"I know what I told you. Have you at least made contact with Mick Jarvas and the Chink astronaut?"

"I haven't seen Commander Lin yet at all. He's been out of

the office; they say he's in Houston, doing something about getting ready for the repair flight."

"I've got one other name for you. Christo Papa—Papathana—"

"The Greek fellow, right. From Cyprus."

"Well, there's a file on him, only I haven't accessed it yet. It's been crazy here." She hesitated, then said, "The thing is, they found the President's press secretary, only he was dead."

Dannerman was scandalized. "Dead? Cripes, Hilda! That was supposed to be a strictly commercial snatch!"

"So something went sour. The word isn't out yet; the President's going to announce it at a news conference in the morning. Meanwhile, everything's pretty screwed up, so it'll be a while before I can get more. And keep after Jarvas."

"He isn't exactly a sociable type."

"*Make* him sociable, Danno. Didn't I tell you this assignment is *priority*? Do I have to teach you all over again how to do your job? And, look, see if you can get into some of the technical part of the work there. You're not going to find much out while you're running the coffee machine."

Dannerman followed orders as best he could. He didn't achieve much with Cousin Pat's bodyguard, though he tried getting Jarvas to go with him for lunch or a beer. He got a frosty turndown. Jarvas didn't socialize outside the office. At lunchtime he went out only with Dr. Pat Adcock, and on the rare occasions when she lunched on sandwiches in her office he preferred to go out and eat alone.

Dannerman did better with the other instruction. It occurred to him that the databanks for astrophysics were reached in just about the same ways as the ones for critical studies on American playwrights. When he pointed out to Pat Adcock that he could be more use in research than fixing squeaky drawers, she reluctantly agreed to allow him to do an occasional literature search.

That was useful. It gave him a good reason to talk shop with his coworkers, and, when Harry Chesweiler found out he spoke good German and at least halting French, the planetary astronomer was delighted. "Hell, boy," he boomed, his mouth full of a bagel, "you can do something for me right now. Pat's been after me to check out some little CLO she's interested in—"

"A what?"

"A CLO. A comet-like object. I don't know why she's getting interested in it now—it came through a couple years ago—but it does have some unusual characteristics. She wants to know its orbital elements for some reason, and I've got all this Ganymede stuff to work up. We don't have any data for the sectors and times she's interested in, so you'll need to check some of the other observatories. Use my screen if you want to; I'd like to get out early for lunch, anyway."

The good part of checking up on the CLO was that it was more interesting than making coffee, and it didn't really require any knowledge of astronomy. With the information Chesweiler left for him Dan Dannerman began calling up other observatories to beg for copies of any plates they might have.

The main sources, Chesweiler had explained, were out of the country: the German Max-Planck Institut für Extraterristrische Physik, which had both an optical and a gamma-ray observatory still more or less functioning in orbit—gamma rays!—and Cerro Toledo in South America, which had one that observed in the extreme ultraviolet. The woman at Cerro Toledo refused his attempts at French—he knew no more of her own language than the taxi-driver Spanish any American needed—but had good enough English to make clear that, while she was perfectly willing to transmit the plates he asked for, she wanted to be paid; Dannerman took a chance and agreed to the price she asked.

The man at Max-Planck was a cheerful youngster named Gerd Hausewitz. He was considerably more cooperative, especially because Dannerman's German was what he'd acquired in his four years in the Democratische Neuereich. Hausewitz was about to go home for the day, he mentioned—it was nearly six o'clock in Europe—but he promised to get the plates, and Dannerman, feeling cheerful, went back to replacing the wilting flowers on the desk of Janice DuPage.

Talking German again had reminded him of the good times in Europe—of the parts of those times that were good, anyway: the cakes with mountains of *schlag* on the ring boulevards of Vienna, the beer in Frankfurt, the girl named Ilse who had invited him into her bed and then into the secret society called the Mad King Ludwig. It was the Mads he had been working on, but Ilse was a definitely valuable fringe benefit. Undoubtedly she was a terrorist, and almost certainly she had been involved in the group that had tried to spread cholera in the drinking water of the UN in New York, but she was also about the most beautiful woman he'd ever shared a mattress with.

Dannerman took a short lunch hour, and when he came back it was Janice DuPage, the receptionist, who checked his carry gun for him.

"How come?" he asked.

"Checking weapons is my job when Mick's out bodyguarding Pat Adcock."

"Huh. What does she need a bodyguard for, anyway?"

Janice looked at him unbelievingly. "Daniel, what galaxy do you come from? Pat's a good-looking woman. She needs some kind of muscle to protect her from rapists and kidnappers and general scum—not counting sometimes she likes to wear some pretty high-priced rocks when she goes out. Why do you carry a gun?"

He shrugged. "Everybody does."

"And everybody knows why."

He persisted, "So why does she hire a retired kick-boxer who never won a fight that wasn't fixed?"

"Ask him yourself. And some Kraut's been calling you, it's in your voicemail."

Gerd Hausewitz was as good as his word, but before he transmitted the plates he wanted to talk to Dannerman again. "Anything wrong?" Dannerman asked.

The broad face on the screen looked troubled. "Just that it's a funny thing, Dr. Dannerman. You said you were looking for a comet-like object, both in EUV and our gammas? But comets do not radiate in such frequencies."

"I guess that's what makes it only comet-*like,*" Dannerman said equably.

"To be sure, yes. But my superiors were interested that you should ask, and interested also in your Starlab satellite. We understand there is to be a flight to repair it, is that correct?"

Dannerman's expression didn't change, but he was suddenly more interested. "Yes?"

"That would be splendid, naturally. It is a fine instrument. However, we have found nothing in the literature to describe the plans for repair. Could you perhaps send us a copy of the mission plan, if it is not too much trouble?"

"I'll have to ask the boss."

"Of course. But please do. We would greatly appreciate. Is there anything else I can do for you?"

Dannerman hesitated, then took the plunge. "Your gamma-ray observer—"

"Yes?"

"I was just wondering, have there been any unusual gamma

observations lately? In the last couple of years, that is?"

The German looked puzzled. "Unusual? There are of course the bursters, but those occur all the time. Nothing *unusual,* however. Why do you ask?"

Dannerman backtracked swiftly. "It was just something someone said. It's not important. Anyway, thanks for the plates."

After Dannerman passed the plates on to Harry Chesweiler, the German's question stuck in his mind. He wished he knew a little more about astronomy. Did this CLO have anything to do with Starlab? Did the fact that it wasn't a normal comet mean anything? Why was the man from Max-Planck asking about the satellite in the first place?

Colonel Hilda would want the answer to that, too, so Dannerman got into conversations on the subject as much as he could manage. He didn't get much. No one seemed to have access to the Starlab flight plan; Dr. Adcock was handling that directly with Commander Jimmy Peng-tsu Lin. No one really knew just what had happened to Starlab, not even Dr. Artzybachova, though she gave him a frosty look when he asked.

At the end of working hours, when all the employees were lining up at Janice DuPage's desk to collect their day's pay before inflation knocked another two or three per cent off it, he dawdled to ask more questions, with little more success. It wasn't that the people in line with him were unwilling to talk, but what they wanted to talk about was their own special programs—black holes, galaxy counts, red-giant stars, red-shift measurements.

When Dannerman got the conversation onto the prospective repair mission for Starlab they were happy to discuss that, too, or at least to discuss what a newly functioning Starlab would mean to their hunt for organic molecules in interstellar gas clouds, or for the "missing mass" that seemed to concern some of them. Whatever that was. By the time the line carried Dannerman to Janice DuPage's desk he decided he didn't even know what questions to ask until he got more information from Colonel Hilda.

Then, as he was handing his cash card over to Janice DuPage for his pay, she said, "Oh, there you are, Dan. Dr. Adcock wants to talk to you before you leave."

And when he got to his cousin's office she glared at him. "What's this I'm hearing about you? Why are you asking for the Starlab flight plan?"

He wasn't surprised that she asked the question; he had no doubt that Pat Adcock kept an ear to everything that went on in the observatory. "I wasn't asking for myself, Pat. I got some data for Dr. Chesweiler from the Max-Planck people, and they were the ones who wanted to know. I thought it would be, you know, professional courtesy to give it to them."

"Professional courtesy isn't your department. You aren't a professional here, and it's none of their damn business. You don't pass out any information to anyone outside the observatory without my personal approval. Ever. Do you understand that? And, another thing, Janice tells me that you've made a payment commitment to Cerro Toledo for their data; we'll have to pay it, but you ought to know you don't have any authority to do that, either. Dan, this just isn't satisfactory. I don't want to have to warn you again, but— Hold it a minute."

Her screen was buzzing. Dannerman couldn't see the face on it, but he recognized Harry Chesweiler's voice. It sounded excited. "I've got your orbital elements for the CLO, and they're damn funny. There's definite deceleration, and—"

"Wait, Harry," she ordered, turning back to her cousin. "That's all, Dan. You can go. Just be more careful in the future."

He shared the elevator going down with two of the scientists, arguing over what the search for WIMPs really signified. They seemed close to coming to blows, so he interrupted. "What's a WIMP?"

They paused to stare at him. "Weakly interactive massive particle," the postdoc who'd been talking to him about the missing mass said.

"Oh, thanks. And, say, long as I've got you, there's something else I've been wondering about. If there's a comet that radiates in gamma and EUV, and it is slowing down as it comes toward the Sun, what does that mean?"

The other man laughed. "Means it isn't a comet, that's all. Maybe it's one of your fucking WIMPs, Will."

"Jesus," the postdoc said, "what are you telling him that for? You know it couldn't be a WIMP. Maybe some old spacecraft?"

"You know of any old spacecraft that would be coming in toward the Sun, Will?"

"So it's probably just a screwed-up observation. Anyway," the man said, getting back to his own subject, "believe me, WIMPs are definitely out there, and they make the difference; they're why the universe isn't going to expand indefinitely."

Dannerman gave up. He was glad enough when they came to the ground floor and he could get out. This debate about whether the universe would continually expand, or rebound to a point again, was sort of interesting, but not, as far as he could see, in any way relevant to any of the questions he was working on.

And, as far as he could know, it wasn't, of course. Because, of course, at that point Dan Dannerman had still never heard of the eschaton.

That night there was a call waiting from the lawyer, Dixler, begging him to have lunch with him the next day. That was a puzzle. Dannerman could think of no reason the lawyer would want to talk to him, and even fewer reasons why he would want to spend an hour with the man. But when he had reported in to Colonel Hilda she said, "Do it. See what he wants."

"It sounds like a waste of time to me."

"So? We're the ones who're paying for your time, if we want you to waste it then you do it. Maybe he knows what your cousin is spending her money on."

"What's that about her money?"

"She's liquidating assets, and it isn't just to pay off her lawyers. I'd like to know why. Something else, Danno. You didn't mention the query from Max-Planck about Starlab in your report."

He stared at her. "Oh, Christ, you've put a tap on the observatory lines."

"No tap is allowed without a court order, you know that, and we can't apply for one without taking the chance that she'll find out about it," the colonel lectured him. "Of *course* we put a tap on their lines. I don't like this questioning by the Krauts, though. What do you suppose their interest is?"

"You could ask the Bay-Kahs," he suggested.

"No, I couldn't, even if everybody wasn't going ape about the press secretary. But I did get some data for you, like on that old lady, Rosaleen—uh—"

"Artzybachova."

"Sure. I think you ought to cultivate her. She's an instrument specialist; it says in her file that she helped design the original Starlab project. Is Starlab what she's working on there now?"

"I don't know what she's working on. She always blanks her screen before she lets me bring her tea in."

"You need to get into their system, Danno. Your cousin's keeping secrets, and that's where she's keeping them, I bet."

"Are you telling me you can't break her code?"

"It's a closed circuit. Get in. And, listen, Danno, I've been checking your file and you haven't been on the range for nearly two weeks."

"I'll fit it in."

"Damn right you'll fit it in. You want to keep your skills up. Martial arts, too, Dan, because you know what occurs to me? It occurs to me you'd make a pretty good bodyguard for your cousin."

He protested, "Mick Jarvas already has that job."

"Maybe something can be arranged; I'll work on it. Any questions, outside of the usual one?"

"You mean the usual one that asks you what this is all about?"

She sighed. "Yes, that's the usual one, all right, and the usual answer is still no."

That was it. She wasn't going to tell until somebody higher up authorized it. That didn't surprise Dannerman; but what did surprise him was that, when he finally did get a clue, it came from that old fart of a family lawyer, Jerome Dixler.

The place the lawyer had chosen for lunch was a small private club way downtown on Gramercy Park. The place appeared to have a theatrical history. When Dannerman checked his twenty-shot and carryphone at the cloakroom—the gun was no surprise, but he was a little astonished that the club did not allow phones to ring in their dining room—he was informed that Mr. Dixler hadn't arrived yet. He spent ten minutes in the lounge, studying full-length oil paintings of famous members, all actors of a century or more ago whose names were familiar to him only from long-ago courses at Harvard. When the lawyer showed up he was out of breath.

"Real apologies, Dan," he panted. "The traffic gets worse every day and that driver of mine— Well, I did make it. Here, let's get to our table and order something to drink."

Dannerman was mildly flattered, more intrigued, by the fact that Dixler had put himself out to try to be on time. Still, he didn't get to business right away, whatever his business was going to turn out to be. While the waiter was bringing cocktails the lawyer went over every item on the menu, discussing the provenance of the basic foods that went into it and the way the club's chef prepared it. Dannerman knew he was meant to feel courted. Clearly Dixler had taken him to a pretty expensive place, although Dannerman's own menu was bereft of prices for anything. He wondered just what it was that the lawyer wanted from him that justified this kind of entertainment.

Dixler was in no hurry to get to it. As soon as the orders had been placed he said brightly, "Well, then, Dan. How're you getting along with dear little Pat?"

"Well enough. I don't see much of her in the office."

Dixler clucked. "That's a pity. You know Cuthbert always hoped you two kids would get together someday."

"Him, too."

"I beg your pardon?"

"Nothing. Someone else said the same thing, just the other night, but I don't think it's going to happen. For one thing, Pat never got in touch with me after Uncle Cubby died."

Dixler gave him a wounded look. "You never called me, either, Dan. I hope you're not holding a grudge about that problem with your inheritance."

"There wasn't any problem. There just wasn't any inheritance by the time it got to me. You explained it all when I got back from Europe. As executor you liquidated the estate."

"Had to, Dan. It's the law. I'm sorry it worked out the way it did, but I put the whole bequest into government bonds the way I was supposed to; it's not my fault inflation was so bad there wasn't much there when you got home. If you'd kept in touch while you were in Europe—"

"Yes, everybody's in agreement about me, aren't they? Pat told me I should have kept in touch, too. Well, I'm not blaming anybody." Dannerman wasn't, either, not really; there wasn't any point since there wasn't anything that could be done about it now. He changed the subject. "Anyway, it didn't work all that well for Pat, either, did it? I hear she's having her own money troubles."

Dixler looked startled. "How'd you hear that?" Dannerman shrugged. "Well, I suppose offices gossip. It's true enough. I don't think I'm violating lawyer-client confidentiality if I say that divorcing two husbands cost her a lot."

"Ah," Dannerman said, nodding. "I guess you handled the divorces for her."

The lawyer winced. "Really, Dan, that's unkind. I did the best I could for her. No attorney can do more than his client lets him, and she—well, she didn't provide me with the best cases, you know. That's about all I can say with propriety. Wouldn't say that much, you know, if you weren't family." He worked on his salad in silence for a moment, then came to the point. "Let me take you into my confidence, Dan. I guess you wondered why I asked you to come down here."

"I suppose it's because the club is sort of historic, and the food's good," Dannerman offered politely.

"Historic, sure; they say John Wilkes Booth used to eat in this very room. If you like history. I don't; and there's good food in plenty of places that are a lot more convenient. There's only one reason I keep my membership in this place and that's because nobody I know ever comes here. It's private. What I wanted to talk to you about is confidential, and in a way it does have to do with Pat's financial situation. You see—" He hesitated, then put his fork down and got it out. "There are some funny rumors going around about what your cousin's up to. I mean this repair mission on that Starlab orbiter. It's not just that the observatory wants its telescopes working again. People seem to think there's more to it. In fact, some people say there's some kind of technology in Starlab that isn't supposed to be there. The kind that might be worth a lot of money to whoever got his hands on it."

Dannerman kept his expression blank, but his level of interest suddenly elevated. "How can that be? Starlab's just an old astronomical satellite."

The lawyer shrugged. "Whether the rumor is true or not, it appears that your cousin thinks it is. She's spending pretty heavily out of what's left of her personal fortune to get what she calls the repair mission going."

That was a good deal more puzzling than enlightening. "Why does she have to spend her own money? You read me Uncle Cubby's will. Unless I heard wrong, it seems to me he left the observatory pretty well financed."

Dixler shook his head. "She has to account to the board for anything she spends out of the endowment. If she wants that mission to fly she's got a lot of off-the-books expenses to deal with. I wouldn't call them bribes, exactly. But not exactly legitimate, either, if you know what I mean. She doesn't want to have to explain them to the board, so she's been dipping into her capital to pay them out of her own pocket. She's been buying uncut diamonds, too."

For the first time Dannerman was startled. "Uncut *diamonds*?"

The lawyer shrugged. "For what purpose I do not know. She certainly doesn't plan to wear them, and she's got better inflation hedges than diamonds already." He shook his head. "Dan, I don't have to tell you, that's not like her. So she must have some pretty powerful reason—and there are these rumors."

"What do the rumors say, exactly?"

The lawyer said shrewdly, "That's what I'm asking you to find out. You work there; you should be able to get the facts on it."

Dannerman quelled a sudden impulse to laugh in the man's face. "You're not asking me to be a *spy*, are you?"

"Oh, no! Nothing like that! I wouldn't ask you to *pry* into your cousin's affairs. All I want you to do is keep your ears open . . . and, of course, give me a call when you find anything out."

"So you can figure out some way to cut yourself in on the profits—if there are any?"

Dixler flushed, but he controlled his temper. "My reasons," he said, "aren't actually any of your business. If you want to take a guess about them, you're welcome, but I don't choose to discuss the subject."

"Let me think about it," Dannerman said. The lawyer waved graceful permission with one hand, and began to talk about what a fine man Cuthbert Dannerman had been and how charming Dan and his cousin had been as children. Dannerman listened but didn't need to say much; Dixler was conducting the conversation by himself. Only when the meal was finished and they were getting their checked belongings at the cloakroom did the lawyer say:

"What about it, Dan?"

Dannerman was listening to a message that had come with his carryphone and gun. He looked up. "What?"

Dixler lowered his voice. "I said, will you do what I'm asking for me? I can make it worth your while, Dan."

"*How* worth my while?" Dixler shrugged and was mute. "Well, I'll do what I can," Dannerman said ambiguously. "Now, if you'll excuse me, I have to run. Looks like I've got an appointment I hadn't expected."

"Fine," said Dixler. "I'll be waiting to hear from you."

As Dixler got into his limousine Dannerman waited for the doorman to produce a cab. He was thinking hard, but not about the lawyer's offer. He was listening again to the message that had been on his phone. What it said was:

"Dr. Adcock will be returning to the observatory some time after two-thirty. You should be waiting at the street entrance before she gets there."

There wasn't any signature, but there didn't need to be: the message had been addressed to him as "Danno."

He made it by two-thirty, but with only moments to spare; but it didn't seem he had needed to hurry. The sidewalk outside the building was as crowded as always, but there was no sign of his cousin. Not at two-thirty, not at two-forty, not at almost three.

Dannerman leaned against the side of the building between two storefronts to keep his back covered; he had no doubt there were pickpockets among the horde of pedestrians. There was a policeman moving methodically down the block, making the sidewalk vendors pack up their wares and move on. He gave Dannerman a searching look, as he did the four or five other idlers who were standing around, doing their best to look as though they were waiting for someone. Some probably were. One at least wasn't, because as soon as the cop was ten meters away the man strolled over to Dannerman. Out of the side of his mouth, not looking at him, he muttered, "Smoke? Get high? Want to have a good time?"

"Get lost," Dannerman said. He looked at his watch. He had stretched his lunch hour a good deal longer than Cousin Pat would approve; if it happened she had come back a little earlier than expected, and was up in her office wondering where he was—

She wasn't. He saw a taxi roll up before the building entrance, and Pat Adcock and her bodyguard got out.

Dannerman wondered just what he was supposed to do, but not for long. Two of the idlers had moved quickly toward the curb. As the cab was pulling away one of them jumped Mick Jarvas from behind, the two of them falling to the ground; Dannerman heard a sickening crunch that sounded like a bone breaking. The other grabbed his cousin, snatched her necklace, knocked her down too and began to run—straight at Dan Dannerman.

Dannerman's reflexes were fast. "Hai!" he shouted, and stopped the man with a full body block. The mugger squawked, and then lost his voice as Dannerman spun him around and got an arm around his throat. The other mugger got up from where he had left Jarvas writhing on the sidewalk and started over to him; then, as Dannerman turned to face him, releasing the man he had captured, the two turned and ran, disappearing into the crowd.

As Dannerman helped his cousin to her feet and handed back her necklace she looked at him with shaky wonder. "Well, thanks, Dan," she gasped. "You're pretty handy in a street fight, aren't you? And you even got my beads back."

"Just glad I was here, Pat," he said modestly.

"So am I." She turned to the policeman who was trotting toward them at last, sweaty in his body armor and looking annoyed. It was only when she had finished reprimanding the officer for not being present when needed and ordering him to call in for an ambulance for groaning Mick Jarvas that Cousin Pat finally remembered to revert to type. "One thing, though, Dan. I'm glad you happened to be here, of course. But you do know, don't you, that you're supposed to be back from lunch no later than two. And it's a pity you let those muggers get away."

He didn't answer that. He especially didn't tell her the reason, because he didn't want to mention that while he had the "mugger" in a choke hold the man had gasped aggrievedly, "Come on, Danno! Don't be so fucking rough!"

CHAPTER SIX

Dan

On the way home that night, Dannerman stopped to do what he should have done days earlier—put in his once-a-month hour's practice on the firing range at the YMCA. As long as he was there he put in another hour on the exercise machines to keep his muscle tone up. When he got home he was hot and sweaty, but the guns had to be cleaned.

His practiced fingers knew how to do that without much direction from his brain, so he put something on the screen to watch while he cleaned the weapons. He hesitated over the choice. One of his store of Elmer Rice plays, for the fun of it? Some of the briefing tapes Hilda had downloaded for him, for the sake of duty? He compromised on looping the two messages from space again; maybe they had something to do with his assignment, as the colonel had hinted, but anyway she'd stirred his curiosity.

He did the easiest weapon first, the registered twenty-shot, his eyes on the screen. Even slowed down to catch details, the first space message gave no more information than it had the first time he saw it, in the Neuereich. The universe expanded and collapsed; and that was that.

He paused before running the second message, because the stink of his bomb-bugger was getting to him. Once the chemicals in a bomb-bugger mixed they produced not only thrust for the bullets but a god-awful smell; he rinsed the whole weapon, firing chamber and all, in water with neutralizer added, then carefully added enough of each chemical to top them off from the canisters hidden under his bed. Then he turned on the second message and began to clean his ankle gun.

He didn't get far. There were angry voices just outside his door. One was his landlady, Rita, in a bad mood; the other, whining and apologetic, belonged to one of the upstairs lodgers, Bert Germaine. When he opened the door, Rita diverted her attention from the lodger to Dannerman. "I didn't see you in the kitchen," she said accusingly. Then, wrinkling her nose, "What's that smell?"

"I guess it's the low-power loads they make you use on the YMCA range. Sorry about that."

She shrugged, turning back to look for the other lodger. But that conversation with the other lodger was over, because Germaine had taken advantage of her distraction to sneak away. "Little bastard," she said morosely. "I ought to kick his ass right out of my condo. Can't pay the rent, oh, no, but he always has a couple dollars for lottery tickets every day."

Dannerman took the hint. "Let me settle up."

"Oh, honey," she sighed, "I wasn't talking about *you*. You're the best goddam tenant I have, you know that. Only how can I make ends meet when I have to put up with deadbeats like Germaine?"

"Look at the bright side, Rita. Maybe he'll win his hundred million dollars, then he'll pay everything he owes all at once."

"Maybe pigs will fly. Dan," she said, looking him over, "when was the last time you got a haircut?" He shrugged. "You really ought to take more pride in your appearance, a good-looking young fellow like you. Which reminds me," she added. "There was a girl here looking for you."

"Oh?" he said, wondering: Colonel Hilda? Somebody from the office?

"Said her name was Anita. Said to tell you they missed you at the theater. Is she the one I used to see here sometimes, like a month or two ago? Not that I'm complaining about your having guests," she added hastily. "You pay your rent on time. I'm not going to worry if you have somebody visit you now and then, and one thing I will say for you, Dan, the ones I've seen have always looked pretty respectable. Not like the hookers that little bastard Germaine tries to sneak in. He's always got the money to pay them, you bet; and still he says he can't pay his rent!"

When he was safely locked in his room again Dannerman didn't start the tape again. He was thinking about Anita Berman.

That was not an enjoyable subject—not meaning Anita herself, who was about as enjoyable a female as he had ever dated, but the fact that he would soon have to do something about her. The troubling question was, do what? He didn't really want to break off their relationship. But she was beginning to sound serious, and that was something he couldn't afford.

Then Hilda's call came in on the coded line and he put Anita Berman out of his mind for the moment. He started in right away with the colonel. "Thanks a lot for setting me up this afternoon. You could've told me about it first."

"What for? I knew you could handle it. Now Jarvas is out of the way for a while, right?"

"I guess so. They were still at the hospital when I left."

"He's out," she said positively. "His arm's broken. So tomorrow morning you go in to your cousin and see if you can get his job."

"You broke his arm on purpose."

"Damn straight we did. So now his job's open, because what's the use of a bodyguard with a broken arm? Get it. Her bodyguard goes wherever she goes, so you can keep tabs on her when she's out of the observatory. Now, let's hear your report."

There wasn't much to say, until he got to his lunch with the lawyer. She scowled at that. "Him, too. Maybe we should sell tickets."

"You don't act surprised at what he said," he pointed out.

"You mean because this Dixler thinks your cousin's trying to make some money out of the Starlab? But we already knew all that, of course."

"Hell, Hilda, I didn't! So now that I know that much, how about telling me the rest?"

She shook her head. "Don't hassle me about that. What else?"

He hesitated. "One thing. I want to go back and visit at the theater. They're opening *The Subway* tomorrow night and I want to be there."

She frowned again. "Is that wise? The only reason we let you do that theater crap was because it made good cover on the Carpezzio job, and that's over for you. Don't get the two things mixed up."

"It's personal, Hilda."

She sighed and surrendered. "That goddam Berman woman, right? Well, I won't say no, but if there's any fallout it's your ass, Danno. All right, I've got some orders for you. We can't get through your cousin's encoding; we need a key. That Greek fellow—"

"Papathanassiou."

"That one. He probably has it, and I've got his data packet; I'll pass it on to you. Couple of others, too, but the Greek's is the one that looks good. You ought to be able to get something out of him."

"Blackmail him, you mean?"

"Whatever. And that Chinaman we were interested in, Jimmy Lin. He's coming back tomorrow morning, so you want to get on him, too." She reflected for a moment, peering past him.

"Did you clean your clothes after firing your bomb-bugger? Once you fire one of those things the stink stays, so everybody's going to know you've got a hideout gun."

"I will," he promised; then, "Hey! You've had me followed!"

"Well, sure. If we didn't do that how would we know if anybody else was following you? You're clean, so far—and, don't forget, the first thing you do in the morning is see if you can go for Jarvas's job."

But, as it turned out, that wasn't an option. Somebody had forgotten to tell the bureau's arm-breakers that Jarvas was left-handed; and when Dannerman put his card in the turnstile at the observatory entrance the next morning his cousin Pat was ahead of him, and beside her, punching out the combination to summon an elevator, was Mick Jarvas, a translucent cast on his right arm.

"Morning," Dannerman said, trying not to grin.

"And good morning to you," his cousin said, smiling. She reached over to touch him on the shoulder—not affectionately, exactly, but a lot more amiably than before. "You surprised me yesterday, old Dan. For an English major, I mean," she said. "Listen, come see me this afternoon. I've got an errand for you to run."

"Sure thing, Pat." He might have asked what kind of an errand, but he didn't get the chance. As they stepped out of the car at their floor she almost bumped into a large, sand-colored man with short black hair who was waiting there.

"Why, Jimmy," she said. "I didn't expect you so early."

"I just dropped off some of my stuff. I have an appointment downtown to check in at the embassy in half an hour," the man said, holding the elevator door open.

"Well, I won't keep you," Pat said. "You know Mick Jarvas,

of course? And this is my cousin, Dan Dannerman. Commander Jimmy Lin."

Dannerman hadn't had any clear idea of what he expected a Chinese astronaut to be like, but Jimmy Lin wasn't it. The man was taller than he had imagined, and a lot huskier; he wore a flowered Hawaiian shirt, and shoes that, Dannerman was pretty sure, would have cost him a month of his observatory pay. "Glad to know you, Commander," Dannerman said, automatically extending his hand.

But the People's Republic astronaut obviously didn't share the pleasure. He didn't accept Dannerman's hand. He didn't even speak to him. He gave him a long, hard look, then turned to Pat Adcock. "I'll be back before lunch," he said. "We can talk then."

"I've got a lunch date; make it this afternoon," she said, gazing after Lin as he let the elevator door close behind him. Then she turned to Dannerman with a mildly puzzled look. "He's usually chummier than that. You didn't forget to shower this morning, did you?" He shrugged. "Well, let's get to work; you can sort that out later."

Dannerman would have to sort that out, somehow, if he was going to carry out the colonel's orders, but it was going to be harder than he'd thought. He hadn't expected that kind of unprovoked hostility from Lin; and he was going to have to come up with something better than a broken wrong arm to get Jarvas out of the way. And then, as he checked his weapon with Jarvas, there was another curious thing. The bodyguard gave him a long look, partly abashed, partly pugnacious, but, though he seemed to want to say something, he didn't get it out.

There was one thing Dannerman could do, though. Hilda

had kept her promise and transmitted the background packets on the observatory employees who had turned up in the sin file. Two of them were unlikely to help: the astrophysics grad student three weeks past her period and frantically sending faxes to her boyfriend, now in Sierra Leone; Harry Chesweiler, identified as a former member of the Man-Boy Love Association. But the packet on Christo Papathanassiou did look good. The old man had got himself picked up for questioning about a terrorist assassination back in the old country. That, Dannerman thought judiciously, could be made to work—whether or not Papathanassiou was actually guilty of anything.

Dannerman couldn't do anything about it for the first couple of hours that morning, because he was kept busy with his nominal observatory duties. And then, when he went looking for the Cypriot, Papathanassiou was nowhere to be found. He wasn't in his office. He wasn't in with Pat, or in the room of number-crunchers all the scientists used to set up their mathematical models. When Dannerman looked into Rosaleen Artzybachova's cubicle he wasn't there, either, and the old lady herself was, incredibly, doing push-ups on the floor. "You want me?" she called, looking up at Dannerman.

"Actually I was looking for Dr. Papathanassiou."

"Try the canteen," she said; and that was where Dannerman found him, attacking a wedge of some unfamiliar kind of pastry smothered in heavy cream.

He looked defensive. "One has to keep one's blood sugar up," he said.

"Good idea," said Dannerman. "Mind if I join you?" And when he had a dish of sherbet for himself he said, "I was kind of hoping I'd run into you, Dr. Papathanassiou. I was looking at those tapes from space again last night—"

"Those odd-looking alien creatures? Yes?"

"And I just didn't understand about this Big Crunch."

"Ah," Papathanassiou said, gratified, "but really, it's very simple. The universe is expanding; in the future it will collapse again; that's all of it. Of course," he went on, "the mathematics is, yes, rather complex. Actually it was the subject of my dissertation in graduate school, did you know that?" Dannerman did, but saw no reason to say so. "It was necessary to use symplectic integrators to predict the next fifty quadrillion years of motion in only our own galaxy. You've heard of the three-body problem? What I had to solve was the two-hundred-billion-body problem."

He tittered. Dannerman pressed on. "But what I don't understand is, when the universe collapses again, what does it collapse *to*?"

"Ah." The astronomer ruminated for a moment, licking cream off his upper lip. "Well, you see, when everything has come together again great velocities and pressures are involved. First all matter is compressed. Then the atomic nuclei themselves are compressed. They become a new form of very dense matter which is stable—well, temporarily stable. Are you following me so far?"

Dannerman nodded, not entirely truthfully.

"Excellent. Interestingly, some workers once thought that sort of thing might happen in a particle accelerator. They called that state 'Lee-Wick matter,' and they feared it would be so dense that it would accrete everything else into it. Perhaps, do you see?, even turning the whole Earth into Lee-Wick matter." He wiped his lips with a napkin, grinning. "They were incorrect. No accelerator can reach those forces, though at the Crunch—"

"Yes?"

"Why, then," Papathanassiou said, nodding, "yes, perhaps it could be possible. Not in the form of Lee-Wick matter, no; one is pretty confident now that that doesn't exist after all. Rather it would be in the form of strange matter. That's to say, matter made from quarks—do you know what a quark is? Well, never mind; but strange matter would be very dense indeed, and it would keep on getting denser and denser. You cannot imagine how dense, Mr. Dannerman."

"Like a black hole?" he hazarded.

"Far denser than even a black hole. It would encompass the entire universe, you see, for as soon as it began to form it would transform everything around it into strange matter. Do you know our story of King Midas and his touch of gold? Like that. But only for a tiny fraction of a second, because such matter has a net positive charge—no electrons, you see—and so it tries to fly apart, like a bomb. Have I answered your question?"

"Well, yes." Dannerman cleared his throat. "That part of it, anyway. But it's funny you should mention a bomb."

Papathanassiou's cheerful expression faltered. "I beg your pardon?"

"Someone was asking about you," Dannerman lied. "He mentioned bombs? And a brother?"

The astronomer's smile was gone. "I don't understand. Who was this person?"

"I don't know. Greek, I think. You know that bar downstairs? I was having a cup of coffee, and he sat down next to me and asked if I knew you. Do you think I should mention it to Dr. Adcock?"

"Dear God, no!"

"I mean, so she can find this man and make him stop. He said some very unkind things about you, Dr. Papathanassiou."

"No! Please, no," the astronomer begged.

"Well," Dannerman began, then paused as his communicator beeped at him; there was an incoming call on the observatory system. In any case, he thought, that was a good place to stop; the hook had been planted, and it would be worthwhile to let Papathanassiou worry for a while. "I'd better take my call," he said. "Anyway, I won't say anything to her today. But I need to think this over; maybe you and I can talk again tomorrow? Here? I think that would be a good idea—and, oh, yes, thank you for explaining to me about the Big Crunch."

The call turned out to be Gerd Hausewitz from the Max-Planck Institut again, and he was looking aggrieved. "You promised to supply the specs for the Starlab mission," he reminded Dannerman.

"I know, Gerd. I've requested them."

"It is only that we supplied the data you asked for at once."

"I know you did. What can I tell you? I don't know how it is in your place, but here it takes time to get people to move."

"Yes, of course, Dannerman, but—" He looked over his shoulder and spoke more softly. "—my superiors are quite interested in this matter. They were not pleased that I delivered your material without at once receiving what we asked in return. This could be difficult for me here."

"I'll do what I can."

"Please, Dannerman."

"Yes, I promise," Dannerman said, half turning as he cut the contact. Someone was at his door and, surprisingly, it was the Chinese astronaut, PRC Space Corps Commander James Peng-tsu Lin.

He was wearing a propitiatory smile. "Hey, Dan," he said. "I owe you an apology."

"I beg your pardon?"

"No, really. I was pretty rude this morning, and I didn't mean to be—had to get down to the embassy and all that red tape, had a lot on my mind. So let's start over, okay?"

"Glad to, Commander Lin—"

"Just Jimmy, all right? Listen, what I was thinking, are you free for lunch? Looks like we're going to be working together for a while, and I like to get to know new people when they come to work here. Especially if they're Pat's cousin. They tell me there's some pretty fine ethnic food just around the corner—?"

"That'd be fine," Dannerman said, with pleasure. Whatever had turned Lin around was a mystery, but it was also a break: you didn't often get a subject volunteering to let you interrogate him. "I'll get my stuff and meet you at the elevator."

And then, as he picked up his twenty-shot weapon from Mick Jarvas, another little mystery solved itself. Jarvas was in the men's room, but when he came out he looked almost cheerful until he saw Dannerman waiting for him. Then he gave Dannerman that peculiar look again as he handed over the gun. He didn't let go of it.

"Is there something you want to say to me?" Dannerman asked, holding the barrel while Jarvas held the butt—he was glad to see the safety was firmly on.

Jarvas's eyes were on the ground, but Dannerman thought he muttered something. "What did you say?"

Jarvas looked up angrily. As he let go of the gun at last, he managed to get it out. "About that business in the street yesterday? I just said thanks."

Jimmy Lin was in the waiting room, busily chatting up the receptionist. In the elevator he said appreciatively, "I have to say your cousin Pat doesn't mind hiring other good-lookers. How'd you like to do the Twin Dragons Teasing the Phoenix with that Janice lady?"

"The what?"

The astronaut guffawed. "The Twin Dragons Teasing the Phoenix. It's an old Chinese expression. It's like, well, like when a lady has two gentleman paying attention to her at once." He grinned sidelong at Dannerman. "Just a joke, you know. Phew, what a mob." He led the way along the block to turn the corner, moving rapidly. When he noticed that Dannerman was lengthening his stride to keep up with him he said apologetically, "Sorry, I guess I'm always in a hurry. It's a genetic fault; my dad was the same way—except with the ladies, of course. Anyway, here's the place."

To the surprise of Dannerman, who had been preparing himself for Chinese food, the ethnic restaurant was not Oriental at all. What it was was Tex-Mex. The place was almost as crowded as the sidewalk, but Lin had a whispered conversation with the waiter and money must have changed hands; they got an immediate table. "I hope you like this stuff, Dan. I guess I got an appetite for it in Houston. First time I was there this lady from El Paso introduced me to it, then I introduced her to the Jade Girl Playing the Flute. Aw," he said, grinning, lowering his voice as he glanced at the waitress who was hovering just out of earshot, "that doesn't mean anything to you, does it? It's another of those old Chinese expressions. One of these days I'll show you some books that were written by my great-great-I-don't-know-how-many-greats granddaddy, Peng-tsu. I got my middle name after him; the old man's kind of famous, in some circles, anyway. He was a Taoist sage two thousand years ago—I'd have to say, a pretty *horny* Taoist sage—and he wrote some dandy books on what he called 'healthful life.' His idea of health, though, was to prong the ladies as often as he could and make up a list of all the ways there are of doing it. Well, enough of my sordid family history. Let's go ahead and order, we don't want to keep that good-looking little cowgal over there waiting, and then you can tell me all about Dan Dannerman."

And that was the way it went. It didn't take Dannerman long to realize that the astronaut was as interested in pumping him as he was in finding out about the astronaut. They didn't talk shop. They talked the way long-lost friends talk when they catch up on each other's lives after years of separation. Jimmy Lin wasn't reticent about himself. Garrulous would've been more accurate; in the first half hour Dannerman learned that the Lins were a wealthy old Hong Kong family who moved to Beijing after the reunification and got even richer there, as the People's Republic discovered the wonders of entrepreneurialism. Jimmy Lin himself had been educated in America, of course. That, along with the fact that he spent a lot of his spare time in his father's place on Maui, accounted for his accent-free American English. Then, instead of going into the family business, he'd been accepted for astronaut training. "But," he said, sighing, "I'm no credit to my ancestors. The top brass fired me out of the astronaut corps a year ago—they had some damn political charge." He looked ruefully embarrassed. "What they called it was 'left-wing, right-wing zigzag deviationism,' if you can imagine that. But actually about half the corps got dumped at the same time for one pretext or another. My opinion, they just decided there wasn't any money to be made in space anymore, so they cut back. So now I have to scratch for work." But after every little datum he supplied about himself he paused inquiringly to give Dannerman a chance to supply a little quid for his quo. He was fascinated by Dannerman's interest in the little theater in Brooklyn. ("Coney Island! Wow! That's really what you call Off-Off-Off Broadway, isn't it? I didn't think *anybody* went to Coney Island anymore!") He was searching about Dannerman's years in Europe—Dannerman was glad he'd been thorough about covering his tracks with the Mad King Ludwigs—and sympathetic about the fact that, although Dannerman and Pat Adcock had inherited the same amount from Uncle Cubby, Pat had actually got hers and Dannerman's had shrunk to invisibility through inflation before he collected it.

But of the repair mission to Starlab he would say nothing at all. "The thing is, Dan," he said, all good-natured candor, "I'm in line to fly that bird. Provided I don't screw up with your cousin and, well, she just doesn't want it talked about yet." He glanced at his watch. "Well, this's been great, but we better get back to the office. I hear Pat's got a job for you to do this afternoon."

When Dannerman was summoned to his cousin's office, though, the first thing she said wasn't about the errand. It was "What the hell did you promise the Germans?"

He shrugged, less interested in the question than in the fact that Mick Jarvas was standing there beside her desk, looking truculent again. "They asked for information about the Starlab repair mission."

"They can't have it."

"All right," he said agreeably, "but can I give them a reason?"

"No. Well, hell, I guess you have to say something. Tell them we've got a problem, you don't know exactly what it is, but it'll all be cleared up in a week or so."

It seemed to Dannerman that his cousin had a lot in common with the colonel. He ventured, "Meaning when you get back from your Starlab trip?"

She glared at him. "Who told you I was going to Starlab? Just do your job," she ordered. "No, wait a minute, I didn't mean for you to go. I need something delivered to the Florida embassy. You're going to take it, and it's important. I'm sending Mick along with you, just in case."

Jarvas stirred. "I can handle it all by myself," he muttered.

She ignored him. To Dannerman she said, "Give me your

belly bag." When he unsnapped it and handed it over, puzzled, she dumped the entire contents on her desk.

"Hey!" he said. There was personal stuff there, his cash card, his ID, the key cards for the office and the condo.

"Shut up," she said. She unlocked a drawer of her desk and took out a small, soft-sided leather satchel. She stuffed it into his belly bag; it fit, but just barely. She thought for a moment, then put his ID back.

"You can pick up the rest of your stuff when you get back, Dan. What I want you to do, take this bag to the Floridian embassy and give the bag to General Martín Delasquez personally. Nobody else, understand? No matter what they say. It's to be hand-delivered, and he's expecting it. Wait for him while he checks it out, and when he says it's okay you can come back here. Mick, give him his gun."

"Right, Pa—Dr. Adcock," the bodyguard rumbled, pulling the weapon out of his pocket. "Come on, Dannerman."

In the elevator he was fidgety, glaring at Dannerman. Just before they reached the ground floor he asked, "Do you know what this is about?"

"Don't have a clue."

"Neither do I. Listen. Maybe you're not as big a prick as I thought you were, but my orders are that that package *stays* in your belly bag until you hand it over to the guy it's meant for. No peeking. I don't want to have any trouble with you."

"You won't," Dannerman said, meaning it. He didn't want to cross Jarvas just when the man was being nearly human. In any case, he was hoping that the subway ride would give him a chance to engage Jarvas in conversation.

But that didn't happen. Jarvas was working at the business of being a bodyguard. He stayed close to Dannerman, keeping anyone else from touching him even on the subway, his good hand always near his own weapon, and he wasn't talkative. When the train speeded up to pass what some terrorist had done to the Fourteenth Street station, all lightless and covered in dark green radiation-proof foam, Jarvas crossed himself awkwardly with the arm that was in a cast. Dannerman considered mentioning to him, as a conversation opener, that he really had nothing to worry about, the residue from the terrorists' nuclear satchel bomb was no more dangerous than the general atmospheric levels—as long as you didn't linger there, of course. But as soon as he opened his mouth Jarvas gave him a warning scowl.

He closed his mouth again, and followed Jarvas meekly as they got out at Chambers Street.

The Floridians had their place on Embassy Row, just like the rich foreign countries. Theirs wasn't one of the big-money establishments—it wasn't anything like the Swedish embassy on the corner, twelve stories high and immaculately kept, and of course not a patch on the embassy of the United Koreas across the street. But then Florida was stretching a point to have an "embassy" at all, since it wasn't really an independent nation. At least not in name.

The Floridians took themselves as seriously as one, though. Both Jarvas and Dannerman had to turn over their guns even before they got to the scanners in the vestibule, and then Dannerman had to turn over his ankle gun as well. Jarvas gave him a scowl for that; at least, Dannerman thought with resignation, the scanners hadn't picked up the bomb-bugger. Then they had to sit for half an hour in a sort of barred quarantine chamber before a guard was available to escort them to the office of Major General Martín Delasquez Moreno. Jarvas sat like a stone, a scowl on his face. After a moment Dannerman decided to improve the time; he checked his mail, wiped it all, then accessed a news broadcast. But he had time only for a couple of items before the door guard leaned in and ordered no electronics.

Then they just sat.

When the armed guard came for Dannerman he pointed to Jarvas and said, "You stay."

"Hey! I've got my job—"

"Your job is stay here. Come on, you."

Leaving the fuming Jarvas behind was a surprise for Dannerman, but not altogether unwelcome. It occurred to him that, without Jarvas by his side, it was a chance to sneak a quick look into the leather bag; but it really wasn't, with the armed embassy guard watching every move.

When he got to the office of General Delasquez the man seemed surprisingly young—probably a relative of somebody high in Florida's government, Dannerman supposed. He was wearing the full dress uniform of a general of the Florida State Air Guard, and when he shooed the guard out with an offhand gesture the man was meek to obey. Delasquez closed the door. "Hand it over," he ordered; and then, when he had the leather bag in his hands, "Turn around. This is not your concern."

But by then what was in the satchel was no longer much of a secret to Dannerman, because he'd felt its contents as he took it out of his belly bag. It felt like a few dozen pebbles. It wasn't pebbles, though. When the general had finished his inspection and had locked the bag in a drawer and told him he could turn around again, he forgot to put the jeweler's loupe away, but by then Dannerman had figured out that they were gemstones, almost certainly the diamonds Jerry Dixler had mentioned Pat was buying.

"Wait," the general ordered, and keyed on his phone. Dannerman couldn't see the picture, but he knew his cousin's voice when she answered. "Your application has been received and is satisfactory, Dr. Adcock," the general said. "The documents

will be processed immediately." And then, to Dannerman, "You
can go."

With their errand completed,
Jarvas loosened up a little. He listened almost politely as Dannerman answered his questions about what had happened in the
general's office, then actually managed a grin. "Got that done,
anyway; your cousin'll be happy about that." Then he stopped
short in front of the Swedish embassy, eyeing the curbside vendors. "Hey, Dannerman, how about some candy? I've got kind
of a sweet tooth."

"Not me, but go ahead." As he watched Jarvas haggling with
the woman at the pushcart he wondered how Jarvas got away
with his drug habit; the candy addiction was a tipoff, and so was
the fact of his mood swings. In some ways Cousin Pat didn't
seem to be as sharp as he'd thought. But it was good that Jarvas was mellower; maybe on the way back he would be more
talkative.

The other good thing in his future, he thought, was that that
night he could go back to the theater. He must have smiled, because the guard outside the Swedish embassy gave him a suspicious look before going back to eyeing the vendors and loafers
along the crowded sidewalk. Dannerman kept getting nudged
as people bumped against him, but if any of them were pickpockets, as they likely were, he had nothing left in his belly bag
worth picking.

He felt droplets of cold water hitting the back of his neck and
looked up; the meticulous Swedes had permanent crews at work
in hoists overhead, to keep the building washed down. Even so,
they were just barely keeping ahead of the pollution. As he
moved away he felt someone touch his arm. It was a young boy,
no more than fifteen. *"Vill herrn växla? Vägvisare?"* he hissed.

Dannerman shook his head, but the boy persisted. *"Vill ni knulla min syster? Ren flicka, mycket vacker."*

Dannerman realized the boy had taken him for a Swedish tourist. "Asshole," Dannerman said cheerfully. "I don't want your sister, and besides I'm an American."

The boy changed gears without a blink. "Okay, sport, how about a little American happy time? Sticks, ampoules, mellow patches, I can get you anything you want."

"No sale." And then, as Jarvas came toward them, munching on caramel popcorn, he said, "You can try my buddy there. He might be in the market for some dope."

It was a light impulse, and he regretted it. The boy took one look at the expression on Jarvas's face, and then dodged across the street to try his luck with the Koreans. And all the way back in the subway Jarvas stood cold and angry beside Dannerman, and wouldn't say a word.

CHAPTER SEVEN

Dan

There was one job remaining for Dannerman to do that day. It was a fairly nasty one, and not one he looked forward to, but it was best to get it over with. So at quitting time Dannerman went looking for the Cypriot astronomer, Christo Papathanassiou. The man was standing over the screens in his office, preparing to shut them down for the day. When he saw Dannerman in the doorway he gave him a quick, apprehensive look. "Sorry to bother you, but I need to talk to you for a minute," Dannerman said. "I've got a problem."

Papathanassiou sat down again, stiffly waiting. "See, Dr. Papathanassiou, I'm in a little trouble with my cousin, and I don't want to make it worse. When I went down to the lobby to get something for Dr. Chesweiler that man was there and he started up again."

The astronomer still didn't speak. He didn't look surprised at what Dannerman was saying, only sadly resigned.

"And now," Dannerman went on, "I'm really worrying about not telling my cousin about it. You see, what the man says— well, he says you've been mixed up with some bad business. You have a brother—I think he said the name was Aristide? Yes. And this Aristide was implicated in an assassination on Cyprus. A Turkish tax collector, I think he said. Shot in the back as he was opening his own front door."

Papathanassiou stirred. "I know of this case, yes. A very sad business. But it was long ago, more than five years, and Aristide is only my half-brother. My father's youngest son, by his third wife. We were never close, so what has that to do with me?"

"Well, Aristide's on Interpol's wanted list, and it seems they have some idea you helped him get away."

Papathanassiou nodded somberly. "I was aware they had that idea. I was questioned at the time, of course. That is all. Never since. But how does it happen, Mr. Dannerman, that you know so much about Interpol?"

"Who, me? Oh, I don't know anything about Interpol," Dannerman said quickly. "That's just what the man said. But if Pat finds out I knew about this and didn't tell her she'll be even madder."

"Madder about what?" Papathanassiou inquired.

"Well, that's where I have this problem. She wanted me to get some data for her, and I said I'd already done it. Actually I hadn't. And now I can't remember the specs for what she wanted, and I can't ask her, because I'd have to admit I lied about doing it already, and I can't look them up because they're in her secure file. So what I wanted to ask you, Dr. Papathanassiou—"

The old man held up his hand. "Permit me to guess," he said. He didn't seem angry or surprised, only sorrowful. "I imagine what you want is for me to give you the access code for the secure file. Simply so you can carry out Dr. Adcock's orders, of course. And then, I imagine, you will no longer feel it necessary to tell her about this other matter."

"Well . . . yes. That's about it," Dannerman agreed, and did not enjoy the expression on the astronomer's face.

It was a long subway ride to Coney Island, and at rush hour the trains were packed. It hadn't taken long, after Papathanassiou left—without saying good-bye, Dannerman remembered—to access the secure file and dump it all into a coded transmission for the National Bureau of Investigation office. But it hadn't left time for anything like a leisurely dinner—at least, not if he wanted to get to the theater early. The best Dannerman could do was to pick up some falafel and a juice box, figuring he could stave off starvation on the way, and then there just wasn't enough elbow room in the standing-room-only subway car to eat them. They were at lower Manhattan before he was able to squirm his way to the corner of the car. He managed to eat his dinner there on the long stretch under the East River, doing his best to avoid spilling hummus on the luckier seated passengers around him, but he took no pleasure in it. For one thing, all that congested body heat had caused all the high-tech micropores in the garments of his fellow passengers to open, and the collective odor was not appetizing. More than that, there was the depressing business with Christo Papathanassiou. Dannerman could not help empathizing with what the old man must be feeling. Hilda was right about one thing anyway, Dannerman admitted to himself. He had the bad habit of letting himself feel what his victims went through. In a way, it was an asset for a professional spook. It had certainly made it easier for him to get along with, for instance, Ilse of the Mad King Ludwigs, not to mention even the Carpezzios. But sometimes it made him feel, well, guilty.

By the time the train had come out of the ground and begun to run on the old elevated tracks, Dannerman even found a seat. He took advantage of the time to run through his messages, none of which mattered to him, and then did what most of his fellow passengers were doing: stared blankly into space, or watched the advertisements as they circled around the display panels just under the ceiling of the car. What caught his eye was a commercial for a soft drink with a mild tetrahydrocannabinol content—the obligatory surgeon general's warning ran in inconspicuous type under the prancing cartoon figures, along with the legend "Not to be sold to anyone under 14." The figures, comically struggling with each other for the soda, were the seven aliens: the Sleepy with its red-shot eyes and pursy little three-cornered mouth, the Happy with its ominous shark-toothed grin, the Bashful, the Doc—all of them, in their sanitized and anthropomorphized Disney-like forms. As cartoons, the creatures were funny and not at all threatening. But suppose, Dannerman thought, suppose the real creatures were somewhere not far away, possibly as close as Starcophagus. Suppose the messages from space had in fact been warnings. Suppose the creatures were actually a clear and present danger that the world really needed to be warned about. Dannerman remembered the little song the taxi driver's Grumpy doll had sung—"Hi-ho, hi-ho, to conquer Earth we go, we'll steal your pearls and all your girls, hi-ho, hi-ho." But it might not be a joking matter.

Dannerman dismissed the notion; it was simply too fanciful, and, besides, he had nearer concerns. He leaned back, closed his eyes, and thought about just what it was that he was going to say to Anita Berman.

There were a million ways of breaking off a relationship. The trouble was that they all started from the same point: you had to *want* the relationship to be broken off, and Dannerman was a long way from being certain of that. It was the job that mandated the break, not his personal wishes. Although the life of an NBI agent was surely full of interesting incidents, there was a part of Dan Dannerman that sometimes thought wistfully about what it would be like to live a more settled existence. To have a home of his own, for instance. In something like a four-room apartment somewhere in the outer suburbs, with a regular job that didn't require him to move somewhere else on short notice. A home that he could share with someone else on a more or less permanent basis. With someone, for example, who was a lot like Anita Berman. . . .

That wasn't a useful speculation, either. He wasn't going to resign from the Bureau, for what else would he do with his time? By the time he got to the stop for Theater Aristophanes Two he had managed to bury that line of thought along with imaginings about the aliens and the memory of his conversation with Christo Papathanassiou, and was only looking forward to an evening that was all his own.

The people who got out with him were a mixed lot; Coney Island wasn't the worst neighborhood in Brooklyn, but it wasn't the best either. It was not what you would consider a natural place for a theater, but the old Ukrainian Orthodox church they had converted into Theater Aristophanes Two had one great advantage. It was cheap. It was a sound building, too, because the Ukrainians had done their best to make the area livable—built a church, tore down the worst of the burned-out tenements, turned some of the vacant lots into vegetable gardens. But when the Ukrainians moved out and the immigrating Palestinians, Biafrans and Kurds moved in, the neighborhood went sour again. The new people apparently didn't go in for farming—maybe there weren't any farms in Palestine or Iraq? Anyway, now there was little behind the chain-link fences but burdock and trash, and the church had lost its congregation. The theater group had been able to pick it up for a nominal rental and a lot of sweat equity—it needed the sweat work, because it had been looted twice and flooded three times in Atlantic hurricanes. On warm evenings it still smelled a little like low tide at the beach. It wasn't very big, either. Maximum seating capacity was not quite two hundred. That had its good aspects; it was easier to fill than a bigger house, and most of all it kept the theatrical unions from bothering the group . . .

even though it also meant that Theater Aristophanes Two had no chance at all of ever turning a profit.

But that, of course, wasn't what they were there for. The members of the group were there because theater was in their blood—or because it was what they were trained for and nothing better offered itself.

Dannerman arrived early. The lobby doors were locked; but when he knocked the "manager," Timmi Trout, peered out of the ticket window and came out to let him in. "Dan," she said, pleased, "hey, we thought we'd lost you. I should've known you'd be here for the opening, anyway. They're still rehearsing—it's a mess, because we open in an hour, and that idiot Bucky Korngold's out of the cast because he got himself arrested yesterday on some damn drug charge. Can you imagine?"

Dannerman could imagine very easily. Practically everybody in the group had a day job, of course. Bucky Korngold's had been dealing drugs; he was one of the people Dannerman had been investigating in the Carpezzio matter. He said, "Mind if I go in and watch?"

"Of course not." She hesitated. "Anita's going to be real glad to see you, you know. She's been kind of worried about you . . . but, hey, you'll talk to her yourself. Go on in."

He did, and took his seat in a back row as inconspicuously as possible. The cast wasn't so much rehearsing as shouting at each other for missing cues and stepping on each other's lines—normal enough for a final rehearsal at Aristophanes Two—and he saw Anita Berman at once. For one thing, she was the prettiest woman on the stage: slim, tall, red-haired, with a deep, carrying voice that was perfect for unmiked theater (and of no use at all in the heavily enhanced productions on Broadway).

She saw him right away, too. When she caught sight of him at the back of the theater she looked startled, then perplexed, then gave him a tentative, not quite forgiving, see-you-in-a-minute wave. And it wasn't much more than a minute before the director abandoned his attempts to get the performance running like clockwork. "Go back for makeup, all of you," he ordered. "A bad dress rehearsal means a good show, they say. Maybe you can take comfort in that. I know I will."

And Anita Berman jumped down from the stage and ran up the aisle to meet Dannerman. It was clear she'd made up her mind for forgiveness. "I'm real glad you're here," she said, putting up her face to be kissed.

She clung to him for a moment, then pulled back to look at his face. "I guess we've kind of been playing telephone tag."

"I'm sorry about that," he said, meaning it—meaning at least the "sorry" part. "I've got this new job and it keeps me really on the jump."

"I figured it was something like that. I guess you're making a lot more money there—?"

"Maybe soon, anyway," he said vaguely. "But it takes all my time. Matter of fact, I'll have to be going out of town pretty soon."

"Ah," she said. "For very long?"

"I don't know that yet."

She was silent for a moment, then said, "Dan, dear, listen. I've been thinking about us. I know some men still like to be in control, and maybe—well, if you think I was rushing things, talking about moving in together—"

"That's not it," he said uncomfortably. "Look, you need to get ready for the performance and we've got a lot to talk about. How about if I meet you after the play?"

She gave him a sudden smile. "That'll be fine, Dan. Come backstage and we'll go to the cast party. You can tell me all about the new job and your trip. I'll be waiting for you."

So Dannerman had the whole duration of the play to decide on a story about where he was going on the trip he had invented on the spur of the moment, and how long he would be away.

There was a funny thing about that, if only he had known it. It was part of Dannerman's tradecraft as an NBI agent to tell selected fragments of truth in order to deceive. For a change, this time it was the other way around. Although he didn't know it yet, the deception was truth. He was indeed going away, in fact very much farther away than he could ever have imagined.

Fidgeting in his seat while waiting for the curtain to go up, Dannerman was trying to decide what to do about Anita Berman. He didn't *have* to break up with her. Well, not just yet, anyway. Sometime, yes, because a permanent, committed relationship was out of the question for anybody in Dannerman's line of work. The worrisome part was that, he was pretty sure, the longer he waited the worse it would be for her when the break did come; and how bad was he willing to make it for sweet, pretty Anita Berman?

When the play began, he was glad to put that question out of his mind; what was happening on the stage held his interest. Maybe the old adage was right; the blunders of the rehearsal had disappeared and the cast was flawless in the first act of *The Subway*. Anita was beautiful even in her 1920s bargain-basement flapper costume, and whoever the actor was who had taken over for poor Bucky Korngold, he didn't miss a beat.

Even the play itself was going well with the audience. *The Subway* was definitely one of Elmer Rice's more squirrelly works, and Dannerman was the one who had first urged it on the group. It was ideal for them. It was short. It used a large cast—always an asset for an Off-Off-*Off*-Broadway theater, when everybody involved wanted to get on stage where some slumming big-time media critic might just possibly think their performance worth a few seconds' commendation in a review. The play was cheap to produce, since it only required one impressionistic—and therefore inexpensive—set. Most important of all, *The Subway* was just about totally forgotten. No major company had given it a production in close to a hundred years, and so the troupe didn't have a million library tapes floating around out there to compete with.

He had also vowed to the group that *some* critics, at least, would be sufficiently intrigued by a long-lost classic of "modern" American theater to make the long run out to Coney Island to see its revival. He was happy to see that he had been right about that. He was pretty sure that at least six or eight of the audience members were actual critics. None of them were smiling, but he didn't expect that. Critics didn't smile. The important thing was that they weren't walking out, either.

Then, when the first act ended, at least two of them were actually clapping. Well, the whole audience was enthusiastic in its applause—not surprising, since a good half of its members were in some way related to one of the actors—but it was a good sign. In the intermission crowd that packed the lobby—once the vestry, when the place had been a church—Dannerman attached himself, as inconspicuously as possible, to a woman he was nearly sure was a TV talk-show host, trying to overhear what she was saying to her companion. But she was only commenting on the buskers on the sidewalk outside: two Arab kids tap-dancing while a third, in an "I ♥ Allah" T-shirt, worked the intermission crowd for cash. He started for another potential critic and was annoyed when someone touched his arm. He turned to face a short, plump woman who was placidly gazing up at him. "Why, Danno," she said, "it really is you, isn't it? Nice to run into you like this. Why don't we step outside for a little air?"

"Damn it, Hilda," he said. "What the hell are you doing here?"

She didn't answer that, but then she didn't need to. She simply steered him firmly out of the doors and around the corner to where a large truck was parked at the curb. The liquid-crystal display on its side glittered with the words NIITAKE BROS. MOVING & STORAGE, but Dannerman knew it was not going to be any ordinary moving van.

It wasn't. It turned out to be a complete mobile NBI surveillance station, with a Police Corps master sergeant saluting smartly as Colonel Hilda Morrisey brought him in.

"It's time for us to do a little business," she said cheerfully. "Take a pew, Danno. Want some coffee? A beer? We're pretty well stocked here, and Horace'll get you anything you want."

"What I wanted was to be left alone for one damn evening with my friends."

"Another time, Danno. How's it going?"

"As well as can be expected, considering you picked Korngold up the day before the opening."

"Not me. *They,*" she corrected. "They picked everybody in the operation up, but I wasn't involved. I've been off the Carpezzio business as long as you have, because your cousin's is more important. Let's have your report."

She absorbed the news about the Floridian general and the diamonds without comment, but winced when he told her that the "muggers" had broken Mick Jarvas's wrong arm. "We'll have to do that another way," she said resignedly. "You've got to get his job, because she's going out to Starlab and you're going to have to go with her."

He goggled at the woman. "Into *space?* Nobody goes into *space* anymore!"

"She does; that's what she was bribing the general for. And she would've taken Jarvas along for muscle, but we'll have to change that."

"You want me to go into *space*?" he said again.

"Why are you making such a big deal out of this? Lots of people have gone into space."

"Not the Bureau! And not recently for almost anybody."

"Well, until recently the Bureau didn't have a reason."

He looked at her more carefully. "Something's happened," he said.

"That data from your cousin's file happened, Danno," the colonel said triumphantly. "I knew there'd be something there. You know what it was? Synchrotron radiation!"

He said impatiently, "Cut the crap, Hilda. I don't know what that is."

"Well, neither do I, exactly. But that's what started your cousin off. Seven or eight months ago the observatory was trying one more time to reactivate the satellite, and they detected a burst of this synchrotron radiation coming from it."

"But you said to check into *gamma* radiation."

"I know what I said. The agent who passed the word along must've gotten it wrong; anyway, the word is it's definitely synchrotron, not gamma. There wasn't much of it. It lasted just for a few seconds. But it was definite, according to your cousin's analysis, and the thing is, there isn't supposed to be anything on Starlab that could cause it." She paused, studying his face. "So you know what that means? Something's been added to Starlab."

"Are you going to tell me what that is?"

"I'll show you, as much as we know. Horace? Will you start the simulation now, please?"

The sergeant touched one button, and the inside of the truck body went dark; touched another, and the simulation tank at the front of the body lit up with a picture of Starlab, sailing along in its perpetual fall toward Earth, with its ruff of solar panels soaking up photovoltaic power to run the instruments that were no longer responding, and its huge collector eyes staring unseeingly out at the universe.

"As you can see," Hilda instructed, "it's big. That's because it was designed to let astronomers live there for weeks at—"

"I've seen all this, Hilda. It's no secret. Christ, they've got a model of the thing in the observatory waiting room."

"Don't rush me, Danno. We're coming to what you haven't seen. This is stuff we got from your cousin's observatory records. She had this whole segment deleted from the public bank—decided to keep it a secret, I guess—but once our technicians knew what to look for they had no trouble retrieving it. This is enhanced imaging, otherwise you couldn't see anything at all. Watch that little thing coming in from the upper right."

"I see it." It was a nearly featureless lump, by comparison with the huge Starlab no bigger than a football. It slipped past the great solar vanes and gently caressed the sheathing of the main body of the satellite. It didn't bounce away. It stuck where it touched. Then, while Dannerman watched, the object draped itself to the curvature of the shell. In a moment it was almost invisible again, except as a nearly imperceptible swelling of the hull.

"So what the hell is it?" Dannerman demanded. "Space junk?"

"Did that look like junk? It didn't crash into the satellite, did it? Looks to me like it *docked* with the son of a bitch."

"What then?" As the idea struck him: "Does it have any connection with the CLO?"

"Good question," she said approvingly. "I ran that past the experts as soon as they dug out the clip on the object. They said no. They said this thing was way too small to be taken for a comet, although they couldn't turn up any later observations of the object; lost it somewhere, I guess. But they didn't exclude the possibility that this thing had come in on the CLO and been dropped off."

"Like a probe?"

"I guess. Anyway, they're pretty sure it is some kind of an artifact."

"Well," he said reasonably, "if it's an artifact somebody would have to put it in orbit. Who's been launching spacecraft lately?"

"Nobody. Not openly, anyway."

"Some terrorist bunch?"

"God, I hope not. If there's some kind of technology that can launch an artifact without anybody detecting it we need to know about it. If terrorists got hold of it . . . well, can you imagine what it would mean if the Mads or the Irish or the goddam Basques could put up their own satellites?" She shrugged expressively, then added, "But maybe that would be better than the other possibility, at that. Your cousin seems to think it's extraterrestrial."

"But that doesn't make any sense, Hilda! If she thought that, why would she keep it a secret?"

"Money," she said shortly.

"From what, damn it?"

"Oh, Danno," she sighed, "you know what your trouble is? You just don't think like a normal human being. You aren't greedy enough. Think about it: some kind of technology that can produce synchrotron radiation where there isn't supposed to be any. The brains tell me that it can't be done without a big particle accelerator—those things that run out of subway-tunnel kind of things, fifteen or twenty miles long. So that means there has to be some pretty hot hardware up there. If it's alien, it's worth money to whoever finds it. For us, on the other hand, it doesn't matter whether it's from some weirdo ET or somebody on Earth; we want it."

"So let the Bureau send a mission up to get it," Dannerman said reasonably.

She shook her head. "That's one option, sure. But maybe we can't. It's tricky. Starlab's private property; your uncle paid for it out of his own pocket. Maybe we could get around that—that's what we've got lawyers for, for God's sake—but then there's the other problem. We don't want to alert other people to what's going on. The goddam Europeans might send up a mission of their own if they knew we were after something; they can move faster than NASA, and you know there's no security there. And anyway the goddam Floridians still control the launch facilities."

"So?"

"So—*probably*—the final decision hasn't been made, because too many of the top people are all tied up with the press-secretary thing—so probably we want to let her go ahead, but send one of our own along to make sure we get first crack at whatever's there."

"Ah," said Dannerman glumly. "Like me, you mean."

"Exactly like you, Danno, so you have to take Jarvas's place. I've got an idea about that. Sergeant? Kill the display and let's have some light again while we brief Agent Dannerman on what he's going to do for us."

As she turned to get something out of a locker, Dannerman tardily remembered the other thing that had been on his mind. He sneaked a look at his watch.

It was late. The play would be long over before he got away from the colonel. And so he wouldn't be keeping his promise to meet Anita backstage; which meant that probably that particular problem had already settled itself.

CHAPTER EIGHT

Dan

When Danny Dannerman was eight years old, spaceflight was still a going business. Young Danny was a pretty normal American kid, too, so naturally he did a lot of daydreaming, picturing his grown-up self as one of those grand spacefaring adventurers with sharp uniforms, rows of ribbons, the look of eagles on their faces and all. But that was then. Then he was a child. As he was growing to become a man, the space program was dwindling at almost the same rate of speed—few human heroes but a lot of machines; then, as money began to run short, fewer machines, too. Even instrument launches got rarer and rarer, and the dream dried up.

Until now.

Now it had become not only real but *personal,* and Dannerman had never reckoned on anything like this. When he joined the National Bureau of Investigation he knew, as every rookie knew, that the work could take you anywhere in the world; but it had never occurred to him that it might someday take him right out of it. All the way home from Coney Island, in the subway train sparsely occupied by drunks and sleeping homeless people, he thought about what he had let himself in for. Climb into a giant kind of sardine can and let them lock it shut behind you. Lie there, strapped in and helpless, while a few dozen exploding tons of fireworks blasted you, hard as a hammer blow, right off the surface of the Earth. Oh, the idea was exciting, all right; but it kept him awake for an hour after, very late, he finally got to his narrow bed in Rita's condo, and then he dreamed all night of spaceships and hideous, sharp-toothed aliens and a long, terrifying fall out of orbit. He didn't know what final smashup he was falling to. The dreams never got that far. But all night long he was falling, falling; and when the speaker clock woke him at 6:45 (the only time he could expect to beat his neighbors to the shower) he was edgy and unrested.

And then, as he was getting ready to leave, Hilda called. "You're awake. Good. You've got a busy day ahead of you, Danno. I should've told you there wasn't much time. Now there's no time at all."

"What are you talking about?"

"I'm talking about your cousin, what do you think? She got all her papers signed last night. She's planning to launch tomorrow."

The news beat Dannerman to the office. By the time he arrived, half the observatory staff was clustered in the reception room, all chattering. "What's going on?" he demanded, as Janice DuPage checked his sidearm. "Where's Jarvas?"

"In Dr. Adcock's office. So're Dr. Artzybachova and Commander Lin. They're going up to the orbiter, Dan!"

"Up to the Starcophagus?" he asked, hoping to learn more than the colonel had been able to tell him.

Even in the excitement of the morning she took time to give him a reproving look. "To the *Starlab*, right. We don't use that other word, remember? Anyway," she went on, the spirit of the morning taking over again, "she's going to make an announcement as soon as everyone's here—that'll be any minute now—but that's what it is, all right. I saw the documents myself when they came in. Isn't that wonderful, Dr. Papathanassiou?" she added, as the old man came up to hand her his ancient Uzi.

"Yes, quite wonderful," he said, managing to avoid noticing that Dannerman was standing right beside him.

"It calls for a celebration," said one of the postdocs. "Is there any money in petty cash, Janice? Maybe Dan could go out and get some supplies—"

"I'll ask Dr. Adcock as soon as she's made the announcement," Janice promised, and someone else predicted:

"She won't want to spend the money."

"So what the hell," the postdoc said happily. "We'll take up a collection. God! To have observing time on Starlab! You don't know what that's going to do for my T-Tauri count!"

But they did know; they all did know, because almost all of them had observations they wanted to make, and only the skimpiest budget of hours Pat Adcock had been willing to buy for them on the Keck, or the big twin instruments in Arizona, or even the ancient radio dish at Arecibo. They didn't need party "supplies." They were all partying already, and when the interoffice channel lighted up and Pat Adcock's flushed face appeared on all the screens there was a cheer from everywhere in the observatory.

Pat had to have heard it, even locked in her private office; she looked startled, then grinned. "I guess you all know what I'm going to say already," she said. "Well, it's true. The mission is on. We're taking off tomorrow; in seventy-two hours we'll be on Starlab. Dr. Schneyman will be in charge while I'm gone—and—and wish me luck, all of you!"

But she hadn't said what kind of luck she wanted. Dannerman wondered what she was going to tell them all if she got back with a fortune in new technology, but the old orbiter still out of commission . . . but it wouldn't matter, of course. If she was right—

If she was right, the whole world was going to change, and Dannerman himself would be part of it . . . provided, that is, he reminded himself, he did what the colonel wanted him to do and won the chance to go along.

He patted his belly bag, where the pouch Hilda had given him was packed away. What he needed now was a chance to use it.

Pat had firmly vetoed the notion of a party, but not much work got done at the observatory that morning anyway. Word of the mission had got out. Janice was kept busy on the phone, fending off calls from well-wishers, listening to complaints from the downstairs security guards, besieged by reporters with their tinycams who wanted statements from Dr. Adcock. When Pat took her crew out to an early lunch most of the staff took off, too, determined to celebrate even if they had to do it at some nearby restaurant. The observatory finally began to quiet down.

It was time for Dannerman to do his job; all he needed was for Janice DuPage to cooperate. He lurked around the reception room, waiting for her to leave her desk for a moment. It didn't happen for a long time. She seemed fixed at her desk, making him wonder what sort of bladder the woman had. But finally, with hardly a quarter of an hour before Mick Jarvas would be back with his charges, Janice stood up, put the elevator door entrance on lock, picked up her purse and moved toward the washrooms.

Dannerman didn't wait. As soon as she was out of sight he was in the gun locker. A coded computer file might defeat the skills the Bureau had taught him, but a simple locker was not a serious challenge. In thirty seconds he had the locker open, peering past the gun racks until he found Jarvas's private cubbyhole. And when he had it open, there, in among the candy bars and the anti-inflation trade goods and the porno disks, was a package, unmarked, with three sealed medical-looking patches that, he knew, did not contain any physician-prescribed medications.

Bingo. Dannerman pulled the patches out, stuffed them in his belly bag and replaced them with three of the ones Hilda had given him the night before. By the time Janice returned from the ladies' room he was innocently watering the reception-room plants and realizing that he had not left himself enough time to eat lunch. No matter. A missed meal was a small enough price to pay for the mission.

J arvas was predictable. As soon as he had escorted his charges back from lunch he made a beeline for the gun locker, then for a cubicle in the men's room.

Ten minutes later Dannerman knocked on the lintel of the office where Jimmy Peng-tsu Lin was conferring with Pat Adcock. "Excuse me," he said. "Jimmy?—Commander Lin, I mean? I hate to bother you, but Mick Jarvas is acting kind of funny out here. He's a pretty big guy, and I wonder if you could give me a hand with him."

That brought them both to the doorway, where they gazed incredulously at Jarvas. Who was dreamily waltzing up and down the corridor, pinching the ass of Rosaleen Artzybachova in passing, grabbing unsuccessfully at the breast of Janice DuPage. Rosaleen was laughing; Janice was only annoyed. As he neared Pat Adcock's office she found her voice. "Come in here, Jarvas!" she commanded.

"Sure thing, sweet buns," he said amiably. "Hi, Danny. How's it going, China boy?"

Pat looked bewilderedly at Dannerman as he was closing the door behind them. "What happened?"

Dannerman shrugged. "My guess, he must've got his hands

on some extra-powerful dope. You never know what they're going to be selling you on the street."

The bewildered expression changed to anger. "Crap! Mick promised me he doesn't do drugs anymore. I couldn't have a doper for a bodyguard."

"Oh? Well, why don't we just ask him to take his shirt off?"

"Aw, Dan," Jarvas said, suddenly pouting. "I thought you and me were friends."

Pat looked from one to the other, then made her decision. "Do what he says, Mick."

"I don't have to. I got pers'nal privacy rights, don't I?"

She turned to Dannerman. "Take it off him, Dan."

Dannerman looked at Jimmy Lin, who spread his hands; evidently personal combat wasn't one of his specialties. It wasn't something Dannerman would have sought with somebody like Mick Jarvas, either; but the former kick-boxer was giggling. Apart from good-naturedly pushing at Dannerman's hands he hardly resisted as Dannerman pulled the tabs of his shirt loose, *zip*, and slid it down over his back.

On Jarvas's rib cage, just under his right armpit, there was one of Hilda's inconspicuous, flesh-colored patches.

Jimmy Lin chuckled. "Well, what do you know? He really is mellowed out."

"Oh, shit," said Pat, too disappointed to be furious. "What am I going to do now? He can't escort me in that condition."

Jarvas gave her a happy grin. "Course I can, hon. Little joy never hurt me. Just makes my reflexes sharper and all."

He might as well not have been in the room; Pat, biting her lip, didn't even look at him. "I was counting on him," she told the air.

It was the cue Dannerman had been waiting for, but Jimmy Lin forestalled him. "If you need a new bodyguard, Pat," he offered, "what's the matter with your cousin? He's handy enough with his fists, you tell me."

"Danny? For a *bodyguard*?" Pat Adcock stared at him, then at Dannerman. "I guess you're big enough," she said thoughtfully. "What kind of gun do you carry?"

"Twenty-shot spray with quick-change clips. Same as always."

"Are you sure you know how to use it? Oh, right, you were rotsy in college, weren't you?"

"Protsy, actually."

She sighed and made up her mind. "I don't really have much of a choice, do I? All right, Dan-Dan, I guess you're about due for a promotion. How would you like be an astronaut for a while?"

Not much work got done in the observatory that afternoon, either. At least not by Pat Adcock and her spacefarers. As soon as they'd sent Jarvas, sniveling, back to his home in the company of one of the larger postdocs, Pat declared herself through for the day. "Take me home, Dan. I've got to pack. You better take an overnight bag, too."

"Sure thing, Pat. I'm new at this, though. What sort of stuff do you pack to go into space?"

"How do I know? I've never done it before either. I guess they'll give us all the space stuff we need at the Cape, but we'll be gone five days, according to the mission plan, so take whatever personal things you think you'll need. And, oh, yes, don't forget your gun."

"You're expecting trouble?"

She didn't answer. Just, "Don't forget, I want you back at six A.M. to get us to the airport."

Six o'clock, Dannerman thought dismally on the ride up to Pat's Yorktown condo. That meant getting up not much after four; it was a long way from Rita's Riverside Drive place to Yorktown. But at least he could make it an early night.

As soon as he had reported his success to Colonel Hilda Morrisey he went looking for his landlady. "I'm taking your advice and getting out of town for a while, Rita," he told her.

"Hey, great! Where are you going?"

"Florida," he said, and stopped her lecture on how nasty the Floridians were since they got their own government by taking out his payment machine. "I'm not sure how long I'll be gone, so I'd better pay a week or so in advance. I don't want you throwing my stuff out into the street."

"Oh, Dan! I wouldn't do that," she protested, "not even if you were away for even a month."

"It won't be that long," he assured her. "I'm sure of that."

CHAPTER NINE

Dan

The captain's voice woke Dannerman as the plane was making its approach to the José Martí airport outside the Cape. He hadn't intended to sleep. He hadn't realized he actually was sleeping until he woke up, saw the red light on the seat back before him to show that the airbag had just been armed and saw Pat Adcock stirring beside him. "Look there," she said, yawning as she gazed out the window. "That's our Clipper." There it was, gleaming ceramic white, forty meters tall, with work trucks and people busy around it.

So it wasn't a dream. It was real. That was the ship that was going to lift Dannerman and the others right off the solid planet they had been born to, and all those childish fantasies would become fact.

"Are you scared?" his cousin asked him, giving him a searching look.

"Oh, no. Well, not really *scared*. Are you?"

"Certainly not," she said. "Going into space isn't what worries me. Uncle Cubby brainwashed me pretty well, you know; it was his dream, only he never could pass the physical to make it on his own, and I guess he infected me. That's not what's bothering me."

He looked at her with new interest. "But something else is?"

"Well, yes." She squirmed around to look back at Jimmy Lin and Rosaleen Artzybachova, in their own seats a few rows back. "For one thing, I don't know if I can trust Lin," she said moodily as she straightened again. "Delasquez, either. That's why I want you along, Dan. Keep an eye on those guys while we're up there."

"But they're the pilots you picked," he said reasonably.

She shrugged. "I had to take what I could get. Just be careful about them, okay?" She peered up and down the length of the plane. "Do you suppose it's too late to go to the can?" she asked.

It was. The stews were cruising the aisle, checking seat belts and picking up empty glasses. He said consolingly, "We'll be on the ground in a moment."

"Yes? And then what?"

He said, surprised, "Then there'll be a chance to get to the ladies' room right away."

She gave him a pursed-lips look. "That's right, you've never been in Florida before, have you?"

He hadn't understood what Pat had meant by that, but as soon as they were off the plane it became clear. The passengers were not permitted to step off the plane and go freely about their business. The passengers were immediately herded into long lines for customs inspection—well, it wasn't called "customs," exactly, since Florida wasn't really an exactly independent country, however determinedly they insisted on their own laws and practices. The processing was just as thorough, though, and the first step was that one of the agents collected everybody's carry weapons. Dannerman hated to give up his twenty-shot, but all the more seasoned Florida travelers seemed to take it as a matter of course. The agent tagged each gun and gave the owner a claim check—"So you can redeem it, señor, when you leave our beautiful Free State." Then another set of agents searched methodically through everyone's bags and pockets. For a moment Dannerman thought they might even insist on a body-cavity search as well, but it didn't come to that. It was bad enough, though; the inspector gasped in outrage when she patted him down and found his ankle weapon.

She held the gun in her hand and gave him a severe look. "This is contraband weapon," she announced. "It is conceal. This is not permit in the Free State of Florida. It must be confiscate." She beckoned to a state policeman, who patted his own gun to make sure it hadn't fallen out of its holster as he strolled toward them.

The cop waved all four of the party over to a little quarantine ghetto while the customs agent and her supervisor debated the matter in Spanish. Pat was irate. Rosaleen Artzybachova waited patiently for a resolution to the problem. Jimmy Lin showed amusement. "Danny, Danny," he said reproachfully, "don't you know any better than that? When you go to Florida you leave your own gun at home. Nobody brings a gun to Florida. You don't need it. You can always pick up another on the street—there's not a block in the state where you can't buy anything you want."

Dannerman didn't answer. He did know better; he just hadn't wanted to part with his service special.

"It's all right," Pat announced, waving in relief to a tall man who had appeared at the customs desk. Although he was wearing a different uniform this time, gleaming dress whites with clusters of ribbons at his chest, Dannerman recognized General Martín Delasquez. He spoke rapidly to the customs agents, then approached them, looking grave.

"What a pity, Dr. Adcock," he said to Pat, ignoring Dannerman. "Your man has attempted to break our law. Therefore he is forbidden admission to our state. However, I believe that we can avoid the legal penalties. I have arranged that he will be placed on the first return flight to New York, and the rest of you may proceed to the staging area."

"Oh, no!" Pat Adcock exclaimed. "I want him with me."

Delasquez shook his head politely. "But it is impossible, you see?" he said reasonably.

"Maybe not," Dannerman said. He had been watching Delasquez carefully. The general looked at him for the first time.

"You spoke?" he asked, his tone frosty.

"Yes, I did, General. You know what I bet? I bet you have enough authority to get us all through these bureaucrats, don't you, General?"

Delasquez said coldly, "It is apparent that you do not understand the gravity of your situation."

"I bet I do. For instance, I bet I know what would happen next. I bet while I was waiting for the next plane the cops would ask me a lot of questions. I wouldn't want to lie to them, either. And if the subject of our first meeting came up I'd have to tell them anything they wanted to know—you know, like the articles I delivered to you in New York?"

Delasquez did not respond for a moment. He studied Dannerman in silence, then turned to Pat Adcock. "Who is this man?" he demanded.

She shrugged. "He's my cousin."

"And do you know what trouble this could cause?" She didn't answer, only shrugged again. Then Delasquez smiled. "Well, what harm can it do? It is only a technical violation, after all. I think I can persuade the authorities to let you pass."

"And get our guns back for us, too, please," Dannerman added.

CHAPTER TEN

Dan

The flight started tamely. The takeoff thrust was not much worse than some of the high-speed scramjets Dannerman had taken to cross an ocean, but the Clipper was still being an airplane then.

He hardly noticed when the takeoff jets switched over to the higher-speed contoured flow, but then the time came when the scram cut over to rocket thrust, and he noticed that, all right. That was *real* acceleration. He was squashed into his seat for four long minutes. His belly sagged, his head drooped, he realized for the first time that even his eyeballs had weight on their sockets. Then he fell forward against his chest straps as the thrust cut; he was suddenly weightless, and they were on their way.

It was about then that Dannerman realized that space travel took a long time to happen . . . and that while it was happening there was nothing much to do. What he wanted to do was to get out of his seat and roam around the Clipper, but he had been warned against that. He quickly saw why. Every course correction brought another jolt, not nearly as violent as the first but unpredictable for either time or direction. Then the gimbaled seats tilted, the motors roared, and you were lucky if you didn't bite your tongue or bash your head.

A window, at least, would have been nice. He didn't have one. All he had was the tiny TV screen on his armrest, but all it showed was black, empty space. By his side Rosaleen Artzybachova sat with her eyes placidly closed, maybe even napping; well, spaceflight was nothing new to her. She could not have been comfortable; her feet rested on a pair of gray metal boxes, lashed to the seat supports, and so her knees were squeezed almost into her belly. Just ahead, but out of his sight, Pat was in the third-pilot seat, trying to talk to Delasquez and Lin at the controls; Dannerman couldn't make out the words, and if the pilots answered he couldn't hear.

In the seat next to him Artzybachova opened her eyes and gazed at him. "Are you all right?" When he nodded, she asked politely, "And how are you enjoying spaceflight? Is it what you expected?"

"Well, no. Not exactly. I thought we'd have to go through more training—"

She laughed. "Like high-G conditioning in those awful old centrifuges? Drills for emergency actions? Thank heaven, we don't do that anymore. We don't wear spacesuits, either."

"I noticed that." What Dannerman himself had on was the slacks and jacket he had put on that morning. Dr. Artzybachova and Jimmy Lin were wearing one-piece coveralls, General Delasquez the combat fatigues of the Florida Air Guard.

Dr. Artzybachova was still being grandmotherly. "Are you hungry? I brought some apples and I believe there are other things on board."

"Hungry? No."

"And you don't have to pee or anything? You should've gone before we took off."

"I don't," he said shortly, but she had put the idea in his mind. He quelled it, for there was an opportunity here to be taken. "Dr. Artzybachova? Can I ask you something? Is there something, well, peculiar about what we're doing?"

She gave him an amused look, pale eyebrows raised. "Define 'peculiar.'"

He chose his words with care. "This is supposed to be a simple repair mission, right? But there are all these rumors—"

"What kind of rumors?"

He spread his hands. "Something about some kind of radiation from Starlab that wasn't supposed to be there? I don't understand that very well, Dr. Artzybachova; I was an English major. And something about those messages with the Seven Ugly Space Dwarfs?"

"You are very skilled at listening to rumors, Mr. Dannerman." It wasn't a compliment.

He pressed on. "I get the idea that that's really what this mission is about. Something *alien* on Starlab? Something that might be worth a lot of money. Pat wouldn't talk to me about it—"

"That is not surprising," the old lady observed.

"I guess not. Will you?"

Dr. Artzybachova studied his face for a moment, considering, while the Clipper rolled itself into a new position. "I suppose it could do no harm now. In a little while you will see what we all see—whatever that turns out to be. Or it will turn out that there is nothing worth seeing, and then we will simply try to determine what repairs might make Starlab function as originally designed again. So," she said, sighing, "yes, the rumors are true. Fifteen months ago your cousin's observatory detected a burst of synchrotron radiation from Starlab. No one else appeared to observe it, but then no one else was actively trying to reestablish communications with the orbiter. So she called me at my dacha. I flew at once to New York. We examined all the logs of instrumentation changes and, no, there simply was nothing on Starlab that could have produced that emission. So we performed a data check."

Dannerman pricked up his ears; this was new. "What kind of data check?"

"A fortunate coincidence: the Japanese were getting ready to replace one of their old weather satellites, so they did a census of everything in orbit—to select a safe slot for their satellite, you see. One of their instrument people was a former student of mine. From her I got all their obs of astronomical satellites—including Starlab. When we massaged the data it became clear that there was a steady flux of very low-level radiation coming from it, in several bands—none of it compatible with the presumed dead-board status of the satellite. In addition, optically, there was a blister on the side of the satellite that didn't belong there. Finally, just recently we got another indication. There was a comet-like object—"

"Yes, I know about the comet-like object."

She regarded him thoughtfully. "Yes, I suppose you do."

"And what all this adds up to?"

"Oh, Mr. Dannerman," she said, sounding less patient, "I have no doubt that you know that, too. All the evidence taken together, there is strong reason to believe that something extraterrestrial has established itself on Starlab."

"An *alien*?"

She looked pensive. "Probably not a living one, no. At least I hope not. More likely some sort of automated probe. But definitely some sort of technology that is not terrestrial in origin."

A quick course correction spun their chairs around; the old lady grimaced and closed her eyes. Evidently she had finished her story.

But Dannerman hadn't finished thinking about it. It sounded wholly preposterous, but this apparently sane woman seemed to give it credence. He cleared his throat. "Dr. Artzybachova?" And when she opened her eyes again, "I can see that new technology might be worth a lot of money. But what do you do with it when we find it?"

"*If* we find it. But that I cannot say until we see it, of course. That is what I am along for, me and my instruments." She tapped one of the boxes with a toe.

"I was wondering about them," he said.

She smiled. "Of course. Did you think I could examine what we find—whatever we find—by smell, perhaps? Although it may be that none of these instruments will be of any use, since we have no data on what might be there."

"But you must have some idea—"

She raised her hand amiably. "But, Mr. Dannerman—Dan, may I? And please call me Rosaleen; it was a notion of my mother's when I was born. She was much taken with the wife of your American president and gave me a name as close to hers as she dared." She paused, then finished her thought. "But, Dan, I really don't know what will be on Starlab, you see. I only have hopes. I hope that there will be some useful-looking devices which I can remove and bring back for analysis. Do you know the term 'reverse engineering'? For that, so that perhaps they can be copied in some way. Will that happen? I don't know. Will there be anything alien in Starlab at all? I don't know even that much, either; it is all hopes. It is quite possible that, even if there is something there, it will be so unfamiliar that I will not dare to try to remove it. Or there may be nothing at all. In either case, we will have done all this for nothing."

He looked at her. "Seems like a pretty long shot, the way you describe it."

"Ah," she said softly, "but think of the payoff. If we win our bet there will be unimaginable benefits, and not just in money. I would not have left my comfortable summer place in Ukraine just for the money, only for the chance to learn." She looked pensive for a moment, then smiled. "Whatever it is, we'll find out for sure when we get aboard. Now, Dan, if you'll excuse me,

we should be coming around toward North America again and
I'd like to check the uplinks for news."

Dannerman must have drifted off
to sleep again, in spite of everything, because the next thing he
remembered was Jimmy Lin's cheery hail. The astronaut was
swinging weightlessly toward them, hand over hand, pausing to
float in space upside down by Dannerman. "So how do you like
micrograv?" he asked amiably; then, glancing at Artzybachova
and lowering his voice: "Tell you one thing, if my great-great
had ever gone into orbit he would've had to write three or four
new books. You don't know what screwing is until you try it
weightless."

Rosaleen turned to him, her arms still waving in the graceful
flow of tai chi. Ignoring the astronaut's remarks, she asked, "Are
we getting close to Starlab?"

"Not too far. That's why I'm going to the head now; if we
have to wear those damn suits I won't want to need to pee. I
recommend the same to you two, soon's I'm through. But don't
stay out of your seats any longer than you have to, okay? And
sing out when you're both strapped in again. The general claims
he ranks me, so he's doing most of the piloting, and he has a
heavy hand with the delta-vees."

Dannerman's bladder was signaling to him with increasing
urgency, but he didn't get his turn for a while. He deferred to
Rosaleen Artzybachova out of politeness, and then to General
Delasquez because he wasn't given much choice when the pilot
came back and pushed his way past; then to his cousin out of
politeness again. By then his fidgeting was becoming conspic-
uous. Dr. Artzybachova, observing it, did her best to distract
him. "Have you seen?" she inquired, reaching over to adjust his

screen. It was displaying something tiny and oddly shaped, but when she turned up the magnification it became a satellite with antennae and solar collectors poking out in all directions.

"Starlab?" he ventured.

That amused her. "No, of course not. It is simply a dead old orbiter, I think a military one, and probably Russian; but it is interesting, is it not?"

Oh, it was interesting enough, as a souvenir of the days when wars were actually fought between nations, instead of between legions of police on one side, and on the other a horde of criminals and a few squads of slippery terrorists. He cast a longing look at the toilet, but Pat was still locked inside. "Well," he said to the Ukrainian woman, forcing jolliness into his tone, "was there any interesting news in the uplinks?" Dutifully she rehearsed the principal items for him: England's MI-5 had caught a dozen Welsh freedom fighters redhanded in possession of nuclear materials; some Sikhs at the Marseilles airport had machine-gunned Moslem pilgrims en route to Mecca; and in Washington the President had finally announced the death of his kidnapped press secretary. Hilda would be going crazy, he thought; but he didn't think it long. The door to the toilet was opening, and he was already unbuckling himself to go there.

Pat was looking baffled when she finally came out, and when Dannerman got his chance at the toilet he saw why. The writing on the cubicle wall wasn't graffiti. It was instructions, a complete tech manual to the use of a micrograv toilet, and it took a bit of doing. As he was finishing up with the complex flush maneuver he heard squawking from outside. He hurried back to his seat, Rosaleen waving him on; and there, spinning slowly on the screen, was an orbiter that he recognized because he had spent so much time studying its pictures. There was no doubt about it. Just disappearing from view between the solar-collector struts and a communications dish was the blister that might, or might not, have come from outer space. The construction was *immense*.

"So that's Starlab," he said.

"Of course it is," Rosaleen said fretfully. "And, look, the optical mirror has been left uncovered all this time—who knows how much damage it's taken from microjunk impacts?"

"There's a little ship attached to the side," Dannerman observed.

"Yes, the ACRV—the Assured Crew Rescue Vehicle. It was supposed to take crew back to the Earth in an emergency, but poor Manny Lefrik never got a chance to use it."

"Manny Lefrik?" Memory clicked the name into place: the astronomer who had died on Starlab. "Did you know him?"

She sighed. "Of course I knew him. Very well, in fact, and on this very satellite; Jimmy was quite right about making love in microgravity." And then, noting the expression on his face, "Oh, Dan! Can you not believe that I was not always a million years old? But buckle yourself in quickly; there will be much maneuvering now. Hurry!"

She was right about the maneuvering. Docking was tricky, with a lot of swearing in three languages from the pilots up ahead as they jockeyed the spacecraft to its port. But then there was a faint metallic crunch and a shudder, and a cry of satisfaction from Pat Adcock. The Clipper had mated with Starlab.

Beside him, Rosaleen Artzybachova was busily removing the containment straps from her instrument cases. "Let me help you," Dannerman offered.

She hesitated. "Yes, perhaps it would be better if you took one. But do be careful with it!"

"Stay put, you people," Delasquez called from up front. "We're checking the life support."

But Starlab's systems were apparently working, even after all these years; the internal pressure and temperature were all right—a bit chilly, maybe, Jimmy Lin suggested, but they wouldn't need the suits. ("Thank God," Rosaleen muttered gratefully. "I hate trying to get in and out of those things.") Even the lights were working—some of them, anyway. Enough.

Then the arguments started. Pat wanted somebody to stay behind in the Clipper, preferably one of the pilots. "For Christ's sake, why?" Jimmy Lin snarled.

"Just in case."

"Just in case, screw that. Nothing's going to happen here, and anyway Dannerman can stay on board if you want him to. I'm going in."

And he did, Pat right behind him; even encumbered with one of the instrument boxes Rosaleen Artzybachova squirmed ahead of Delasquez, who was angrily stuck with going through the shutdown checklist. In spite of Lin's suggestion, Dannerman was not far behind. As he squeezed through the docking port, tugging his own massive toolbox, he heard Rosaleen's shocked voice—"Do your mother! Everything's all *different*!"

CHAPTER ELEVEN

Dan

It wasn't what he had expected. He hadn't expected Starlab to be so warm, but it was. That was passive heating, Rosaleen said, only sunlight. He certainly hadn't expected it to stink. But it did, a rancid, pervasive odor, part chemical, part almost like cinnamon. Was it the decaying body of the abandoned astronomer? Not likely. It wasn't really a spoiled-meat smell, and besides the mortal remains of the lost Manny Lefrik must have long since finished all the decay that was possible to him.

But that was not the greatest shock. Rosaleen Artzybachova had been right. It was all different. The views of the Starlab interior he had studied displayed gray metal cabinets, sunshine-yellow and warm red walls, patterned wall hammocks. Those things were still here, most of them, but to them had been added objects that the schematics had never displayed: green-flecked lumps of transparent matter, like lime Jell-O, with glittering sparks of gold and diamond light flickering within it; a great copper-colored pillar, six-sided, that gave out perceptible warmth; a huge cupboard sort of thing with a door that slowly swung closed when Dannerman tried to peer into it—things for which he had no easy name. There had been structural changes, too. Even some of the walls were gone. The partitioned space of the original had been opened up, and here and there, all about, stuck at crazy angles from the remaining walls, were the machines that were like nothing Dannerman had ever seen before. The more he looked the stranger they got. He saw some that were palely luminous, some velvet black; they were rounded or jagged-edged, some with brightly glowing dots on the surface that flickered and changed as he watched, some faintly crackling or humming. None of them looked *normal.*

"Jesus," he said. "I guess you were right, Pat. That's not any human stuff."

Pat's face was glowing in triumph. "Effing well right it isn't, Dan-Dan! It's *alien.* And it's *ours!*"

"But what do those things *do?*"

"What's the difference? My God, Dan," she said happily, reaching out to caress the pinkly glowing surface of one of the machines, "once we get this stuff back and figure out how it works—can you *imagine* what it'll be worth? We'll make a bundle out of this."

"If we can move it," Rosaleen Artzybachova muttered, trying to fasten her instrument box to a handhold on the wall while, like everyone else, she was distractedly staring at everything around her. "Pat, I recommend you do not touch anything until I have had a chance to study it. The rest of you, too."

Pat pulled her hand back; beside her, Jimmy Lin was doing the same thing. "What's the problem?" he asked.

"How do I know what problem there is? Perhaps there is no problem at all, or perhaps if you touch it it will fry you to a crisp. If you want to experiment I suppose it is your right, but I would prefer that you help me."

"Me, too?" Dannerman asked, trying to keep his own instrument box from bumping into anything; in the micrograv environment it weighed nothing, but its mass made it hard to handle.

"Oh, Dan," Rosaleen sighed, "what help could you be? At least the others have some experience with instrumentation. No. Go and explore."

"I'll go with him," Pat said suddenly.

"You also want to be a tourist? And, General Delasquez, is that what you are indicating, too, with that scowl? Well, why not? If there are too many unskilled helpers here it will be worse than none at all, so go. Look for old Manny's body; perhaps we can give it a decent burial in space while we are here."

"And maybe get rid of some of the stench," Martín Delasquez growled.

The old woman ignored him. "Or perhaps you will meet some interesting stranger, and then you will come back and tell us. If you can."

A few meters down the main transverse Pat stopped and consulted a scrap of paper from her pocket. The general gave her a suspicious look, but brushed past her to go off on his own. "Let him go," Pat muttered without looking up. "Maybe he'll see something we don't. Let's see, we follow this transverse to the second junction—"

Dannerman drew the obvious inference. "You're looking for something specific."

She glanced after Delasquez's disappearing form and lowered her voice. "Right you are, Dan-Dan. I want to see where that blister was attached, from the inside. Come on, I think I know where I'm going."

The way you got around in the effectively gravitationless Starlab was by pulling yourself along by the handholds spaced along the walls, or by hurling yourself like a slow-moving projectile from point to point. Neither Dannerman nor Pat was up to projectile standards, so progress was slow.

They didn't speak. Pat was concentrating on the chart in her hand, Dannerman thinking about the implications of Rosaleen's final remark. If artifacts had been added to Starlab, as they had, someone had to have put them there. And it was at least a reasonable possibility that that someone was still there.

Dannerman kept his eyes peeled as they drifted along the passages. Ears, too, but there wasn't much to hear. Even the chatter between Rosaleen and Jimmy Lin became inaudible after the first few turns. Apart from the cryptic noises that came from the alien machines, the only sounds Dannerman heard came from Pat and himself.

When Starlab's designers planned the satellite they allowed for weeks or months of occupancy by its observers. That meant they had to make arrangements for living quarters. So they did, but they were not lavish. The residents weren't given rooms. What they had—Dannerman perceived as he pulled himself through the square-sided passages of the observatory—was no more than coffinlike cubicles. The things were doorless, though fitted with stiff fabric panels to provide at least the illusion of privacy, and they were small—smaller than any broom closet Dannerman had ever seen, and not much more elaborate.

There was more of Starlab than he had expected. For Pat, too, it seemed—when, twice, she paused to look uncertainly around and when, once, she had to retrace her steps for half a dozen meters. Dannerman assumed she was lost, and the way she muttered to herself made that assumption plausible. "But it ought . . . ought to be . . . right *here,"* she murmured, touching a bare spot on the corridor wall; and then, "Hell! It *is!"*

Is what? Dannerman asked, but only silently. He didn't have to say it out loud because Pat was already demonstrating the answer. Her fingers traced the lines that made up a hexagonal shape on the wall; the lines were new, bright metal. "They cut a patch out here. Then they entered. Then they welded it up again."

"Who 'they'?" Dannerman asked.

She gave him a look of mild surprise. "The people who brought this new stuff aboard, of course."

"Then *where* they?"

There was less surprise this time, but more visible worry. "Yes, that's the question all right, isn't it? Probably there wasn't a living 'they' at all, Dan, just some robot probe machinery."

Dannerman made a neutral sound. In his view, the word "robot" did not exclude some mean-tempered clanking thing that could be quite as unpleasant to meet as any of the Seven Ugly Space Dwarfs. "One thing, though," he said.

"What?"

"If all the machinery we've seen came on the thing that looks like a blister—probably from the CLO, I guess—how did it all fit?"

Pat opened her mouth to answer, and then closed it again. Obviously it was a hard question. The amount of unfamiliar gadgetry in Starlab could easily have filled a dozen objects the size of the blister. Some of them were far too large to have been squeezed through the space traced on the wall, as well.

"I don't know," she said at last. "Maybe—"

But whatever the "maybe" was going to be, Dannerman never heard it. She stopped in midsentence, turning toward a sound that came from one of the corridor openings; and so did Dannerman, his hand on his twenty-shot.

What appeared in the corridor wasn't an alien. It was General Martín Delasquez—who also had his hand on his gun, and a look of alarm on his face.

His expression cleared. "Oh, it's only you," he said. "I thought it might be whatever's been eating the corpse."

"The corpse?" Dannerman repeated.

"The dead astronomer, Manny something? I found his body."

"Well, that's not so surprising; we knew that he died here, so his body had to be somewhere around."

"Sure you did. But did you also know that his head was missing?"

Rats," Rosaleen Artzybachova informed them. "A headless corpse? Of course it is rats. They go wherever human beings go. It is not surprising that some managed to get aboard Starlab somewhere along the line, or that they would mutilate a corpse."

"And then disappear," Jimmy Lin suggested sardonically.

"And then die of starvation," she corrected him, "or of plague, or whatever. Or possibly they have not disappeared at all but are still aboard. Rats are excellent at avoiding attention."

"But—" Pat began, unconvinced.

"*But,*" Rosaleen overrode her, "in any case they are not our problem. Our problem is merely to detach some of these artifacts and stow them on the Clipper."

Pat nibbled her lower lip in silence. Martín Delasquez, looking at the single cobalt-colored metal lever that Rosaleen had so far detached, said, "You aren't doing very well at that, are you?"

Rosaleen Artzybachova swung around to confront him. "You have some criticism? Would you like to do this yourself? No? That does not surprise me. It is much easier for someone like you to complain than to try to understand how these things are interconnected, or what will happen if we separate them."

"But someone like me," Delasquez said, "does not claim to be an expert on instrumentation. You do, do you not? Isn't that why you are here?"

"I'm earning my way," Rosaleen said grimly. "And I'm not getting paid for my services twice."

Delasquez looked insulted. "Are you referring to the gems I was given? But those were not for me! They were to make it possible to get clearance on such short notice for this flight."

The quarrel distracted Pat Adcock from her thoughts of corpse-eating creatures. "Oh, hell," she said, "what are you fighting about? There's plenty to go around, just as we agreed."

Jimmy Lin cleared his throat. "I think not," he said politely. "You know what I think, Pat? I think we're going to have to refigure all that."

"The hell with that!" she said sharply. "We made a deal, and we're sticking to it. Remember, Starlab's my satellite! Well, the observatory's," she qualified, "but as far as you're concerned that's the same thing. Starlab was built and launched with my uncle's money, so it's private property. Mine."

Lin gave her a long, bland look. Then he shrugged—not in the manner of someone who is convinced, only in the manner of someone who has decided not to pursue the question for the moment.

However, Dannerman decided as he watched the squabble, Lin was not going to put it off forever. Then there was General Delasquez, silently listening. He was another who was presumably looking forward to renegotiating their arrangements.

Pat Adcock was taking charge. "Right, then. Rosaleen, what do you think? How long will it take you to get this stuff detached?"

"First I have to figure out what it is, Pat."

"Well, damn it, do it!"

The old lady pursed her lips. "I kind of agree with Jimmy," she said. "Why don't we talk about how we're going to split it up?"

"Rosaleen! Not you, too!" Pat bit her lip, then surrendered. "All right. We can settle this after we land. What we have to do now is pick out the likeliest items and shift them to the Clipper. When we land in California I've got a crew—"

Rosaleen interrupted her sharply. "California?"

Pat said apologetically, "I'm sorry I didn't tell you before,

Rosie. We couldn't go back to the Cape, though, could we? The vultures would be waiting to snatch it all away. Anyway, it's all arranged. I've got a crew and a chopper waiting in California. We'll offload as fast as we can and get the stuff to a safe place, and then—"

"We're not landing in California," General Delasquez said.

"Damn it, Martín! You agreed!"

"I have reconsidered the question. We will return to the Cape."

Dannerman sighed softly, because he knew what was coming. The four of them were regarding each other like stray tomcats, paying no attention at all to him.

Pat gave the general a sour look. "Don't be foolish. The arrangements are all made," she said crossly.

Delasquez shook his head. "No. I have also made arrangements. The State of Florida can make good use of this technology. We have suffered under Yanqui tyranny long enough; with this we can have full independence at last."

With the gun in his hand Dannerman spoke up. "And a little something extra for you personally, Martín?" he inquired politely.

That was when it all got rough. Delasquez fumbled for his own gun, tangled in the incongruous gilt-leather holster. Jimmy Lin was also reaching for something, no doubt a weapon of his own, but he didn't get very far. Rosaleen was perched just behind him, still holding the rod of blue metal; she didn't stop to speak but swung it and caught Lin on the side of the head.

"Oh, no, you must not," said a new voice.

Dannerman barely registered the fact that the voice was unfamiliar; he had Delasquez in the sights of his twenty-shot.

Then there was something like a flash—a tingle—a sudden sense of falling, and the weapon never did get fired.

CHAPTER TWELVE

Dan

A while later—he had no idea quite how long it had been—Dannerman blinked and opened his eyes. The other four were stirring around him, and they all looked bewildered. They were in the Clipper, though Dannerman didn't remember going there. He had a recollection of his gun being in his hand, though he wasn't sure why. He glanced hastily around, in case it was floating in the nearby air. It wasn't. He observed General Delasquez looking around in the same befuddled way, and, beyond him, Jimmy Lin, looking perturbed as he rubbed the side of his head. "What the hell happened?" he asked.

Rosaleen Artzybachova said shakily, "I think I must have had a touch of micro-G vertigo."

It looked to Dannerman as though they all had. Everyone seemed dazed, and Pat was weeping softly. "All for nothing," she whimpered. "Hell."

Jimmy Lin said pensively, "Bad enough there wasn't any of that alien technology; even Starlab's own equipment is ruined."

"Ruined," Rosaleen Artzybachova echoed. She sounded more than dazed, Dannerman thought; in fact, really ill. It was her age, most likely, he decided. But she kept on doggedly with the litany of loss: "Electronics fused, power supply ruined—there must've been a plasma arc. A big one. There's nothing left worth salvaging. Might as well start back. We can't do any good here."

Dannerman was scratching the back of his neck—as, for some reason, so were the others—as he was peering into the pilots' screen at Starlab's hull. He pointed at the bulge that had no business being there. "I really thought that was going to be something interesting," he said.

"Just some kind of sticky space glop, I guess," Jimmy Lin said. "All right, get strapped in. We're ready to undock."

Despondently, the five of them took their places, ready for the long return flight to Earth. . . .

CHAPTER THIRTEEN

Dan

And at the same time, but a very long way away, Dannerman blinked and opened his eyes . . . and squawked in unbelieving outrage. In a place he had never seen before, he was being held firmly by two people in Hallowe'en trick-or-treat dress—big ones, with a froth of white concealing their faces and an astonishing number of arms—while a smaller one in a different costume was interestedly, but inexpertly, undoing the flaps of his clothing to undress him. Shouting around him made him look about; all four of his companions were similarly held and two of them, Jimmy Lin and Pat, were already naked. He bellowed, "What the hell *happened*?"

He wasn't asking anyone in particular, but the goblin who was taking his clothes off gave him an answer—sort of an answer. It seemed to have the body of a large chicken; it gazed up at him out of mournful huge kitten's eyes and worked its slack jaw for a moment, and then it spoke. "Do not struggle. The handlers may damage you."

And Pat Adcock cried, half laughing, "My God, Dan! It's Dopey!"

CHAPTER FOURTEEN

Pat

Yes, the chicken with the cat's face did look like the Dopey the transmission from space had warned against; and the pale, bearded giant that never spoke was likely enough the Doc; and that was a subject for wonder; but Pat had other things on her mind. Pat Adcock had had fondly held hopes blighted before. Never like this. She had been so *close*! After all those interminable, exhausting weeks of court battles and conspiracy there had been that one great, exultant moment when it looked as though all her dreams were paying off. . . .

And then, *bam,* reality hit her right between the eyes and these bizarre creatures from a nightmare had snatched all the triumphs away.

But it wasn't a nightmare. Even that consolation was denied her. Improbable as it was, the Dopey was real, the whiskered Doc was real, the space aliens truly did exist and they had taken Pat Adcock prisoner. It was almost more than she could take in—the astonishment, the incredible strangeness of it all—but the wonder was diluted by fear. And diluted again by discomforts of several kinds, including her increasingly urgent need to go to the bathroom.

It was all more than she could handle, because nothing like this captivity had ever happened to Pat before. She had never been in jail. She had never in her life been restrained against her will in any way at all, unless you counted the times her nanny had made her sit in a corner for some five-year-old's wickedness. She wasn't prepared for it, and she didn't like it at all. She didn't like the six-sided chamber that was their prison, like a scaled-up honeycomb cell the size of a backyard swimming pool, or the bright mirrored surfaces that reflected their own naked bodies whichever way they looked. She didn't like being naked, for that matter—at least, not under these circumstances. Pat was not a prude about her body, but she had always been selective about whom she displayed it to. She especially didn't like the fact that there were no private spaces inside the cell, not even a toilet. About that she was, indeed, quite prudish.

She was not the only one suffering from affronted modesty. That dedicated sexual athlete, Jimmy Peng-tsu Lin, sat with his back against a wall, his bloodied head down in shame, hugging his knees to his chest to conceal as much of his privacy as possible. Dannerman and the general were less obvious in their discomfort, though the general, she saw, had a lot to be discomforted about. Lacking the built-in corsets of his uniform, his body sagged and bulged in unexpected ways. Both men, she observed, did their best to turn away from whomever they were talking to. Only Rosaleen Artzybachova seemed unaffected— very likely, Pat thought with interest, because she stripped down pretty well, for a woman of that age. All that exercise appeared to have paid off. Pat resolved to try a bit more of it for herself when she was back in her real life. . . .

If she ever was.

There did not seem to be a very high probability of that. They were well and truly captured, all five of them.

They were all responding in the same way, too. All five of them—well, all but Jimmy Lin, who was fully occupied in nursing his bashed head and his embarrassed nudity—had immediately begun to check the mirrored wall, centimeter by centimeter, looking for a doorway, perhaps, or at least some sort of gap. There wasn't any. "I guess we're stuck here," Dannerman said at last, and no one disagreed. All they could do was ask each other unanswerable questions and complain—"pissing and moaning" was the term Dannerman had used. It wasn't a good choice of words. Pat was uncomfortably aware that they had so far really done only the moaning part.

From all the questions a few facts were established early. They certainly were not on Starlab anymore, because gravity pressed them down as it had on Earth. They almost certainly were not on their own Earth, either, because of that same gravity. It was Rosaleen Artzybachova who noticed it first, but then they all agreed. They seemed to weigh a little less, pressed a little less heavily on the soles of their feet when they stood, perhaps could even jump just a bit higher, than they had for all their previous lives.

"Also," Rosaleen went on, "you will notice that we are breathing quite normally."

Pat frowned. "Yes?"

"Which means that the atmosphere here contains approximately an Earth-normal partial pressure of oxygen. I imagine the rest is probably nitrogen. Some inert gas, at any rate; and not helium or carbon dioxide, because we would know it if so, from the effects on our voices or our alertness. All the other inert gases are comparatively rare, so I believe," she said thoughtfully, "that it must be nitrogen." She reflected for a moment, then added, "The temperature is a bit warm—more like North Africa than New York, I would say—but still in a livable range."

Jimmy Lin looked up at her to make a face. "So, Dr. Artzybachova, put it all together and tell us what we need to know. Where are we?"

"Not on Earth, of course," she said at once. "Perhaps we are on a planet, I am not sure of that, but in any case not a planet of our own solar system—too much gravity for Mars or Mercury, not enough for any of the gas giants. And, of course, not on Venus, because the heat would have killed us at once. There are other possibilities. Perhaps we could be on a spaceship undergoing constant acceleration, but I doubt that also—I believe we would hear the rockets."

"If they use rockets," Dannerman offered.

"A good point," Rosaleen agreed. "But I think I do hear something. Perhaps motors somewhere? It doesn't sound like rocket engines. So we come back to the one clear fact: we are not on Earth."

Of course, that question was not seriously asked in the first place. They didn't really need much proof that they weren't on Earth, because the proof was right before their eyes. Nothing on Earth was like their cell, and nothing on Earth looked like the creatures who had disrobed them here.

There was argument about that, too: What were the creatures? Were they really the Seven Ugly Dwarfs from the space message? Rosaleen polled the group. Jimmy Lin had no opinion on that, partly because he was distancing himself from the others with his embarrassment and his sore head, and mostly because, he said, he had spent much of his recent time in a place where they did not pay a great deal of attention to such cartoons, namely at the Jiuquan space center in the People's Republic of China. Martín Delasquez didn't think their captors really resembled the figures from space, either, but there was no doubt in Pat's mind at all. It was simply statistically unlikely, she was sure, that two unrelated sets of such bizarre creatures could turn up at once.

She noticed that Dannerman took little part in the discussion. He was restlessly checking the cell out, not saying much, until abruptly he announced: "I'm hungry."

So, Pat realized once he mentioned it, was she. And wanting other creature comforts, too. "And I wish I had something to drink," she said wistfully, thinking of the silver decanter of ice-water always on her desk.

Rosaleen said, "I'm sure we all feel the same way, but the less fluid you take in the less you will have to discharge. Which we all must do." She looked around at the others, almost smiling. "We do not have a choice, you know. Shall I be the first?"

She paused for a moment, but no one answered; no one had a useful answer to give. "Very well," she said, and walked purposefully over to one wall, where she squatted down without further remark.

"Oh, hell," Pat said unhappily. "Hey, guys. At least you could all turn your backs." Jimmy Lin raised his head long enough to laugh sourly, glancing at the mirrored walls. Dannerman paid no attention—very conspicuously and politely paid no attention. He redoubled his study of the mirror wall, but by the sense of touch only, his eyes half closed against any impolite reflection. Martín stood by him, watching.

"There's nothing to see in the wall," the general pointed out.

"Nothing I can find so far, anyway," Dannerman said obstinately. "But those goddam bug-eyed monsters walked right through it, so there has to be something."

Rosaleen finished her task matter-of-factly and stood up. "That wasn't the wall where they came in, anyway. They came through the one next to it, where Pat's standing."

Which started another argument, even more pointless. Which wall? How could you possibly tell which wall, anyway, when they all were identical? There was no mark of any kind on any of them, not even a seam where two panels joined. Pat ran her fingers wonderingly over the smooth, warm surface herself. It looked as though it should be glass-hard. It wasn't. As she pressed her fingers against it the tips actually entered the wall, faintly dimpling it as they might a surface of modeling clay, but they penetrated no more than, perhaps, a millimeter or so. She tried harder, finally pressing with all her weight. No good. She could get fingernail-deep into the surface and no farther. And she could find no sign at all that it had ever opened up to let the extraterrestrials through. If she hadn't seen the creatures walk right through it she would not have believed it possible.

Jimmy looked up unhappily. "Tell me something. Suppose you did find a way to get through that thing, even got all the way out of here?" he said. "I don't think you ever will, but what if you did? What would you do then?"

"Then," Dannerman said, "I'd figure out what to do next, but we'd be that much ahead. As long as we're stuck in here we can't do anything at all."

Jimmy shrugged, but said nothing. Neither did anyone else; some truths were too obvious to be argued.

Then, "But this is interesting," Rosaleen called from her place at a far wall, gazing at the floor.

"What is?"

Rosaleen gestured to where she had relieved herself. "The urine is disappearing. Look, there is only a trace now, and it is getting less."

Even Jimmy Lin got up to see that. It was true. The tiny pool of pale liquid was dwindling, and a moment later it was gone. Martín Delasquez hesitated, then stopped to touch the floor where it had been. "Dry," he reported. He didn't need to. They could all see for themselves that there was no trace of urine, not even a faint stain on the milky-white, slightly resilient flooring.

"Well," Rosaleen said encouragingly. "At least we seem to have a sewage system."

Martín scowled at her. "But still no food and nothing to drink."

She shrugged. "And nothing we can do about it, either, is there? Meanwhile I am quite tired. I think I will try to sleep."

Pat watched, incredulous and almost admiring, as the old

woman lay down on her side, curled in the fetal position, folded her hands under her cheek and closed her eyes. "You know," Pat said, "I could use some sleep myself."

"We all could," Dannerman said. "But one of us ought to stay awake."

Jimmy giggled. "Are you talking about setting sentries? To guard against what?"

"Against I don't know what," Dannerman said, "but that's the exact reason why I think one of us should stay up. I'll take the first turn, if you like."

Martín Delasquez said heavily, "Yes, I agree we should set a guard and, yes, we might as well sleep, since we have nothing better to do. Perhaps we will think more clearly when we are refreshed, so, very well, let us— Wait! What is that?"

He didn't have to ask; they all saw what was happening at the same time. A patch of one wall clouded momentarily, then bulged into a pair of figures as the Dopey and a Doc came through. The Doc was carrying small parcels in several of its arms; the Dopey gestured, and the Doc began setting the parcels on the floor as the wall closed seamlessly behind them.

Dannerman wrinkled up his nose. "That's what I was smelling on Starlab!" he said, staring at the Doc. "It was that thing!"

All the captives were standing in a defensive clump now, even Rosaleen, watching warily. Pat Adcock sniffed. Yes, there was a queer odor, not entirely unpleasant—part of it like something from a spice rack, part something sour and distasteful. There was no doubt that it came from the extraterrestrials. She stared at them, realizing for the first time just how unhuman they were. The Dopey was not at all human in form—torso like a Thanksgiving turkey's, but a big one; its prissy little feline face at the level of Pat's chest. It wore cloth-ing—a sort of pastel-mauve muumuu—and it carried a kind of muff made of coppery metal mesh. After it had signed an order to the Doc it put its hands back in the muff before Pat could get a good look at its fingers. There was something odd about them, but she wasn't sure what. Then, as it turned slightly, she saw that the muumuu had an opening in the back from which protruded a scaly, iridescent, spreading tail as colorful as a pea-cock's.

Pat felt at least a hint of reassurance from the fact that the Dopey was wearing a garment. Clothing implied civilization; civilization implied some possible, however remote, hope that there could be some sort of meeting of the minds between them. The one they called the "Doc," on the other hand, was almost naked except for a sort of cache-sexe over where she supposed it kept its genitals. It was also very big. More than two meters tall, Pat guessed, at least twice as tall as the Dopey—of course, the snapshots in the message from space had given no indica-tion of scale. And it was not in the least human. The word that crossed Pat's mind was "golem." The thing stood on short, bent legs, like the Greek version of a satyr, but no satyr had ever had six arms, two huge, thick ones at the top, four lesser ones spaced along its torso, and all tipped with sharptaloned paws. Now that she had a better look at the creature she saw that the white beard was not a real beard: the strands feathered out, more like fern fronds than any kind of animal hair. A cluster of the same sort of growth peeped out from the jockstrap garment.

The Dopey worked its slack little mouth for a moment and spoke. "You stated that you required food. These are food, I think."

That took Pat by surprise. "You speak English," she said. It sounded like an accusation; the alien didn't reply.

"Stupid question," Martín reproved her. "He just did speak English. You, then. Will you tell us why we are here?"

"You are here," the creature said, "so that you may be learned." Its voice was shrill and grating, as much like the cawing of a parrot as any human speech, but the words were clear enough.

"Learned what?" the general demanded. The Dopey didn't reply. "For whom?" No answer for that, either, and Rosaleen tried her luck:

"Can you say how we got here?"

The Dopey considered. "Not at present. Perhaps later," it said at last. Pat thought it seemed to be waiting for something, but didn't pursue the thought; she had other things on her mind. Food, for one thing, and she wasn't the only one. Jimmy Lin was rooting around in the sparse collection: mints, apples, corn chips—she recognized the provenance; it was what they had had on their persons in the Clipper. It wasn't much. It was welcome, though; she selected an apple, carefully excavated a bruised spot with a thumbnail, then bit into it. It was as moist as she had hoped.

Jimmy was less pleased. He was muttering dissatisfiedly to himself in Chinese, then looked up at the Dopey and snarled, *"Wo zen mo nen chi zhe zhong dong xi!"*

The alien didn't miss a beat. *"Ni bao li zhi you zhe xie,"* it replied. Every human jaw dropped at once, and Pat cried:

"You speak Chinese, too!"

"Of course. Also Cuban-Floridian Spanish and Dr. Artzyba-chova's Galician dialect of Ukrainian, as well as a number of other human languages. This was necessary for my work on your orbiter. One moment."

It turned to the wall. Almost at once the mirror bulged and admitted a pair of Docs, carrying a large metal object. They set it down and stood waiting. The Dopey said, "You now have all you need. Now you are simply to go about your affairs in the normal way. You may breed if you wish."

That appeared to be all it had to say. It turned and left through the wall, the Docs silently trooping after. Dannerman sprang to the wall as soon as they were through, but, as before, the wall flowed like mercury around the departing aliens, and re-formed as solid as ever.

Well," Dannerman said encouragingly, "at least now we have something to eat. Jimmy? What was that you and the BEM were talking about?"

Lin was looking amused—at least an improvement, Pat thought, over his sullen withdrawal of before. "I was just complaining about the food. I didn't expect an answer, but then he said—in perfectly good Mandarin—that it was all there was among our possessions. But what about the other thing he said, Pat? Are you ready to start doing the breeding bit?"

She said simply, "Shut up." She was watching Rosaleen Artzybachova, who was examining the metal object the Docs had carried in. It seemed to be a rectangular, fauceted tank, with pipes dangling from it that led nowhere. Rosaleen cupped one hand and held it under the faucet; when she twisted the lever, water came out. She sipped it and nodded.

"I think it's the portable-water recycler from Starlab," she reported. "It appears there is some water in the tank, and it tastes all right. However, I suggest we use it carefully. There's nothing here to replenish it; in Starlab it had a condenser to collect moisture from the air and a still for wastewater from the toilets but, as you can see, those have been disconnected and left behind."

"And, of course, we don't even have regular toilets anyway," Jimmy smirked. Pat scowled at him. But that was not all bad, she thought; she was not enthusiastic about drinking water that had come from a toilet, no matter how meticulously it was treated and distilled. But when she said as much, Dannerman laughed.

"And where do you think that water came from in the first place? Anyway, it looks like they're going to take care of us. Maybe the Seven Ugly Dwarfs aren't so bad after all."

"But they are still the ones the broadcast warned us against," Rosaleen reminded him, and no one had any answer for that.

CHAPTER FIFTEEN

Pat

Of all the things Pat Adcock missed, the ones she would least have expected were clocks. They had none. There wasn't any day or night in their cell; the white glow came always unvarying from the ceiling. She felt time dragging for her, with nothing to do, but the only clues the prisoners had to measure how much of it was passing were their own internal ones—the number of times they (unenthusiastically) ate some of the scraps the Dopey had given them, or slept (uncomfortably stretched on the bare cell floor), or, when the remorseless demands of their metabolisms made it necessary, did their best to come somewhere near the impossible wish to urinate and move their bowels in private.

It was not a kind of existence Pat Adcock had ever expected for herself. Not Patrice Dannerman Bly Metcalf Adcock, who had never in her life gone hungry, except in the occasional struggle to get rid of a few extra pounds, who had, from tiniest childhood, always lived a life of privileged security—well, reasonable security, if you didn't count the natural hazards everyone faced from street violence or random terrorist acts. Pat was accustomed to being a person of position. She was entitled to give orders to nearly two hundred people, as the operating head of a reasonably prestigious scientific enterprise. She was also used to all the perquisites that went with being more or less rich.

What Pat Adcock was used to was being an organism efficiently adapted to the ecological niche she occupied. She had all the skills necessary for that life; knew how to juggle budgets even in runaway inflation; how to discourage a date who wanted more intimacy than she cared to give—and how to motivate one who didn't; how to find a clean and comfortable ladies' room at need, wherever she was; how much to tip a headwaiter and when it was best just to give him a smile; how to—

Well, how to *live,* in the particular world she was designed to live in.

But not in this new world, which seemed to call for skills she didn't have and didn't know how to acquire. So nothing in Pat's previous life had prepared her for the present confinement and privation, not to mention the humiliating aspects of their captivity. Naked, weaponless, surrounded by the mirrored walls—wherever she looked six Pats, or sixty times six Pats, looked back at her, dwindling as the reflections became more distant. They were penned like abandoned dogs in an animal shelter, waiting to be adopted—or to be put to death. Nor did they have any more control than a stray dog over their future. They could tell time only by events. Only in their case the events weren't inspections by possible new owners, they were occasions like the time when they got the food from Starlab, and the time when they were at last given back their clothes, and the frightening time when they killed the Dopey.

No circumstances were ever so bad that a little human effort couldn't make them worse. As their tempers grew short they became quarrelsome. Pat snapped at Martín Delasquez for snoring, Dannerman and Rosie Artzybachova withdrew from the others, each busy at some not discussed thoughts of their own, while Martín and Jimmy Lin argued fiercely over whether the lack of blankets to sleep on was worse than the lacks in their limited larder, and whether mints, apples and corn chips represented a diet they could survive on. For Pat, who was trying to force herself to down one more meal of that sort of trash, it was the last straw. "Oh, shut up, you two, for God's sake. Dan, what's the matter with everybody?"

It was a rhetorical question, but she could see him making the effort to give her an answer. "It's prisoner neurosis," he said. "You see a lot of it in jails; that's why you have so many murders in prisons. Actually, it's the policeman's best friend, because when people are hiding out from the cops, after a while they just can't stand each other. That's when they do something foolish and get caught."

Jimmy was listening with a half smile. "You know all about that, don't you, Dannerman?" he said.

Dan gave him an opaque look. "It's common knowledge. Psych 101, or don't they teach that in Chinese colleges?"

Lin met him stare for stare, then shrugged. "Actually, I got my bachelor's at the University of Hawaii," he said, and dropped the subject. Pat frowned, chopping a bruised part out of the apple she had just picked up; there was something going on between the two of them, but she couldn't guess what. Jimmy was being his usual irritating self, of course, but Dannerman—well, what was Dannerman up to, exactly? He prowled their cell for hours at a time, then sat silently, seeming to be trying to work something out, though she couldn't imagine what.

Rosaleen was talking to her. "Do you notice anything about the apples?"

Pat looked at the fruit, puzzled. "Well, I think that's the second or third I've had with a bruise in the same spot."

"Really," Rosaleen said thoughtfully. "That I hadn't noticed. What I was talking about was how many are there. I never packed that many."

"And actually I only had one package of corn chips," Pat said.

"I don't understand. Are they raiding a supermarket some-where?"

"If they are, they could give us a little more variety," Martín said sourly.

Dannerman speculated, "Maybe they figure that's all we need, since that was all they found on us."

"Or maybe they have some way of multiplying the food—you know, loaves and fishes," Rosaleen said. "But they could find something better to multiply. There's stored food in Star-lab. If Dopey—" She hesitated before she said it, but they did need a name for the creature. "If Dopey can bring the potable water still from the orbiter he can bring us some of the food, too."

"Or," Jimmy Lin said, "he could bring us a bed, maybe one of those four-posters with curtains that come down? So we could get on with that breeding he was talking about?"

Pat gave him a freezing look. It was nice that Jimmy seemed to be coming out of his funk, but she didn't want him starting anything that could not be properly finished. As a matter of fact, the subject had been on her mind from time to time. This en-forced intimacy was stimulating glands that she didn't really want stimulated just then. She thought almost wistfully of ex-husband Ferdie Adcock—not of that son of a bitch of another ex-husband, Jerry Metcalf, who had been a disappointment in all areas, including the bed. Ferdie, on the other hand, had been a truly rewarding lover, in almost every way a fine choice for a mate . . . if only she had been able to overlook his unfortunate habit of keeping his amatory skills current by constant prac-tice—on two of their maids, on the assistant cook, on an occa-sional picked-up professional and, most troublesome of all, on several of her (formerly) best friends.

But Ferdie was far in the past and even farther away in space.

As to the nearer candidates—well, she thought, simply as a speculation; there was no intention to do anything about it, of course—there was General Delasquez. Not counting the flab, he was a powerfully proportioned·man, though too bossy in his disposition to be a really first-rate choice. Jimmy Lin himself? Yes, she admitted to herself, under some circumstances the Chinanaut might have been a definite possibility. Even on Earth it had once in a while crossed her mind to wonder just how much of the know-how of Jimmy Lin's great-great he might have inherited. Of course, there were problems with Jimmy, too, one of the most annoying of them being the prospect of becoming just one more scalp on his boastfully long list. That wasn't necessarily a total disqualification. Pat Adcock was not a jealous woman, except with husbands. In the case of a casual lover that sort of thing might have been bearable—under normal conditions. However, under normal conditions they wouldn't be stuck with an audience of three interested onlookers while they got it on.

Which left only one—still purely theoretical—contender. Dan.

Actually, she conceded to herself, watching Dannerman move about the enclosure out of the corner of her eye, there wasn't really much wrong with her cousin, if you overlooked his habit of thinking private thoughts he didn't choose to share with anyone. Dan wasn't a bad-looking man. He wasn't a stranger, either. They had been pretty close at one time, and if they hadn't gone off to separate schools the two of them might sooner or later have decided to become a lot closer. Dan was a definite possibility, she thought—still purely theoretically, of course.

But, under the circumstances, she was determined that it had to be theoretical. Without privacy, making love with him or with anyone at all was simply out of the question—at the moment, anyway, she added to herself . . . and then noticed Jimmy Lin's knowing grin as he watched her covertly eyeing Dannerman.

They kept making small, but inexplicable, discoveries about their cell. Rosaleen pointed out a curious thing about the floor. It not only soaked up and removed their biological wastes, it did the same for trash of all kinds—their apple cores, for instance. Throw them on the floor, and an hour or so later they were gone. Yet the floor was selective about what it caused to disappear. Their food supplies were scattered on the floor, for lack of any better place to put them, and they were never touched. "It discriminates," the old lady said, sounding pleased—well, the cell was, after all, an interesting machine. "Also we must have used all the water the tank could hold by now, but if you notice it's not empty. Somehow the water is being replenished."

"Have you noticed that we don't stink very much, either?" Jimmy Lin put in. That was also true, Pat realized. Add the open "toilet" to the fact that bathing was impossible, and the air of their cell should have been pretty ripe. It wasn't. Their air was constantly being changed. The shadowless light that came from the ceiling was less of a puzzle—even on Earth there were such wall installations that glowed in much the same way—but the greater mystery of the walls resisted all explanation. "Talk about making money from alien technology," Martín said bitterly. "Do you have any idea what that kind of hardware would be worth for prisons? Let the guards walk in and out, but keep the convicts secure?"

Rosaleen, doing leg lifts with her hands pressed against the wall in lieu of a barre, gave him a look. "It would be worth a great deal for many things far more useful than prisons, actually."

Jimmy Lin laughed. "You have something against prisons, Rosie?"

"Yes," she said. "Now more than ever, but always. We had enough experience of prisons in Ukraine. My mother's uncle was taken away to one when he was fourteen years old; he didn't come back until he was sixty-two, and dying. Also my mother's father, my grandfather, who died there. We learned much about prisons in my family from my great-uncle, because he had many stories to tell."

"Did he have any good advice to give?"

"About escaping? No. About how to survive, yes; my great-uncle said the important thing was to go on doing what you should be doing if you were free—as much as you possibly can, that is. Some things would naturally be impossible."

Pat made the connection. "That's why you do your exercises every day?"

Rosaleen hesitated. "That is one reason, yes. The other reason— Well, that is not important. What is important is to keep a sense of purpose. In my great-uncle's case he constantly continued his education; he had been taken right out of school when they arrested him. He organized classes with the other prisoners and at night, instead of sleeping, they taught each other what they knew. Before he died he could speak French, German, Georgian, some English and Japanese and even a little bit of Hebrew. He was pretty nearly in Dopey's class as a linguist, almost, and that wasn't all. He could recite poetry for hours—Mandelstam, Okujawa, Shakespeare, Petrarch—and he knew the names of all the kings of England and France, in order. And much more. But he didn't spend much time thinking about escaping. There would have been no point in running away from the camps, you see, when the whole country was a prison."

"Much like our own situation," Jimmy Lin said sourly; and no one had anything to say to that.

When Dopey came again the three men were sleeping restlessly on one side of the cage, and Rosaleen was teaching Pat tai chi. They were trying to be as quiet as possible, but when Pat saw one of the wall panels begin to cloud she called out at once. By the time Dopey was inside the men were getting up, bleary-eyed but curious.

"You asked for the food from Starlab," Dopey said. "Also blankets so that you may sleep in more comfort." The parade of Docs that followed him began setting down racks and cases of objects.

"Hey," said Jimmy Lin, for the first time in their captivity looking almost pleased. He began sorting through the new rations even before the Docs had set their burdens down and trooped out. Besides the blankets, the Starlab ones hemmed with metal rings to keep them from floating away, there were scores of food packets of all kinds. Some were in pop-open cans, some sealed in plastic. Freeze-dried, radiated or canned, they needed no refrigeration, and they came in many varieties. Pat saw packages labeled "omelette" and "fried tomatoes" and any number of vegetables: green beans, white beans, red beans, pickled cabbage, raw cabbage, beets. There were soups, stews and quiches; there were powders that were dehydrated fruit juices or coffee, and Pat was suddenly aware of just how hungry she was. She wasn't the only one. Martín held up one opaque plastic sack, reading the label wonderingly: "What is 'hassenpfeffer'?" he demanded, and Jimmy Lin exulted: "Look! There must have been some Chinese on Starlab; there's bok choy! And rice, and I think these other things are dim sum!"

The only one not poring over the larder was Dannerman. He was gazing at Dopey. "What's the matter, Dan?" Pat asked, but he didn't answer her. He said to the alien:

"You heard what we said about the larder on Starlab. You can hear everything we say in here, can't you?"

The creature inclined its mournful head, the equivalent, Pat thought, of a nod. "Of course. That is my assignment. I am tasked to monitor you. Also to provide you with everything you need so the observation can continue as long as possible."

Pat looked up from the canned ham in her hand. "You aren't doing a very good job of that. Why don't you give us back our clothes?"

"To provide you with what you *need*," Dopey said firmly.

"Well, we need clothes. Tell him, Dan," she said, but Dannerman was looking thoughtfully at the alien. It was Rosaleen who picked up on the question.

"Clothing is a definite need for us," she declared. "We are not animals. We will be definitely harmed by prolonged exposure. Also there are items that we carried in our clothing which are essential to our survival—medications, for instance."

Dopey hesitated, then did a curious thing. He jammed his little paws deep into the copper-colored muff; his eyes closed, he seemed to be listening to voices unheard by the others. Then his eyes opened and he declared, "The clothing will be brought."

"That's more like it," Jimmy Lin said, his mouth full of something he had seized from the food supplies. "How about answering some questions for us, too? Where are we?"

"You are in this pen. You do not require more information than that."

"Well, then," Martín Delasquez tried, "at least tell us what you're monitoring? What do you want us to do?"

"Simply to continue as you are," Dopey said, as though that should have been obvious. Then, as the walls opened and three burdened Docs came back in, he added sharply, "Do not touch your clothing yet!" It was not really a necessary order. They couldn't have, anyway; the three Docs had formed in a line between the captives and the pile of clothing. Dopey paid them no further attention, but began carefully examining each garment. As he finished with one he tossed it past the Docs to be claimed—a brassiere for Rosaleen Artzybachova, a single sock, a pair of men's undershorts claimed by Dannerman. The underwear came first, because, Pat thought, it was the easiest to check out. As Dopey came to the outer garments he was more thorough, investigating pockets, running his long, tapering fingers over seams to see if anything was concealed inside them. He was looking for weapons, it seemed. He found them, too: two guns and a bomb-bugger in Dannerman's effects, a gun and a knife in Martín's, more guns from the others, even two little switchblade knives from the garments of Rosaleen Artzybachova. "Christ," Pat said. "We were all ready to fight a war!"

"I simply took routine precautions," Jimmy Lin said defensively, watching as Dopey pulled a sixty-shot sidearm out of his jacket.

Rosaleen spoke up, to the Dopey: "That's just a pen! Please let me have it."

The Dopey didn't respond, except to turn the pen over a few times, then take it apart. Evidently he decided it would not make a good stabbing weapon; he tossed it over and turned to everyone's shoes. That took longer. He ran his fingers inside each shoe, apparently measuring to see if there was enough thickness anywhere to conceal a weapon. On one of Jimmy's shoes he hit pay dirt: the heel unscrewed, and inside it was a coil of razor wire.

"Hell," Jimmy said, and resignedly went back to getting dressed. They were all doing it, now. It was surprising, Pat thought, how much more formidable Martín Delasquez looked once he had his military camouflage jacket on again, gold braid with its embroidered general's stars. For Pat herself getting dressed again after so long bare was less pleasant than she had imagined. The waistband of the slacks was uncomfortably tight; the pantyhose unpleasingly constricting; and her feet seemed to have swelled, because it was an effort to get them into the shoes.

The three Docs abruptly turned as one and left, carrying the confiscated weaponry; and it was only then that Pat realized that while they were dressing Dopey had slipped through the wall and was gone.

"Damn it," Dannerman said. "I was hoping we could ask him some more questions."

"Which he probably wouldn't have answered anyway," Pat said. "So let's eat!"

The canned ham had been cold and greasy, the pita bread Pat ate with it dry and leathery, but her belly was full. Eating made a difference. Being clothed made a difference, too; Pat couldn't help feeling that things were taking a turn for the better. Maybe only a very small improvement, with a very long way still to go, but everybody seemed cheerier. Martín in uniform stood taller than before, and what they had received was not merely food and clothing. Dopey had returned all their pouches and belly bags. Pat was pleased to get her watch back and her rings, less pleased to have the packet of tampons that she always carried in case of emergency; it reminded her that her period would be coming along sometime soon, and that one pair of tampons would not be adequate to her needs.

Rosaleen held aloft a small bottle. "My painkillers," she said exultantly.

"Were you in pain?" Pat asked wonderingly.

"Dear girl, at my age one is always in pain; exercise helps a little, but these are better—though they do not solve the real problem. May we not discuss it, please? I have a suggestion."

There was something in Rosaleen's tone that made Pat anxious to hear more, but she didn't press the point. "Yes?"

"Let us make an inventory of all our possessions. Dan, since you still have your screen, perhaps you can keep the tally."

Her tone made Pat curious. "Dopey didn't return yours?"

Rosaleen pursed her lips. "He probably thought it contained a weapon."

Delasquez laughed. "And, of course, it did. What, simply a sharp little blade, for emergencies? He took mine too, for the same reason."

"And left us no weapons at all," Jimmy Lin said. Something in his tone made Pat give him a closer look. But when she started to ask him, Dannerman cut in.

"Hold it," he commanded. "Of *course* none of us have any weapons—but if we did"—he glanced meaningfully at the wall—"we had probably better not mention them out loud. Let's get on with the inventory, shall we?"

It didn't take long. There was Rosaleen's multicolor pen (but nothing to write on with it but some coarse wrapping paper from the food larder) and a reading glass; a collection of key cards and IDs from all of them; a nail clipper; two pocket combs; some loose coins—very few, because hardly anyone carried cash. That was it. Most of them had left their more interesting gadgets in the lockers at the Cape. "No weapons there, anyway," Jimmy said ruefully. "I guess if we put all our coins and stuff in a sock we could make a cosh." Dannerman gave him a warning look, prompting him to add quickly, "Although there's not enough mass there to do any real harm to anybody anyway."

Pat could restrain her curiosity no longer. "Rosie? What's this 'real problem' you're talking about?"

Rosaleen shrugged. "I don't suppose there's any need to keep it secret; it is simply that there is nothing that can be done about it. Painkillers are not the only medication I need. I have a good many other troublesome conditions. They are well controlled by implants, but the implants need to be refreshed from time to time—beta blockers, polyestrogens, most of all the implant that helps to ward off Alzheimer's. I don't suppose any of you have anything like that on you?"

General shaking of heads. Jimmy Lin, his mouth full of rice, offered, "I have allergy medicine. I don't suppose that would help?"

Rosaleen shook her head, unsurprised. "Not at all. I doubt you'll need it, either; there may be allergens around here, but not the ones you've needed it for. So," she added, "I have some weeks at least, conceivably even some months, before the implants wear off, then— Well, let's look on the bright side. By then we may all be dead anyway."

CHAPTER SIXTEEN

Pat

What Pat Adcock discovered—what millions of jailed men and women had discovered before her—was that prison reduced life to fundamentals. There were no decisions to make or crises to meet; the high spot of the day was eating.

Their larder was a mixed bag. The fruit juices were good, once you mixed them with water—she could have wished for an ice cube or two, but they were certainly drinkable without. There was even real wine. It wasn't very *good* wine, but it came in little plastic cups, which could be rinsed out and used for other things. No beer, though, which annoyed Jimmy Lin, and the coffee was a disappointment. Not only was it at the same temperature as everything else they had, but it was the European kind of coffee, heavy on chicory and made from beans burned black. Only Martín and Rosaleen seemed to enjoy drinking it.

Still, things were looking up a little. Not counting the fact that she was tired of seeing herself reflected in the cell's walls no matter where she looked; if anything could make her crazy, she thought, it was those mirrors. Not counting the fact that Jimmy Lin had formed the annoying habit of following her around, brushing against her in a pretty unmistakable way; but at least now she had clothing.

But none of it was good enough.

Time was passing, and it was all *wasted* time. Pat Adcock had little practice in time-wasting. She was used to a world in which she always had something to do, usually more to do than she had time to do it in: work to get done, plans to make, social obligations to fulfill, amusements to seek. Here she had nothing. She even missed the annoying everyday flow of sales messages on her comscreen and the solicitations of street panhandlers. Pictures from her childhood flashed through her mind, the images of pacing polar bears and sullenly squatting gorillas from Sunday zoo trips with Uncle Cubby or her parents. The parallels hurt. "We're zoo animals. We have nothing to *do*," she complained. "It doesn't make sense."

Dannerman shook his head. "No, you're wrong there. Everything makes sense to somebody."

"Even this?"

"Even anything. People used to talk about senseless crimes—like murdering some eighty-year-old guy on welfare to steal his shoes; they think it makes no sense to kill somebody for so little. But to the guy who did it, it made perfect sense. He wanted the shoes."

"Thank you for the lecture, Dr. Dannerman," Jimmy Lin said.

Dannerman said stubbornly, "I'm only saying that all this must make some kind of sense to Dopey and the others, from their point of view. All we have to do is figure out what their point of view is."

"It sounds like you're taking their side, Dannerman," Martín rumbled.

"Oh, hell, why are people always telling me that I'm taking the bad guys' side?"

"What people?" Martín asked, puzzled.

"Different people." He didn't elaborate. There was something there he didn't want to discuss, Pat was sure, though she couldn't imagine what. "Anyway," he said, "I'm just trying to understand what's happening. Probably they want to know more about us before they reveal themselves."

Pat asked, "How much do they have to know? Isn't that why

Dopey was hanging out in Starlab all that time, eavesdropping on Earth?"

Martín said heavily, "Maybe that is not enough for them. I am remembering what the old sailing-ship explorers used to do when they encountered new indigenes. They would kidnap a few and take them aboard their ships to look them over. Your Christopher Columbus—" he began, and then stopped, scowling. They all heard it: a distant sound, almost like a shriek, faint and far away. "What the hell was that?" he demanded.

No one answered until Rosaleen shrugged. "If this is a zoo," she said, "we may not be the only animals on exhibit."

"It sounded human to me," Jimmy said uneasily. Dannerman said nothing, but he was frowning. Pat thought she knew why. The scream had sounded human to her, too. In fact, it had sounded a lot like the voice of Dan Dannerman.

The scream didn't come again. They listened; they tried to be as quiet as possible so that they might hear, but there wasn't much to hear. Dannerman reported that he had heard, might have heard, a faint hum that could have been distant machinery. Pat herself thought she caught a whisper of speech—of a voice of some kind, anyway. When she reported it Dannerman shook his head. "I didn't hear anything like that. Did it sound human?"

"How can I tell? I thought it sounded as though it were asking for something."

To her displeasure, Jimmy Lin took that to be a cue. He moved closer to her. "Perhaps it was asking for something which I too would like," he said, one hand casually resting on her shoulder.

The man was making her uncomfortable. She shrugged herself free. "Knock it off, Lin."

"But why?" he asked reasonably. "I am aware that such things are better conducted in privacy. I would prefer it so myself, but what can we do? Modesty is pointless here."

"The point," she said, "is that I don't want to make love with you, Jimmy. If you're looking for a comfort woman, look somewhere else."

"Hey!" Rosaleen said good-naturedly. "Where do you want him to look, exactly? I've been out of the comfort business for forty years."

"But what else is there to do?" Jimmy Lin asked in a tone of reasonableness. "It is a perfectly natural thing, and also good for you. My honored ancestor said it all in his book. He said it was unhealthful to go for very long without sex, and all my life I have done my best to follow his advice."

Rosaleen said pleasantly, "If you need to masturbate no one will prevent you. If not, perhaps you won't mind if we change the subject."

He glowered at her. "To what?"

She hesitated before she spoke. "I've been thinking about those messages from space. You see, I think most of us took those pictures of aliens as some kind of a joke, perhaps some satellite controller with time hanging heavy on his hands. Very well, that was a mistake. Now we know better about that, but what about the rest of the message?"

"What rest?"

"The original pictures. The scarecrow creature crushing the universe at the time of the Big Crunch. What do you suppose that means?"

Dannerman said, "I asked one of the astronomers the same thing. He thought it meant that we were being warned against something that was supposed to happen after the universe has finished expanding, and fallen back and contracted again."

At least, Pat thought, they were on a subject she knew something about. But she frowned. "That kind of speculation doesn't make any sense. Nothing could happen after the Big Crunch. It's like wondering what the universe was like before the Big Bang. The answer is there wasn't any. That sort of thing isn't science, it's metaphysics."

Rosaleen shook her head. "You know more about that than I do, Pat, but even I know that some quite good scientists have speculated about the subject."

"Arm-waving. Smoke and mirrors," Pat said dismissively.

"But perhaps for the aliens it isn't."

Pat shrugged. It was true that cosmologists had built any number of pretty speculations about the origins and end of the universe—she had spent many boring hours learning about them in graduate school—but they had always seemed idle day-dreaming to her.

Martín shared that opinion. He said impatiently, "There is no point in thinking about such things. The trouble is simply this: We have been kidnapped. That is not a speculation, it is a fact. Governments have considered such things an act of war."

Jimmy said, "Fine. Now, if you'll just let them know about it at the Pentagon, I'm sure they'll have a rescue fleet here right away."

Martín glared at him. "You are very good at sarcasm, Lin. Less good at taking action. We should do *something*."

Rosaleen attempted to defuse the antagonism. "Very well," she said, "since no one else seems interested in trying to inter-pret the meaning of those messages, I agree that Martín is right. We should do something else. What is available to us? When we were discussing what people in prison on Earth do I am afraid I distracted us with my reminiscences of life in the old Soviet Union. So let us try again. Is there some action that is possible for us to take?"

Jimmy said sourly, glancing at Dannerman, "Why don't you ask the expert?"

Pat frowned. "What do you mean, expert?" But Dannerman seemed unsurprised: He was already answering the Chinanaut.

"First thing," he said, "if I had any specific ideas, I don't think I'd say them out loud. Remember Dopey hears everything that goes on. But if you want general principles I don't see any harm in discussing them—just in the abstract, of course."

"Of course," Rosaleen said impatiently. "Well?"

"What prisoners do depends on what they want to accomplish. If their primary goal is to escape, they do things like digging tunnels, they hide themselves in bags of waste, they get weapons, or make them, and force a guard to take them outside. Or they take hostages for the same purpose. Or they go on a hunger strike—of course that only works if the people on the outside care whether they live or die."

Martín demanded, "Which would you recommend?"

"What I would recommend," Dannerman said, "is that we don't talk about this any more."

"Fine," said Jimmy Lin caustically. "Your advice is that we do nothing, then. Is that why you spooks couldn't even catch the guys who kidnapped the press secretary?"

Dannerman opened his mouth angrily, then glanced at Pat and closed it again. He didn't answer. He simply turned his back and walked over to survey the food store.

There was an undertone here that Pat couldn't identify. She wasn't enjoying it. "What's going on here, Jimmy?" she demanded.

He jerked a thumb at Dannerman. "Ask him."

"Hell," she said, and marched over to Dannerman's side. "Dan, what's Jimmy talking about."

He stood up and popped a cup of wine before he answered. "How do I know?"

"I think you do know. Why does he call you a spook?"

Dannerman shrugged. "Maybe because I was in protsy in college—you know, the Police Reserve Officers Training Corps."

"Not good enough, Dan. That was a long time ago. What about now?"

He took a long pull of the beer before he answered. Then he sighed. "All right, Pat. I don't suppose it matters anymore, and it's the truth. I work for the National Bureau of Investigation."

It was no more than she had guessed, but she felt adrenaline shock flood through her body. "You're a *spy*!"

"I'm an agent of the Bureau, yes. I was ordered to find out what was going on with you and Starlab—"

"Dan!"

He looked remorseful—no, not remorseful; stubborn and sullen. "Well, Jesus, Pat, what did you expect? This was major stuff. As soon as the rumors got out, the Bureau had to find out what you were doing."

"Bastard!" she said, scandalized. "I wouldn't have believed it of you! You come to me with a hard-luck story about needing a job, and all the time you're a goddam spy. Honestly, Dan, what did I ever do to you? Are you still pissed off because you didn't get your share of Uncle Cubby's money?"

"It wasn't a personal matter. I had orders."

"Orders to do what? To steal whatever there was on Starlab for the damn Feds?"

He said uncomfortably, "Well, I suppose that's one way you could put it."

"Is there some other way? So tell me, just how far were you prepared to go for the good old Bureau, Dan? Liquidating me if necessary, for instance?"

"Oh, hell, no, Pat. What kind of a person do you think I am? I've only, uh, shot two people in my life, and I couldn't help that; both of them were doing their best to kill me at the time. Nobody ordered you liquidated."

"And if they had?"

"They wouldn't," he said stubbornly, and that was all he would say.

When Pat curled up on the floor with her face to the wall and her eyes shut tight, she didn't go to sleep. She wasn't planning to. She just wanted to be alone for a bit, as alone as you could get in this place. The National Bureau of Investigation! Everybody knew what that was all about—cloak-and-dagger stuff, with all too much emphasis on the dagger. Now her own cousin turned out to be one of them.

It wasn't just Dan Dannerman, she told herself, feeling abused. Every last one of her comrades had in some way betrayed her trust—Delasquez and Jimmy Lin trying to hijack the goodies on Starlab for another country, even Rosaleen Artzybachova hitting her up for a bigger share of the pie. If Pat Adcock had been a weeping woman she would have allowed herself a few tears of self-pity. As she wasn't, she simply went to sleep.

When raised voices woke her, nothing had improved. She lay with her back to the room, unwilling to turn around and join the others, while Martín and Jimmy Lin were arguing about the food. "But it is nothing but party leftovers," Jimmy Lin was complaining. "It's the stuff nobody wants to eat. What kind of people would have ordered all this stuff?"

Then there was Rosaleen's voice, patiently trying to keep the peace: "There were astronomers from a dozen different countries on Starlab in the early days. I imagine each chose the sort of menu they preferred."

"And ate all the good stuff, and left the remainders for us."

Then Martín's voice, deeper but equally irritated: "I am tired of breaking my teeth on bricks of filthy, uncooked Russian stew."

Rosaleen offered, "I've told you, if you do what I do and soak it for an hour or so it gets softer. A little."

"And then it is cold grease."

She didn't try to deny it. "Try the fruit compote, at least."

"I've had enough of the fruit compote," Jimmy Lin said. "Who knows how long this stuff has been in storage, anyway?" Pat turned away from the familiar bitch session. She had her own feelings about the dehydrated beef (or was it goat?) Stroganoff. She found herself thinking wistfully of a fried-egg sandwich, perhaps with a couple strips of crisp bacon, on whole-grain toast. Or a fresh salad, lettuce with the dew still on it, perhaps some slices of avocado, maybe even a few curls of green pepper. . . .

There wasn't any help for it. She got up and headed for the food, ignoring her companions. That wasn't hard to do. Rosaleen had begun quietly exercising, off by herself, and Martín and Jimmy had moved away to whisper together over the water tank. Only Dannerman was by the larder, and he looked apologetically at her but didn't speak.

Neither did she. She was not yet ready to talk to the duplicitous spy, Dan Dannerman. Ignoring him, she took her time studying the available choices, reading labels, peering at the foods that were visible through glass or plastic. None of them looked attractive, but there were many she hadn't yet tried. She settled on a packet of irradiated chili; at least it would not require soaking to be chewable.

Martín had been right; cold, it was fairly nasty. She had turned her back on Dannerman as she ate, but was not surprised to hear his voice. "Are you still mad?"

She didn't answer. "Because," he said, "I'll apologize if you want me to."

She didn't answer that, either, and apparently he gave up. When she finally peeped around he was over with Rosaleen, doing his best to learn some of her exercises. That was another annoyance for Pat. It had been on her mind to do the same thing, because she could feel herself gaining fat on their preposterously unbalanced diet, but how could she do that while he was there?

The worst part was that it seemed all four of them had decided that Pat was in a bad mood and better left alone. As long as they were ignoring her how could she effectively shun them? She went back to the larder, for lack of anything better to do . . . and was glad when, while she had almost decided to try some more of the damned fruit compote, the patch on the wall suddenly fuzzed and bulged and Dopey came in, oddly without Docs. He was pushing ahead of him a thing that looked like a portable top-loading washing machine. It moved easily on spherical bearings. "This device is to heat your food, as you wish," he said. "If you put things into it they will become hot. This is not the device from your Starlab, however. That object was far too primitive to be of any use here."

They all clustered around while he demonstrated the use of the cooker. Pat hadn't forgotten that she wasn't speaking to any of the others, but put that matter on hold for a while. Operating the cooker looked simple enough. You put things in from the top and left them for a while, and in a minute or two they were hot. When Rosaleen reached to take the container of spaghetti and meatballs out Dopey stopped her. "No, be careful! You will do yourself harm if you put a part of your body into the device. Use these." He plucked a pair of sticks from under one arm and showed them how to lift the packets out without putting their hands in the cooker. Rosaleen eagerly popped the packet open and sniffed the steam that was coming out of it. "I think it's actually too hot to eat!" she said happily.

"It will cool if you wait for a moment," Dopey informed her. "In any case, this instrument will be useful when you have renewable food supplies in the next phase."

Dannerman was suddenly alert. "What next phase? What's going to happen?" Silence. "Well, when will it happen?"

Dopey looked evasive—or simply uncertain; how could you tell with a kitten-faced chicken? "That is unclear. That sequencing is not my decision to make. There are also—" He hesitated. "—some technical problems which have hampered communications."

Pat asked the question for all of them. "What technical problems are you talking about?"

Dopey turned his large kitten eyes on her, then did again the thing with the muff: jammed his hands into it, gazed vacantly into space for a moment, then said, "There are bad people who would harm our project. I may not say more at this time."

"What kind of bad people?" No answer; only that continued stare. Pat bit her lip. The alien was at least answering some questions now, but she was running out of the right questions to ask and Dopey was volunteering little. Nor was she getting much help from her fellow prisoners. Out of the corner of her eye she noticed that Delasquez and Jimmy Lin, though they seemed to be listening intently, were strolling slowly around behind the alien. It crossed her mind that they were up to something.

Not in time.

By the time she began to guess what that something was, and long before she had even begun to decide what, if anything, to do about it, Dopey was turning to leave. The wall began to cloud, preparatory to letting him through.

He didn't get that far. "Grab him!" Delasquez shouted, hurling his weight against the milky place in the wall. Lin did as ordered—threw himself on the alien, who squawked once in astonishment and then was still.

If Delasquez was trying to escape, he failed. The wall was not deceived. He struck against it and was hurled violently back into the cell, as the wall turned mirror-bright again against him. Delasquez didn't walk away; he was catapulted backward, staggering into the pile of Dopey and Jimmy Lin on the floor. He sat down heavily on top of them and gasped dismally, "Mother of God, that hurt!"

From beneath him Lin, breathless and equally dismal, begged, "Get off me." He struggled to his feet and backed away, Delasquez at his side, the two of them looking apprehensively at the alien.

Dannerman gave them both a hard look, but said nothing as he knelt by Dopey's side. "Is he breathing?" Martín asked.

"I don't know. It didn't feel like it," Jimmy Lin said uneasily.

"Maybe he just had the breath knocked out of him," Martín offered, but Dannerman looked up and shook his head.

"Knocked out of him for good, I'm afraid. I don't know much about his anatomy, but there isn't much doubt about it. He's really dead."

Ever since they had been taken captive there had been no times for Pat Adcock that she could think of as really good, but there had never before been one quite as bad as this. She had a pretty good idea of what was done to zoo animals who murdered their keeper. Was it going to be done to them?

Dannerman was saying, "Well, that was stupid," and even Rosaleen was looking reproachfully at the two, Jimmy Lin shamefaced, Martín belligerent but—crossing himself? Pat couldn't be sure. The general's right hand was fingering the left shoulderboard of his uniform jacket as he answered.

"It was your suggestion, Dannerman," Delasquez said.

"Bullshit! I never said anything about attacking Dopey!"

"You spoke of taking hostages. Well, we decided to try it. The other part, trying to crash out, that was my own idea, I just thought of it at the last minute."

"Obviously it wasn't a real good idea," Dannerman said. "Taking a hostage wasn't much better. That only works if you don't kill the hostage."

"His death was simply an accident. How could we know the thing was so delicate? In any case, it's done. And we have an opportunity." The general reached down to the corpse—but with his left hand, Pat saw in puzzlement; his right hand was still close to his lapel. He was trying to pick the coppery metal-mesh muff from Dopey's slack hands.

"Wait!" Dannerman cried warningly, but too late. As soon as Martín's hands touched the metal he screamed, jolted erect and fell unconscious to the floor.

"Damn fool," Dannerman snarled, leaping to his side. But ancient Rosaleen was there before him, her ear pressed to the general's chest.

"No breath. No pulse," she reported. "Electrical shock, I think. Dan, do you know CPR?" She didn't wait for an answer, simply bent her mouth to the general's for artificial respiration. Dannerman didn't speak, either, as he dropped to his knees and began pounding a fist rhythmically on Martín's chest. Beside Pat Jimmy Lin was muttering to himself, but it was Pat who caught the first flicker of a reflection in the mirror wall. "Watch out!" she cried as a pair of the great, ungainly Docs came lumbering in. But the creatures paid no attention to their prisoners. If there was any expression on their white-bearded faces Pat could not identify it; they were strictly businesslike. They bent down to Dopey's body, disentangled his fingers from the coppery muff and bore it away through the wall without a sound, leaving the corpse abandoned behind.

Rosaleen had paid no attention, continuing to breathe for the general. Pat watched, nervous, unsure of what to do; she knew what CPR was, of course, but she had never seen it done before, had not expected it to be so violent. Beside her Jimmy Lin was glumly watching. "What do you guess they'll do to us now?" he asked the room in general. No one answered.

It was a good question, Pat thought dismally, shifting from one foot to another. The two Docs had shown no punitive intention, but then the Docs never spoke, never seemed to show any independent thought or emotion at all.

Then Dannerman sat back on his heels, regarding the patient. He placed one finger at the base of Martín's neck and held it for a moment. "It's irregular, but it's beating," he informed Rosaleen; and then, as she lifted her head for a moment, Martín gasped and coughed and opened his eyes, staring wildly about. He struggled to sit up, but Dannerman pushed him back. "Stay put," he ordered.

"What— What—" Martín tried.

"You got yourself killed, Martín," Dannerman informed him, "Lie still for a while. I think you'll live, but don't push it." He tested the pulse with a finger again; then, Pat was puzzled to observe, Dannerman's fingers moved to the lapel of Martín's uniform jacket, as though feeling for something. When he stood up he looked almost amused, but all he said was "Keep an eye on the walls for me while I see if Dopey had anything we can use." He walked over to the corpse of the alien and looked down at it. The slack mouth was open, so were the eyes; the peacock tail, half erected, seemed to have lost some of its scales.

"Are you going to search the body?" Pat asked.

He gazed at her for a moment. "Unless you'd rather do it

yourself? Don't worry. I've done it before, though of course the others were at least human."

"Be careful," she begged. He nodded and knelt beside Dopey's corpse. The creature had worn only the one garment, and, though Dannerman poked at it—diffidently at first, then with more assurance as there was no punishing electrical shock—it seemed to have no pockets. It did have some sort of decoration, things like glassy buttons sewn on it; Dannerman tugged at them experimentally. The Dopey had also worn a bangle over the base of its tail, and a wristlet of the coppery metal, but Pat caught only a glimpse of them as Dannerman completed his search of the corpse.

He sat up and shrugged. "I guess he carried everything he had in that muff," he said. "At least, I can't find anything."

"Maybe he carried some stuff internally," Jimmy Lin offered.

"Good thinking, Jimmy. Do you want to give him a body-cavity search? Because I don't think I'd like to."

"I wonder why the Docs didn't take his body away?" Rosaleen mused, squatting beside the semiconscious Martín.

Dannerman shrugged. "Maybe they'll come back for it. Maybe we'll wish they would, because I imagine it's going to decay pretty rapidly."

Rosaleen nodded, then checked herself, staring at the body. "Perhaps not," she said. "Look at that!"

Pat peered at the dead alien, and saw what Rosaleen meant. Something was happening to the corpse. The bottom of it, where it touched the floor, was soaked with a dark brown liquid, and Pat noticed a sharp, nasty smell, as of some foul brew cooking on a stove.

Dannerman knelt for a closer look. "The floor's dissolving it away," he announced incredulously.

"Please, Dan, don't get too close to it," Pat pleaded.

"Don't worry," he said dryly. "Although it's kind of interesting. That's a great waste removal system; I bet if I lay down right next to Dopey the floor would leave me alone—but, no, I'm not going to try it." He stood up and looked around. "How's the patient doing?"

Rosaleen was supporting Martín's head while holding a cup of water to his lips. "Seems to be improving. He opened his eyes and looked at me."

Dannerman nodded. "So the question now," he said, "is what we do when, and if, somebody takes a dim view of this. Do we just take our punishment, whatever it is? Or do we try to fight back?"

"What have we got to fight with?" Pat demanded.

He looked at her quizzically. "Whatever we can find," he said.

From her post by the patient Rosaleen called, "I do not think that fighting back would be advisable. Not now, anyway."

"I think you're right," Dannerman agreed. "After all, if they want to hurt us they wouldn't have to get into hand-to-hand combat. They wouldn't even need weapons. The easiest thing would be just to leave us here until we run out of food and starve. Speaking of which," he said, "why don't we see what cooking can do for some of those rations?"

Pat stared at him unbelievingly. "You want to *eat* now?" she demanded. "With this dead body turning into mush right here?"

"Well," he conceded, "maybe we might as well wait until it's gone. It seems to be going pretty fast right now, anyway."

Indeed it was, Pat saw, as she gazed down on it, holding Dannerman's arm for reassurance; more than half of Dopey had already turned liquid and been sucked away. The smell was still there, but no worse than before; and actually, Pat admitted to herself, Dannerman was right. The process was kind of interesting to watch, not to mention that it implied a kind of technology she had never before imagined. "Just one more damn thing," she murmured to Dannerman, "that would have been worth a fortune if we could have taken it back to Earth."

Dannerman looked down at her, seeming almost amused; tardily she remembered that she wasn't speaking to him. She looked away. Dopey's body was nearly gone, one of the little arms sticking up and then collapsing into the general mulch. Pat frowned. Something was missing. What had happened to the wristlet? "Dan?" she asked. "Did you notice—"

But he was giving her a scowl and a quick headshake. Puzzled, she opened her mouth to complete her question . . . just as the wall turned milky again.

They all spun around to face it as another Dopey walked in— this time not alone. Two of the golem-like Docs followed him and stood silently protective behind him as the Dopey glanced incuriously at the almost disappeared remains of his own body, and then said in reproach, "You should not have done that."

CHAPTER SEVENTEEN

Pat

"But they *killed* you," Pat gasped; and, "Yes, they did," Dopey confirmed, sounding impatient. "Please. One moment." It did not seem to be a subject that interested him greatly. He turned his great eyes on the two Docs, who instantly moved forward to pluck Martín out of Rosaleen's hands. Naturally the general squawked and protested; naturally it did no good. One of the things picked the general up from behind, the two great upper arms holding him, the other four restraining his arms and legs; the other golem methodically stroked and patted Martín all over, each touch lingering for a moment and then moving on. The whole process took no more than a minute or two. Then, without warning, the Docs dropped Martín sprawling. They retreated to stand, silent and impassive, with their backs to the wall, apparently no longer interested in their environment.

"Yes," Dopey said, as though one of the Docs had reported to him—but Pat hadn't heard a sound, "the examination shows that General Delasquez is not seriously injured. It will not be necessary to replace him, as it was me due to your ill-advised action."

"About that," Jimmy Lin said at once, swallowing hard. "You know that was just an accident, don't you? I mean, we didn't want to *hurt* you. . . ."

Dopey gave him a severe look. "Whatever your intentions, your action caused the loss of some data, which I must restore for this copy. Please inform me of the nature of our discussion just prior to my death."

They all looked at him blankly. "You want to know what we were talking about?" Jimmy ventured.

"Yes. That is what I said."

"Well," Jimmy said, trying to remember, "actually, I don't think it was anything much—"

"Except," Rosaleen cut in swiftly, with a hard stare at Jimmy Lin, "that you were explaining this whole matter of 'copies' to us."

"I was?"

"Oh, yes, absolutely," Pat said, picking up her cue. "Is that why you aren't angrier about getting killed by those idiots? Because you're just a copy?"

Dopey looked almost offended. "I do not understand the term 'just' in that context. Of course I am a copy. We are all copies, are we not? How else could we have been transmitted here from your Starlab?"

"Transmitted?" Rosaleen repeated, fumbling in the dark. "Then—well, then that means we didn't come here in a spaceship?"

Dopey seemed amused. "Indeed not. That is a strange notion, Dr. Artzybachova. Persons do not travel on spaceships. That would be impossible for almost any person, yourselves included, since the transit times would be greater than your life span, due to the limitation imposed by the speed of light. As an astronomer, you at least must know that, Dr. Adcock."

"Oh, right," Pat said, nodding vigorously, trying to help the process on. "That's what you were explaining to us. Please go on."

The funny thing was that he did go on. Pat did her best to keep an expression of pure exultation from her face: it was, after all, the very first time they had been able to trick their captor, and that in itself promised at least some hope for the future. The other prisoners listened in silence: Rosaleen concentratedly frowning; Martín frowning also, but probably about something else; Jimmy Lin merely curious; and Dan Dannerman—well, something was going on with Dan, too, Pat thought, because the man seemed abstracted, and he appeared to be turning something over and over in his pocket as he listened.

She postponed the question of Dan Dannerman, because what Dopey was saying was certainly fascinating. It seemed there was some sort of great search going on, all through the universe, for intelligent races. Automated probes had been sent out on the quest in uncounted numbers; they traveled slower than light, because there was no way for ordinary matter to go faster. But then, when some sort of civilization was detected, a "terminal" was set up and observers like Dopey were "transmitted" to a listening post; and when "specimens" like themselves were obtained they too were "transmitted" for further study—

"Hold it!" Pat commanded. "What do you mean, 'transmitted'? Not even photons can exceed light speed."

Dopey said patiently, "I did not use the word 'photons.' The transmissions are carried by a different particle, the name of which—" He hesitated, while his fingers moved rapidly in the muff. "—is 'tachyons' in your language."

"Oh, my God," Pat breathed, remembering her days in graduate school. "Tachyons! Yes, I've heard of tachyons. They were, what's his name, Gerald Feinberg's theory, right? Particles for which the speed of light was a limiting velocity, yes, but a *lower* limiting velocity, so that they could travel only *faster* than light."

"Precisely," Dopey confirmed. "It is the nature of tachyons that the lower the energy the faster they move. The carriers used in this case are quite low in energy and thus have a virtual velocity of—" He hesitated, the long fingers moving inside the muff. "—of somewhat more than one hundred thousand of your light-years per second."

Pat gasped. "Good God! But I'm pretty sure scientists looked for the things, and they were never found."

"Indeed," Dopey said politely. "Perhaps your scientists should have looked harder."

Rosaleen was shaking her head. "But how could you transmit *objects* on these carriers?"

"Not objects. The object is analyzed, so that a sort of—I believe you would call it a 'blueprint' is made, and that is what is transmitted. And, of course, once the blueprint exists copies may be made as desired."

"Like you," someone said.

"Precisely," said Dopey, seeming gratified; the class was beginning to understand its lesson. "Such occurrences are quite common in my situation. In fact, in my time on your orbiter it was necessary to discard and reconstitute me—" He paused to think for a moment. "—at least twenty-five times. You realize I was there for six years four months, observing, and there is damaging radiation in the environment."

"But," said Rosaleen, reasoning it out, "if it was that important, why have you stopped?"

"Stopped? Why do you think the monitoring has stopped? There are automatic machines still in place to carry out the assignment, of course." He seemed to be tiring of the conversation. He shoved his paws into the copper muff and his eyes went vacant again, and then he said, "If there are no other questions—"

"Wait," Martín said thickly, pushing himself up. "Don't go yet. I have something else to ask about your, ah, your purposes in kidnapping us." He hesitated, glancing at his fellow captive. Pat instantly thought he looked suspicious . . . a suspicion that was confirmed when Delasquez rattled off a couple of high-speed sentences in Spanish: *"Si ustedes están interesados en establecer relaciones, no pierdan su tempo con esta gente. Mi gobierno en Florida les ofrecerá mejores condiciones."*

"Hey!" Jimmy Lin yelled. "None of that! Talk so we can all understand you!"

Martín gave him a frosty look. "Why? I was merely asking if they were checking us out as a precaution, before proceeding to make contact with the rest of the human race."

Dopey said politely, "Actually that is not an accurate translation, General Delasquez. Your precise message was, 'If you are going to want to establish relations, don't waste your time with these people. My government in Florida will give you a better deal.' However, that contains an incorrect assumption as to the purpose of this operation."

Dannerman glared at Martín, who glared defiantly back, but then closed his eyes and went to sleep. Or pretended to, Pat thought angrily. Dannerman turned to Dopey. "Then what is the purpose?"

Dopey was silent for a long moment. "I do not think I may discuss that. Moreover," he added, sounding sorrowful, "I believe that you have not been candid with me about our discussions before General Delasquez and Commander Lin leaped on me and crushed me to death. That is not fair. Please do not attempt to deceive me again. Also," he added, turning toward the wall, but looking over his plume at Dannerman, "please also learn that you must not attempt to steal things which do not belong to you and you do not understand."

It sounded as though the message was meant for Martín Delasquez—but then why was he looking at Dannerman? Before Pat could ask, Dopey was gone through the opening wall. A moment later the Docs followed.

"I guess the conversation's over," Dannerman said wryly.

Pat sighed. "You know what would be nice? It would be nice

if he would, just once, say good-bye when he goes." And then she turned to the unfinished business of Martín Delasquez. "Bastard," she said. "What were you trying to do?"

Delasquez would have had a harder time of it—Pat would have seen to it herself—if he hadn't abruptly pressed his hand to his forehead, staggered and sat down. "Pardon," he said. "Perhaps I am not entirely recovered. In any case I was merely attempting to establish contact in another way, in the hope that something could be gained for all of us."

"Sure you were," Jimmy Lin sneered. Pat opened her mouth to tell the general a few more home truths about himself, but then closed it again. What was the point? Dannerman seemed to have lost interest in the subject; his hands were still turning something over in his pocket, and his expression continued to be abstracted.

For a while the others pressed Pat for all she could remember about these "tachyons," but it wasn't much; she had said just about all she retained from those long-ago courses, and after a few minutes Rosaleen turned to something more useful. She had been experimenting with the cooker Dopey had brought, and ten minutes later there were heavenly smells of decent meals coming out of the thing.

The reality was as good as the aroma. Pat had forgotten how fine a cup of hot Irish stew could taste. Even Martín recovered swiftly enough to cook up and devour some sort of fried-banana thing. It wasn't until they were all on their seconds that Rosaleen cleared her throat. "Patrice?" she said. "Were there not some studies, long ago, about how to produce these tachyon things Dopey was talking about?"

Pat swallowed and thought for a moment. "Studies? But the tachyons were never found."

"Yes, you said that," the old lady said patiently. "But I do recall some speculations on the subject. It was while I was studying at the high-energy institute in Kiev; we were analyzing the instrumentation of the synchrotron, and the instructor mentioned, purely for our entertainment, I am sure, that someone had once suggested faster-than-light particles could be generated with a sufficiently powerful instrument."

"With a synchrotron?" Pat said, and then, "Oh! That radiation from Starlab!"

Rosaleen nodded. "Exactly."

Then Pat had to explain what they were talking about to Martín and Jimmy Lin, who had heard nothing about synchrotron radiation being observed from the orbiter. Dannerman, on the other hand, listened for only a moment, then said, "I think I'll take a little nap."

He wasn't the only one. Martín was losing interest in the discussion; he lingered only for a few moments, then silently removed himself to a side of the cell and lay down, closing his eyes. Rosaleen yawned. "A full belly makes a sleepy brain," she said. "Do you think one of us should stay awake?"

"Not me," said Jimmy Lin; so Pat volunteered. It wasn't that she wasn't drowsy herself; it was that she had something else on her mind. Not Martín's treachery; not what Dopey had told them, astonishing though that was; the thing that was preoccupying her thoughts was the delicious fact that, at last, she had her comb back. It was what she had yearned for—well, one of the things, anyway—and while most of the captives had stretched out to nap away their full bellies Pat knelt before the mirror wall, carefully drawing it through the tangles of her hair.

That was one good thing about the place, she thought. You

never had to hunt for a mirror. The bad thing was what the mirror revealed. Pat gazed discontentedly at the dark roots on her hair, the smudges of unidentified filth on her blouse, the circles under her eyes. What was even worse was that she was uncomfortably aware that she didn't smell very good, either. The hoarded drops of perfume from her carryall were running low, her little deodorant stick was long gone—and in any case the deodorant paste had left her unwelcome thatch of armpit hair sticky and tangled.

What she needed was a bath. She thought longingly of a slow soak in a hot tub, with scented bubble-bath foam rising high over the steamy water . . . and, yes, then also a wardrobe of clean clothes to put on afterward. Even a bar of soap would be fine. She thought of all the million little soap chips she had thrown away over her lifetime because they got to be too small to bother with. She would have paid a high price for any one of them right now.

A stirring a few steps away from her attracted her attention. It was where Dan had settled himself to sleep, but he didn't appear to be sleeping. He had taken off his jacket to wrap it over his head—well, that was a sensible enough thing to do, to keep the light out—but she saw that he had one hand up inside the garment, right in front of his face, and the hand was moving as though he were doing something with it inside the jacket.

Pat informed herself that whatever he was doing, it was none of her business. Picking his nose? Something equally distasteful and private? Not to mention that she wasn't really speaking to the man. . . . But it went on for a surprisingly long time, and curiosity overcame her scruples. "Dan?" Softly, so as not to wake the others. "What are you doing?"

The motion stopped. A moment later Dan's head popped out, regarding her. "It's nothing," he said.

"Well, sorry. I just thought—"

But he was shaking his head as though to tell her not to pursue the subject. Baffled, she watched as he wrapped the jacket around his hand and stood up. He looked as though he were pondering something. When she opened her mouth he shook his head at her again, then seemed to come to a decision. He touched the wall with one hand, then raised the other, wrapped in the jacket, to press against it. He held it there for a bit, frowning, then slowly moved it up and down.

He seemed to be expecting something. Whatever it was, it didn't happen. He shrugged and sighed. . . .

And then something did happen. The wall puckered and opened just where his hand was. A moment later a great fist—a Doc fist, taloned and immense—poked through and snatched the garment from his hand. "Shit!" he said, jumping back.

"What—?" Pat began, but almost at once the wall puckered again, the fist reappeared, it dropped the jacket on the floor and was gone again.

Dannerman looked angry. He picked up the jacket and shook it free. "The bastards," he muttered. "I guess they saw what I did after all, and now they've taken it away from me."

CHAPTER EIGHTEEN

Pat

Pat didn't think she had screamed when that fist poked through the wall, but she must have—must have made some sort of noise, anyway, enough so that a sleeper or two woke and saw something going on. Then their questions woke the rest. "It was the wristlet, wasn't it?" she demanded. "You took it off Dopey's body!"

He admitted it with a nod. "I had one of those glass buttons, too," he said. "Did you know they glow in the dark? Under my coat I could see it easily; and the bracelet looked like metal, but it was soft. Rubbery. It slipped right off when I pulled at it."

Rosaleen was looking at him curiously. "What did you think you were going to do with them?" She had wakened totally and quickly, as though there were no difference between sleeping and waking for her; Pat wondered if that was what it was like to be old.

Dannerman shrugged. "I didn't know. It occurred to me that maybe they were a sort of key to the wall, so I tried that out—"

"Didn't work, did it?" Jimmy Lin growled. "Now you've got them even madder at us."

That was more than Pat could stand—this from one of the men who had actually killed the first Dopey! But, surprisingly, it was Martín who came to Dannerman's defense.

"You are wrong, Lin," Martín said heavily. "He was quite correct. It is the duty of a prisoner of war to try to escape, by any means possible." He hesitated, then added, "I beg your pardon, Dannerman. You are not as useless as I thought. Now I think I will go back to sleep."

The entertainment was obviously over, so, more slowly, Jimmy and Rosaleen Artzybachova followed his example. Dannerman sat awake, leaning against the wall with his eyes half closed. After an indecisive moment Pat sat down next to him. He raised his head to look at her. "Are we friends again?" he asked hopefully.

Pat considered. "Well," she said, "not active enemies, anyway. Right now I'm a lot madder at Martín than I am at you."

"So is it all right if I say something?" When she nodded he cleared his throat and added, "I want to apologize. I'm sorry about lying to you and all. Will you believe me when I say I never wanted to do anything to harm you?"

She thought about that for a moment, then shrugged. "We'd have to get into a definition of what 'harm' means, wouldn't we?"

"Well, I mean *personal* harm. I admit what I was doing might have kept you from making a lot of money, maybe—"

"Damn straight it might. Important money. Money I needed, as a matter of fact; my second divorce came pretty close to cleaning me out." She thought about that might-have-been money, then relented. "Let's let it drop. Tell me, though. How'd you get into the spy business in the first place?"

"You mean, how did a nice guy like me get into a racket like that?" He grinned. "It just happened. I was in protsy in college, I told you that. I didn't think it would last past graduation, but they called me up."

"Into the army?"

"Not the army," he said wearily. "I keep telling you; it was the *Police* Reserve Officers Training Corps. I guess I was a natural for them, with my background—well, you know how we grew up. Golden kids, private schools, all of Uncle Cubby's rich power-broker friends hanging around when we spent our summers at his place. So I made a lot of contacts, and then when I grew up I had entry into all kinds of places. Sometimes that was pretty useful for the Bureau."

"I suppose," she said thoughtfully. "What the hell were you doing in protsy in the first place?"

"Easy credits . . . and, well, yes, there was also a girl. . . ."

She laughed out loud. A couple of the sleepers stirred, and she lowered her voice. "That's the story of your life, isn't it? Was she the one you brought to Uncle Cubby's for Christmas just before your father died?"

"No, that was a different one," he admitted. "You had a guy there, too. Was he the one you ran off and married?"

She gave him a sharp look, then smiled. "No. Actually not even close. Well, maybe neither of us is that much different from Jimmy Lin, just a little less outspoken about it." She nestled against him comfortably, then remembered to pull away.

He turned to look into her face. "What's the matter?"

She said uncomfortably, "I don't think I smell very good right now."

"So join the club."

"Damn it, Dan, I don't want to be in that club! I'd give anything for a bath—or at least for a little more water and somebody to chain Jimmy Lin up while I sponged myself off." She paused to smother a yawn. "Hell. Tell me something, Dan. Do you see any way of ever getting out of here?"

He gave her a warning look, but only said, "Did you notice how that thing reached right in to where I was standing to grab the stuff?"

"Meaning they're watching us?" She shuddered involuntarily, looking about. Well, she hadn't really ever doubted that they were being observed, but still—

On the other hand, getting out of this place was definitely the central concern in her mind, and she couldn't let it go. "So the walls have ears. Right. But do you have any ideas?"

He considered the question for a moment, then picked his words with care. "I hope so, Pat. There has to be something."

His tone struck Pat as somber. "But you have thought of what that is?"

"If you mean something that could help us escape," he said, glancing at the ceiling, "no. Not really. What I'm thinking is that there are all these people back home who don't have any idea they've been watched all this time."

There was an expression on his face that Pat couldn't identify—stubbornness, worry, concern? Something of all of them, plus a kind of determination she had never before associated with Cousin Dan-Dan. "I have a duty," he said, and stopped there.

In the silence she leaned back against him, wondering. It had never occurred to her that a cloak-and-dagger spook might be driven by conscience and concern as much as by—well, by whatever misguided adolescent yearning for colorful action might make a person get into that line of work. It was a new feeling for Pat. Not a bad one. It made him a lot easier to be comfortable with. . . .

Which she was. Comfortable. In spite of everything; comfortable enough to be definitely drowsy. When she yawned, he did, too. "We'll figure something out," he said. "Right now I'm sleepy."

And so, Pat realized, was she. It occurred to her that it would be nice for them to untangle themselves so they could stretch out, but by the time she had got that far in her thinking she was already asleep with her head on Dannerman's shoulder.

What woke Pat up was someone talking. The person was intruding on her dream, and she didn't want to let go of it, especially not because of the green-skinned woman playing a musical instrument who was intruding into it. When she opened her eyes she discovered her head was in Dannerman's lap and Jimmy Lin was grinning down at them. She sat up abruptly. "What did you say?" she demanded fuzzily.

"I was asking Dan what you were doing. Looked like the Jade Woman and Flute bit to me. Of course, Dan claims it didn't happen, but then old Dan's a real gentleman about a lady's honor, isn't he?"

"Damn you," she said. "Can't you turn off your testosterone for a while now and then? What is it, do you get a kick out of making trouble?"

His expression changed to belligerency. "Are you talking about the accident? Well, you know what? I'm not sorry we killed the little son of a bitch, even if it didn't take. Sooner or later I'm going to find some way to make him give us straight answers, and if he won't do it I wouldn't mind killing him all over again."

Dannerman was sitting up straight now, glaring at Lin. Pat was pleased to see that he was getting angry, too, but a little disappointed, too, when she realized that the anger wasn't at Lin's smarmy remarks. "You're an idiot," he said flatly. "If you really wanted to do something like that you're sure making it hard by advertising it ahead of time."

Lin shrugged and stalked away. Dannerman hesitated, then patted Pat on the head, easing it off his lap. "I've got an idea," he said, and got up without saying what the idea was. What he did was only to head for the stack of miscellaneous supplies Dopey's golems had brought.

Pat gazed after him, her back propped against the wall, knees hugged to her body. She was thinking about the connotations of being patted on the head. "Pat on the head" was a metaphor for tolerant dismissal and there had been a time, in her rad-fem undergraduate days, when any male who ventured such an act did so at his own peril. But she didn't feel tolerated, and certainly she didn't feel dismissed. What that casual touch had felt like was affection. Maybe even *sexual* affection. Tentative, yes, but under the circumstances about as forthright as was feasible. Under other circumstances . . .

Under other circumstances, Pat told herself wistfully, something nice might come of that; but not under these.

She shook herself and stood up, curious about what Dannerman was doing. He had borrowed Rosaleen's multicolor pen and was busily printing something out on a scrap of wrapping paper from the Starlab booty, shading what he was writing with his other hand. Rosaleen Artzybachova was sitting cross-legged nearby, watching him curiously. When Dannerman saw Pat standing over him he complained, "The damn ink smears on this stuff."

"That's what wrapping paper is like," she agreed. "What are you writing?"

He paused to add a word, then covered the sheet with his hand. "You could call it a diary," he said. "We don't have much privacy here, and there are some things I'd just as soon not advertise to the world."

She frowned. There was something odd about his tone. "So we can't see it?"

"Oh," he said. "I didn't say that. I guess a few friends could take a look."

"Like me?" Rosaleen offered. "It's my pen."

"Why not?" Dannerman said. "Only do it like this, please." He cupped the scrap in two hands and lifted it to his eyes, opening the hands at the thumbs just enough to peer inside. "Can you do that?"

Rosaleen gave him a baffled look, but did as instructed. "Thank God for radial keratomy," she muttered. And then, "Oh."

She closed her hands again over the scrap, looking at Dannerman with interest before she passed it to Pat. "You know the drill," she said. "I hope your near vision's in good shape."

It wasn't, particularly, but when Pat had done as ordered, opening narrow slits between fingers for light, she managed to make out the blurry scrawl:

If anybody has any useful ideas for escape etc let's share them like this.

"Oh," Pat said, too. "I see what you mean." By then Martín and Jimmy Lin were clamoring for their own turns, and Dannerman was already writing something else. When he passed it to Pat it said:

Concealed weapons? I have flex. glass knife in belt. Martín, what's in lapel? Anybody else?

By then they were all industriously writing little messages of their own, squabbling over their turns at Rosaleen's pen. "Hold it," Rosaleen ordered. "Let's make sure everybody sees everything. How about if we pass them around in alphabetical order—Adcock, Artzybachova, Dannerman, Delasquez, Lin. Then you can dispose of the messages when you're finished with them, Jimmy."

"How?"

"I don't know, swallow them, maybe?"

Lin looked rebellious, but Dannerman said, "Maybe we can burn them up in the cooker?" And when they had all seen the first message he gave it a try; it worked. The crumpled scrap of paper became ash, and he teased it out and ground it into powder with his heel for the floor to remove.

By the time they had finished taking inventory they had discovered they possessed a remarkable little armory: Dannerman's glass blade, Martín's plastic stiletto, a garroting cord from Jimmy Lin. Even Rosaleen had a pair of knitting-sized needles in her boots; apologetically Pat admitted to being the only one who had entered the Clipper without fallback arms.

But when they had exchanged all the information they had to offer, secure from the prying outside eyes, the temporary euphoria subsided and she felt let down. It was nice to know that they had some weapons. But what was the good of weapons when they had no plan to use them?

Passing secret messages around was a kind of pleasure Pat hadn't experienced since high school, but it palled. There was really nothing for them to say, and besides they were all getting hungry again.

While they were cooking their individual meals Rosaleen was investigating the cooker. "There must be a power source for this thing somewhere," she said puzzledly. "I can't find it. Maybe it's in the base? The rest of it's nothing much but sheet metal."

"Funny sheet metal," Martín rumbled. "It isn't even warm on the outside."

"Like a microwave," Pat offered.

Rosaleen shook her head. "It's not a microwave. Those vegetables Jimmy put in were foil-wrapped, and it didn't spark. I don't exactly know what—oh, hell!" Tardily they all smelled the scorching as the container of beef stew inside began to burn.

"Damn," Dannerman said. "I had my mouth all set for that stew." But it was powdery ashes before they could lever it out, and in the long run Martín simply picked the cooker up and shook them out of it for the floor to dispose of.

It was Martín, then, who noticed another curiosity. "Look here," he said, pushing at the device. "The wheels don't roll anymore."

Pat looked and discovered that they weren't actual wheels, anyway; they were just metal balls. When she pushed at the gadget hard enough it slid sluggishly over the rubbery floor, but the wheels weren't turning. "But it rolled easily enough when Dopey pushed it in," she said, perplexed.

"Maybe," Rosaleen said thoughtfully. "Or maybe they never did turn. I think we've got another piece of that far-out technology we were looking for here."

"For all the good it will do us," Martín said grumpily.

Dannerman and Pat took their food over to sit against the wall. Dannerman was deep in thought—probably, Pat supposed, about ways of getting them out of their prison cell. She hoped so, anyway. She was just getting used to the fact that her own cousin was a gumshoe; the annoyance was fading, curiosity was beginning to assert itself. She said, "Feeling talkative, Dan?"

He blinked at her. "What? Oh, sure. What's on your mind?"

"Well, you told me that after college protsy they drafted you into the army—all right, the protsy—"

"Had to be the protsy, Pat. They had snappier uniforms and no thirty-kilometer hikes."

"Then what?"

He chewed reflectively for a moment. "Well, when they called me up it turned out they didn't need any more people in uniforms. They needed undercover ops. They thought I'd do just fine mingling with the white-collar criminals and the yuppy terrorists. I objected. I said I didn't want to spy on my old friends, so they said, sure, we can give you something else. And they did." He shook his head wryly. "They ordered me to infiltrate one of the ultralight plane gangs in Orange County—you know, like the Deadly Force and the Scuzzhawks? The gangs that had been taking over little towns and scaring the hell out of the citizens? It meant wearing the same leathers for three or four weeks at a time and never taking a bath—not all that different from here, you know? Except that there were occupational hazards. The reason they needed gang infiltrators so badly was that they were having a pretty high attrition rate with the agents that managed to get in at all. All kinds of casualties: one plane crash, two ODs—and one guy who was found washing up with the surf. It didn't take me long to call in and say that, after all, I thought investigating tax frauds and radical-chic terrorists was more along my line of work."

Jimmy Lin had settled down nearby, listening intently. Pat gave him a glance, then grinned at Dannerman. "I think you made the right pick. I can't really imagine you as a Scuzzhawk. But, look, that was eight or ten years ago, at least? And you didn't quit when your hitch ran out?"

He said simply, "I found out I kind of liked it."

Fascinated, Pat persisted. "What else did you do?"

"Whatever they told me to do, pretty much. That outfit I used to work for in New York before I came to you—that was drugs. And I did a lot of antiterrorist stuff, too: the Free Bavarian movement, the Spanish guys that blew up Nelson's column in London, all that."

"And you'd go in and make friends with them, and then the end result of all these adventures was you put somebody in jail."

Dannerman gave her an injured look. "Only the bad guys."

Pat looked at him wonderingly. "Dan-Dan," she said, "you

know what I think about you? I think you didn't keep on being a spook for the money. I think you did it because you want to protect people. You're a kindergarten teacher, you know that? José pees on Elvira's milk and cookies, so you give José a good swat—but you're doing it for his sake as much as for hers."

Dannerman looked as though he was getting hot under the collar. "Somebody has to keep the peace. Do you have any better way of doing it?"

"No," she said, studying him analytically. "I don't. Actually, I think it's kind of sweet." He shrugged. "You weren't that kindly a kid, you know. What happened? Do they teach compassion in the spy school?"

"Not exactly. We did take a course in sensitivity training, but basically it was to teach us how to manipulate people." He looked at Jimmy. "Of course," Dannerman said, "I'm not the only one with experience in this area, am I?" Lin was silent, waiting, watching Dannerman's face while the bowl of goulash was cooling on his outstretched thighs. "I mean," Dannerman went on, "you knew I was an agent. You had to find out from somewhere."

Lin sighed. "If you're asking if I'm a professional spook like you, the answer's no. But, yes, I did know. They told me at the consulate, first thing, as soon as I got back from Houston. That's why I started cozying up to you." He glanced penitently at Pat. "See, Pat," he said, almost pleading, "I want to go home, I mean without getting arrested. They've got a warrant out for me at Jiuquan. It's a chickenshit political charge, but they're serious about it; jail's involved, and, trust me, you don't want to be in a Chinese jail. They told me I could square it by performing a little service for the state. So, I ask you, what could I do?"

Pat didn't answer that. Instead, she asked, "What's this Jewchoon place you're talking about?"

"Jiuquan," Dannerman corrected. "It's the Chinese space

center, like our Cape and Huntsville and Houston all rolled into one." Then, to Lin, "Tell you what. Let's change the subject, all right? No hard feelings. We all did what we had to do . . . and look how much good it's done any of us."

Time passed. Pat was interested to discover that time kept right on passing, even when there really weren't any events to mark the passage. Oh, there were a few slow, but visible, processes of change. All three of the men were developing tacky-looking beards, and Pat's own axillary growth was no longer scratchy stubble.

But very little *happened*. Once or twice Dopey put in a brief appearance, not talkative, seeming harried. Sporadically someone would have a notion and commit it to paper to be passed around, but none of the ideas seemed to go anywhere. Sleeping, eating, defecating took up just so much of their time, and the rest hung heavy. Pat was mildly pleased to discover that she could beat any of the others but Rosaleen at chess, once Rosaleen had made a wrapping-paper board, and while she and Dannerman were playing their hundredth game Jimmy Lin was attempting to fabricate a deck of playing cards out of more scraps of the paper towels. "At least I might have a chance to win something at poker now and then," he said sulkily.

Pat rocked back on her heels as a thought struck her. "It's your move," Dannerman said.

"Wait a minute. Give me the pen and a piece of paper, will you, Jimmy? Something just occurred to me."

And she began to print: *Would it do any good if we tried to get Dopey into a game of something?* She was just about to hand it to Dannerman when Jimmy called: "Hey, looks like Dopey's coming back!"

Indeed the mirror wall was turning milky again. Caught with

the scrap of paper in her hand, Pat stared about, looking for a place to hide it. There wasn't any. Desperately she popped it in her mouth and began to chew.

She forgot to swallow when she saw what was happening. Dopey was indeed entering through the wall, but he wasn't alone. He was leading two other human beings through the wall.

"Hey!" Jimmy Lin shouted in delight. "Naked women!"

So they were, being shepherded into the cell by a pair of Docs, looking terrified and angry at the same time. Each of them was rubbing the back of her neck with one hand as she clutched her bundle of clothing with the other. "You said," Dopey explained, "that you required additional breeding stock."

They looked very familiar to Pat Adcock. She swallowed the lump of paper as she stared at them, clutching Dannerman's arm. "Sweet Jesus," she gasped. "They're both *me!*"

CHAPTER NINETEEN

Pat

It was frightening, it was unbelievable, but Pat had to face up to the fact that it was true. These two women were indeed herself. They were two precisely identical copies of Dr. Patrice Adcock—oh, a lot cleaner, yes, and a lot less frayed-looking, but in every other way exactly herself. Their voices were the same. Their appearance was the same. The way they were hurrying into their clothes—Dannerman politely looking away, Martín impolitely observing, Jimmy Lin frankly ogling—was just the way she had done it when she first got clothing again. And when she asked, "Where the hell did you two come from?" what they answered was just what she would have said:

"Starlab." They said it in chorus, too, and then stopped short to stare at each other—to stare at everything around them. "Jesus," one of them began, a half-second before the other, who paused to let the first one finish with the flip side of Pat's question. It wasn't "Where did you come from?" but "Where in God's name are we?"

That got several answers; the habit of talking in chorus was contagious, Pat thought. Jimmy Lin, giggling, said, "You've been abducted by space aliens," and Rosaleen said compassionately, "That's a long story," and Dannerman proposed, "You go first, please? Tell us everything that happened. It might be important. Then we'll tell you everything we know."

As Pat Adcock listened to her duplicates talk she discovered a strange feeling in herself. It was pride. She was proud of herself—of her two new selves. They were less than an hour in this bizarre and terrifying new place, and yet they were managing to tell a coherent story. Oh, with repetitions and interruptions, of course—many interruptions—but it showed, she was gratified to think, some real strength of character.

The first thing her two duplicates remembered was waking up; they had been lying on what the first new Pat described as a kind of army cot and the other as a morgue slab. There were aliens all around them, and they weren't just the Dopey and the Docs that stripped them and convoyed them to the cell. "I saw one of the ones they call 'Bashful,' " the other said. "You know, the ones with the big eyes and the dewlaps that cover their faces? He was doing something with a big machine that looked kind of like a refrigerator. What? Oh, I don't know what, but he was making lights go on and off—the lights were in that green jelly stuff, you know? Like we saw on Starlab. A *lot* of it was like on Starlab." They hadn't observed their surroundings very closely, because as soon as they were awakened they were unceremoniously stripped by the Docs. And their necks hurt, they said, rubbing them reminiscently. "Let me see," Rosaleen ordered, and Jimmy Lin chimed in, "Me, too!"

"Knock it off," Pat said wearily, elbowing him out of the way. She and Rosaleen bent to inspect the nape of the women's necks. "Here?" Pat asked, touching a vertebra.

"Up a little higher. There." Pat and Rosaleen studied the hairline—how neatly trimmed, Pat thought with a twinge of jealousy—but there was nothing to see.

"Maybe you bumped yourselves," Jimmy offered, crowding in to look. But they denied that.

Then, yes, the Dopey and the Docs had gone through their clothing and handed it back to them. "There was a whole pile of other clothes there," one remembered, and the other confirmed it.

"I saw something with a lot of braid on it—it looked like that jacket you're wearing, Martín. All in a heap, with a lot of other stuff. No, they weren't doing anything with it; it looked like they just tossed it there."

"Maybe they're making clean clothes for us," Pat said hopefully.

"Maybe." And then they were marched down a long, busy passage, lined with bizarre things that probably were machines, they thought, to the point where they saw all the rest of the captives. "Wall? No. I didn't see any wall. Not from the outside, not until we were inside here. No, it didn't look like glass. It didn't look like anything at all. All I saw was the bunch of you, playing cards or something, but it didn't look like you saw us . . . and then we were here and there were these big damn mirrors all around us."

"And those machines?" Rosaleen asked. "What did they look like?"

But she didn't get much of an answer. They had been too full of other questions for close study. One of the devices they passed was making a kind of coffee-percolator sound, one of the new Pats remembered, and the other said another one was giving off heat; but, "Just weird, you know? Like the stuff on Starlab." Then she pleaded, "Our turn now. What *is* this place?"

Pat took over. "Come over and sit down," she offered. "Want something to eat? Jimmy, make us some of that lousy coffee, anyway."

Pat Adcock, who had been an only child, had never had any experience with this sort of thing. She had never had sisters before, much less identical triplets. She

was astonished to discover how much she liked it. There was
something warmly pleasing about sitting with the two new ver-
sions of herself, the repulsive coffee cooling untasted in their
hands, while she took over the job of briefing them.

There was a lot to be told. Pat had not realized just how much
she and the other captives had had to learn in all those long days
in the cell until she had to summarize it all for the two new Pats:
their capture, their imprisonment, their futile attempts at escape—the whole disheartening story. It was bad enough for the
original five captives, even worse for the new arrivals . . . who,
Pat thought, not only had the shock of finding themselves in
this bizarre new predicament, but also of suddenly being inex-
plicably part of a perfectly matched set of three.

They took it well, increasing Pat's pride in them. Took it well
most of the time, anyway; not counting their outrage when she
explained the toilet arrangements to them. They were almost
(though not quite) as repelled when she told them that everything they did, all the time, was watched from outside the cell.
"They have no right!" one of them exclaimed—barely before the
other.

Pat sighed, sparing a quick look at Dannerman, who had written something on a scrap of paper and was holding it covered,
impatiently waiting. "They have the power," she said. "I don't
know about 'rights.' Except that we don't have any at all." And
to Dannerman: "Is that what I think it is?"

"For the new ones," he said, handing it to Pat. She glanced
at it: it was what she had expected, a synopsis of the parts of the
briefing that were not to be spoken out loud.

She showed the newcomers the technique of managing to read
it without ever letting it be exposed to hostile eyes. When the
first one read it she said nothing, just looked affronted and unhappy when she passed it to the other. When the other finished

she giggled wanly. "Passing notes back and forth," she said, "it's like being in school again."

"Only school was never like this," the other one agreed, and Pat marveled: they were thinking the same thoughts she had thought. Well, they would, wouldn't they? Being the same person . . . except for being a lot cleaner.

Which made her think of something. She glanced at the other captives, all of whom had edged close to listen in, and lowered her voice. "Listen," she said. "They left you your perfume, didn't they? Could one of you spare me a couple of drops?"

They could, and Jimmy Lin stepped closer, inhaling. "Ah," he said, "that's really fine. I'd almost forgotten what a woman was supposed to smell like."

Pat gave him a look of disgust. "Shoo," she ordered, and then, more politely, "All the rest of you, could you just leave us alone for a bit? So we can get used to this?"

The other three considerately took themselves over to the cooker, but Lin looked rebellious. "Who are you to give me orders, Ice Queen? Maybe these other ladies appreciate a little male attention."

"We don't," one of the others said briefly. "Get lost." When he moved sulkily away she stared after him. "What's the matter with him?"

"He's horny."

"Well, sure he's horny. He's always been horny, but he didn't use to act like that."

"Ah, no," Pat said, remembering. "Not quite as forthright, anyway. But that was then. You were his boss then. Now that doesn't matter anymore."

The other Pat was staring after Jimmy, who was now sulkily demanding his share of what was coming out of the cooker. "Speaking of that kind of thing . . . well," she said, now almost whispering, "excuse me for asking, but I don't suppose any-body's actually getting any, are they?"

"In this goldfish bowl? I wish."

"Because," the other went on, "I couldn't help seeing the way Dan-Dan looks at you, you know? Is something new going on with you two?"

Pat had to think about that one. "I wouldn't be surprised," she said finally, surprising herself. "He's not really a bad guy when you get to know him . . . I mean, not counting that he's a goddamn spy."

That took explanation, too. Every-thing did, not helped by the fact that the new arrivals not only looked the same but talked at the same time, with the same words, and then stopped and stared at each other. "Hell," Rosaleen said at last. "We've got to do something about telling you apart. Let's start by naming you. You"—the original—"you're Pat. And you"—the one nearest her—"you can be Patricia—"

"It's Patrice, actually," the two new ones said together.

"All right, Patrice. And you're Patsy."

The third one looked rebellious. "The hell you say! Nobody ever calls me Patsy!"

"Oh, come on," the Patrice said soothingly. "It's not so bad and Rosie's right about needing names."

The Patsy scowled. "So why don't you be Patsy, then?" Then she surrendered: "Oh, well, I guess it makes no difference, but you owe me."

"Fine," Rosaleen said, smiling for the first time. "That's set-tled: Pat, Patrice and Patsy. Now, hold still." She was pulling out her multicolor pen. "Just so the rest of us can know which of you is which I'm going to put a little beauty spot on your fore-heads."

"Hey!" both of them protested at once.

Rosaleen overruled them. "It's just for now; it'll wear off by the time we think of something better. Let's see. We'll do blue for you, Pat, just to be fair. Red for Patrice; and I'll do green for Patsy." And then, mimicking Dopey: "Are there any questions?"

She was talking to the Pats, but it was Jimmy Lin who spoke up. "I have one. Which of you is going to be the lucky girl who gets me?"

Pat opened her mouth to chastise him, and then closed it again. What was the point? Better just to ignore him, she thought, and, hostesslike, was about to ask her new best friends if they were ready to eat again when something happened. It sounded like a distant *crump* of a blast—thunder? an explosion?—and a moment later that constant, featureless white light from overhead dimmed and reddened. It only lasted for a second. Then it was bright again.

"What the hell was that?" Patsy asked.

Nobody had an answer. Patrice asked, "Does that happen a lot?" and Pat shook her head.

"Never before," she said. "It sounded like something blew up."

Rosaleen Artzybachova said, "Did you feel the floor shake?" Dannerman thought he had; none of the others were sure. But there wasn't any doubt that something had happened, and, though they chewed the subject over the next half hour or so, all they could agree on was that they didn't like it.

Except for Jimmy Lin. Who said, grinning weakly, "How about that? Just *talking* about sex I can make the earth move for you."

Whatever it was, it didn't happen again. By their second day—well, by the time they woke

up from their second sleep after their arrival—the two new Pat
Adcocks were at least no longer speaking in chorus. Nurture had
triumphed over nature. There hadn't been many differences in
their experience, and those only small ones. Patsy had burned
her hand trying to learn how to use the cooker; Jimmy Lin had
been a little too forthright when he managed to get Patrice
alone—well, not "alone," but at least a couple of meters from
any of the others, enough for him to deem the privacy adequate—and it had wound up in a screaming match. Things like
that. But however little the differences had been, they were
enough to set each of them off on somewhat different trains of
thought.

What all the Pats had, and kept, was a preference for each
other's company. They ate together. When one of them had to
use the toilet the other two stood protectively before her, glaring the three males down. They slept nestled next to each other,
woke at the same time, whispered to each other. Within the
small group of captives they had become a separate subunit. It
was, Pat thought, a little reassuring to have two companions
whom she could trust absolutely, since they were herself.

The other four were not as pleased. Dannerman and Rosaleen
embarked on a chess marathon, doggedly ignoring the three Pat
Adcocks. Martín Delasquez hardly spoke to anyone, retreating
into sleep, or pretended sleep, for hour upon hour, while Jimmy
Lin went the other way. He was hyperactive, Pat thought. He
seemed hardly to sleep at all. He kibitzed the chess players, tried
unsuccessfully to get Martín to play some other game with him
and, of course, did his best to talk sex with any or all of the three
Pats. If they were worried about getting pregnant, he offered,
the revered ancient Peng-tsu had the answers for that, too. "We
could do Approaching the Fragrant Bamboo, for instance," he
said. "That's doing it standing up, you know? And Peng-tsu says
you can't get pregnant that way. You don't believe that? All

right, then there's always the Jade Girl and the Flute, or The White Tiger Leaps—that one," he said, with a wink, "I don't want to tell you about, but any time you like I could show you."

All that sort of talk had long since become pretty stale for Pat, but the two new ones were more tolerant. They let him talk. Anyway, Pat thought, that was better than Jimmy's other main occupation, which was feverishly writing out notes with ideas for doing something—going on a hunger strike, capturing Dopey and torturing him until he did whatever they wanted— maybe using some of the concealed weapons they still possessed, maybe by dunking his limbs or tail into the cooker. Pat wondered if the man was going insane. When he passed around the suggestion for cooking Dopey's plume, on the grounds that that was bound to hurt but unlikely to kill the creature, he was almost trembling with excitement; but then, a few hours later, he was talking enthusiastically about some of his ancestor's other sexual proposals . . . when the wall clouded and Dopey came in.

As always, he was bombarded with questions as soon as he appeared: "Why were you gone so long?" from Jimmy Lin; "What was that explosion?" from Dannerman.

One answer did for both of them. "There was an incident," Dopey admitted, his fingers working nervously, his bright tail dimmed and still. "It caused some problems for a time, but it has been dealt with. Now I have some news for you—"

Pat wasn't letting him get away with that. "What kind of incident?" she insisted.

He hesitated, staring around at them with those great eyes. Then he spoke to Dannerman. "In your previous life you were assigned to dealing with 'terrorists,' is that not correct? That is, with criminal persons who performed violent and destructive acts? Yes. Well, it is something of that sort here. I can say no more about it, except that the criminals have been, ah, neutralized."

"Neutralized how?" Jimmy asked suspiciously, but Rosaleen overrode him—probably, Pat thought, because she didn't think they would like to hear the answer.

"Never mind that," she said. "What he means is, are these the same 'criminals' who were interfering with your communications?"

"Yes, precisely. The terrorists."

"I see. And perhaps the same ones who transmitted the message that described you people as destroying the universe?"

For a moment Pat thought that Dopey was going to relapse into his trance state again; it seemed to be a troubling question. But then he made a breathy sound—almost a sigh—and said, "Yes. They are the same. Through trickery and violence they managed to infiltrate the link to your Starlab for a brief time. Of course, I observed their transmission at once and was able to jam the rest of it."

"But then they did it again," Dannerman offered.

Dopey said mournfully, "Indeed. This time I failed to observe it, as they had caused the death of one of me. But my replacement dealt with them. No," he added, waggling his head against the next burst of questions, "that is all I may say on that subject. But I have received new instructions for you. I am instructed to accelerate your program, and so a device is being prepared which will give you more complete information—"

"Device? What kind of device?" Rosaleen demanded.

"It will be explained when it is ready," he said severely. "Please do not interrupt. I have further instructions. I am directed to provide you with whatever additional matériel from your Starlab you require—except, of course, anything that can be used as a weapon."

"Why are you being nice to us?" Martín asked suspiciously.

"I do not make these decisions. I simply carry out instructions. If there is anything in particular you wish, simply inform me, now or later. Otherwise I will use my own discretion."

"We don't have room for anything else in here!" Pat put in.

"Yes. That has been anticipated. Other accommodations are being prepared for you." He paused, eyes closed, fingers busy in the muff. It looked to Pat as though he was getting ready to leave, with a million questions unanswered; Rosaleen evidently thought the same, because she spoke up.

"Tell me one more thing. Are you going to bring any more of us here?"

"More copies of you here? I know of no such plans. It is possible, however, that there will be other human beings. Two additional human missions to Starlab are currently being proposed, and of course if they reach the orbiter they, too, will be copied for study. Now I must go."

He turned, then paused to look back at Jimmy Lin. "One more thing. Please do not give any more thought to the plan of capturing and torturing me. I do not think you could succeed, but if you did it would be very unpleasant for me, and it would do you no good at all."

CHAPTER TWENTY

Pat

Pat Adcock was deep in sleep when the sound of her own voice yelling jerked her awake. It didn't come from her own throat; it had to be one of the new Pats, and she jumped to a conclusion. "Is that damn Jimmy trying something?" she demanded, sitting up and rubbing her eyes.

But it wasn't Jimmy Lin. It was one of the Docs, and the person shouting was Patsy, hanging by one arm from the Doc's grasp. "Damn you," she cried, shaking herself free. "Don't grab a person like that!"

The Doc hesitated, glancing at a second Doc standing stolidly by. "Where's Dopey?" Pat demanded; no one answered, and he wasn't there. The second Doc, which was holding some sort of metallic object, didn't speak, of course: They never did, as far as Pat knew; perhaps couldn't. Or simply had no reason to. What it did was make a gesture, and at once the first one abandoned Patsy and casually reached out for the arm of the nearest other human—it happened to be Jimmy Lin—holding him firmly while the other jammed the object down on Lin's head.

"Hey!" Jimmy squawked in alarm, reaching up with both hands to tug it free. In vain; the Doc's grip was firm. Pat thought for a moment of trying to rescue the Chinanaut from whatever new torture the Docs had devised. She could see the thing plainly now: a sort of helmet, made of the same coppery mesh as Dopey's muff. On Jimmy's head it looked almost like a garish wig, cut along the lines of one of those flapper hairdos of the early twentieth century, what they called a "French bob," she thought. And while she waited Jimmy stopped struggling.

"Hey," he said again, sounding startled but now—astonishingly—almost pleased. "There's a Frenchman talking to me. He's saying—no, just wait a minute, I'll translate for you when he's done."

"I speak French," Rosaleen said eagerly—only the first to make the claim; she was quickly followed by all three Pats and both other men.

Jimmy waved impatiently for silence. "He isn't speaking French. He's speaking Chinese. Shut up so I can hear."

"Chinese!" Martín muttered angrily, as the two Docs left as wordlessly as they had come in. One of the Pats—Pat thought it was Patrice—complained:

"That is *so* inconsiderate!" Both of them were echoing Pat's own thoughts. Chinese, for God's sake! Dopey was showing even worse judgment than usual. But there was nothing to do about it but wait until Jimmy Lin was willing to talk to them.

Evidently the Frenchman's message was short. After a moment Jimmy took the helmet off and gazed at them. "Well," he said, "that was interesting. It didn't actually tell much, but—hey!" Martín had grabbed the helmet from him. Jimmy reached to take it back, but Martín fended him off and settled the thing on his own head. "Now, what's the use of doing that?" Jimmy demanded pettishly. "You aren't going to understand Chinese, Martín."

Martín said triumphantly, "He isn't speaking Chinese! He's speaking Spanish."

"But that's impossible," Jimmy protested. "He was speaking quite excellent PRC Chinese, with a well-educated accent, though there was a trace of the Beijing tones—"

"Be quiet!" Martín thundered. "I can't hear while you're making all that racket! Also, I know who this man is. I will tell you all about it if you will simply let me listen."

Looking petulant, Jimmy Lin did as ordered, but the others didn't. Under the dark eye-patches of the helmet Martín was scowling at the noise, but he said nothing more until it was over. Then he took the helmet off and held it in his hand for a moment.

"The man speaking, he is Hugues duValier. He's a navigator with Eurospace; I met him once at Kourou. What he is saying is a communication meant for everybody in the world. It sounds as though they finally got their own Starlab mission off."

"What did he say?" Dannerman demanded.

Martín shook his head. "Try it for yourself. Since he is so unexpectedly versatile, I am curious to see if perhaps this time he will speak in some language you can understand."

"Hey!" Pat cried as Martín handed the helmet to Dannerman. "What happened to alphabetical order? Who said all the men go first?"

"What happened to women's rights?" Patrice chimed in, and Patsy added:

"Oink, oink, you sexist pigs."

But Rosaleen said, "It's faster if we don't argue. Let him go; we'll all get a turn." And Dannerman placed the helmet on his head.

CHAPTER TWENTY-ONE

Dan

Dannerman settled the thing on his head as rapidly as he could; he wanted to see this linguistic marvel, wanted even more to find out just what the Frenchman had to say. The helmet didn't fit particularly well and it was heavy. The goggles—opaque eye-shields, actually—dug into his flesh over the cheekbones, but they did their job. He could see nothing but blackness, could hear the sounds from his companions only faintly through the thickness of the helmet.

Then the blackness dissolved. Dannerman was looking at a man dressed in an astronaut's EVA spacesuit, helmet tucked under one arm, and the man was looking directly back at him. It didn't look like a broadcast. It seemed that the man was standing before him, solid in three dimensions, seeming almost near enough to touch. When the man spoke he sounded as though the conversation was one-on-one. He said:

"Hello, ladies and gentlemen. You may recognize me. I am Colonel Hugues duValier, and I am speaking to you from the astronomical observatory called Starlab. I am not alone here. I am in the company of a person who has a message of great importance for everyone on Earth. I cannot show him to you at this time. However, he is a friend, and he has given me the responsibilty—and the privilege—of delivering his message to you.

"You will remember that some time ago these two broadcasts of alien origin were received all over the world." A screen appeared beside the figure, displaying the two old space messages one after another. "Some people thought these were some sort of a joke. Others came closer to the truth, imagining that they were warnings of an extraterrestrial invasion. That is both true and false. There is a threat of invasion by evil people, that is true. What is false is that the evil ones are not the ones shown in the messages. The evil ones—the people who are even now planning to attack our planet and do us all great harm—are the ones who sent those first false messages in order to deceive you. These brutal creatures are called by a name which is difficult for me to say; it sounds like the 'Horch.' They possess a very high technology, particularly in weaponry. They have fought many wars, over long ages of time, and in them they have succeeded in destroying many other civilizations in other solar systems. Only a few races have been able to defend themselves against the Horch. Some of them are the people whose pictures the Horch sent to you—pretending they were enemies—but they are in fact the ones who can help you defend yourself against these attackers. Their name is even more difficult to pronounce; my friends here call them 'Beloved Leaders.' You already know what they look like, from the deceitful transmissions the Horch sent. What I will show you now is a picture of a Horch."

The image of the astronaut flicked out of sight and another being appeared. It didn't look like a picture. To Dannerman the creature looked as though it were actually standing there, no more than a yard or so away from him. It was taller than Dannerman himself, and gazing threateningly at him. It was certainly not from the gallery that had already been displayed, though equally ugly. Stocky body, wearing metallic armor. Long lizard head on a long and supple neck, with a lipless mouth filled with sharp teeth. Instead of arms it had two boneless limbs, like an elephant's trunk, fraying into half a dozen digits at the ends. In one "hand" it carried an axe, in the other a spiked club. It was, in fact, the very model of the kind of alien invader you would never want to see appearing out of your skies.

The image shrank to a picture inset on the screen and the colonel appeared again, looking grave. "I have been shown the evidence, which is indisputable, and so I now know what terrible things the Horch can do," he said somberly. "They will do such things to us, too, if we let them, and we have no defenses of our own that could withstand them. Still, we have been offered strong allies. With the help of the Beloved Leaders—as these friends are called—we can defend ourselves.

"Without them we are doomed.

"That is all I can say now. In twenty-four hours I will speak to you again, and then I will give you more details about the choices before us. Until then . . . please. Be warned."

The picture went to black. The message was over.

Thoughtfully Dannerman removed the helmet. "He spoke to me in English," he announced. "Rosie? Why don't you take a shot and see what he does for you?"

"Thanks a lot, Dan," Pat said with annoyance.

He shook his head. "You'll get your turn. Wait till we've all seen it." He settled himself on the floor and waited, staring into space.

Then Patsy, last to have her turn, took the helmet off and shakily, "Wow. That was an ugly one, all right."

Dannerman had been thinking. He said, "Something strikes me as peculiar. The astronaut spoke to me in English; was it the same for you Pats? Yes, I thought so. Rosaleen?"

"Why, yes. He spoke in Ukrainian. With a few Russian words, actually, but his accent was good. Why do you say that's peculiar? Clearly this is an announcement transmitted to everyone on Earth, like the others; naturally they would want it to be in languages everyone can understand."

"That's not the peculiar part. Did you see duValier's lips move?"

"His lips?" She looked puzzled, but Jimmy Lin was quicker. "You're thinking it was lip-synched for each of us?" he demanded. "No. Forget lip-synching. Maybe you could get away with that for European languages. Mandarin Chinese, no. DuValier was actually speaking those words, Dan."

Dannerman nodded. "But that wasn't exactly what I was thinking. What I'm thinking is that it *wasn't* lip-synched, and that's the part that's hard to understand. Martín? Did this Colonel duValier know all those languages?"

Delasquez looked indignant. "That ass? No! I was astonished to hear him even speak Spanish. I do not even know how he succeeded in getting a spacecraft on course to Starlab, he is such a notorious fool."

Pat was looking at Dannerman expectantly. When he didn't speak she prodded. "What's your point, Dan?"

"I wish I knew. The whole thing sounds funny."

Patrice nodded. "I know what you mean. If I saw that on TV at home I'd turn it right off. 'Beloved Leaders,' for Christ's sake! Only—well, if what he says is the truth . . ."

Jimmy Lin finished the sentence for her. "Then," he said, "the world is really in the deep shit."

CHAPTER TWENTY-TWO

Dan

Dannerman didn't have to be told that the world was in trouble. It always was. That was the reason it hired him and others like him, to do their best to protect it against itself.

Now here was the biggest threat of all, and shouldn't—he asked himself—shouldn't he be doing something about it? There was only one answer to that for Jim Daniel Dannerman. The question wasn't *whether*. It was *what*.

And to that he had no answer. Every other time he had found himself in harm's way he had known exactly what he wanted to accomplish. If he'd been in any doubt, Colonel Hilda Morrisey or someone like her would have spelled it out for him at the briefing. There was always a hierarchy of defined objectives. First, you stayed alive. Second, you got the evidence. Third, you called in the strike force and watched the malefactors being led away.

Here there was no briefing to tell him what to do. There was also no evidence to get, no way to get out and no strike force waiting to be called. And here the stakes were higher than they had ever been before. It was the entire population of Earth who were at risk now—Hilda herself, and sweet Anita Berman from Theater Aristophanes Two, and his landlady Rita, as well as everyone at the Dannerman Observatory . . . as well as everyone else he'd ever known in all his life, villains and colleagues and civilians alike. He wondered what they were doing now. He wondered how much comfort they could take in the promise of help from the "Beloved Leaders."

And he wondered, too, just how much help those Beloved Leaders had any real intention of giving. There just wasn't enough data! He knew nothing useful of those shadowy figures, had no idea what sort of bizarre alien personality traits motivated them. And had little reason to believe that benevolence was among them.

He opened his eyes when he heard Pat raising her voice. She was saying something harsh to Jimmy Lin, who was grinning as he held her by one arm. She wrenched herself free, saw Dannerman looking at her and came over to sit beside him. "Bastard," she said.

He didn't take it personally, but, "You mean Jimmy?" he asked, just to make sure.

"Who else? You'd think he'd have enough decency to give it a rest, the way things are."

"I take it he was hitting on you."

"Me, and Patsy, and Patrice—he doesn't care. He just wants to get laid. He said—" She hesitated, then shook her head. "He said what he always says, so what's the use of talking about it? Forget him." Then she looked apologetic. "Did I interrupt something?"

"Nothing that was going anywhere," he admitted.

"Well, if you're sure . . . Listen, I've been wanting to ask you something, Dan. What did you mean about it's being funny?"

"Funny? Oh, right. I almost forgot. Well, it is funny. Why would Dopey show us that message?"

"Why? Hum." She thought for a moment, then said, "Yeah, I see what you mean. Dopey doesn't do anything that doesn't do him some good, so what good can that do him?"

"That's the question, all right. I don't suppose you happen to have an answer?"

"I wish I did. I wish I knew how much of it to believe, too."

"So do I." Dannerman thought about telling her some of his

own doubts, but there wasn't much point; they weren't clear in his own mind. Anyway, he saw that Pat was glaring again at Jimmy. Who was standing over the cooker, waiting for his next meal to heat, and leering at them.

"Bastard," she said again. "Not that I don't understand how he feels. It's been a long time—but here? With everybody watching? Although I have to say he thought about that part, too."

"Oh?" said Dannerman, surprised to find a sudden interest growing.

She looked at him, her expression unreadable. "Well, yes. Like in an airplane, you know, when you get a couple of blankets from the stew. There are all those blankets from Starlab. Then— well, did Jimmy ever explain the Rabbit Nibbles the Hare to you?"

"Frequently," he said—surprised again to find that he was feeling just a tiny bit of unexpected jealousy. "Is that what you and Jimmy talk about?"

"It's what Jimmy talks about," she corrected. "All the time." She was still studying his face as she added, "But, listen, Dan, just for the record—I mean, in case you're interested—Jimmy and I never actually did anything. Not now, or ever. The only thing I ever wanted from Jimmy Lin was for him to help me make a lot of money."

One more surprise: the feeling of relief. But, "Always thinking of the big bucks, aren't you?" he chided. He meant it lightly, but her expression changed.

"I don't want to be poor," she said.

"I'm sorry—"

"No, you were right. I wanted the bucks. That's why I wanted Starlab so badly."

"Our dear old family lawyer told me you had made some bad investments," Dannerman said, remembering.

"Did he now? Our dear old family lawyer has a big mouth,

but that wasn't it. Well," she said, reconsidering, "I did make one real bad investment, maybe. That was Ferdie. My ex-husband—the sweet one. He'd spend the whole day lying naked by the pool, communing with nature, when he wasn't writing poetry. Ferdie was very Zen; made me learn my mantra and everything. But after a while I got tired of having this big, healthy man around the house who couldn't even remember to flush his own toilet, but I couldn't let him starve, could I? So before the divorce I endowed this lectureship for poetry and got him put in charge of it. I figured that would keep him eating for the rest of his life."

"And your generosity bankrupted you?"

"Well, not directly. It cost me a bundle, but I had plenty left . . . but, on the other hand, yes, I guess it did, because after I'd laid out the cash to finance the lectureship—and, believe me, Dan-Dan, I was generous—the next thing that happened was Ferdie's lawyers came to see my lawyers and said, 'Okay, now that we've got that out of the way, let's talk about how we're going to divide up the community property.'"

"Skunks," he said. The diffuse light that came from nowhere made her unkempt hair radiant.

"Lawyers," she corrected. "He got some really good ones working for him, I'll say that much. They had every last thing I owned on their database. I had to give him half—which meant I had to sell off a lot of stuff that I didn't really want to sell, to keep the house and the personal stuff. But Ferdie really was a sweet man." She stretched and yawned. "Now you," she ordered.

He considered. "What do you want to know?"

"Everything. Especially about the women. Start with whoever it was who kept you from collecting Uncle Cubby's inheritance."

He leaned forward and lifted her hand to kiss, and the hell with who might be watching. It was the first time in a long time—maybe, he reflected, the first time ever—that he'd had this kind of boy-girl talk without having to lie through at least some parts of it, to cover up what he was really doing. But now there was nothing to lie about. "That would be Ilse, I guess. In a way, anyway. She was in the Mads—"

"The what?"

"The Mad King Ludwigs. The Bavarian secessionist movement. Well, the terrorists; that's what they really were. I was undercover, investigating them, when Uncle Cubby died, and I'd cut all my links with home. We were on the run, Ilse and I, although I always kept my team leader informed. And Ilse finally must've rumbled me. Or someone else did, and tipped her off."

"Who were you running from?"

"The Bay-Kahs—the Bundes Kriminalamt. The cops. They were after us because we'd tried to blow up the Kunstmuseum as a protest. I made sure the bomb didn't actually go off— maybe that's what made the Mads suspicious—but we had to get out of there. Anyway, one night Ilse and I had a lot to drink in this pension in the Alps. Now that I think of it, I was the one doing most of the drinking. Then I just went to sleep, not a care in the world, and when something woke me up an hour or so later, in the middle of the night, Ilse was gone and four big bastards with hockey sticks were crashing through the door after my blood. I knew them all. They were *aktion*—the organization's muscle men. I'd seen them doing their stuff at demonstrations, but I hadn't expected them to be coming after me just then."

He leaned back, meditating. "You know how you're never prepared for the really big challenges? If you knew something like that was coming up you'd get a good night's sleep first and make sure your reflexes were all tuned. . . . Mine weren't. I was still half in the bag and all tangled up in the bedclothes, and there I was."

"But you overpowered them anyway."

"Oh, no. I did break the arm of one of them, but the other three beat the shit out of me, until Hilda got there."

"Another of your women?"

That made him laugh. "Jesus, no. My team leader. She'd been surveilling the building. When she saw Ilse come out and the leg-breakers go in she decided she'd better make sure I was all right. Which I was, after I healed up for a while, though I had to stay out of sight for a month or so—the Mads had planted a couple people in the police, and they had to be collected first." He scratched himself. "Hilda had intercepted the lawyer's notice about the estate," he added, "but she didn't pass it on, because she didn't want to blow my cover."

"Poor bastard."

She was yawning as she said it, which made him yawn too. "Dirt poor," he agreed drowsily. Well, except for what the Bureau had been putting away for him, but he couldn't collect that until he retired . . . which didn't seem like a very early probability . . . unless, he corrected himself, you considered that in a way he was, perforce, pretty much retired already. . . .

His thoughts were going in circles again. He abandoned them and let himself drift off. It was getting to be a habit to fall asleep with Pat Adcock on his shoulder, he thought, and couldn't decide whether it was a good one or not.

His body had its own opinions. When Dopey appeared again and roused the whole cell Pat's proximity had started a few glands flowing; and Dannerman woke with a major erection and the rapidly dissipating recollection of some more than normally erotic dreams. Beside him Pat was scrambling to her feet. "Come on, Dan!" she urged him.

"In a minute," he said, waving her away. By the time he felt fit to stand up everyone else was clustered around Dopey and his two Docs as they dispensed more largesse.

"I have brought you more blankets and food," Dopey said unnecessarily. "You do not presently need them, I am aware, but there is always the risk that supplies may be temporarily interrupted. Meanwhile, I have some urgent business."

"What kind of business?" Patsy asked, but was outweighed by two or three others demanding to know what kind of "temporary interruptions" Dopey was talking about.

"Merely more of the difficulties we have already experienced," he explained. "They will be dealt with. Now, as to the more important matters—"

But Rosaleen, poking around in the mounting heap of supplies the Docs were lugging in, had more important matters of her own. Arms akimbo, she faced Dopey angrily. "We need more than food and blankets," she said. "We need medical supplies. We need—"

"We need to know what's going on on Earth, too," Patsy put in.

Dopey said defensively, "I cannot promise that. I do not have authority to make such promises. I have in fact asked those who decide for permission to provide you with additional data, but I have not received an answer. You do not understand how difficult things have become."

"I don't *care* how difficult things have become."

"But, you see, at present I am unable to reach the ones who could give permission. Just at present, that is to say."

"Everything's 'just at present,' " Jimmy Lin sneered, and Dannerman, looking at the stack of food packages, had a comment of his own:

"You must expect us to be here for a long time."

"That is also not for me to decide, but the reason for the large quantity is that I do not know when I will be able to get more.

I have said this. Now we must deal with the urgent matters. Do you have any questions about the announcement made by your Colonel duValier?"

Dannerman was surprised that that was the "urgent" business, but it was Pat who spoke up. "We've got plenty of questions, but they're not about Colonel duValier. For instance, these 'Horch' the colonel talks about in what you transmitted to the Earth. Are they related to the problems you're having?"

Dopey didn't answer immediately. Dannerman expected him to thrust his paws into the muff and go again into the thinking-it-over trance, but he merely looked pained—as much as a kitten face can look pained. Finally he announced, "There is a disjunction here. You are correct in one respect. The Horch are indeed responsible for our problems, because they are evil. They have performed acts of terrorism which have caused great hardship for us. You will understand what terrorists are like, Agent Dannerman, from your own experiences with Colonel Hilda Morrisey. The Horch are criminals in much the same way as your human terrorists, but far more dangerous than any you can imagine. However, you have made a false assumption."

"Which is?" Dannerman demanded.

"That message has not been transmitted. The reason for that is that Colonel duValier has not yet arrived on Starlab."

"Hah!" Jimmy Lin shouted. "I knew it! It was a damn simulation."

"The problem was not understood," Dopey admitted. "It will be corrected."

Something was bothering Dannerman. He asked, "Why bother with simulating somebody who isn't there? If you wanted to send a message that seemed to come from a human being, why not use one of us?"

Dopey hesitated again. "That would not be effective," he said, and would not say why. The only subject that he seemed willing to discuss was what their reactions had been to the message, and when they began asking questions in return—what would be in the second message? What other languages would it be delivered in?—he did not respond at all.

Not until, at a venture, Pat asked, "Are we in personal danger from these Horch?"

That made Dopey pause to think once more. "At this time, no," he said at length.

"Oh, fine," Patrice muttered. "You're making me feel all cuddly warm and protected."

"I understand you. That is sarcasm, meaning the opposite," Dopey said. "You will, however, be protected."

"By you?"

"I? No, of course not I. That protection will come from a far more advanced race than my own."

"Meaning," Dannerman asked, "those odd-looking scarecrows we saw on TV?"

Dopey winced. "That was an unfair picture our enemies transmitted. The Beloved Leaders come from a light-gravity planet and thus are rather frail in physique."

He paused as Jimmy Lin made a sound of disgust. " 'Beloved Leaders,' " Lin sneered.

Dopey looked inquiring. "Your tone of voice indicates disapproval," he said.

"You damn bet it does! 'Beloved Leaders' is what the old Koreans called their dictators. That's not a good name, Dopey."

"Thank you," the alien said. "That too is useful, although I am not sure that a change will be permitted. At any rate, because of their evolutionary heritage the Be—the persons in charge, that is, would not be on a planet of this mass."

"So they're not really going to be around to save us?" Jimmy Lin demanded in alarm.

But that was one question too many. Dopey evidently had

what he had come for. Without farewell, he turned and disappeared into the mirror, which re-formed seamlessly behind him, like a puddle of mercury closing over a stone.

Dannerman stared after him for a long minute, though there was nothing to see but his own reflection in the wall. He was puzzling over something, and it showed. "What's the matter?" Pat demanded. "You still wondering why he showed us that message?"

"Actually no," Dannerman said. "I think that's pretty obvious now, isn't it? He's using us to be his sneak-preview film critics, getting our reactions before he puts the thing on the air. No, it's something else." He hesitated for a moment. Then, "Tell me something, Pat. When we were talking I mentioned Hilda to you, didn't I?"

"Sure. Your boss in the Bureau. I remember."

"But did I ever say her last name? No, I didn't think so. So how did Dopey know that it was Morrisey?"

CHAPTER TWENTY-THREE

Dan

So Dannerman had one more puzzle to add to his collection. He was certain he'd never mentioned Hilda Morrisey's last name, and the Bureau did not advertise the names of its personnel. And it was not information that could be picked up from the monitored broadcasts.

But Dopey had known it.

In fact, Dopey seemed to know quite a few of the things they had never spoken aloud. How? There was one easy answer to that: Someone might have been sloppy in concealing some of the notes as they read them or passed them around. But that didn't explain Hilda Morrisey, and Dannerman didn't believe it anyway. What he believed was that Dopey possessed sources of information they didn't know about.

Whatever those sources might be.

He snorted in disgust—muffled quickly, because he didn't want Pat, or any one of the Pats, to come over to see what was bothering him. That had happened twice already, and he had waved them away. He wished he didn't have to. He wanted badly to talk it over with the others, because someone else, Rosaleen maybe—well, any of them—might have a clarifying insight he had missed. But if even the eyes-only note-passing was compromised, they would simply be giving more information to Dopey, or Dopey's masters.

Would that matter? Would that sort of information be useful to them? Dannerman could form no satisfactory answer to that, either, but it was simple basic tradecraft to deny as much information as possible to the enemy, and—

His thoughts were interrupted by a new sound. Something had begun squealing shrilly, somewhere. When Dannerman raised his head he saw Patrice holding the helmet in her hand, looking puzzled. "I think it wants something," she said.

"It wants one of us to put it on, of course," Rosaleen said crossly. "Give it to me."

Evidently she was right. As soon as she had it settled on her head the beeping stopped. By then most of the others had converged around her, clamoring to know what she was hearing. Rosaleen didn't take the helmet off, only held up her hand and said, "Relax. It's basically the same message, but with a few— improvements. Give me a moment."

"Then this time we do it in alphabetical order, remember?" Pat reminded them. "Pat comes before Patrice or Patsy, so I get the first look."

Jimmy Lin emitted a long, exasperated sigh, Martín muttered something that sounded obscene. Dannerman only waited; he was as impatient as anyone, but he accepted the fact that it would go faster if they didn't argue. When all four women had had a look—each looking puzzled, even faintly disappointed, when they were finished—his turn came. As soon as the helmet was on his head and the eyepieces in place the figure of the French astronaut popped into being and began to speak. *"Messieurs et mesdames,"* it began, *"je m'appelle Colonel Hugues duValier, peut-être vous me connaissez, et je suis—"* And then the French language was drowned out by another voice, overriding the colonel with unaccented American English:

"Ladies and gentlemen, I'm Colonel Hugues duValier. Maybe you know me; I am an astronaut at present in orbit on the astronomical satellite known as Starlab. I have a message of the greatest importance for everyone on Earth—"

It was the same message as before, but reworked to remove their objections. The colonel wasn't risking any distractions to his audience by speaking in many tongues; there was a simple voice-over, the same thing viewers heard on any newscast anywhere in the world. The phrase "Beloved Leaders" was still there, but modified to: "they are called 'Beloved Leaders,' but we can know them simply as the forces which have so far—and very successfully!—born the brunt of the attack." When Delasquez and Jimmy Lin had had their turns Dannerman asked about languages, just to clear up one final point. The answers were the same as before, Ukrainian for Rosaleen, American English for Dannerman and the Pats, Spanish for Delasquez and Chinese for Jimmy. "But this time," Rosaleen said, "the Ukrainian was all Ukrainian. They corrected some of the Russian words."

Dannerman nodded thoughtfully, but said only, "Fast work. Dopey must have real good production facilities."

When he stopped there, Pat gave him a perplexed, maybe even an unfriendly, look. "Is that all you have to say about it?"

He shrugged; Jimmy Lin answered for him. "What's to say? We're just Dopey's damn test audience, aren't we? And we did our job for him. He listened to everything we criticized, and he changed the message around to suit. Now—" He turned and faced the wall, cupping his hands around his mouth. "—are you listening, Dopey? Okay, then listen to this. You got it right this time. It's fine the way it is, so don't bother us with any more revisions; just keep the food coming." He turned to Dannerman, grinning. "Does that about cover it? Because if it doesn't we could—"

He didn't get a chance to finish the sentence, because he was interrupted. Abruptly the ground began to tremble. Everyone who was standing suddenly began to reel; Jimmy grabbed Martín Delasquez's shoulder to steady himself, nearly bringing them both down. "Oh, hell," Jimmy grunted, his voice as shaky as the floor. "They're doing it again."

The odd thing, Dannerman thought, was that this time he hadn't heard any explosion, just the sudden uneasy twist and slide in the floor beneath him. But the tremor was a big one. Some cans of something or other on top of their stacks of supplies were jarred loose and clattered to the ground. Rosaleen sat down abruptly. There were yips of surprise from at least two of the Pats. Then it was over.

No. Not quite over. Just as everyone opened their mouths to tell each other that this one had been an unusually bad one, all right, something else happened. The mirror walls flickered and changed color. Jagged streaks of bright red danced around them like slow lightning flashes; that permanent diffuse pale glow from overhead darkened and their only light came from the radiant walls as they turned lurid orange in one spot, blotchy bright red in another. For a moment they seemed to go almost transparent, and through the nearest one Dannerman saw, or thought he saw, a shadowy ziggurat of bright metal. A Doc was standing there transfixed, all of its arms raised toward the sky in what looked like abject terror.

Then the colors faded. The faint visions from outside clouded and disappeared. The steady overhead glow returned, the walls became featureless mirrors again and everything was as it had been before. Everything but the prisoners, at least; but they were all shaken and bewildered. "What in the name of God was that?" Martín Delasquez angrily demanded of the room at large.

Rosaleen was the one who tried to answer. She was getting back to her feet, wincing, with one of the Pats helping her on either side. "I think it must have been some kind of a power failure," she said soberly. "I do not think that is a good sign."

At least they had a new topic of conversation to keep them busy for a while. In fact, they had two of them. One was the debate on what caused the tremor, why the power had seemed to fail and make the walls go all weird—some new questions, some just repetitions of the familiar ones about just what the hell was going on here, anyway. Whatever it was, it clearly was something that mattered to them. It made Dopey jittery and, no doubt, it threatened their own fragile security as well. But that particular discussion had nowhere to go; all anyone had to contribute was unanswerable questions and speculations, none of them very satisfactory.

The other area of discussion, Dannerman thought, was more productive. During that momentary lifting of the veil some of the captives had caught glimpses of what lay beyond the wall. None had had time for a clear view, but most had seen something. What they saw depended mostly on which way they happened to be facing. Patrice and Jimmy Lin were out of it, because they had been looking the wrong way and hadn't seen anything at all, but each of the others had at least a hazy impression to report.

It was Rosaleen Artzybachova who interrupted the hubbub with a suggestion. "Listen, please. Each of us should do his or her best to draw what we saw before we forget. Then we can compare notes."

Patsy bobbed her head at once. "Good idea," she said, reaching for Rosaleen's pen, and then paused long enough to give Dannerman a questioning look. "Is it all right for us to do it this way? Or should we be trying to keep the drawings covered?" she asked.

Before Dannerman could respond Martín answered for him. "Why do you ask Dannerman for permission?" he asked, giving Dannerman an unfriendly look. "It is obvious that there is no point in hiding such drawings. Who can doubt that Dopey knows what is outside the wall far better than we do, so what information could he gain?"

Patsy was still looking expectantly at Dannerman. He shrugged. "I guess that's true," he said, though his own reasons had little to do with what Dopey already knew, and a lot with whether all their secretive note-passing had served any useful purpose.

When they began drawing it turned out that Martín had seen the same metallic tower as Dannerman, though it was hard to recognize the thing in the man's crude, kindergarten-style drawings. Rosaleen, on the other hand, produced a workmanlike engineer's view of what looked as much like a row of file cabinets as anything else Dannerman had ever seen. ("They were tall, though," she said. "At least three meters, and there was something fuzzy that I couldn't make out on top of them.") Pat and Patsy had had the benefit of a year of art in college, and both provided neat sketches—an elongated, two-domed metal object for Pat, looking a little like a steel camel hunkered down to the ground; for Patsy a broad corridor between more rows of the file-cabinet objects, with something that might have been a vehicle a score of meters away. "It wasn't moving," she said, "but I'm pretty sure it was some kind of a car. And there was somebody, well, something, standing outside of it."

Patrice, looking on enviously, commented, "You know, it looks a little like the way Dopey brought us in here."

"I thought so too. And the person, or whatever, that was standing there—it could have been a Doc. Like the one you saw, Dan."

He nodded abstractedly, his attention on the handful of drawings. Patsy was still watching him, her expression quizzical. "Dan?" she said. "Are you all right?"

He looked up. "What? Oh, sure."

"You're not talking much."

That was the simple truth, not to be denied; but he wasn't yet prepared to say why. "I've got something on my mind," he said, truthfully enough; and then, when Patsy suggested maybe he should write it down, he could think of nothing better to say than "Not yet."

All three of the Pats were looking at him, the expressions on their faces less friendly than they had been. They thought he was being hostile, he knew, but could think of nothing useful to do about it. Rosaleen, who had been watching silently, felt the tension. She coughed. "If I can propose something we ought to do?" she suggested. "Each of you, which way were you looking when the wall went transparent? If we compare notes maybe we can make a kind of map of what's around us."

It was a sensible proposal. As they all began trying to recall just which way they had been facing, they included Dannerman in the conversation civilly enough; but that was as far as it went. And when, some time later, Pat began to yawn, she didn't look toward Dannerman. All three of the Pats curled up close together, and Dannerman did not sleep that time with any warm and pleasing head on his shoulder.

By the time he woke up Rosaleen had completed making a fair copy of the map their collective glimpses had produced. Of course it wasn't complete. In the center Rosaleen had drawn the hexagonal cell they were in, with each side numbered counting clockwise from their main point of reference, the area they had set aside as latrine. Dannerman's tall tower was at Side Two. There was nothing at One or Three except Rosaleen's small, neat question mark; Four was the cabinet things she herself had observed, next to them at Five Patsy's broad corridor and at Six Pat's angular steel camel.

He handed the chart back to Rosaleen with gratitude. "Good work," he said.

She nodded, and forbore to ask any questions. She turned away—not hostile; simply accommodating his desire to be silent—and limped back to show it again to the others. Dannerman watched her go with a frown. How long had Rosaleen been limping? And how long would it be before this very old lady began to show other signs of distress? If a chance ever came for them to escape, would she be able to take it?

And if she couldn't, would they be able to leave her here?

They were not pleasant thoughts. It was a relief to be distracted from them when the helmet began its plaintive beeping cry once more.

By the time it was Dannerman's turn all four of the women had already heard the message, and in each case their expressions ranged from shock to incredulity. Pat, who went first, ordered everyone who followed to hold all comments until they'd all seen it; they grumbled, but they obeyed.

Then Rosaleen handed it to Dannerman, her face bleak, and when he put it on the colonel appeared at once.

"*Mesdames et messieurs,*" Colonel duValier began, and once again the voice-over took up the message in unaccented American English:

"Ladies and gentlemen, this is the most important message you will ever hear. Some of it will startle you even more than what you know already. Some of it you will find very difficult to believe. I found it so myself; but I was given proof that I could not deny, and our friends from space stand ready to give those same proofs to you.

"What it concerns is Heaven.

"That startles you at once, doesn't it? I'm sure that many of you believe in God and His Heaven, just as I do; and I'm equally sure that, like me, you consider that that sort of thing is a religious matter, not a scientific one. But what I now know is that it is both.

"What our friends from space have discovered in their scientific investigations—which are far more advanced than our own—is that at a time in the far future, a very long time from now, something very strange will happen. At that time every intelligent being who ever existed in the universe will come to life again, and then will live forever. In scientific terms that is called the 'eschaton.'

"There is also another name for it. It is what we ordinary people have been used to calling 'Heaven.' "

He paused, staring seriously at Dannerman. "Yes," he said, "you heard me correctly. We are talking about Heaven. The very Heaven that priests and religious leaders of all kinds have told us about. You see, it's real, and our new allies have discovered definite scientific proof of this fact.

"I cannot explain all this to you now. I am not qualified, and there is no time. For our eternal life in Heaven is threatened, and the people who are threatening it are the ones I told you about earlier, the Horch. I warned that they intended to conquer the Earth. I did not say that their reason for doing so— just as it has been their reason for conquering, and often for wiping out, countless other intelligent races in the past—is so that when the eschaton arrives they, and they alone, can be the dominant race, who will be able to rule everyone else . . . forever."

The colonel smiled sorrowfully, then waved a hand. A screen appeared, showing the second message from space: the expanding and contracting universe, with the scarecrow and the Seven Ugly Dwarfs. "Do you remember this picture?" he asked. "Probably you didn't understand it when you first saw it. Neither did I, but now it has been explained to me. The diagram shows the universe expanding, then contracting again as it reaches its maximum growth and then falls back. It is at that point at the end of the final contraction, when the Big Bang has been replaced by the Big Crunch, that the eschaton will occur.

"You see, the message that picture tried to convey is true— that part of it, at least. But one part of it was a lie. It was sent to you by the Horch, in order to deceive you. It is the Horch, not our friends from space, who want to dominate the eschaton. And they are ruthless enough to subjugate or destroy every living thing that stands in their way.

"That is all I have to say to you at this time, except for one thing. It is now up to you, the people of Earth, to decide whether you want to invite our friends to come to Earth. If you do, they will display for you all the proofs I have mentioned. They will do more than that for you if you wish; they will give you freely of their immense store of knowledge.

"However, first you must, of course, have time to think all this over. Then I will speak to you again, and tell you what they propose. Until then, au revoir."

The figure went to black. Slowly Dannerman removed the helmet. "Wow," he said, and handed the helmet to Delasquez. Obviously everyone who had already seen the new message was burning to have something to say about it, but they managed to keep quiet until Jimmy Lin, at the bottom of the list, had his turn.

Then they all began to talk at once. "What a load of bullshit," Jimmy Lin said scornfully. "Heaven, for Christ's sake!" And Martín complained:

"It is blasphemous to talk of Heaven in that way!" And Patsy began:

"Yes, sure, but—listen, Dan-Dan, ever since I heard it there's something I've been trying to remember. Pat? Patrice? Didn't we have something in college about—"

But by then Dannerman knew what he had to do. "Hold it!" he ordered. "All of you! Don't say another word."

That was more than Martín Delasquez could stand. He said angrily, "Who are you to be giving us orders, Dannerman? I have had enough of being bossed around by you!"

But Rosaleen put her hand placatingly on his arm. He was fuming, but he listened to her. "Please, Martín," she said. "I'm sure Dan has a reason for this. Let's listen to what he has to say."

Martín looked darkly suspicious, Jimmy Lin looked only hostile, but both of them kept quiet. So did the Pats, waiting while Dannerman thought out what to do.

After a moment he nodded, satisfied. "Here's the point," he said. "Evidently Dopey wants information again. He must think we have some, or he wouldn't go to this trouble, and I guess we do. But let's not give it away."

He raised a hand to prevent questions, then turned and faced the mirror wall, just as Jimmy Lin had done earlier. "Dopey," he called. "You hear us. None of us is going to say or write another word about that message until you agree to our terms. If you want us to tell you everything we know or think—I mean tell you out loud; no more secrets; we'll talk it over in your presence, and you can ask as many questions as you like—if that's what you want, then come here and let's talk. But it's going to cost you, because this time we aren't going to do it for nothing!"

CHAPTER TWENTY-FOUR

Patsy

The Dr. Patrice Adcock they were calling "Patsy" (she was willing to answer to that name, because she didn't have any choice about it, but she never *ever* thought of herself that way) was angry. She sat Buddha-like, her legs tucked into the lotus position, glowering at the world. She knew she shouldn't be angry. She conceded to herself that Dan-Dan had some reason for ordering them to be quiet, and she supposed those orders might make sense. Why should you give away what you might be able to sell? All the same, she wasn't used to being told what she could or could not talk about.

What she was bursting to talk about was that whole "eschaton" business. It was right on the tip of her tongue, if only she could compare notes with Pat and Patrice to goose her memory along. That ancient and ill-recalled episode had been a very minor item in her education, no more than a grace note in some course she had taken for easy credits. She could almost see the face of the professor who had talked about it. It was the young dark one with the bedroom eyes—what was his name?—and he hadn't called it the eschaton. Something like—oh, yes. The "Omega Point." Whatever that was supposed to be. But she was pretty sure that it was precisely the thing that Colonel du-Valier had been blathering about in the message on the helmet.

Farther than that, however, her unaided memory would not take her.

It was perfectly obvious to her that everybody else was dying to talk it out, too. Well, of course they were. Was it even remotely possible that this notion of eternal life ten-to-the-zillionth years in the future could be *real*? Or that some hideous creatures from outer space might be doing their best to turn that eternal heaven into some kind of perpetual hell?

The whole thing was ridiculous.

The other thing about it was that it was also, just possibly, quite true.

In any case, she couldn't help thinking about it, and neither could any of the other six captives. It put a damper on all other subjects for conversation. The seven of them did their chores, completing Rosaleen's inventory, cooking and eating their meals, using the "latrine" when there was no way to avoid it; but what they were thinking about was this eschaton thing. If only Dopey would show up! Then maybe Dan could work out some kind of deal with him and then they could all talk freely, and maybe scratch that burning itch to hash the subject out.

But Dopey didn't show; and time wore on.

As she was beginning to get sleepy she said something about Dopey's absence to Pat, who had nothing useful to say in return. "How would I know why he doesn't come? Maybe that power glitch is screwing things up for him."

"Well, sure, but there must be something else going on. It couldn't be just the glitch; he got that new duValier message out to us after that happened, didn't he?"

"Beats the hell out of me," Pat said irritably. "Anyway, maybe we're not supposed to talk about that, either."

Pat wasn't the only one who was short-tempered. Everybody was getting antsy under the burden of Dan's rule of custody of the mouth. Then, when they were all getting sleepy, Pat didn't join Patrice and herself. Instead she nestled up next to Dannerman again, just as before; evidently his silence was now understood and thus forgiven. And as Patrice was settling herself down she glanced at the two of them, and then whispered to

Patsy, "What's *she* got to be pissed off about?"

It was a fair enough question. Pat had Dan-Dan, and what did the other two of them have?

There was certainly some jealousy there. There was also quite a lot of sisterly (or sort-of-sisterly) loyalty. To be fair about it, Patsy thought justly as she drifted off to sleep, you couldn't really say that Pat actually *had* Dan-Dan. Not in the total lack of personal seclusion that was their present condition. Patsy wondered drowsily if they could talk Dopey into giving them a few more of the helmets, because if everybody but Pat and Dan were wearing a helmet there would be at least the illusion of privacy while they got each other, as they were obviously yearning to do. Or maybe she and Patrice could patch together some of the blankets from Starlab and make a kind of a screen to hide the lovers as they went to it. Or—

Or maybe somehow, miraculously, the U.S. Cavalry would come charging over the hill with bugles blowing and pennons flying, and wonderfully carry them back home; and then the two of them could do whatever they damn pleased . . . and so could she, with whoever was handy . . . and . . .

And then the world would be fine again, but none of that was actually going to happen. The cavalry wasn't really coming to rescue them, was it? Their future was very uncertain but definitely dark—if the seven of them turned out to have any real future at all—and when Patsy finally did succeed in falling asleep there were tears on her cheeks.

They slept, and they woke up, and they spent most of another long day of trying to keep from talking about the things that really *had* to be talked about. And when finally Dopey did appear, without warning, simply walking in through the mirror, he said only, "I was delayed."

"We understand that you were having problems," Rosaleen said courteously. "You needn't apologize."

He looked flustered, Patsy thought; his peacock tail was rippling in dark colors and the expression on his furry little face was troubled. But he said firmly, "I did not apologize. I simply stated an explanation. I am now prepared to transact business with you on the basis you proposed."

Everyone was listening intently, and Patsy thought they all looked delighted—well, so did she. But Dannerman was making sure of the terms. "No holds barred?"

Dopey looked faintly puzzled. "I assume that what you mean is without reservation. I agree to that. However, I must tell you that there are things I cannot do, because at present they are physically impossible to me. The Horch terrorists have caused serious interruptions in our communications with the Beloved Leaders, and even certain of the resources of this base are temporarily not available to me. But please, you must help me to evaluate the message for Earth."

It was what Patsy had been waiting for; she opened her mouth eagerly, but Dannerman raised a hand. "Wait one," he said. "If your communications are down, what's the point?"

"They will be restored," Dopey said doggedly. "Please. Do not argue. Remember that you are not indispensable."

"Sure we are," Jimmy Lin said, his face angry. "You need our input."

"But not necessarily from your particular specimens, Commander Lin. Do you not realize that it would be possible to produce new copies of all of you, copies who would remember nothing after being taken from Starlab, and extract the information from them?"

"What I realize," Dannerman said firmly, "is that if that were what you wanted to do you wouldn't be talking, you'd be doing it."

Dopey looked irresolute. "It is true that there are at present some difficulties in this respect," he admitted. "Very well. I agree. Now tell me—"

"No, no! You first!"

The creature didn't like that. The lips on the little kitten face were drawn back—almost, Patsy thought, as though he were going to hiss at them. Then he relaxed. "I will agree," he capitulated. "What do you want from me?"

"Information!"

The little paws drummed impatiently on the muff—not inside it, Patsy observed, and realized that in this interview, unlike any other, Dopey was not keeping his hands in the muff. Was there something wrong with the thing? "Be more—" Dopey stopped as there was another ground tremor. A mild one, this time, Patsy observed gratefully, but was surprised to see the way Dopey reacted: his tail went all dark, his eyes were fastened on the wall, there was something like fear on the little feline face.

But nothing happened to the wall. Dopey's fan slowly began to regain its color. "Be more specific," he ordered. "And hurry."

"All right," Dannerman said. "What's wrong with the wall?"

Dopey paused to think. "The terrorists have done some damage to our systems," he said at length.

"The whole truth!" Pat snapped. "You promised!"

"But that is the whole truth," Dopey said, seeming surprised. "Do you wish to know details? Very well. Approximately, ah, nineteen of your days ago the Horch succeeded in transporting some of their weaponry into our base; since then there has been fighting. Each time their attack has been defeated, and each time they succeeded in transmitting new forces and attacked again. Much damage has been done, and communication with the Leaders has been interrupted."

"Who's winning?"

More hesitation. "I do not know," Dopey confessed. "I have

no doubt that in the long run our Beloved Leaders will prevail, but as your sage John Maynard Keynes once said to your president Franklin Delano Roosevelt—it was on a documentary broadcast while I was still on your Starlab—the trouble with the long run is that in the long run we are all dead."

"I'm glad to see you've kept your sense of humor," Dannerman said caustically. "I'm only surprised to discover that you have one. More details!"

"But I do not know any more details," Dopey said in surprise. "I know nothing of weaponry. Many of our people are dead now and much has been destroyed; that is all I can tell you. In any case, now it is your turn. Are there errors in the second broadcast?"

Dannerman looked rebellious, but gave in. "Not as far as I know. Nothing significant. Did any of the rest of you notice anything?"

No one had. "That is good," Dopey said gravely. "Now, about your comments on the eschaton—"

I f Patsy had been prudent—if all the Pats had—they might have held out for more information from Dopey. They weren't. Pat and Patrice were as eager to talk as Patsy, and it was Pat who got in first. "We heard about it in a history-of-science class in graduate school. The professor—"

"Dr. Mukarjee," Patrice supplied eagerly.

"Yes, that's the one. He told us about some scientist a long time ago, just before the turn of the century, I think it was, who claimed the same thing. Only he didn't call it the eschaton—"

Patsy raised her hand, excited and impatient. "The Omega Point! That's what he called it."

Pat gave her a grateful look. "How smart of you to remember that! Anyway, it was the same thing—universe expands, universe contracts, Big Crunch, everybody reborn in heaven."

Then they stopped, having run out of recollections. "His name," Dopey insisted. "Who was this scientist?"

The Pats looked at each other. "Tinker?" Patrice hazarded.

Pat frowned thoughtfully. "I was going to say maybe Doppler. Something like that." Patsy just shook her head.

"That is not satisfactory," Dopey complained. "Now I must try to have a data search conducted through that primitive equipment on Starlab. Have you nothing else to add?"

They looked at each other again. "Nothing," Pat said, and Patrice said:

"Only something Dr. Mukarjee said. He said that was just another example of the ways most cosmologists went kind of loopy after a while."

"That is not a useful datum," Dopey declared, but Dannerman cut in.

"Sure it is. Now you know he was a cosmologist; that ought to help identify him. Anyway, that's all we've got, so now let's talk about—"

But what it was Dannerman wanted to talk about he didn't get a chance to say. The ground shook, the wall flared again, the sound of distant thunder drowned out his words.

This time the display lasted for many seconds. No one spoke, though Dopey was whimpering softly. Patsy, eager to take advantage of any new visions that might come through the wall if it happened to go transparent again, faced it unblinking through all its swirling changes of color. It didn't. It cycled rapidly through the entire spectrum, then resumed its milky mirror sheen. She turned just in time to see Dopey's plume vanishing through the mirror as the creature sped away.

"Oh, damn the thing," Pat said feelingly. Rosaleen was more tolerant.

"He's frightened," she observed. "I don't blame him. If we knew everything he knows we might be terrified, too."

"I'm already terrified as much as I can handle, Rosie," Pat said. "Well. What do we know that we didn't know before?"

The answer to that, Patsy thought, was "damn little." She listened as the others tried to piece meaning together from what Dopey had told them, but there wasn't a lot of meaning there. All right, things were even worse than they had expected; but what kind of news was that?

She scowled at her own reflection in the mirror wall, half listening to what the others were saying, mostly filling with resentment. For just a moment there she had been reminded that she had another life, a life in which she was not a helpless pawn stranded in a demeaning captivity, but a responsible human being who held an important job. She was, for God's sake, a highly trained *scientist*. It was time for her to act like one, she told herself. It was time to stop being so damn *passive* and start to take *action*. . . .

The problem was, she could not think of any productive action to take.

She looked at the others. Dannerman, at least, seemed to be actually doing something, even if only going over everybody's recollections, repetitively, demandingly. Maybe, she thought, that was the way he had learned to interrogate witnesses in spook school. Was there any point in it? Did it matter how much they learned, when there was nothing they could do about it, anyway?

A snarling, buzzing sound interrupted her. It interrupted everyone else, too. It was not a sound any of them had heard before, and so it took them a moment to realize that it came from the helmet.

"What the hell," Dannerman said.

"I think it wants to be picked up again," Patrice said.

Jimmy Lin said nervously, "You sure? It sounds like it's broken to me. Could be dangerous."

"Oh, for God's sake," Pat said in exasperation, snatched the thing from the floor and pulled it on over her head. . . .

And then a moment later, she gasped, "Hey! It's a damn *Horch* and it's trying to tell me something!"

CHAPTER TWENTY-FIVE

Patsy

Whatever it was that Pat was seeing, it was brief. Hardly more than a minute or two; and when she pulled the helmet off her head, her expression both astonished and bewildered, and handed it to Patrice, it was without a word. Not without a struggle, though. Martín was already grabbing for it, but Pat pushed him away. As was right and proper, Patsy told herself, even in that moment; at least now they were doing alphabetical order again. And was quick to take the helmet when Patrice, as startled and uncertain as Pat herself, handed it to her.

The most astonishing thing Pat had said was true. It was a Horch that faced her in the simulation space. It was not at all the same Horch that Colonel duValier had displayed, either. This one carried no vicious-looking weapons, wore no armor, seemed much less evil. But it was certainly a Horch, all the same; and how such a thing could manage to use the device of the Beloved Leaders she could not guess.

Nor had time to.

The Horch didn't speak. It gestured—with both its boneless arms and with its sinuous, long neck as well—toward a corner of the field of view, and immediately a picture appeared there. Patsy was looking at a street scene in what, she knew, had to be a city, though not any kind of city she had ever seen before. The street itself was not a mere strip of hard surface. It was a moving ribbon of what looked like liquid metal, on which what looked like great, multicolored dragonflies danced, and now and then launched themselves into the air to fly into doorways set into tall buildings, high in the air. The buildings were alabaster and goldenrod and fleshy pink, some of them (it seemed to Patsy) a dozen stories tall. All this was what she saw in the first eye-blink, and she had no time to study details. Almost at once the view pulled back, as though the camera were rising to the sky. *Through* the sky; accelerating, it flew higher and higher until it was out of the planet's atmosphere entirely, looking down on the whole planet, pale blue and tainted white, as from orbit.

Then a spacecraft came into view, coppery-red and glittering, and the point of view approached it, entered it as though the ship's hull were only mist, showed the inside. A Beloved Leader swam languidly in zero-gravity there, the very scarecrow of the original message from space. It waved a fragile arm at its viewscreen, and something—*something*, something huge and dark and craggy—came plunging from nowhere at the planet. It blazed an eye-searing meteor trail through the atmosphere, and when it struck the surface it exploded with the power of a billion nuclear bombs.

And that planet died before Patsy's eyes.

No time to think about that now, either; immediately she was looking at another street scene (different street, dense with fast-moving vehicles; different buildings; different beings, these looking like wraiths with heads like sunflowers), but the story was the same. Pull back into space, see a Beloved Leader negligently take aim on the world, observe that world destroyed. And instantly there was another. And another, and another—the pace speeding up, the planets all different, the end always the same. And then—

And then the velocity slowed. A world appeared in the field of view that she recognized at once. It was the world Patsy had always known: their own Earth, northern hemisphere. Down toward the fringes that approached the equator she could see the hook of Italy, the wedge of India with Sri Lanka hanging like a teardrop from its tip, the narrow Red Sea. And when the view went inside the object in orbit this time it was not an alien spacecraft. It was an orbiter she recognized: their own Starlab! And there was no giant asteroid plunging toward the planet—not yet—but what was happening inside was even more frightening. There was no Beloved Leader present. What there was was Dopey, clinging to a wall while a pair of Docs worked over a human figure spread-eagled against a bulkhead. The Docs were doing something to the back of the man's head. Then they drew back. The human figure turned itself—it was Martín!—and silently pulled itself to a lineup, joining Dannerman, Jimmy Lin, Rosaleen and Patsy herself. The Docs herded the humans, who moved like zombies, into the Clipper, and it dropped away en route to the planet.

That was it. The picture went black.

They had all seen the same thing. They had all had the same reaction. "So the Horch want us to believe that the Beloved Leaders are mass murderers," Dannerman said meditatively. "Which, of course, is what the Beloved Leaders want us to believe about the Horch."

"So where does that leave us?" Jimmy Lin demanded. No one answered, but of course the answer was obvious, Patsy thought. They were left right where they had been all along: in their cell.

"But, if the Horch are telling the truth, Dopey also sent copies of us back to Earth," Rosaleen said. "Why would he do that, do you suppose?"

"We will damn well ask him that," Martín said, his face grim.

"If we see him again," Dannerman said.

That alarmed Patsy. "Why? Do you think he's going to abandon us?"

"I think he may not have much to say about it," Dannerman

told her. "If things are as bad as he says— *Now* what does the thing want?" he added, as the helmet snarled at them again.

Martín was the nearest; he picked it up. "There's only one way to find out," he said.

Pat was outraged. "You're doing it again! It's my turn first!"

Martín looked at her contemptuously and, without replying, jammed the helmet down on his own head.

"Damn the man," Pat snapped in Patsy's general direction. Patsy didn't answer. All these things that were happening were coming a lot too fast for her comfort—yes, and a hell of a lot too weird, too. She couldn't sort them out. Beloved Leaders killing planets: all right, she was perfectly willing to believe that that was what the Beloved Leaders did. It wasn't good news, but at least it was comprehensible; they were being warned. But what was the meaning of sending copies of themselves to Earth! That was *scary*.

Then everybody fell silent as Martín Delasquez slowly lifted the helmet off his head. He stared at them blankly until Jimmy Lin snapped, "Well?"

"Yes," Delasquez said, organizing his thoughts. Then he took a deep breath and delivered his report. "What I was seeing—it was, I think, the VIP dining area at Kourou."

"Kourou? in South America?"

"The European launch center," Delasquez confirmed. "That's what it looked like, anyway—I did a six-month exchange mission there once. But what is astonishing—I was seeing it out of my own eyes."

Rosaleen was the first to react. "Your *own* eyes? But how do you know it was you?"

"It was. I saw my Academy ring on my hand—and I know my own hand. And there were all kinds of European Space Agency people there too—at other tables—I think I even saw Colonel duValier—but I wasn't with them. I was at a table by myself, except for one other man. He was in uniform, and he carried a sidearm, and he wasn't eating. Didn't even have a plate in front of him. He was just watching me. It was—" He hesitated, trying to think of the right word. "It was—It was very *unpleasant.*"

"Let me have that," snarled Jimmy Lin, reaching for the helmet. Pat was ahead of him. She snatched the thing from Martín's slack grip.

"My turn!" she snapped, and put it on.

Martín was paying no attention. "I could taste the food," he said wonderingly. "I was eating an omelette, one of the kind with vegetables in it? And there was the shell of a papaya on the table—I could still taste it—and a brioche. Quite good coffee, too. And hot; it almost burned my tongue."

Rosaleen was listening intently. "You could taste and feel? So it wasn't just a television picture?"

"It was just as though I were there," Martín insisted. But by then Patsy wasn't listening anymore, because Pat had claimed her attention. She was making sounds of distress, and Patrice was standing anxiously beside her, begging to know what was wrong.

Then Pat moaned, gasped and pulled the helmet off as though it burned her. "It was all woogly!" she cried, suddenly white-faced and shaking. Patrice put her arm around her; if Patrice hadn't, Patsy would have, because she had never seen Pat look so shaken. "I guess I was on Earth, all right—partly, anyway. But I was in jail!"

And of course there were about a million questions about that, but Patsy didn't wait to hear the answers, didn't even wait to find out what Pat meant by being "partly" on Earth. She went right to the source. Snatched the helmet out of Pat's hand, pulled it over her head, snapped the goggles into place—

It was a good thing that Pat's complaints had prepared her, at least a little bit. Even so, the shock was almost paralyzing as she found out what Pat had meant by "woogly."

She wasn't seeing one scene. She was seeing two of them—no, not merely seeing; she was *present* in two different places. Feeling, seeing, hearing, smelling; all the senses were involved. And everything was doubled. In one scene she was seeing herself with the helmet over her head, saw Pat—right up close, as though she were holding her in her arms; no, she *was* holding Pat in her arms, because she could feel Pat's body shaking. And at the same time, in the other scene, she was looking at a bare room with bright lights, a small table with nothing on it, a straight-backed plastic chair, dun-painted walls without any pictures or ornamentation of any kind. She saw all this second scene from a recumbent position, because she was lying on a hard, narrow cot, curled up on her side with her open hand under her cheek, but wide awake. She was staring into space. And she could see the door to the room, all right, and, yes, Pat had been perfectly right.

There were steel bars on the door. She was definitely in some kind of a jail.

When Patrice took her turn—no argument about who was next this time, not even from Jimmy Lin; everyone wanted to know what the "woogliness" was all about—she reported seeing the same thing. Two separate scenes. Both wholly real, in every sensory way. The only difference was that in the scene that corresponded to their cell, she saw Patsy there instead of herself.

"Dopey said they were monitoring our copies," Rosaleen said meditatively.

"But like this? Seeing with our eyes?" Pat was still shaken. "It gave me a damn *migraine!* Only—" She hesitated, remembering. "Only what I saw was three different scenes, not two. Two of them were here, from different angles; it was the other one that looked like a jail."

"Damn well *was* a jail," Patrice said feelingly.

Rosaleen sighed. "Yes," she said, following out some private thought process of her own. "It must be so."

"*What* must be so?" Patsy demanded, and Rosaleen looked at her with compassion.

"It explains much," she said. "These copies of us that the Horch showed us, the ones the Beloved Leaders made and returned to Earth? They were fitted with some sort of transmitters to pass on everything they saw and felt—"

"How?" Jimmy Lin asked.

"Oh, Jimmy, what foolish questions you ask. How do I know how? With a magical incantation, perhaps, or perhaps they implanted a tiny broadcasting station in the left nostril—who knows what kind of technology is here?"

"Damn," Dannerman said feelingly. "I see what you mean, Rosaleen. That's how Dopey knew the name of my boss, Colonel Morrisey."

"Yes. And much more," Rosaleen said. She turned back to Patsy and Patrice. "And when, in kindness, Dopey provided us with you two, he first turned you into observing devices—"

"Hey!" both of them said at once.

"Yes. And so now, at least, we know just how Dopey was able to read all our little secret messages that we passed around with such care. You two read them for him. Whatever you saw he saw too."

In these last two days Patsy's life had been violated in more ways than she could count—the violation of the nudity taboo when she was first brought in, the endless privacy violations that came with everyone being huddled together in the one common pen for everything—for sleeping, for eating, even for going to the damn *toilet*.

But this latest violation was something new. Until now she had had the illusion that at least her private central self was intact. Now that illusion was destroyed. Some weird creature somewhere—not just Dopey; who knew what other bizarre beasts were eavesdropping as well?—some*body* was seeing and feeling everything she did.

And beyond doubt was still doing it. It was, she told herself, an intolerable situation . . . except, of course, that she had no choice but to go right on tolerating it.

CHAPTER TWENTY-SIX

Patsy

If the others had taken the news as hard as Patsy, they didn't show it. They were all clustered around whoever was wearing the helmet at that moment, every one of them demanding another turn. It was like Christmas at Uncle Cubby's, with every child demanding the one best toy at once. Even Dannerman and Rosaleen, though Dannerman had reported resentfully that his turn had been a washout, since as far as he could tell he was simply in bed asleep. (Which, Patsy thought, supported her own feeling that it was the middle of the night—assuming they were in the same time zone.) And Rosaleen had seen nothing at all, didn't even share Dannerman's conviction that the reason was that she had been asleep.

But then there was Jimmy Lin.

His turn lasted longer than any of the others were willing to tolerate. He clung to the helmet, trying to wave them off with his arms; and when at last he took it off he was beaming. "You guys had me worried," he said. "You know, armed guards, and jail cells, and all that? But I was just fine. I'm pretty sure I was in Jiuquan—the Chinese space center? And I was in my old Fiat electric? Driving somewhere from the base? I know that road; it hadn't changed much since the last time I was there. I could see the launchpads way off by the hills—oh, there's no doubt about it; that's where I was. And I was in uniform; I could see the sleeve of my tunic. It looks like I got a promotion, too, because I was wearing full commander's stripes."

"I thought you got kicked out of the astronaut corps," Dannerman objected.

Jimmy scowled at him. "Well, I did. But I know what I saw, so I guess they reinstated me. Anyway, I wasn't alone in the car, and I don't know for sure where the two of us were going, but I think we were planning on having a pretty good time. Oh, and the language we were talking in was *Chinese*."

"What were you talking about?" Dannerman demanded.

Jimmy gave him the ghost of a smile. "What do you think we were talking about? It was a *date*, man!"

"Old reliable Lin," Martín groaned. "Always right there with his gonads blazing."

"Don't be so envious," Jimmy said, enjoying himself. "Let's see, what else? It was maybe late afternoon, I think. Probably we were just coming from a shift at the base. I was kind of hungry, but I was also—well, Martín, yeah, I have to admit that I was feeling kind of horny, too."

Rosaleen had been listening intently, but now she frowned. "What I don't understand," she said, "is—assuming it's true that they've planted bugs in our copies—how come we're receiving anything from them? Dopey said they'd lost their communications."

"Maybe only with the Beloved Leaders at their headquarters, wherever that is?" Patrice put in.

Dannerman nodded. "That could be it. Remember, Dopey also said something about using the Starlab equipment to track down the Omega Point man? He may not have contact with his Beloved Leaders, but apparently he still does with Starlab."

Rosaleen considered that. "It sounds plausible," she said, and hesitated. Then she reached for the helmet. "I think I would like to try another turn for myself."

That made everyone quiet down. Jimmy handed her the helmet without a word. Rosaleen carefully settled it around her head and fumbled with the opaque goggles until they locked in position.

She was silent for a moment, while everyone waited. Then she removed the helmet again. "Yes," she said in a colorless, conversational tone, "there is nothing there but blackness for me." She handed the helmet to the person standing beside her, who happened to be Martín, and added, "I can think of only one explanation. There is no copy of me on Earth."

"But we saw you being sent there in the Horch message!" Pat said worriedly.

Rosaleen did not respond to that, except to say, "I think I would like to rest for a while."

Then a most surprising thing happened. Martín took the helmet from Rosaleen's hand, but he didn't put it back on. He laid it on the floor and, instead, took Rosaleen Artzybachova's arm and helped her over to a position by one wall. He settled blankets around her until he was sure she was comfortable.

Patsy stared. Could this be *Martín*? For a moment she almost toyed with the thought that when they weren't looking Dopey had somehow slipped a doppelgänger general in among them in Delasquez's place. Well, that was fantasy, sure; but to find General Delasquez caring for somebody else was almost as fantastic.

By the time he came back the others were gathered around the cooker—all but Jimmy Lin, who had seized the chance to get back in the helmet. Martín didn't speak. He stood over the pile of rations, staring down at it, but making no move to take anything for himself.

Impulsively, Patsy spoke to him, keeping her voice low so that the others might not hear. "That was nice of you, Martín."

For a moment she thought he wasn't going to answer. He reached down and selected a ration packet at random. Then he said, "My mother was like that. Quite old, but active, alert, in fact a very brilliant woman . . . until her sister died."

"Her sister died?" Patsy repeated. The man was being even more difficult than usual.

He studied the packet for a moment, then slit it open with a thumbnail. "They were quite close," he said. "Then afterward it was quite different for my mother. Her condition deteriorated very fast."

He looked up at Patsy for the first time. "I see you don't understand," he commented.

"No. You're right. I don't."

"But this must be very similar for Rosaleen. You see, there is no copy of Rosaleen on Earth, although we saw her being sent there. How can that be? Because, of course, the Rosaleen who returned to Earth has died."

Died.

Patsy stole a look at Rosaleen, lying with her eyes closed and only a part of her face visible among the blankets. What could that feel like, losing one of yourself? Patsy tried to imagine how she would feel if Pat died, or Patrice, but she didn't try for long. The thought hurt, with kinds of pain Patsy had never felt before.

Something else was troubling her, too. It felt like guilt. Rosaleen's exposed face was gray. Although she had stood as erect as ever while they were talking, Patsy remembered that Rosaleen had been biting her lip, and when she turned away she had limped worse than ever.

That was where the guilt lived. It was her fault, after all—that is, it was Dr. Patrice Adcock's fault—that the old woman was here in this place, a place that certainly was not a good environment for an ailing woman in her—what were they?—at least her nineties. Maybe more. Rosaleen had been comfortably retired to the leisure of her Ukrainian dacha, as at her age she had every right to be, until Pat called her in for this mad venture, with its even madder consequences. If she died as a result of all this—

Patsy finished her meal and lay down to sleep, hoping to blot out some of the things that were on her mind. She did not want to think of Rosaleen's dying, and she was glad when at last she seemed to be drifting off to sleep.

The sleep didn't last long; what woke her was another groundshake—not big, but enough to rouse her. She opened her eyes in time to see the wall doing its magic trick. The bright mirror was streaked with glowing pink and red, the colors shimmering over the surface like oil on a pool of water. The display lasted for a dozen seconds; then the swirls of color disappeared. It didn't turn transparent this time, and a moment later the wall was a bright and unflawed mirror again, and nothing had changed.

The others were all awake, Martín and Rosaleen standing by the cooker; Patsy covertly studied Rosaleen's face, but it showed nothing but fatigue. Jimmy Lin was holding the helmet in his hand, his expression thunderous. "What a time to lose contact!" he cried; and, as soon as things had settled down again, hastily jammed the thing back on his head.

Patrice gave him an unfriendly look, then turned to Patsy. "I think the son of a bitch is getting laid in China," she muttered. "Did you get enough sleep? I took another turn while you were out and I was—we were—still in that jail, and nothing was happening. Except that I was dressed and sitting in the chair. Just sitting there, with, I guess, nothing to do. Martín did a little better, though."

"I will tell her," Martín said. He fished a ration packet out of the cooker, juggled it a moment in his hands before passing it on to Rosaleen and made sure that the old lady was able to handle it before he told Patsy what he had observed. He had been standing at a lectern at the front of a briefing room, while some other astronaut at another lectern was going over a 3-D virtual of the interior of Starlab. "It didn't look the way we saw it when we were there. It was, I imagine, the way it had been before Dopey's people rearranged it. And every once in a while someone would ask me if that was how I remembered it, and I said yes." He hesitated. "That isn't the truth, of course. I must have been lying to them. But I didn't *feel* like I was lying. And that guard with the gun was sitting right behind me."

That was interesting, but Patsy had nearer concerns. She drew some water from the tank and rubbed it over her face, then used the space they had set aside as the latrine, leaving the others to argue with Martín as to how he could tell whether or not his copy was lying. She didn't listen. She was thinking about Rosaleen—and thinking, too, at the same time, that splashing a few drops of water on her face was all well enough, but, God, what she would give for a real *bath*. Not to mention some clean clothes. Not to mention—well, everything that made civilization worth having.

By the time she was as presentable as she had any way of getting Jimmy Lin was out of the helmet and his face wore a broad grin. "That," he announced, "was *great*. Listen, I'm not one to kiss and tell, but—"

"Do not tell, then," Martín said savagely.

"Yes, but honestly—"

"Shut up," Pat ordered.

"Ah," said Jimmy, understanding at last. "I'd just be rubbing salt in the wounds, eh? Well, I can see how you feel, but I have to say—no," he corrected himself, catching Pat's glare at him. "I guess I don't have to say. But you know what I'm thinking."

And he turned and headed for the cooker. Over his shoulder he called, "The dinner was great, too. Gave me an appetite."

"Son of a bitch," Patrice said moodily, and changed the subject. "Patsy? Did you hear about Dan-Dan?"

"What about Dan-Dan?"—looking at him.

Dannerman said reluctantly, "I guess it's important enough to tell. All right. About half an hour ago I took a turn in the helmet. I was awake, all right. I was getting dressed. And I had a hell of a hangover."

"What were you celebrating, do you know?" Patsy asked curiously.

"I don't think I was celebrating anything at all. I think my duplicate is in the deep shit. I was wearing a collar, you see."

"Collar?"

"The tracker kind," he said impatiently. "The kind they put on you so they always know where you are. So they can hear everything you say, and everything anybody says to you."

"Oh, hell," Patsy said, suddenly sympathetic. She wanted to put her arm around him, checked the impulse with Pat standing right there. "So you're in trouble, too?"

"House arrest, I guess. Pretty much the same as Martín and you."

Pat turned to Patsy. "Any ideas? Can you figure out why we're all in trouble back home—all but Jimmy, anyway?"

"Maybe," Dannerman offered, "it has something to do with what Martín is saying about lying to them."

"But why would we all be lying?" Patrice asked reasonably. "I mean, all but Jimmy, I guess. What reason could we have?"

Dannerman shrugged. No one said anything for a while, and Patsy looked around the cell. Martín and Rosaleen were talking quietly over by the cooker. Jimmy Lin was sitting with his back to the wall, hands locked behind his head, a broad, reminiscent grin on his face.

Pat was looking at him, too. "Bastard," she said. "But, hey, think about it. Suppose we could get this little piece of technology back to Earth! Suppose we put these bugs into, I don't know, maybe a couple of vid stars, boy and girl—or boy and boy, or whatever; listen, any kind of preference anybody had. And then we could rent out helmets while they were getting it on. Can you imagine what kind of money people would pay? Mad sex, any kind of sex, without all that trouble of actually having to find Mr. Right and then getting a motel room and all . . . and no worry about catching something or getting pregnant or— Well," she said hastily, aware of Dannerman's eyes on her, "I mean, simply as a commercial venture."

"I know what you mean," he said kindly. Then he added, "I was thinking of something, too. I was thinking, what if the Bureau had this technology? Then they wouldn't have to get people like me to infiltrate terrorist groups or criminal gangs or whatever. Just catch one of the gang, stick a bug into him, set him loose. From that moment on everything he saw or did would go right to the Bureau."

"Oh, Dan!" Patrice said in dismay. "Do you know what you're saying? It wouldn't have to be just criminals! What if some government used that to keep track of everybody, all the time? Talk about your police states!"

And Pat said meditatively, "Maybe that isn't a kind of technology we would want to bring back, after all."

Silence for a moment, and then Dan said, "I wonder if we have a choice. I wonder if that might not be some of this wonderful stuff that the Beloved Leaders are going to give the human race if they're let in."

Then there was more silence, a lot of it, as everybody thought about that. Until Patsy sighed and shook herself. "Maybe I should take another turn in the helmet," she said, and accepted the device as Dannerman handed it to her.

As soon as she was locked in the pictures flashed before her, just as before—the same doubled images: herself in the helmet as seen through Patrice's eyes, and at the same time the bare cell on Earth. There, she discovered, she seemed to be eating breakfast. Some machine-scrambled eggs, far overcooked for her taste, some dry toast, a cup of weak coffee. She didn't much like the taste of the food. Even less liked the dizzying duplication of images, which threatened to give her a headache. She closed her eyes to shut them out for a moment, and discovered that made no difference; she could feel that her eyelids were clamped shut, but she was still seeing both scenes.

Maybe, she thought, there was a way to ease that particular problem, at least. If Patrice were simply to keep her eyes closed and sit as still as possible while she herself was in the helmet, wouldn't that cut down on the "spillover"? It might be worth a try, she thought. And was on the point of taking the helmet off to tell her so, when the floor shook again under her feet. She staggered. The helmet images blurred and distorted, but through Patrice's eyes she could see that the wall was flaring again.

By the time she got the helmet off it was a kaleidoscope of color and the ground was still shaking, slow, remorseless swings back and forth. Patsy sat down abruptly to keep from falling— as everyone else was doing—and they watched the light show on the wall in fascination and fear. It flickered through the spectrum, settling on a dull red that felt as though it were actually radiating heat. . . .

Then—it disappeared.

There was no color at all where the wall had been. The smooth, resilient floor had turned into a pattern of closely woven metal strands. The ceiling, too, had changed; the even white glow was gone. Where it had been there was now a mesh that looked like bleached burlap, through which a pale light filtered from somewhere else. The same light illuminated the scene beyond the walls: Rosaleen's "file cabinets," the broad corridor along which Dopey had brought them to the cell, the two-domed metal object and all sorts of other things, too many and too strange to take in at once. Nothing obstructed her view.

Everybody was up and staring now. And Jimmy Lin, standing at the urinal, reached out with one hand to where the wall had been. He pulled his arm back slowly and turned, blinking, to the others. "There's nothing there," he said. "There isn't any wall at all anymore."

CHAPTER TWENTY-SEVEN

Patsy

There was a story Patsy remembered about a lion in a zoo. For ten years that lion had paced restlessly back and forth in his cage, snarling at the bars. Then, one day, the keeper was careless. He went away and left the door open. When the keeper was gone, the lion padded over to the door, and sniffed at the air of freedom for a moment ... and then turned and lay down in the farthest corner of his cage, his head on his paws, his eyes squeezed shut, until at last the keeper came back and closed the door.

That's you, Dr. Pat-known-as-Patsy Adcock, she told herself. You've been pissing and moaning about wanting to get out of here ever since you arrived. Now you've got your big chance. There's nothing to stop you walking out of here whenever you like. Well?

But she hesitated.

So did everyone else, all of them staring apprehensively at the vista around them, strange machines and distant gleams of light and, from somewhere, a pall of smoke drifting over them. No one moved ... until Jimmy Lin, glancing wildly back at the rest of them, took a deep breath, then carefully stepped over the little puddle of his own recent urine and walked through the space where the wall had been. Not far. Just a step or two, actually, before he stopped to stare around. But he was definitely *outside*.

That did it for Patsy Adcock. If Jimmy Lin could do it she certainly could. She turned and marched resolutely out into the space she had never seen before. Behind her Pat called worriedly, "Hey, watch it, hon! What're you going to do if the power comes back on and you're stuck out there?"

That stopped Patsy, frozen on one foot, until she remembered. "No, it isn't like that," she called back. What she remembered was how it had been when Dopey brought them to the cell. It was a one-way wall. They hadn't even seen the thing as they approached from outside, had simply walked into the space where the others were clustered, and had then been astonished to see the wall of mirrors bright and impenetrable behind them.

Everyone was staring after her. She saw Rosaleen, her face still gray, crossing herself, and Martín standing with his mouth open, and Dannerman experimentally poking his own arm through the space where the wall had been. And she took a deep breath, looking at the bizarre structures around her, and said to herself, Okay, sweetie, now you've got your freedom. Use it!

Or (the echo sounded in her mind) lose it.

Things were happening in that outside world, now revealed to them. Patsy sniffed acrid smoke, heard distant, and sometimes not so very distant at all, crashes and pops from whatever it was that was going on just out of sight. Jimmy Lin, greatly daring, had ventured, a step at a time, five or six meters down the broadest of the passages, Patrice close behind him and Martín and Rosaleen peering after them. Dannerman and Pat were on their knees at the margin of their cell, poking at something on the floor. When Patsy drew close she saw that where the base of the mirror wall had been there was now only a shiny line of alternating coppery and colorless segments, each less than a centimeter long. "It wasn't real," Pat marveled, looking up at Patsy. "The wall, I mean. It wasn't *solid*. It was just some kind of projection, and when the power went off it just disappeared."

"And so did the floor," Dannerman added. "Not just our floor. Look outside here." The floor on the other side of the boundary was the same metal mesh as inside, or most of it was. But a few meters away there was a section that looked as though it had been repaired with ordinary cement—not recently, either; the patch was stained and potholed. Actually, everything looked pretty helter-skelter to Patsy. Some of the machines looked naked, as though they had been meant to have some sort of case or cover. (The mirror walls they'd seen on the way in? Maybe so, Patsy thought, because she could see the same buried hexagonal lines as surrounded their cell.) Some looked very old, corroded with time.

"It's a mess," Jimmy Lin reported, returning. "There's a machine out there that looks as though it ran itself to destruction—bearings scorched, housing popped off—like a car engine that ran out of oil."

"I don't think they used oil," Patrice said.

Rosaleen said thoughtfully, "I wouldn't be surprised if they used some kind of energy to reduce friction—like maglev, you know? Or something like the balls the cooker moved on, and when the power went off—"

"The cooker!" Jimmy Lin interrupted, looking stricken. And when they put it to the test it was what they had feared. The packet of chili Pat dropped in sat there at the bottom of the well, unwarmed.

"Oh, hell," Jimmy said, contemplating another period of uncooked food. And of worse; at a sudden thought he picked up the helmet and tried it on, then morosely set it down again. "No power there, either," he said. "What do we do now?"

Dannerman had a prompt answer. "I think," he said, "that somebody ought to go out and see what's going on."

"Are you volunteering?" Pat asked. "Because if you are, I'll go along."

Dannerman looked pleased, then frowned. "Better not," he said reluctantly. "I won't go far, and it's easier if I do it alone."

"Don't you want to eat something first?" Rosaleen asked.

"Put some in to soak," he ordered. "I'll eat it when I get back." And turned and left without looking at Pat again.

When Dannerman was out of sight Pat stared after him for a moment, then sulkily took over the job of opening packets and filling them with cold water to soften. Patsy looked at her with compassion. She was pretty sure that exploration hadn't been the only thing on Pat's mind, or on Dannerman's, either; if ever she had seen two people with a strong compulsion to get off by themselves it was they. But Dannerman, Patsy thought, had been right; he had the skills of his Bureau training and Dr. Pat Adcock did not. Score one for responsibility in the face of temptation.

She joined Pat at the task of preparing food. It wasn't a job she really enjoyed, but it had one great advantage: it was a task she was confident she could handle. And confidence in dealing with everything else in this challenging new environment was absent from her frame of mind. Were the others as stunned— well, say the word: as *frightened*—as she was? She couldn't tell. They didn't seem to show it if they were . . . but on the other hand, she told herself, probably she wasn't showing that total interior terror either.

By the time her job was done the others were clustered at the base of the things that looked like file cabinets (though if they had drawers, nothing any of the captives could do had managed to open one). As she joined them she heard Rosaleen say, as she stood with one hand on Martín's shoulder, "Listen. Am I wrong or have the explosions mostly stopped?"

"There aren't very many now, anyway," Martín agreed, looking up at the top of the cabinets. "I wish I could get up there. I might be able to see something useful."

"You can't," Pat said positively. "You're too big to lift. But I'm not. If you guys give me a hand I think I can make it to the top."

It turned out that, indeed, she could—not easily, and not without a couple of near misses that threatened to drop her to the floor. But she did it. Stepped from Jimmy Lin's crouching back to Martín's hunkered-down shoulders. Braced herself with her palms against the cabinets as the general slowly rose. Got her arms across the top of the cabinets and, with both men pushing from beneath, scrambled on.

Patsy heard a faint sound of crunching as Pat got to her feet, examining the legs of her slacks. "It's a mess up here," she reported, panting. "There's scratchy stuff all over, like spun glass, but not that hard; there are big balls of it on some of the tops, but a lot is just broken into powder."

"I think that might be what I saw before," Rosaleen called. "Is it orange? And luminous?"

"Orange, yes. Luminous, no." Pat raised herself on tiptoe, shading her eyes to gaze in the direction the others had gone. "No sign of Dan. I can see where the smoke's coming from, though; it's a fire—I can see the flames—but not very big, and a long way off. And around in the other direction"—as she turned—"there's—hey! There's sunlight! Real sunlight, I'd bet a million dollars on it, and—oh, my God—*trees*!"

"Trees?"

Patsy couldn't say which of them had incredulously repeated

the word—maybe it was all of them—but Pat was positive. "You damn bet they're trees, and not too far away, either. Closer than the fire." She appeared at the edge of the cabinet, peering down. "Do you think some of us should go take a look?"

"No," said Rosaleen firmly. "Not now. Wait till Dan comes back." Because, she didn't say, Dan was the only one of them who seemed to have an actual plan—or, Patsy thought, if not a real *plan*, at least the determination to keep trying to find things that would be useful to them.

And then she thought what it would be like if Dan didn't get back, and shuddered.

CHAPTER TWENTY-EIGHT

Patsy

It was foolishness, Patsy scolded herself—yes, and it was gender treason as well—to allow herself to feel so lost simply because Dan Dannerman was away.

It was also embarrassing, because the other women in the party were clearly not as troubled about it as she. All three of them were asleep, even Pat, while Jimmy was morosely poking at the machine that looked like a two-humped camel, just outside the cell boundaries. (Poor Jimmy, she thought, almost sympathetically; he was taking the loss of the helmet hard. But of course it had had more to offer him than anyone else.) Martín was flat on his back, hands locked behind his head, open eyes regarding their tattered ceiling with incurious distaste. Once more he had positioned himself next to the sleeping Rosaleen. At least, Patsy was grateful to him for that; if freedom was an unexpected challenge for all of them, it was a challenge that could hardly be met for Rosaleen Artzybachova. The old lady couldn't move without wincing. Taking part in any exploration was out of the question for her; the ancient body wasn't up to it.

But Patsy's body was, and she was too restless to sit still. "I'm going to look around," she called to Martín, keeping her voice low.

But not low enough. Martín didn't answer but Rosaleen did. "Be careful," she said, not opening her eyes. "Yell if you need us."

Yell if you need us. And what, Patsy asked herself, could a couple of unarmed men and three equally unarmed women, one of them frail and old, do if she should really need help? As well she might, in this baffling combat zone.

That was a thought that should have been frightening. Oddly, she wasn't particularly frightened. Oh, there was a lot of fear, even something not too remote from panic, that sat there at the back of her mind, ready to appear if something startled her, but curiosity outweighed the fear. Everything she saw was a new mystery—not one that she could hope to solve, no, but something to wonder at. That smoke that drifted overhead, sometimes pale, sometimes inky black and stinking with some foul chemical odor. The machines all around—all silent, some in ruin. When she looked up, crane her neck as she would, she could get no glimpse of anything that looked like sky, only layers and layers of construction and mechanical puzzles.

The first time she saw a Doc standing motionless before her she yelped out loud. She couldn't help it.

But the creature didn't move. Its eyes were open behind the fuzzy beard, but unfocused; the half-dozen limbs were hanging loose and still. So it was with the next one she saw, a moment later. It was alive, all right. She could see an artery pulsing in the Doc's throat and it seemed to be breathing.

Patsy couldn't resist. She passed a hand before the creature's eyes, the way they said tourists used to do for the guards at places like Buckingham Palace. It didn't blink.

Patsy was almost smiling as she turned away, and that was when she saw the dead Dopey.

Oh, Jesus, she whispered to herself, staring. The body had been roughly handled. It lay in a pool of sticky dark fluid and its head had been crushed.

But it was smaller than Dopey—smaller than *their* Dopey, at least—and the peacock plume was far more modest: matted and discolored now, but nothing like the great fan that Dopey had worn.

That was enough for Patsy. She turned on her heel and headed back to the company of the others. Rosaleen was standing at the perimeter of the cell, leaning on the useless cooker, Martín close behind. They were both watching for her. "Yes?" Rosaleen said, and Patsy poured out everything she had seen.

"I was frightened," she finished. "I'm sorry."

"But why should you be sorry? Of course you were—" Rosaleen didn't say "scared shitless"; she was kind, and only said "startled."

"Thank you," Patsy said, and then was immediately startled again. They heard a faint chittering sound, and when she turned something very strange was coming slowly toward them. It was a round . . . well . . . a round *thing*, turtle-shaped, beach-ball-size. Possibly it was an animal, possibly not. Feathery fronds extended upward from the short-legged body, and clinging to the tip of each frond was a tiny creature, no bigger than a mouse. The little creatures were all peering worriedly behind them, chittering softly to each other; and Patsy was almost certain she had seen them before. That shark-toothed grin on the tiny faces surely belonged to the variety of the Seven Ugly Dwarfs called "Happy." "But I didn't think they would be so small," she said stupidly.

She had spoken softly, but the little things heard. One of the creatures turned and saw the humans staring at them. It squeaked in shrill alarm. All dozen of them turned, toothy mouths wide in fear. There was a chorus of chittering, and they turned their mount toward another corridor and galloped away out of sight in obvious panic.

"My God," Rosaleen remarked behind Patsy, crossing herself. "Patsy? Did it not seem to you that they were running away from something?"

And so it had; but it was Martín who saw what that something was and called, "It's all right. It's only Dan coming back."

In spite of everything, some little part inside of Patsy had been hoping that when Dan returned he would be bringing good news. She couldn't imagine what the good news might be. Certainly not like—like—well, like finding that Colonel duValier's expedition had got to Starlab, and found the transmitter there, and used it to ship themselves and a brigade or two of commandos here to rescue them. She hadn't really expected anything like that, but there had still been a hope that Dan would have *something* to report that might make things look better for the captives.

He didn't. What he had was a bundle of metal rods tucked under one arm, and a discouraging report. "Looks like somebody's dismantling this whole enterprise," he said. "I went about two or three hundred meters down one of the corridors, heading toward where the smoke was coming from. I didn't want to get too close—"

"Thank God," Pat put in.

Dan gave her a glum look. "I figured I had to be cautious," he said, defending himself although Pat obviously hadn't intended an attack. "There was a lot of destruction, some of it still going on. I saw a big damn thing that looked like a school bus—"

"A *bus?*"

"Well, it was all yellow, and it had wheels, or anyway those big ball-bearing things, and it was on fire. I could see it melting, liquid metal flowing out onto the ground like water, and a stink you wouldn't believe. And then there was this other thing right next to it, kind of a pyramid, and it began to burn, too."

"I hope you had the sense to get out of there," Pat said.

Dan gave her a somewhat mollified look. "You bet I did. But wherever I went there was all this wreckage. Oh, and bodies. I saw a couple dead Dopeys and a bunch of others I couldn't recognize—maybe like that thing you said you saw, Patrice? That looked like the Bashful? But these were too burned to tell, and some of them were pretty ripe, too. I think they'd been lying there for days, some of them."

That seemed to conclude the report. No one spoke until Rosaleen said philosophically, "Your food is ready. Me, I think I will get some sleep."

Martín was frowning over the pile of metal rods Dan had dropped. "And what are these things?"

"I picked them up," Dan said, selecting one of them and hefting it. "I thought they might do for clubs. Or spears, maybe. And who knows? We might be needing some kind of weapons before long."

There was another unwelcome thought for Patsy. Weapons. To defend themselves, that was, against some invisible enemy that could melt metal objects without even being seen. Perhaps some of her fellow prisoners could take comfort in having a club to bash somebody with—if they ever came across somebody who could be dealt with by simple bashing—but all the rods meant to Patsy was one more wholly inadequate response to problems they could not really hope to solve.

For lack of something better to do, Patsy picked out a couple of packets of food and carried them over to where Rosaleen lay huddled in silence, next to the water tank. Although the old lady wasn't moving, Patsy didn't think she was asleep. Still, she tried to be quiet as she juggled the food packets, but she dropped one.

It made hardly any noise as it bounced from the mesh flooring, but Rosaleen opened her eyes and looked at her. "Oh, sorry," Patsy said. "I didn't want to disturb you. I thought you might be, ah—"

"Yes? You thought I might be what?"

"Well, praying, I guess."

"Praying?" Rosaleen looked surprised, then comprehending. "Ah. You saw me crossing myself."

"Well, yes." Patsy was embarrassed to have brought the subject up; conversations about religion, with religious people, always embarrassed her. She said, "It's just that— Well, how long have we known each other, Rosie? And I never knew you were religious before."

"Am I?" Rosaleen pondered the question. "I don't think I am, exactly. You might say I'm just stubborn. It's a kind of a family tradition. My mother's grandfather was the metropolitan of Rostov, back in Soviet times. He died in the camps, like a lot of our family, so I kind of go to church every now and then just to spite the memory of Joe Stalin. On the other hand—" She looked wistful, then smiled. "You know, my mother didn't want me to take science courses in school, she thought it would ruin me as a believer. Now, if there's really some scientific proof of Heaven, I'd really like to have had a chance to show it to her."

Patsy suddenly shivered. "You know—maybe you will."

But really, you had to face up to this eschaton thing, she told herself. You can't just go on ignoring the whole subject. Suppose what the French colonel said is real. Suppose it doesn't matter all that much what happens to you here, even if maybe you die. No, she amended herself, that's not a maybe; you damn near certainly will die here, and probably before very long. Okay. Fine. For if the colonel was telling the truth then all that happens is you go to sleep, and next thing you know you're wide awake and healthy and happy and, hey, *immortal*! That wasn't too shabby, was it? Living forever in Heaven . . .

But it wasn't really a very comforting thought. Future immortality was a theory; dying was a *fact*. Not to mention the other thing. Even if the theory was right, what about these damn mysterious Horch? Or, for that matter, about the equally damn mysterious Beloved Leaders?

She shuddered again, and began picking over the stored foods. They were as discouraging to her as ever, but she settled on something that called itself potato soup and set it to soak in cold water; maybe it would turn itself into vichyssoise, she thought optimistically. Then, on second thought, sighing, she picked out a couple of others and set them to soak for when the others woke up.

Rosaleen was giving her a questioning look. Patsy said sorrowfully: "I wish I hadn't got you into this, Rosie."

Rosaleen looked surprised, then gave her a little never-mind headshake. "Oh, don't blame yourself, Patsy. Look at the bright side. I'm not dead yet—here, I mean. Whereas actually, if I understand what has happened, the one of me on Earth isn't that lucky. So perhaps accepting your invitation to come along has produced a net gain for me after all." Then she smiled. "What foolish things we think of. Shall I tell you what has been on my mind for hours now? I have been wondering who might have taken over my old office at the observatory."

Nearby, Patrice confided, "You know, so am I, Patsy. Who do you suppose has taken over ours?"

"I hope nobody," Patsy said with indignation. "This jail thing must be some kind of misunderstanding; when it gets cleared up we'll be back in charge."

"*We* will?"

Patsy looked at her in surprise, then nodded. "Oh, yeah, I see what you mean. That would make a problem, wouldn't it? I mean if we all got back. Anyway," she said, stretching her arms, "I wonder how old Papathanassiou's getting along with his gamma-burster counts. And poor dumb Mick, and all the rest of the guys. . . ."

"And—" Patrice began, and stopped, frowning. Something was moving toward them through the maze of machinery. Everyone was suddenly standing, half of them with metal rods already in their hands.

They they saw what it was: a Doc, walking slowly and gazing from side to side. When it saw them it stopped, immobile, waiting.

And what it was waiting for . . .

That appeared a moment later. It was Dopey, bedraggled, limping along, hurrying fearfully toward them.

"Please!" he begged. "Help me! They'll kill me if they find me!"

CHAPTER TWENTY-NINE

Patsy

There was the world turned upside down for you, Patsy thought, their arrogant little jailer now pleading hysterically for their protection. "It is not safe here," he sobbed, wringing his fussy little hands. "They go about looking for the Leaders' people and they *butcher* us. Also they're destroying everything in the base!"

"The Horch?" Pat asked, moved to sympathy.

"No, not the Horch themselves! What would the Horch be doing in a place like this? It is the machines they've sent, the killing ones . . . and I am very hungry."

Dannerman gave a quick look at Pat—how kindly did she feel to the little freak?—before he said, "I'm afraid we really don't have enough even for ourselves—"

Dopey looked astonished, then indignant. "But I cannot eat your food! No, there is plenty of good food for me in the base, but I dare not go near it—the whole area is swarming with the surrogates of the Horch. You must help me! I have thought this out carefully; what you must do is very clear. You are a very violent race. I am well informed in this respect; remember, I monitored your whole planet for some years. You can fight them, drive them out—"

"With this?" Dannerman demanded, brandishing his spear. "You took our guns away from us."

"But you can have them back," Dopey said eagerly. "I can get them for you. There are better weapons as well. Beloved Leader weapons! Very powerful! As powerful as those of the Horch surrogates, and I will show you where they are."

"If you've got weapons like that, why don't you fight them yourself?"

Dopey looked sorrowful. "The Beloved Leaders' weapons require a great deal of energy."

Dannerman laughed sharply. "And the power's out, so this is all bullshit."

"Bullshit?" Dopey looked trances for a moment, then indignant. "No, certainly what I ask of you is not 'bullshit.' There is a standby power source which is quite adequate, but I dare not activate it by myself. The Horch surrogates would be sure to detect it and then—" The creature shuddered, and added, "Also fighting is not a characteristic of my race. Those others who were fighters were of a different kind, and they are already dead. As I will be if you do not help me now."

Pat gave him a curious look. "You seem to be really scared of dying all of a sudden."

"No," Dopey said. "You have misjudged this matter. I am not afraid of dying. The death of one copy is of little importance when new copies can easily be made. But afraid of failing to carry out the tasks of the Beloved Leaders? Oh, yes, I am very much afraid of that."

"So you'd rather die than fail to carry out your task?"

"No, no! How can you misunderstand me so? To die is no excuse! Do not forget the eschaton!"

Ah, thought Patsy, her curiosity satisfied at last. The eschaton! The eternity of immortal bliss in heaven that waited for them all—assuming the Beloved Leaders were right—but less blissful by a good deal, it seemed, for anyone the Beloved Leaders found wanting in his duties to them.

If it was a fantasy, it was clearly very real to Dopey. He

showed it in his look and demeanor: the plume draggled and gray, the little kitten face wrinkled in worry. Then, impatiently: "Must we stay here and argue? It is not safe here. The Horch surrogate machines may detect us at any time. You must leave the base for a place of safety and wait there; my bearer and I will secure your weapons and bring them to you. It will take some time, as we must go very cautiously and by a roundabout route, but I believe we can accomplish this, and then, once you are armed, I will lead you to the power generator—"

"Hold it," Dannerman ordered. "Go back a bit. What's this about a place of safety?"

"A place of *relative* safety, perhaps I should say," Dopey qualified. "Outside the bounds of the base there is a habitat area which has been prepared for you—it was to have been in a later stage of your experiment, but it is available now. I promise you you will find it quite pleasant, not unlike certain portions of your own planet. Also there are dwellings already prepared. There is clean water in a stream. There are trees and flowers—"

"I knew it!" Pat shouted triumphantly. "I saw them! And they were in the open, with real sunshine!"

Dopey squinted at her in reproof. "There is no sunshine at present," he corrected her, "as it is presently night in this portion of the planet. But you will be safe there, relatively, and I will have the bearer prepare a map to guide you."

"If it's nighttime, how will we find our way?" Rosaleen objected.

"I said it was night. I did not say it was *dark*," Dopey told her, glancing at the Doc. He didn't say a word, or even make a gesture that Patsy could see, but at once the golem stirred itself, pulled out a pen like Rosaleen's—hell, no, Patsy realized; it wasn't *like* Rosaleen's, it *was* Rosaleen's, a copy no doubt made as they copied anything else they chose—and swiftly began to sketch a diagram on a scrap of wrapping paper. "It is not far," Dopey reassured them. "Perhaps, ah, two kilometers. See here"—snatching the completed map from the Doc—"you go that way, past that large orange object, do you see? Then you will see the open space just ahead. Go across this meadow, here, and around this lake, here, and there will be a path. It will lead you to the encampment, and you will wait there until the bearer and I return with your weapons. Then—"

"Stop right there," Dannerman ordered. "Why should we do what you tell us?"

"Why, because that is what the Beloved Leaders would wish," Dopey said in surprise. "Also to save your own lives, since it can be only a very short time before the Horch surrogates arrive here."

"That's what you say," Dannerman said. "We have no reason to trust you. We've seen what you people do."

Dopey looked perplexed. "You have *seen*?"

"On the helmet," Dannerman told him. "Your Beloved Leaders have blown up dozens of planets—"

Dopey looked stricken. "I did not realize the Horch had taken over that circuit," he moaned. "But the people of those planets were enemies! They refused to cooperate with the Beloved Leaders—"

"So you killed them all?" Pat asked in horror.

Dopey said earnestly, "It was not an evil act! Do you not understand? In effect, we merely transported them all, instantly, to their immortality at the eschaton."

Dannerman was staring at him. "Jesus," he said, shaking his head. Then, obstinately: "But you yourself sent copies of us back to Earth from Starlab."

Dopey recovered himself quickly. "So much argument for so little purpose, when time is passing by!" he said in indignation.

"But of course we sent copies to Earth, how else could we obtain primary-source data? The observation units we installed did the copies no harm."

That was too much for Patsy. "Then why the hell are our copies in jail?" she demanded.

"Ah," Dopey said, "yes, I see why you are concerned. But it was necessary to alter the memories of those copies, since we did not wish to prematurely reveal our presence. And then they became suspicious after they discovered the device in Dr. Artzybachova at the autopsy—"

He stopped there, suddenly aware of the way Rosaleen was staring at him. "The autopsy," she repeated, as though she had to say it out loud to make it real.

"Unfortunately, yes," he said sadly. "I am sorry to say that your copy was the first living human subject in which we implanted the device. Of course, we had experimented on the head of the corpse in Starlab. But that was in a very poor state of preservation and we were not well experienced in the procedure when we did your copy, Dr. Artzybachova. I regret it, but your copy did not survive."

By the time Dopey had left with his zombie—urging haste at every breath—all the captives had had a chance to study the map. It impressed Patsy: the Doc had sketched as quickly as it could move the pen, but the result was as carefully drawn as any Geodetic Survey chart. Who would have thought that speechless golem capable of such detail? But the important thing was that everyone agreed that they could follow it. Rosaleen, who had been very quiet, not to say subdued—well, Patsy thought, why wouldn't she be, now that her fears were confirmed?—spoke up at last. "It is all quite clear," she said, her voice colorless, her expression blank. "We should have no problem."

"*If* we go to this place," Dannerman said argumentatively.

Martín scowled at him. "Do we have a choice? You yourself have seen what damage these 'surrogate' things can do."

"Maybe we don't," Dannerman conceded, but his tone was reluctant.

Patsy was studying his face. "What's the matter?" she asked. "Don't you want to leave here?"

He shrugged. "Martín's right about that, we probably can't stay here. It's the part that comes after that that I don't like. The son of a bitch wants us to fight his battles for him! Christ! We don't owe him a thing. It's his fault we're here in the first place."

"But we are here," she said reasonably, "and those Horch surrogates do look as though they're killing everything they can catch. Maybe he's right. Maybe we need to fight them just to stay alive."

He grunted. "You're pretty warlike, all of a sudden."

"I don't want to die any sooner than necessary, is that so strange?" She gave him a disapproving look. "I thought you were the trained killer here. What happened?"

He shook his head. "What happened," he said, "is that I'm well enough trained to stay out of other people's fights, especially against superior forces."

Martín rumbled, "I understand your concern, Dannerman, but we can deal with what comes later later. The question is, what do we take with us when we leave? Food, of course; remember what Dopey said. He cannot eat our food, so we probably cannot eat anything we find there, either."

"How the hell are we going to carry all these things?" Jimmy Lin said, staring at the mound of food containers.

"Well, that I can answer for you," Dannerman said. "We can

use the rods I brought back and the blankets from Starlab to make travoises."

Martín kicked at the rods contemptuously. "Most of those rods are too thick to fit through the blanket loops," he pointed out.

"So we use the others. Let's get on with it."

"Hey," said Patsy and Pat at once, and Patrice added, "It's not that easy. What did Dopey say, two kilometers? Rosaleen can't walk that far."

"Fine," Dannerman said. "She won't have to. We'll make a travois for her, too."

Martín said with disdain, "Using those toothpicks? The thing will come apart in ten minutes, and then you will drop the old lady on her ass. It's simpler for me to carry her."

CHAPTER THIRTY

Patsy

When they started on their trek to their new home, Patsy was filled with worries. What was waiting for them there? Would they be able to follow the Doc's hastily drawn map without getting lost? Would they be able to see where they were going at all, since Dopey had told them it was night outside? But when they reached the edge of the Beloved Leader base—cut as cleanly as with a knife, one moment surrounded by the hulking dead machinery, the next looking out on a sprawl of meadow and woods—at least one of those worries disappeared. They all stopped dead in their tracks, looking up. "Oh, my God," Patsy breathed. "Will you *look* at that sky?"

They all were looking. They couldn't help it. Overhead there were a zillion stars, far brighter than anything she had ever seen on Earth, and far more of them. There were red stars and blue ones, yellow ones, white ones. On Earth star colors were so muted that you had to stare at even, say, Betelgeuse to be sure that it was really ruddy instead of featureless white. Here there was no doubt. The colors were as unmistakable as traffic lights, and nearly as brilliant. There seemed to be at least a thousand stars up there that were brighter than Venus at its maximum from Earth. There were a dozen or more that seemed even brighter than the Moon. Patsy had heard of, but had never seen, starlight you could read a book by. This was starlight you could do brain surgery by.

Next to her Pat sighed. "You know what, friends?" she murmured. "We're definitely not in Kansas anymore."

Two kilometers wasn't much; Patsy had jogged more than that some mornings before breakfast, along the bridle path in the park . . . in the days when Patsy was still Dr. Pat Adcock, who not only jogged but worked out in the gym once a week—most weeks, anyway.

Those days were past. Confinement in that tiny cell had left them all out of shape, and a two-kilometer hike was now a *lot*. They took turns dragging the travoises that were loaded with most of their Starlab food, three of them at a time with Rosaleen limping painfully along when she could and riding on Martín's back when she couldn't, and the other two following behind to pick up whatever rations fell from a travois and toss them back onto the pile.

But there was so much to see! When she was dragging a travois Patsy's eyes were on the sky as much as on where she was going; when Jimmy Lin relieved her to drop back and do pickup she was glad to see who was there with her. "Patrice!" she hissed, trying to keep her voice low enough that the others might not hear. "Do you know what I think? I think we're in the middle of a globular cluster!"

Patrice bent to pick up a pair of soft-plastic packs and tossed them into Jimmy Lin's travois. "So does Pat," she whispered. "We were talking about it before. At first I thought maybe we were at the core of the galaxy, you know? The star density might be about the same. But we'd know that, all right, and—"

"Hey, back there!" Dannerman called. "Pay attention to what you're doing, we can't afford to lose any food." But he had stopped at the edge of a dark lake, setting down the handles of his own travois to consult over the map with Rosaleen and the general.

Patsy would have supposed that Jimmy Lin would be right

up there to take part in the debate, but he lingered when everyone had stopped. "What were you guys saying about a globular cluster?"

Patrice frowned. "Sorry, we were trying to keep it quiet. What about it?"

"Well, to start with, what is it?"

"It's what it says it is. It's a tight cluster of thousands of stars, more or less shaped like a ball. But if that's what we're in, then we're *really* pretty far from home; most of them are in the galactic halo, none of them closer than several thousand light-years."

"Wherever they are, their stars are really jammed close together," Patsy added. "Thousands of them might fit into the space between Earth and Alpha Centauri . . . a lot like what you see up there."

Jimmy craned his neck, then had an objection. "So how do you know we're not in the core of our own galaxy? Christo Papathanassiou told me once—"

"That there were a lot of stars crowded together there, too? Sure there are. But there's something else at the core, and that's a hell of a big black hole. If we were anywhere near that we'd know, because we'd all be dead now from the radiation."

From up ahead, Dannerman was trying to get their attention. "Quiet!" he ordered. "Do you hear that?"

And as soon as they stopped talking, Patsy did. It was a thick slobbering noise, not quite a roar, definitely not friendly.

In a moment Patsy saw what it was. Something was crossing from a patch of shrubbery toward the lake, off to their right, no more than thirty or forty meters away. There were two somethings, one larger than the other. Patsy couldn't make out details, but the heads looked as huge-mouthed and wide-nostriled as a hippopotamus—though wearing something puzzlingly like a mustache. Not really a mustache, she corrected herself; the strands weren't hair; more like the tentacles of an octopus. The bodies, though, were streamlined as a seal's, and they flopped along the ground on their fins like any pinniped. As she watched, the smaller of the two slipped into the water; the other planted itself on the shore and gargled at them again before following the other.

"Christ," Pat breathed from up ahead. "Was I wrong, or were those things wearing some kind of collars?"

"Perhaps they are pets," Rosaleen said dryly. "I don't think I want to try to return them to their owners just now, though. Please, can we proceed?"

They did. They gave the lakeside a wide berth, all of them watching worriedly to see what might come up at them out of the water. But nothing did.

Once past the lake the distance was short. They crossed a meadow—delightfully speckled with patches of phosphorescent grasses, smelling peculiarly of mown wild onions and mint. Once or twice Patsy thought she heard a distant whickering from the woods, and Jimmy Lin startled everybody when he declared he'd seen something flying there. But then they crossed a little ridge, and there before them, laid out in the brilliant starshine, was a valley with a bright stream running through it, and some sort of structures beside the stream.

"They look like tents," Patrice said in awe.

"Yes," said Rosaleen, summoning up the strength to stand for the last little bit. "Dopey said there would be dwellings for us."

"Tents aren't 'dwellings,' " Jimmy Lin complained; and then, when they were closer: "My God, they aren't even tents! They're what you call 'yurts.' Like the things the Uighur ethnics live in, up in Xinjiang Province, you know? And they *stink*."

So they did; as soon as Patsy came within range she smelled it, a long-ago aroma of spice and decay. On the other hand, she was well aware that she herself was far from fragrant, and she eyed the stream water longingly.

She wasn't the only one, though not for the same reason. Behind her Dannerman asked, "Think we can drink that river water?"

Rosaleen was limping after him. "What choice do we have?" she asked, painfully crouching over the stream for a closer look. Most of the others followed. At that point in its course the stream ran over a pebbly bottom, and, in the glory of starlight from that blazing sky, it looked crystal-clear. It also looked empty. If the stream held any population of fish or insects—or of whatever would pass for either in this place—Patsy couldn't see them.

She put a finger in the water and quickly revised her thoughts of a quick bath; that water was *cold.* Next to her Dannerman hesitated, then dipped his cupped hands into the stream. He lifted the water to his nose to smell, then tasted it.

"It seems all right," he said judiciously. "Tastes good, in fact."

That was enough for Patsy. She cupped her hands in the stream, drank; and then realized how thirsty she was and drank more, and then more still. She wasn't the only one, either. Most of the others were following Dannerman's example, until Rosaleen said thoughtfully, "I wonder if we shouldn't have boiled it first."

"Boiled it how?" Pat asked, but Patsy wasn't listening. She was remembering what a case of violent diarrhea was like, learned well from some heavy-drinking and poorly sanitized picnics in her college days. What would that be like here, without any pink medicine waiting in the dorm dispensary to calm the outraged bowels down?

But it was a little late to think of that, and now everybody—no, she corrected herself: every one of the men; the women seemed less bossy—had a plan to offer. "We need to make a fire," Jimmy Lin was saying, and Martín was arguing, "First we must fix up some sleeping accommodations for Rosaleen," and Dannerman was urging that they check the woods out, in case there were surprises there.

"Fire first," Jimmy insisted. "To keep vermin away, and so we can cook some of this crap instead of eating it cold."

"Cook it in what?" Pat asked. It was a reasonable question. Patsy thought wistfully of the score or so of pots and kettles and asparagus cookers and omelette pans in her (seldom-used) kitchen in New York. Would they have to reinvent pottery? Dig out clay? Throw bowls on a wheel, the way she vaguely remembered from one of the less enjoyable courses she'd taken in high school? But Jimmy dismissed all questions. "Get me firewood," he ordered. "Preferably dead stuff that's fallen to the ground; let me worry about the rest of it." And, when there still were arguments, grandly: "Don't forget, I was an Eagle Scout at Kamehameha High."

It was Dannerman who lost out. Exploration, they decreed, would have to wait for daylight; meanwhile Martín and Jimmy Lin had their way. Patsy found herself carting wood from the edge of the forest—ears alert for any sound, eyes searching the dimness—while Dannerman cut it into quarter-meter lengths with the serrated blade from his belt, and Martín drafted Pat and Patrice to drag everything out of the yurts for inspection. Everything the yurts contained was old, fragile and decayed; but there had been things that could only have been pallets that still seemed useful. Well, *maybe* useful. Certainly not comfortable. They were sacks filled with powder that had once been leaves and grasses, along with brittle sticks that still had sharp edges; and they were more than three meters long and less than a meter wide.

They would do. Martín ordered four of them returned to the largest and cleanest of the yurts, three to another—why, Patsy thought, amused, they were doing sex-segregated dormitories! And when he had made sure Rosaleen was comfortable, or as comfortable as she could hope for, he emerged to help Jimmy Lin rasp deadwood into a kind of powder with the little files from Rosaleen's hair sticks. And then Jimmy did his Eagle Scout thing, spinning a stick between his palms against a rock, finally getting a smoldering glow from the friction. And ten minutes later he had his campfire going, throwing out orders in all directions. "Only put in small sticks," he commanded. "Not too much wood. What we want is an Indian campfire—small, so it won't use up our fuel too fast. And now—who's for a real home-cooked meal?"

But no one was. What they wanted was sleep. Exploration could wait, eating could wait— it had been a long day for everyone. For Patsy, too, but somehow she found herself volunteering to take the first watch to keep the fire fed. She had had some idea that, once everyone else was well and truly asleep, she might just dip herself into that brook and try to get at least the surface layers of grime and stench off her long-unwashed body. That notion didn't last; when she tried the water with one toe it was even colder than she had remembered.

Replenishing the fire was about the easiest job Patsy had ever had. Jimmy's orders had been explicit: no more than four or five sticks at a time, none at all until there were no more flames, just glowing coals, because you didn't want actual flames. Patsy debated what to do with the longest sticks, too long to fit in the tiny fire. She didn't want to try to break them for fear of waking the others up, wasn't sure she had the strength to do it, anyhow, and had no idea where Dannerman had left his glassy blade; but then she worked out a simple solution. She laid them across the fire until the middle sections had burned through, then picked up the ends and tossed them in. Nothing to it.

The hard part was staying awake. For the first hour or so little pinpricks of fear kept the adrenaline flowing. Distant whickerings in the wood, the gentle plop of something falling from a tree, a nearby growl (which turned out only to be Martín snoring)—every sound was an alarm. Almost anything, Patsy thought, could leap raging at her out of the trees; but then time passed and nothing did, and the fears, while not going away, changed character. Were they really going to try to take on the might of the Horch killing machines with a handful of popguns? Should they be doing that, anyhow? (Or was Dannerman right about the dangers of taking sides?) And, that biggest question of all, how much truth was there in the promise of eternal bliss (or otherwise) in this improbable eschaton? The questions revolved themselves through her tired brain—with, of course, no answers. She was fed up with the endless supply of unanswerable questions.

But then she had only to lift her eyes to the sky to see the kind of marvel she had never expected to behold. It was—there was only one word for it—*magnificent.* She noticed, as time went on, that the stars were appropriately wheeling across the heaven, just as they should do; that pair of blue-white beacons that had been low on the horizon when they arrived was now gone from view, and on the other side of the sky—she supposed she should call it the "east"—there was a whole new puzzle to gape at. Streamers of pale light stretched among the newly risen stars, some of them almost as bright as the stars themselves, almost enough to make her squint. She realized with a sudden shiver— part excitement, part wonder at being privileged to see such a thing with her own unaided eyes—that she was looking at stars in the very act of stealing gas from one another, a spectacle she had never before beheld except in plates from Starlab or the old Kecks.

She was so absorbed in the sight overhead that she wasn't aware Dannerman was coming up to her until he called her name, and then she jumped. "Jesus, Dan-Dan! What are you doing up?"

"Time to relieve you," he said, following her example and staring toward the east. "What the hell's that? It looks like something you'd see under a microscope?"

Well, it did; all filamentary and webby. But she was glad to be able to explain something at least, when so little was explainable. "They're exchanging matter. Stars can do that when they're close, and some of those are probably nearer each other than Pluto is to the Sun. So you're looking at the naked hearts of stars, Dan. If our models of star evolution are right," she went on, warming to the subject, "some of those stars used to be red giants, but when the gas was stripped away they were rejuvenated. They became what we call 'blue stragglers,' with surface temperatures five or six times as hot as our own Sun. The bad part of that," she began, but Dannerman held up his hand.

"Please, Patsy. Don't tell me any bad parts right now, okay? You better get some sleep while you can. It's almost daylight."

And he was right about that, too, of course. Past the cobwebby gas streamers the far horizon was beginning to lighten; and Patsy felt the sudden weight of her fatigue. Gratefully enough she climbed onto the pallet that had been set aside for her, Pat stirring gently as she came in, Rosaleen moaning faintly in her sleep. It was not a comfortable bed. Whoever made it must have had skins like armor plate, she thought, and closed her eyes.

But she hadn't told him what the bad part was.

The bad part was that some of those cannibal stars would

sooner or later glut themselves on the mass they had stolen from the others. And then there would be a nova, maybe even a supernova, flooding the space around it with radiation of all kinds . . . at the congested distances of the globular cluster.

When might that happen? The astronomical time scale was far slower than the human. Such things might take centuries to occur, but when they did—

When they did, this would not be a good place to be, and the life expectancy of anyone out in the open under that suddenly lethal sky would be short indeed.

CHAPTER THIRTY-ONE

Patsy

Patsy woke up with bright sunlight outside the opening of the yurt and the sound of somebody yelling at somebody, not very near, but not all that far away, either. When she peered out she saw that it was Dannerman who was doing the yelling. The person he was yelling at was Pat, placidly hanging her underwear on a tree branch to dry. "It's just damn *foolish* for you to go wandering off by yourself," he scolded. "Who knows what's out there?"

"But you said yourself we needed to check out our surroundings," Pat said reasonably, adjusting the bra to catch the sun.

"Not alone!"

"No," she said, acknowledging the justice of what he said—but not, Patsy thought, particularly penitent about it, either. "I should have waited till the others woke up. But, Dan, I found this lovely pond just a little way down the stream, and I got a *bath*. Well, sort of a bath—no soap, of course, and it was really cold—but I can't tell you how much better I feel. Maybe the two of us can go out later?" And then, looking past him, "Well, good morning, Patsy. Did you have a nice sleep?"

Damn the woman, Patsy thought. Damn the man, too; they might as well be married if they were going to squabble like that. She didn't answer, simply turned and headed for the bushes. Then, delighting in the luxury of being able at last to pee without an audience, she relented. She was just jealous, she admitted to herself. Not merely jealous of the Dan-Pat relationship, although she was certainly envious of that, but *extremely* jealous of the bath.

On the way back she paused to peer down the stream and, yes, she was nearly sure that, just past where the brook made a bend around a grove of tall, emerald-leaved trees, there was a definite widening. That went right to the top of her list of priorities. Not to be taken advantage of just yet, maybe; she hadn't missed Pat's complaint about the cold, but as soon as the air warmed up a little . . .

It was astonishing how that thought elevated her mood. She glanced up, and there was the sky. The blue sky, with fleecy little muffins of fair-weather clouds scattered around, and the sun. The sun! Of course, it wasn't their familiar sun of Earth; too large, too orangey. But it was a great deal better than that unending featureless white glow they had lived under in their cell, and she was interested to observe that, even in daylight, a scattering of those incredible stars were bright enough to be visible in the sky. This was not an *awful* place, she told herself. It was even sort of pretty: the grove of trees behind her was hung with clusters of things like bright-yellow berries; the spiky ground-cover stuff underfoot that was like grass (but wasn't any grass Patsy had ever seen) was spotted with wildflower dots of color. Most important of all, she was *outside*. Things might be heading for something even worse than what had gone before, but at this moment, Patsy thought, they didn't seem bad at all. So she had a cheery smile for Pat and Dan as she rejoined the group, and another for Rosaleen and Martín Delasquez, doing something with the stack of ration containers. The only ones missing were Patrice and Jimmy Lin, and about as soon as the thought crossed her mind they both appeared out of their respective yurts, Patrice heading toward the bushes without a word, Jimmy yawning, barely glancing at the others, making a beeline to check the condition of his pet campfire.

To Patsy's eyes the fire was behaving just as it was supposed to behave. It was a neat bed of glowing coals, sixty or seventy centimeters across, with only a couple of lately added sticks palely flaming on top. Clearly, however, it did not meet Jimmy Lin's expectations. He pushed the burning sticks together and carefully added two more, just so, muttering to himself. Then he caught sight of Rosaleen. "What are you doing?" he demanded.

She didn't take offense. "We're counting our rations," she said, "and at the same time looking for containers that won't burn if we boil water in them."

"Thought so," he said, patiently superior. "I told you to leave that sort of thing to me, didn't I? What you should do now is find a big empty container and fill it with water, while I get some rocks from the brook."

He made a production out of it, selecting golf-ball-sized pebbles, which he carried back and painstakingly placed on the coals. "Give them ten minutes," he said, wise old expert showing the tenderfeet how to get along in the wild. "Then the rocks will be hot enough; we drop them in the water and they'll have it hot in no time."

"Hey," Pat said, admiring against her will. "More Boy Scout stuff?"

He didn't deign to answer, merely walked off to the shelter of the trees to relieve himself.

"Bastard," Dannerman said, but his tone was tolerant. He glanced at Pat. "Shall we eat something? And then go explore?"

"If Rosaleen's through with her count?" Pat said, looking toward the stack of rations.

"In a minute," Rosaleen called. "Martín's found a couple of other packets—I guess we dropped them."

But Martín was standing a good three or four meters away—how could we have dropped any of the packets over there? Patsy wondered—and his expression was forbidding. He was holding two of what looked like dehydrated stew packets, and staring at the ground.

"Something's been nibbling at these things," he called. "And I think I see what was doing it. Only they're dead."

Jimmy Lin's hot-water scheme worked fine—to be sure, at the cost of some burned fingers, transferring the hot pebbles to the container of water, but in a few minutes the container was gently simmering and meals were coming along. When Patsy got her stew, though, it was lukewarm and only partially softened. It didn't matter. She'd lost most of her appetite when she saw the three little dead creatures—looking a little like lizards, maybe, though densely furred—with their mouths wide open in the rictus of death.

"Different chemistry," Rosaleen said soberly. "I guess I can forget that idea." And when someone asked what idea she was talking about, she explained, "I was thinking we might try some of the fruits from those trees when our rations run out, but if our food kills them, I doubt their food will be any better for us."

Patsy stopped eating to look at the heap of rations. It had not occurred to her to think of it as a nonrenewable resource. She didn't like the conclusions that thought led to. "Rosaleen? With seven of us eating, how long do you think the food will last?"

Rosaleen looked at the tally in her hand. "Let's see, three meals per day per person, that's twenty-one portions a day, divided into, according to this, two hundred and seventy-three portions . . . say, thirteen days. A bit more, maybe."

"And then?"

"And by then," Rosaleen said firmly, "I presume Dopey will have come back with the guns, and we'll have taken over the base and there'll be all the food we want from Starlab."

"Or not," Patrice said.

Rosaleen nodded. "Or else we will probably have been killed in the attempt, so it's not a problem."

"So then why were you counting the food?"

She hesitated. "I suppose because there is always the chance that Dopey won't come back."

It was what Patsy had known she would hear, but that didn't make it any nicer. She pressed the point. "And if Dopey doesn't come back, and that's all there is, how long before we starve to death?"

Rosaleen didn't answer at first; while she was thinking Dannerman spoke up. "Did you ever hear of a man named William Bligh?"

"I don't think so."

"He was the captain of an old sailing ship, the *Bounty*, hundreds of years ago. I guess he was a pretty mean son of a bitch, even for those days; anyway, his crew mutinied. Somebody made a book out of it. I never read the book, but one summer in graduate school I worked for a local theater, and they put on a musical based on it. I sang the first mate, the guy who led the mutiny. He was a man named Fletcher Christian."

"I didn't know you were a singer."

"Who said I was a singer? They weren't fussy about that kind of thing at the theater. Neither was I; they didn't pay anything, but you got to meet a lot of girls there. Anyway, Christian made the mutineers put the captain and some of his loyal crew over the side in a longboat instead of hanging them out of hand. The mutineers gave them two days' rations or so, and Captain Bligh managed to get every man in the boat safely to a British port a couple of thousand miles away. They rowed six or eight weeks before they reached land, and all that time they lived on the little bit of water they could catch when there were rainstorms, and the food that was only supposed to be rations for a couple of days."

She thought that over. Another month or two in this place, with nothing to eat at all? And no realistic hope of rescue? "That's not particularly good news," she said.

Dannerman nodded. "We don't really need three meals a day, though. Two would be enough, I think. That ought to give us another couple of weeks, anyway."

But that wasn't really great news either.

CHAPTER THIRTY-TWO

Patsy

When everyone had eaten, Pat and Dan took off on their mission of exploration. It surprised no one to see that they were walking hand in hand as they left. No one said anything, though—well, no one but Jimmy Lin. "Hey, guess what?" he said, grinning, pointing to where Pat's laundry still hung on the tree. "The lady left her underwear behind. Probably figured it would just get in the way?"

Nobody responded but Patsy, and she said only, "Shut your mouth." She turned her back on him and walked over to where Patrice was sitting cross-legged on the ground, studying some carved wooden objects pulled out of the yurts. "It's none of his damn business what they do," she said—then, lowering her voice, "Although, you know?, he's probably right. How about that bath?"

"In a while," Patrice said absently, looking at a piece of age-darkened wood as long as her forearm, one end flattened and rounded. "Rosaleen wants to go along, but she's resting. Patsy? What do you think this thing is?"

Patsy considered the question. Although the object was worn and chipped at the edges, she was pretty sure of its identity. "I'd say a snow shovel—if they ever had snow here," she hazarded. "Some kind of a shovel, anyway." She squatted beside the other woman, poking through the little pile of artifacts. Most were wood—the shovel, a rod with a pointed, fire-hardened end (too thick to be a spear; maybe a digging stick?), something that looked like a salad fork, several things that didn't look like anything Patsy recognized at all. What wasn't wood was glassy rock—one pretty obviously a sharp-edged knife, the others harder to identify. "They didn't have any metal, did they?" Patsy discovered. "Sort of like the Stone Age?"

"More like pre-Columbian America," Patrice said thoughtfully. "Those yurts are pretty well built . . . and doesn't this look like writing?" She flipped over an oval chunk of wood, and it was true, there were things that looked like wobbly characters incised on the wood. "Makes you wonder who these people were."

But Patsy didn't want to wonder about these unknown people. They were tall and skinny; they lived in tents; they farmed—there was the remains of an overgrown produce plot along the stream—and they were gone. That much they knew, and the only important fact in the lot was the last one. The Skinnies were gone. There was no chance they would ever know anything more about them; but when Patsy said as much, Patrice got a funny expression. "You're sure of that? You don't think we'll all meet up again at the eschaton?"

Patsy gave her a hard look, and got up to put some new pebbles in the fire to heat. That was another thing she didn't want to think about.

Then, when Rosaleen woke up and announced it was time for the adventure of the bath, there was another one. Patrice helped Rosaleen to the "ladies' room" in the bushes; Martín, gathering wood for the fire, decorously diverted himself to a part of the grove they hadn't investigated, and a moment later appeared again, looking perturbed. "There's something odd here," he called. "Come look."

As the others straggled over, Patsy saw what he was talking about. "It just stops," she said, looking in wonderment at the vegetation. It did. The gnarly trees they had used for firewood stopped short, in a mathematically precise straight line; the branches on the near side swooped and dangled in all directions, but on the side away from them the branches were bent at sharp angles. Past them was a growth of quite different vegetation, equally dense, but thick shrubbery rather than trees. There was no point where a shrub crossed into tree territory or a tree branch into the shrubs'.

Rosaleen studied the line of demarcation for a moment, then painfully lowered herself to grub at the ground. A moment later she had revealed the same sort of line that had surrounded their cell, metal and glassy segments alternating. "Do you know what I think?" she said wonderingly. "I believe there used to be one of those walls here."

"I think so, too," Martín confirmed. "And it had to be here for a long time—long enough for the trees to grow up against it."

Patsy was craning her neck to see what was past the shrubbery, and what she saw made her catch her breath. "Look at that," she called. There was open ground there, but planted—planted in regular rows of tall stalks.

"It looks like farmland," Patrice said, staring. "And there's a path—and, hey, what's that thing over there on the ground?"

The thing along the path was definitely a machine. It had three wheels, bicycle-size, though the spokes were wood—the whole thing was wood, as far as Patsy could see, and it had a sort of basketwork thing in the middle. A farm cart? But if there was a farm, where was the farmer?

That was the next shock. There was a stirring among the tall, ruddy-leafed stalks, and a creature appeared, holding half a dozen banana-shaped fruits (or husks, or *something*) and staring at them.

It was nothing Patsy had ever encountered before, though

even at first glimpse there was something about it that looked vaguely familiar. What it looked like was a scale model of one of the ancient big-bodied, long-necked dinosaurs, maybe the kind that was called apatosaurus—though in this case an apatosaurus that was covered with curly hair all over its body, strands poking out from the colorful embroidered shirt and kilt it wore on its tubby, watermelon-size body, and curly bangs that hung over its tiny, lashed eyes—and a very small apatosaurus, at most a couple of meters from the end of the tail that rose behind it to the little head on the end of its sinuous, long neck. It stood on its hind legs, and its front legs—no, Patsy decided, you'd definitely have to call them arms and hands—were holding what it had just collected.

If the watchers were startled, the creature was petrified with fear. It made a sharp mewing sound, dropping its harvest, and flopped itself onto the machine in the path. Patsy saw what the basket was for. It supported the creature's belly as it lay flat, its legs pumping reciprocating levers that turned the rear wheels, its hands on a tiller that evidently guided the wheel in front. As the vehicle rolled away the long neck swayed around so that the fear-filled eyes could stare back at them.

When he was out of sight Patrice shook herself. "He doesn't look like one of the Seven Ugly Dwarfs," she said thoughtfully, "and he's definitely not a Beloved Leader. But I could swear I've seen somebody like him before."

Patsy had the same feeling. She said, "Maybe he's a prisoner like us. Maybe there are other intelligent races of captives around—even those things in the water last night, maybe?"

"Oh, hell, no," Patrice said positively. "This thing had a velocipede and it wore clothes; they didn't."

Rosaleen sighed and turned, automatically reaching for Martín's arm. "Think about it, Patrice. If you live in the water, what do you need with a velocipede? Or clothes, for that matter. People like us wear clothes to protect us against the weather, but there isn't any weather underwater. In any case, it's time for my bath."

Martín looked alarmed. "That's risky. Maybe that thing went to get help."

"Yes, perhaps so," Rosaleen said, "but it's time for me to clean myself up a bit. You've all been very polite, but I really need a bath."

"We'll take a couple of spears along," Patsy promised.

"You'll take me, too!" Martín insisted.

"We will *not*," Patrice said indignantly.

But in the long run prudence won over modesty—what was left of modesty, after those long nude days in their first pen. The compromise they finally reached was that Martín would come along to carry Rosaleen to the bathing pond, while Jimmy Lin stayed behind to keep an eye on the place where they had seen the dinosaur with the velocipede. Then Martín would stay nearby as long as they were in the water; but he would concede enough to their modesty to sit with his back to them. "And no peeking," Rosaleen called good-naturedly as they began to undress.

Patsy was the first to be naked, but she paused before getting into the water, appalled at the sight of Rosaleen's nude body. The woman was *skeletal*. Her breasts, never ample, were mere flaps of flesh; her ribs showed; her hip joints protruded, and so did her knees and elbows.

Patrice had begun helping Rosaleen toward the water; Patsy turned away in embarrassment and splashed in. The water was still cold, but bearable. After the first shock Patsy began to swim. She couldn't help glancing around at the woods every few moments, but, really, there wasn't much to fear. Was there? And it was so wonderful, so *fine,* to be free in the cleansing water after all that time of filth and deprivation. . . .

She rolled over on her back to look back at where Patrice was helping Rosaleen in the shallows. She noticed that Patrice was holding one of Dan's metal spears, and wondered if she shouldn't have one, too—wondered a moment later whether she wasn't being reckless in swimming out so far from the others. Treading water, she looked around.

That was when she saw the tiny pairs of eyes on the surface of the pond, three or four sets of them, nearer to the other bathers than to herself.

She screamed a warning and didn't wait to see if they would respond. She began to swim as fast as she could toward the shore. Yells and screams spurred her on; when she reached the bank she stood up to look. Martín was there already, splashing fully dressed in the shallows, furiously stabbing at something in the water with his own spear. She didn't see the eyes; she did see the water swirling there as though something large were moving under the surface. Patrice was hurrying Rosaleen out of the water, peering back over her shoulder in panic.

Patsy began to run along the bank toward them, pausing to catch up another spear from the stack beside their clothes. Martín might need help. . . .

Martín did need help. Something huge and slate gray erupted from the water behind him; he screamed something—in Spanish, Patsy thought, though she could not make out the words—and fell back into the water. "Oh, God!" Patrice cried. "It got him!"

Patsy didn't hesitate. She splashed into the shallows to where Martín was half floating, half resting on the muddy bottom of the lake. She didn't see the creature that had attacked him. There was a stain in the water—blood? From Martín? But it was some distance away, and the surface was swirling there; something was there and bleeding. When she reached Martín's body it was motionless. Dead? Patsy tried to imagine what it was like to be killed, to die suddenly, without warning. . . .

But maybe he wasn't dead. The spear in one hand, she wrapped her fingers in his long, coarse hair, trying to pull him ashore. The man weighed twice as much as she. She was barely able to move him, and his face was underwater, time passing; if he hadn't been killed by the amphibian he might drown. When Patrice splashed in to join her she let her take over with the task of pulling the general toward dry land, while she remained in the water, on guard with the spear, watching the swirl of bloody water. Across the pond something was heaving itself out of the water; a good sign, Patsy thought hopefully. They were running away. The thing didn't really look like a hippo, more like a walrus; and it galumphed across the ground in its pinniped fashion. It stopped, turning to look at her with those protuberant eyes, then leaned forward, scooped up some mud, formed it into a ball and threw it at her with its finlike paws.

The mud fell far short, splashing in the middle of the pool. Patsy almost laughed at that pitiful display of hostility. Why, they're as frightened as we are, she thought. It did not occur to her that there had been several of the creatures.

She didn't even see the one that was coming up behind her.

She never saw it at all, only felt the sudden touch of something cold on her back, and then the sharp agony of an electric shock; and then Patsy Adcock's question was answered, and she knew at last what it was like to die.

CHAPTER THIRTY-THREE

Dan

Before Dannerman and Pat had gone a hundred meters they weren't walking hand in hand anymore. They were arm in arm. Very soon thereafter their arms were around each other's waists, and their pace had slowed—no longer a march, now an affectionate stroll. They weren't so wrapped up in each other that they didn't take note of what was around them. That was what they were there for: to explore their surroundings. Dannerman observed that the path they were on had once been trodden hard by some creature's feet—but not recently, since it was now broken here and there with clumps of the wiry grass spikes. It was Pat who first saw the trees that looked so much like cherries (though the bright red fruits that hung from their branches were segmented with hard scales like tiny, ruby-colored pineapples), and it was Dannerman who pointed out the hill that rose off to their left, looming a good hundred meters over the surrounding terrain. ("We could climb that and see everything for kilometers around. Maybe next time.") But they both knew that the thing they were most interested in exploring was not geography; and when Pat looked up at Dannerman, he naturally kissed her; and when they moved their faces away the only question was which of them could first get out of their clothes. They wasted no time. The weeks of enforced abstinence and excessive intimacy were all the foreplay they needed.

When they were done Dannerman propped himself up on one elbow to take some of his weight off her body and gazed reminiscently at her face. "You know, I thought about doing this a lot when we were kids."

"Well, so did I," she said, taking his ears gently in two hands and pulling his head down for a kiss. "But right now it's a little uncomfortable. Oh, don't let go of me—let's hug for a while, okay? Only next time," she added as they shifted position, "we ought to bring a blanket. This mossy stuff has some pretty sharp stickers."

After a while they walked a little farther down the path, remembering that they were supposed to be checking out the area for points of interest. They didn't find many. They had their clothes back on, but Dannerman was comfortably aware that they could get them off again quickly enough if they chose. He rather expected they would choose.

It crossed his mind that probably they shouldn't stay away from the others too long—Dopey might come back and then they would have to think seriously about this mad plan of his to reconquer the base for the Beloved Leaders. Or, alternatively, Dopey might not come back at all. Then they would have to think even more seriously about simple survival. But he didn't want to think about such matters just then, because he was too busy feeling good. It was, he decided, about the best he had felt in a long time—certainly since they had boarded the Clipper for the trip to Starlab. Maybe for a good deal longer than that.

Finally it was Pat who had to say, "Maybe we ought to start back."

Dannerman blinked down at her. "Oh, do you think so? I was sort of thinking that maybe we could—"

"Of course we can," she said, patting his shoulder. "It doesn't have to be here. There's plenty of nice secluded spots right near the yurts, so whenever we like we can just excuse ourselves for a bit and—" She paused, looking curiously at his face. "What's the matter?"

"It just seems so, well, obvious," he said.

Then she did laugh out loud. "Oh, Dan-Dan. Do you think there's one soul back there who isn't absolutely sure of what we were doing here? Come on. Let's see if we can get back without getting lost."

But of course they didn't get lost, because they'd never got that far off the well-marked old path, and of course what Pat said was right. Dannerman switched gears without difficulty. He didn't forget the pleasant feeling in his loins, but he remembered to pick a few of the bright red fruits to carry back, just in case, and even before that he was testing strategies in his mind in the event that Dopey really did bring them their weapons.

That was the part of the Dannerman mind that the Bureau training and experience had honed to a sharp edge. He considered the prospects. If, in spite of everything, they were going to get involved in combat with the Horch machines the first thing they would need was more information. They would need to know, from Dopey, just what parts of the Horch machines were vulnerable to a projectile weapon; and they would have to decide how to allocate the available weapons. He had no doubt that Jimmy Lin and the general could handle a gun; the females were iffier. "Pat?" he asked. "Have you ever been checked out on that little gun you used to carry?"

But she wasn't listening. She was suddenly straining to hear something. "What's that?" she asked, her face suddenly worried.

But by then he had heard the sudden distant screaming, too, and he was already beginning to run.

When they reached the bathing pool there was Martín Delasquez, lying on his face by the side of the pond, his feet still in the water, with Rosaleen, naked, struggling to try to turn him over; and just meters away a clothed Jimmy Lin and a naked Pat were frantically trying to pull the limp form of the other Pat, also naked, to dry land.

What he couldn't see was what it was that they were trying to flee from, but the women were shouting the answer to that. The amphibians? How could that be? What were they doing here, so far from their own pond? But then he saw the little eyes, only a few meters from shore, and then there was no doubt. He didn't waste time wondering. He and Jimmy got the inert hulk of Martín Delasquez pulled away from the water, while the two Pats did the same for the third. "Let me," Jimmy panted, taking over from the Pats; once again his Boy Scout training was useful. Dannerman stood guard, knee deep in the muddy shallows at the water's edge, spear ready. When he stole glances over his shoulder he saw Jimmy bending over the motionless woman, doing the mouth-to-mouth and the rhythmic chest-hammering of CPR, while Rosaleen and the other Pats copied his actions on the form of Martín. Which Pat was which? Hard enough to tell them apart at any time, it was impossible when they were naked.

If the amphibians had any intention of attacking on dry land they kept it in check. Dannerman knew they were there, saw water swirling, caught a glimpse or two of gray flesh; but they seemed more interested in getting their own wounded member to the safety of deep water than in the creatures that had stabbed him. Slowly Dannerman retreated to the high ground, spear still ready, but beginning to feel a little safer.

When he looked around Martín was stirring at last, coughing, looking dazedly around, trying to sit up. But the other Pat . . .

Jimmy was still working on her. He kept it up for long minutes, kept it up long past the time when Dannerman could still feel hope. Then Lin sat somberly back on his haunches.

"She's dead," he said. He thought for a moment. "If we had adrenaline, or shock paddles," he began, and then shook his head and repeated, "She's dead."

Dead?

Dannerman felt the word like a physical blow. *Dead.* It did not seem possible. Yes, sure, they had all faced the strong probability that they might all be dead before long, starvation most likely, possibly some other assault from this hostile place. But not now. Not so *soon.*

"Dan?" It was Rosaleen, drawing on her clothes and looking at him. "Don't you think we ought to get out of here?"

He roused himself. "Yes, of course. But—" He hesitated, looking at the two living Pats and the one that lay motionless on the ground. "But *which?*"

The nearest Pat glared at him angrily. "It's Patsy, you fool," she said, and began to cry.

CHAPTER THIRTY-FOUR

Dan

They didn't walk back to the yurts. They fled. As rapidly as they could, all of them craning their necks to watch for pursuit—but Dannerman knew that if the amphibians attacked again there was very little they could do about it. He had organized them as best he could, but under the circumstances his best was not a lot. Martín had turned out to be able to walk, more or less. He was staggering, confused, seeming tranced and bewildered, with little strength in his limbs. But Jimmy Lin supported him on one side and Patrice on the other, and he managed. Rosaleen Artzybachova was making it on her own—not very well, either, but limping after the others with Pat's help; Pat was carrying Patsy's bundled-up clothing, too, and she had a spear to handle as well, since she was all they had in the way of a rear guard against the amphibians.

Dannerman was carrying the body of Patsy. Jimmy Lin had offered, but Dannerman could not let the man touch her damp, cooling and naked body. Dannerman had her cradled in his two hands, each one also holding a spear. Part of the time he walked backward, scanning the path behind them for possible attackers; there were none. One of Patsy's lax arms hung toward the ground. The other lay across her body, as though trying to preserve modesty. But she had no modesty left to preserve. Though her head hung down Dannerman could see that her eyes were open and so was her mouth. Patsy Adcock would never have let herself be seen in so unflattering a pose. She didn't look pretty. She barely looked like herself; she looked only dead.

Dannerman looked away. They had other things to think of. They would have to bury Patsy, which meant somehow digging a grave. He would have to organize some sort of guard duty to watch for a possible attack. What he would do if that happened he did not know; the yurts were simply not defensible. But there would have to be some sort of plan. Useless or not, it would have to be tried.

There was another thought swelling inside him, bursting to come out—well, no, he corrected himself; not a thought exactly. A pain. A deep hurt that he had never experienced before and did not know how to deal with. Sooner or later he would have to let it come to the surface—

But not yet.

As soon as they had crossed the little stream he put Patsy's body down, as gently as he could, and began giving orders. Martín was to be put to bed in one of the yurts, Rosaleen in the other. Jimmy Lin would be the first to stand guard, while Pat searched the yurts for something to dig a grave with. The others listened attentively. They didn't offer objections to his seizure of command. They moved. But they did not, exactly, obey. Jimmy Lin's first care was for his precious little fire, and only when that was fed did he, not Pat, begin looking for digging tools. Rosaleen flatly refused to be shut away from the others, so Patrice hauled a pallet out of a yurt for the old lady to lie on. Then Jimmy returned with a couple of flat-bladed wooden things that would do as scoops, and he and Dannerman began using their metal spears to loosen clods of dirt, while Pat and Patrice silently dressed Patsy's body. They didn't talk much. There wasn't much to say.

Digging a grave took a long time with crude tools, even though Pat and Patrice pitched in, scooping the clods of earth away when Dannerman and Jimmy had loosened them. Dannerman didn't notice the passage of time. He was glad for something to do, because that interior ache was rising willy-nilly to the surface of his thoughts. When the grave got too deep for both of them to be able to dig, he hopped out and let Jimmy stab and scoop while he confronted it.

The problem was this: How did you mourn the death of one-third of a lover?

This stiffening corpse by the side of the deepening grave was *Pat.* True, it was not *the* Pat, with whom he had made love just hours before, but certainly *a* Pat, indistinguishable from the very *alive* woman with whom he had talked and played and shared so much of a life, from childhood on. No, there was no doubt of it. When someone you "loved"—it was the first time he had used that word, even to himself—when someone you *loved* died you had to feel pain. Dannerman did feel pain, a lot of pain. But how baffling it was to see two copies of that beloved woman alive and well and helping to dig the grave.

To be sure, those other two were definitely mourning. There was no confusion in the tears and self-reproach. "If I hadn't panicked and stabbed the thing," Patrice kept muttering to Pat, even while she was scooping away the loose dirt into a pile. "Maybe they wouldn't have done anything. Maybe—"

The maybes were not helpful. Dannerman stood up. "My turn, Jimmy," he called, and replaced the astronaut in the pit. He had barely begun to dig when Jimmy Lin yelled and grabbed for a spear, and when Dannerman turned to look he saw a regular circus parade approaching: four or five of the great Docs, marching toward them, with Dopey perched in the arms of one of them.

"What is going on?" Dopey called fretfully. "Why are you digging holes? I have brought you your guns—it took a very long time to secure them, with much danger. Now there is no time for the digging of holes, since we must hurry and reclaim our base from the Horch!"

D opey didn't take kindly to being told that the conquest of the Horch machines would have to wait. But then, when someone had explained to him what had happened, he was disgusted but surprisingly helpful. "General Delasquez," he remarked, "is forming a habit of electrocution. Fortunately one of these bearers is medically trained; I will have him treat the general."

"The hell you will," Patrice snapped, surprised and angered. "What does that thing know about human medicine?"

"Why, a great deal," Dopey assured her. "It was he who implanted the devices on your Starlab. He will know what to do for General Delasquez—also for Dr. Artzybachova, who, I observe, is also quite unwell."

Patrice started to reject the offer with indignation, but Rosaleen overrode her. She raised herself on one elbow and said, "Let's see what he can do, Patrice. I'm not much use to you this way."

That was all the consent Dopey needed. He didn't speak, but one of his golems bent over Rosaleen, picked her up with surprising gentleness and bore her away to the yurt where Delasquez was raucously snoring. Dopey didn't bother to look after them. He waddled toward the grave, where Dannerman had replaced Lin at the bottom, gazing disapprovingly at Dannerman's digging. "What are you doing? Is this some form of human death ritual? If you wish a hole dug to dispose of the cadaver one of my bearers can do this far more quickly."

Dannerman didn't look up. "We'll do it ourselves," he said shortly.

Dopey clucked in annoyance. "How you waste time," he

complained. "I am very near to the limit of my endurance. We must act at once, or I must rest for a bit."

"Rest, then," Jimmy Lin says. "If the amphibians attack we'll let you know."

"Attack? Why would they attack? Although," he added meditatively, "it is unfortunately the case that they are not truly civilized anymore. They subdue their prey with electric shocks. You have seen such animals on your own planet? I believe they are called electric eels? But it was foolish of you to get so near them. They have no recent experience of land dwellers, you see; they have been isolated in their own pen for many generations. Now that the walls are down they are no longer confined, and who knows where they may wander to?"

No one responded but Jimmy Lin, turning his head to glare somberly at the alien, and all he said was "Shut up."

Dopey looked surprised, but obeyed the command; perhaps he was getting used to it. "Very well," he said after a moment. "It is foolish to delay, but I will rest for a few minutes. Wake me when you are ready for the reconquest of the base."

Dannerman glanced up long enough to see Dopey climb into the huge arms of a Doc. He didn't bother to watch as the huge golem carried him away, another Doc waddling irritably after. He was concentrating on carving out a straight, flat base for the grave.

He lost track of time. He was surprised when Patrice called down to him, "That's good enough, Dan."

He looked up in confusion. All five of his fellow prisoners were standing there, looking down on him, even Rosaleen and Martín. He had not even noticed that they had left the yurt. He peered up at Rosaleen. She was standing straighter, and there even seemed to be color in her face. "What did he do to you?" he asked wonderingly.

Rosaleen gave him the ghost of a smile. "God knows. As soon as the Doc touched me I was asleep. When I woke up, Dopey

was there, lying on the ground—he's exhausted, you know—
and the Doc was doing something to Martín. And then Martín
woke up and we came out here."

"Dopey's still in the yurt?"

"Oh, yes. Sound asleep. Funny," she added. "I didn't even
know he *could* sleep. He snores."

"Yes, yes," Pat interrupted, single-minded and impatient.
"Dan? Do you need help getting Patsy down there?"

"Of course not." He took Patsy's body from Pat and Patrice
and, gently, clumsily, stretched it out at the bottom of the pit.
As he climbed out, Pat jumped in to straighten Patsy's corpse.

At the graveside, Patrice fretted, "I wish we had a coffin. I
wish—do you think we should say some words over her?"

"My mother taught me some of the funeral prayers my grandfather used to say," Rosaleen offered. "I learned them in Ukrainian, but I could try to translate."

But Pat was shaking her head as Dannerman helped her out
of the grave. "I'll say what needs to be said," she said firmly.
"Patsy, we loved you. Good-bye."

CHAPTER THIRTY-FIVE

Patrice

Once you've dug a grave you need to fill it back up again. Patrice knew that. But, as the first scoops of dirt plopped onto Patsy's body, she could hardly bear to look, much less to take part in the work. For the first time she understood why people bothered to box their dead in coffins before they laid them away. The coffins weren't to protect the deceased. They were there for the sake of the witnesses, to spare them the sight and sound of clods falling on a face that was once as alive as their own.

But as each successive shovelful of dirt fell on Patsy's body the shape at the bottom of the hole looked less like a human person and more like some random lump of anonymous earth; and, grimly, Patrice picked up a scoop and took her place with the others.

That earned her a grateful look from Jimmy Lin. "Thanks," he said, and then paused to look back at where Martín and Rosaleen were sorting over the guns. Dopey was returning in the arms of one of the Docs. Jimmy looked at Patrice again, this time pleading. "Listen, you can finish without me, can't you? Because I'd really like to check those weapons out—"

"Go ahead," she said. And beside her, Pat saw the expression on Dannerman's face and added:

"You too, Dan. We'll be all right."

The funny thing was, Patrice thought as the men hurried to join the others, that Pat actually did seem to be all right. She wasn't weeping. She didn't even look particularly unhappy. She was frowning slightly in concentration as she dealt with the task at hand, efficiently sliding her ancient scoop into the dwindling pile of dirt, methodically dropping the clods in place to fill the lowest parts of the rising layers of dirt.

It was a good example to follow. Patrice followed it. It was easier refilling the grave than digging it had been, and then, when it was all in, and they had scraped all the loose dirt possible off the ground, there was a small mound to mark the burial place. Patrice knelt to pat it smooth. She was so absorbed in her task it was a surprise to hear Pat's voice. "Patrice? That's good enough. I'm going to clean up a little."

Another good example to follow, and Patrice followed it. But then, as they knelt beside the stream, she looked over at the others. "Then we'd better see what's going on," she offered.

"Sure," Pat said absently, scrubbing at her hands. The water was cold, and the clayey soil sticky; the dirt didn't want to come off. Then she paused, looking over at Patrice. "Listen. You're not sore at me, are you?"

"About what?" Patrice was honestly baffled for a moment, then clarity came. "Oh, you mean about you making out with Dan-Dan? No, of course not."

Pat didn't seem satisfied with the answer. She was looking at the gravesite. She sighed. "Easy for you to say, maybe," she said. "It might not be so easy for Patsy. She was the one that got killed." Then, just before she plunged her face into the water, she added, "You know what I'm wondering? I wonder if there's any truth to this idea of everybody meeting everybody again at the eschaton. Because if there is Dan and I might have some explaining to do."

As Patrice rinsed the tearstains off her own face she considered what Pat had said. Could it be true that some sort of high-tech heaven was waiting for all of them? For herself, for Patsy—for all of the Pats, including the one on Earth? And for Husbands One and Two (and what would that reunion be like?), and for feckless, ill-tempered Mick Jarvas and all the other people at the observatory, and even for Uncle Cubby, finally getting to see what his heirs had done with his money? Not to mention Hitler and Stalin and Napoleon and everybody else, all the way back to Tiglath-Pilesar and Nebuchadnezzar . . . and Dopey, too, in fact all the Dopeys there had ever been, as well as all the other myriad extraterrestrials in this astonishingly populated universe, wherever found.

She couldn't imagine it. Would Patsy in fact be ticked off at being allowed to get killed? Would it be like the wronged dead of the old superstitions, coming back as ghosts to haunt those who had harmed them in life? Only these wouldn't be the sort of ghosts that contented themselves with dripping blood from an unseen wound, or shrieking pitifully in the night. These would be *real*—at least as real as she would be herself, in this fantastic rising-up time in the remote future.

She lifted her face from the water and stopped herself short. No! It wouldn't be like that at all. If they did see Patsy again, it would be that same Patsy who was themselves. Who knew everything about them and forgave all, just as they forgave themselves—and, for the things that weren't really forgivable, simply accepted them and got on with it.

She laughed out loud and stood up, startling Pat who was drying her face with the hem of her shirt. "No," she said, "if it's all true you won't have to explain. It'll be all right."

CHAPTER THIRTY-SIX

Patrice

The others were gathered around the guns that lay on the ground, spilled out of the coppery-mesh sack Dopey had brought them in. There were far more than Patrice had expected, and as they approached Rosaleen smiled at them. "Pick a couple for yourselves," she invited. "All the guns are duplicated, so there's plenty to go around."

"But what's going on?" Patrice asked. Dannerman and Dopey were confronting each other; still in the Doc's arms, Dopey's face was at a level with Dannerman's, and they both looked angry.

"Oh, what do you think?" Rosaleen said, sounding exasperated. "Much argumentation. Simply listen and you will hear it all for yourself."

Her voice carried to Dannerman, who twitched slightly but stood his ground. "You stay out of this," he ordered Dopey. "We have to consider our options."

"But you have no options!" Dopey squawked.

"Of course we do! Fighting your damn Horch machines for you is only one of them. We can stay here—"

"You cannot!"

"Why not? You've supplied us with guns. We can defend ourselves in case the amphibians come back . . . or who knows what other wild animals might be around?"

Dopey said plaintively, "You speak such nonsense, Agent Dannerman. There aren't any wild animals on this planet."

"Not even the ones that killed Patsy?" Jimmy asked.

"Not even them. They are simply control groups—exactly like yourselves, you see! There are eight different species out here, kept in separate reservations, and they're all intelligent. Some of them have been here for many, many generations. They're all that's left of races that have become extinct in their home planets—it is," he added boastfully, "in a sense, a kind of ecological thing. But no wild animals."

"What about the furry lizards?" Patrice demanded.

"I know nothing of lizards. Perhaps they were food animals for one of the species. No. The reason you have the guns is to deal with the Horch machines. They are quite large. They have high-powered torches and cutting instruments, and their job is to destroy this whole base."

"So let them," Martin growled. "I vote with Dannerman. We stay here."

The little alien squealed in irritation. "But you cannot! You will die if we stay here."

Dannerman said soberly, "Maybe we should take that chance. We may be able to find something growing that we can eat so we won't starve—"

"Not starve!" Dopey said impatiently. "Fry. Here, ask your own astronomers, now that they have finished with this foolish ritual. You should understand the problem, Drs. Adcock. Have you not observed the stars?"

Patrice had a sinking feeling, but it was Pat who spoke up. "Are you talking about dangerous radiation, from black holes, supernovas, all that? But there hasn't been any, or we'd all be dead already."

"Of course there has not been any! That is because the Beloved Leaders long ago established a screen around this entire planet so that all lethal radiation was filtered out. But when the power went down, so did the screen."

That stopped them all. Dopey seized his advantage. "So you see," he said, "you have no other option. No. You must help me. I have given you weapons. I have also provided all these bearers, to carry the excess weaponry and whatever else we need for our task. And, of course, to help with Dr. Artzybachova," he added politely. "Now we must restore power and wipe out the remaining Horch surrogates before they finish destroying so much that took so long to build!"

Jimmy Lin emitted a sarcastic yelp. "What, the six of us? Against machines that defeated your own fighters?"

"But your numbers are not a problem," Dopey said in surprise. "Once the standby power is restored we can make many copies of you, all you need—a whole army if you want them, Commander Lin!"

Lin looked flustered, but Dannerman was the one who responded. "The hell you will! We've had enough of making copies!"

Dopey looked astonished. "You object to this? But why? We need not keep the extra copies forever; once the machines are gone we can simply delete the unwanted ones."

"No!" Pat cried.

Dopey stared at her. "Is this some taboo for your people? Well, perhaps we need not make more copies. It is possible that some of your experimental copies may still be alive."

And there was another conversation stopper. Dopey paused, surprised by the sudden silence as everyone was staring at him.

It was Patrice who asked the question, once more angry and startled—and very nearly fed up with Dopey's habit of dropping unexpected surprises on them. "What experimental copies are you talking about?"

Dopey looked uneasy. "Perhaps I neglected to tell you of them," he said apologetically. "There were only a few. Actually, I do not think many will have survived. There was quite heavy fighting in the laboratory area."

It was Rosaleen's turn to be indignant. *"Laboratory?"*

"To investigate your anatomy and biochemistry, of course. How else could the Beloved Leaders know how best to help your people?" And then, when he saw the expressions on their faces, "I was not personally involved in these studies," he added hastily. "Some of the copies may still be quite fit. Please do not argue anymore! Do you want me to take you to look for these other copies or not?"

CHAPTER THIRTY-SEVEN

Patrice

One thing you could say about Dan Dannerman—Patrice thought as they approached the stark metal structures of the compound—was that he reacted fast. Conquering the wilderness was out; rescuing their other "copies"—if any—was in.

Dopey would not allow them to enter near their old cell; too far to travel in Horch territory, too dangerous. So they traveled a quarter of the way around the compound perimeter before he paused and pointed to a passage. "There," he said. "This way will be safest—though we must be alert and ready for attack at every moment!"

Everyone stopped, while Dannerman conferred with the little creature. Patrice was glad enough for the chance to sit down. All this activity after all those weeks of confinement was tiring. She glanced up at the sky and shivered. That alien sun was setting; those enemy stars were popping out in all their incredible number, and the breeze had turned cold. She touched the butt of the thirty-shot weapon in its holster under her arm and wondered what it would be like to fire at something that would probably be doing its best to kill her. She was not ready for this kind of adventure—

But, ready or not, it was time to move on. Dannerman finished his conversation with Dopey and turned to give his orders. "Two of the Docs will go first. Then the rest of us, spread out, all but Rosaleen—"

"I can walk!" she protested.

"Sure. When you have to you will, but for now one of the

Docs will carry you at the back. And, everybody, *quiet*. Dopey says the Horch machines are not particularly sensitive to sound, but we'll take no chances. All clear? Then let's go."

Patrice shivered again. This time it was excitement, not cold. The last time she had taken part in an invasion of enemy territory she had been ten years old, playing Good Guys and Bad Guys with the Abwyth kids from next door. She was out of practice. She hadn't had a real gun in her hand then, either; probably wouldn't be holding one, ready for action, now, if it weren't for the fact that right in front of her Dan and Jimmy Lin had their guns out. So did Pat, by her side; for them it seemed to be deadly serious.

It didn't seem that way to Patrice. It seemed like just another children's game. Behind the two Docs in single file at the head of the procession and the five humans who were capable—well, more or less capable—of firing their guns were the other Docs. One carried their spare weapons. Then there was another Doc that carried Rosaleen in one of its assorted arms, and the last one carrying Dopey himself. It was a regular circus parade. And why were they in it? Because Dan Dannerman had said so, and what an exasperating man he was. First he warned them all against getting into other people's fights. Then he reversed himself without notice. Now he was—and all the others with him—suddenly a warrior on the side of the Beloved Leaders against the Horch. Patrice gazed darkly at the back of his neck. In a way, she didn't envy Pat for her lover; in some ways Dan was a most unsatisfactory man. Lovers were supposed to communicate. Not Dan Dannerman; you never knew what he was going to be doing next.

But in another way, of course, she envied Pat very much indeed.

She hoped the Doc who was striding ahead of them knew where he was going. Patrice didn't. Nothing looked familiar, except in the way that one patch of desolation looked pretty much like all the others. She had long since stopped wondering about the strange objects they were passing. There was one period, not long after they entered the compound, that she didn't like to think about. First there was a hint of something foul in the air. It became a definite stench—growing, then horribly intense, then gradually fading again—that could be nothing but dead things. She never quite saw the corpses, whatever species they were, but there was no doubt of what she was smelling, and no doubt that there had been a lot of killing somewhere nearby. But after that there was nothing but their slow march, and nothing happening. . . .

Then something did happen.

Between the time Patrice saw the first Doc suddenly turn and begin to run back, squeaking in a shrill soprano, and the time she saw the big silver-colored spidery thing appear from between the orange-colored crystal sphere and the jade pylons and they all began shooting at it, there was only a moment. It was time enough for her to be astonished that the Doc had spoken at all— before that she had never heard one of them make a sound— but then she saw that Dannerman had flung himself to the ground on one side of the corridor, his thirty-shot out and firing, and Jimmy Lin had done the same on the other, and she realized she had to follow their example. It all happened very fast. The Doc was able to run only a few steps before there was this sudden staccato sound, like shrill bees buzzing, *bzhit, bzhit, bzhit*. Patrice saw nothing that looked like either a projectile or a ray, but she saw the effects, all right, as at once the first Doc's head burst open—spray of orange-red blood and tissue flying out in all directions—and then the Horch machine was skating toward them, *fast*, on its spidery wheeled legs. The second Doc leaped forward to catch its fellow—too late—and there was more *bzhit, bzhit* and the whole right side of that one's body exploded, too. But by then everybody was shooting—even Patrice herself, startled at the unexpected recoil from the gun Dannerman had given her and her shots going wild, even Pat, next to her on the ground . . . even Martín Delasquez, standing wobbly but erect in the middle of the passage, but shooting his heavier gun with two hands. They didn't all miss. Pieces flew off the machine. Two of its legs collapsed and it clattered to the ground; a moment later something inside it flared and crackled and it lay still. And behind her, where he had hidden himself behind the massive trunk of the Doc that had been carrying him, Dopey was crying, "Stop firing! The machines do not respond quickly to sound, but it will attract them if you keep on shooting!"

In the sudden silence both Jimmy Lin and Dannerman jumped to their feet and ran to inspect the wrecked machine. Dannerman gave it only a glance, then turned back, leaving Jimmy to kick at the thing suspiciously; Dannerman ran straight to Patrice and dropped to his knees beside her. "Are you all right?" he demanded.

She rolled over to gaze up at him. "I'm fine," she said, "but I'm Patrice. That's your Pat"—who was already getting up and looking toward them—"over there."

The two Docs that had been given the point were both messily dead, but so was the Horch machine. Dopey was fretting. "I should not have used two of them to draw fire. I can only spare one now, but we must not delay. Have you all got loaded guns?"

Dannerman might or might not have been listening; his expression was unreadable. He was standing over the destroyed machine, his gun in one hand, the other arm around Pat's waist beside him. Patrice was standing nearby, somberly watching

them. She did, after all, wish it was she that Dannerman was
holding. It wasn't envy, exactly. She didn't feel any real jealousy
of Pat—she definitely wanted Pat to have someone to hold her,
too; she wanted nothing but good for Pat. But it would have
been better, she thought, if Dopey had produced an extra Dan
Dannerman or two along with the Pat Adcocks. She turned to
look at the others. Rosaleen and Martín were fussing over each
other, while Jimmy Lin checked the magazine of his gun, and
the three remaining Docs were standing quietly, waiting for orders. That was reassuring, a little bit. They had all got through
at least this first firefight—well, all but the two dead Docs.

Dannerman kicked at the dead machine, triangular body
now blazing quietly, the long legs crumpled. He turned chal-
lengingly to Dopey. "If they're that easy to kill, why couldn't
your people handle them?"

Dopey looked defensive. "Because there were so many of
them! They kept coming. Every time we thought we had them
cleaned up the Horch managed to capture another channel and
they sent more of them in and it was all to do over again—and,
finally, we had no fighters left to oppose them. Please, let us
move on; we are very exposed here."

Dannerman shook his head. "Tell me first, how many more
of those things are there?"

"How do I know? A few. Not very many, I think—but,
please—"

Dannerman disregarded the urging. He had another question:
"Are you sure you know where we're going?"

"Out of my own knowledge? No, of course not. How could
I? There is so much destruction, I cannot recognize anything.
But the bearers do, so please hurry."

Dannerman didn't answer right away. He stood there, with
his arm around Pat's waist; he was thinking about something,

but Patrice could not guess what. Whatever it was, he did not choose to share it.

Jimmy Lin was losing patience. "Are we going or not?" he demanded.

"Yes, sure," Dannerman said at last, then kissed Pat and took up his place in the procession as Dopey ordained it. With two Docs fewer to deploy, Dopey ordered the one with the weapons to take the point. Then came Dannerman and Jimmy, then Pat and Patrice and Martín; then the other Docs with their passengers, Rosaleen and Dopey himself.

Patrice's heart was still pounding from the excitement of the fight. She had seen shoot-outs on the television news, of course—just before they left there had been the one between the police and the subway terrorists, when the Lenni-Lenape Ghost Dance Revengers tried to blow up Grand Central Terminal, and there had been at least a dozen other battles over the years—but she had never expected to take part in a gunfight herself. She had never imagined someone (well, something) actually trying to kill her! And herself shooting back!

The funny thing was that she wasn't frightened. It had something to do with having a chance to do some shooting herself; it was certainly far better to be taking action, any kind of action, than just having things happen to her. She rehearsed every moment of the fight critically, looking for things she might have done wrong. She resolved to be ready for the weapon's recoil next time—if there was a next time. She wouldn't miss, she vowed . . .

And almost fired her gun in reflex when the lead Doc suddenly stopped, glanced around, then down at the ground.

Then it moved on a few more meters to an intersection and simply stood there, waiting.

Dannerman and Jimmy Lin were the first ones on the spot,

and they both recoiled. "Oh, Christ," Jimmy moaned. "Makes me want to puke!" It did Patrice, too, as soon as she saw what they were looking at. It was a corpse—not human, not a Dopey or a Doc—or, more accurately, it was about half of a corpse.

"It's a Bashful," Patrice said, recognizing it: one of the ones she and Patsy had seen before being brought to the cell.

"It looks like that other Dopey did, after we killed him," Lin said in disgust. Apparently the built-in waste-disposal system in the flooring had been in the process of disposing of this bit of waste when the power went off.

"Yes," said Dopey, climbing down from his bearer and puffing toward them, "it is one of our fighters, mercilessly murdered by the abominable Horch machines. And, see, he has his weapon with him."

"This thing?" Dannerman asked, picking up the shiny object that lay next to the corpse. He handled it cautiously, Jimmy Lin and Martín fidgeting as close to him as they could stand, both obviously yearning to get their own hands on the thing. Patrice had no such desire. She didn't want to touch it at all; it looked deadly. Clearly it was not designed for a human being. It didn't have a stock; it had a belly plate of some dark red substance that looked rubbery; it didn't have a trigger, but a pair of metal loops, like the finger holes on a pair of scissors. And it didn't have sights.

When Jimmy Lin pointed that out Dopey said impatiently, "Sights? Why would it have sights? Such things are not necessary. When it is aimed there is a beam of green radiation, like a pocket torch—"

"You mean a flashlight?"

"Yes, are they not the same thing? That green ray is not the particle flux itself, only a beam of light to help you guide it, but what you touch with the beam of light will be destroyed by the particle flux. To fire it? Nothing is easier. You put your fingers in those loops and draw them together; the closer they are drawn, the more energy the particle beam carries."

"Like this?" Jimmy Lin asked, experimenting.

Dopey closed his eyes in silent despair. "Yes, exactly like that," he said, obviously restraining himself, "and if there had been any power for the weapon you would have killed Dr. Artzybachova. Please, all of you! I know you are not experienced with this weapon, but you must take care!"

To Patsy's surprise, Dannerman had another of those off-the-main-point questions. "So why are you bothering with us amateurs? Why don't you make more of your trained fighters?"

Dopey looked evasive. "Yes, that would be better in some ways, perhaps," he agreed. "But—"

"But you can't do it, right?"

Dopey hesitated for a moment. "That is true," he said at last. "At this moment. Once we have restored the power—once we have access to the damaged terminals—then it is quite possible that we could do so. But please, let us not waste time—"

Dannerman held his ground. "That's the other thing. So we get the power on, and we kill the rest of the Horch machines for you—"

"For all of us, Agent Dannerman! Your lives are also at risk!"

"Whatever you say. Then what?"

"Why, then we attempt to restore the damaged terminals. If we cannot, we simply wait for the Beloved Leaders to restore communication. Is that not obvious? Now I must insist—"

"Which will be when?"

"Oh, Agent Dannerman, why do you choose this time to ask foolish questions? It will happen when it happens. First the Beloved Leaders must send another physical spacecraft with a new tachyon terminal dedicated to the proper channel. How long will that take to get here? I do not know how long. Since such a spacecraft cannot exceed the speed of light, perhaps very long. But, you see," he added reasonably, "the length of time does not matter. If we grow too old to be serviceable we will simply generate new copies of ourselves to replace us. That will be no problem."

"No problem?" Dannerman repeated, mildly enough.

"Not at all. And we can repeat it as often as necessary. In that way we can continue to carry on our duties here for centuries if that is necessary. Now no more questions! We must go!"

CHAPTER THIRTY-EIGHT

Patrice

Until, without warning, the lead Doc stopped short and stood motionless, waiting for the rest to catch up, Patrice hardly noticed where they were going. She could not get what Dopey had said out of her mind. *For centuries, if that is necessary.* But centuries of what? Of carrying out Dopey's plan? Growing old, in this miserable place? Never going home again? Manufacturing a new Pat Adcock and a new Dopey and a new everybody else when the present ones were too old or too enfeebled to carry on? And then what? Then quietly allowing themselves to die, with the next generation in place . . . and the next . . . and the next. . . .

Whatever joy that prospect might have for Dopey, it had none for Patrice. On the other hand—

On the other hand, she told herself, to test out the implications of it all, those replacements would likely include an allotment of new Dan Dannermans, so that there might be enough of him for Patrice to have one of her own. But then what? Make some more Pat Adcocks, too, so that Martín and Jimmy Lin might have mates as well? (And how would those new Pat Adcocks feel about that?) And what did you say to the new arrival, blinking and confused as he stepped out of the machine: "Hi, I'm Patrice, and we've copied you so that I can get laid now and then. Unfortunately there's not much else to do around here. But welcome."

The thought was comical enough to make Patrice laugh out loud. It wasn't a happy laugh, and it made Pat turn and frown at her. But none of the others heard, because Dopey was pounding his little fists on a machine that looked like a huge, green-enameled refrigerator and shrieking joyously, "That's it! That's the terminal."

Patrice looked around, bewildered. Everybody else seemed excited about it; even Rosaleen and Martín, supporting each other, tottered over to touch the thing, and Pat and Dannerman were hugging each other. "I've been here before," she whispered, so softly that no one heard. But it was true. It had been a different place then, everything working and intact, but it was where she and Patsy had first discovered themselves in this place.

It was different now, and what struck Patrice was the pervasive odor that hung in the air. It was the same decaying-meat stink she had smelled before. There definitely had been fighting around here, she thought. The terminal was intact, and so was everything on that side of the little square they were in. But on the other side ruined machinery and long-dead ashes showed that somebody had been doing something violent not long before. Dannerman turned to Dopey. "You said you were going to bring us to the experimental copies!" he said accusingly.

Dopey looked away from the Doc he was talking to. "The copies? Yes. Their space was quite near here. I do not see them, so perhaps—". He shrugged and returned to the Doc, which silently listened, then moved away.

Dannerman advanced on the alien, his gun in his hand, his expression dangerous. "If there are any human beings here we want to see them. Now!"

Dopey looked up at him, the kitten whiskers trembling, the plume draggled. "Certainly you can look around, Agent Dannerman. If any survive I do not think they would have gone far; this is where their food was kept. But please, remain on guard! The Horch machines were careful not to destroy this terminal,

so it is quite likely one or more will be somewhere near this area
to watch over it. And—"

He stopped, gazing toward the second Doc. Which had
abruptly moved swiftly toward the wreckage and begun to pull
away one of the metal plates. There was movement behind it.
At once everybody turned, guns ready—

A face peered out of the space behind the plate. It was looking directly at Patrice. And, "Oh, God," said yet another Dr.
Patrice Adcock, "you're more of *me*!"

CHAPTER THIRTY-NINE

Patrice

It all evened out in the long run, Patrice thought to herself—wondering if she were going out of her mind: You lose one Pat, you get another to fill the gap. This particular Pat, though, was something special; she had clearly been through hell, even more hell than the rest of them. Her face was haggard, her bearing twitchy. Patrice longed to comfort her.

But reunions had to wait. Dopey had no particular interest in one Pat more or less—his main concern was dispatching one of the Docs to find the standby generator and start it up—and the only interest the new Pat showed in Dopey and his Docs was to stay as far away from them as she could. "First things first," Dannerman ordered. "I want somebody with a gun at every entrance in case one of those things shows up."

Nobody argued, though Patrice would have preferred to fuss over the new Pat, as Rosaleen alone could be spared to do, instead of standing guard, weapon out and ready, where she could see a few dozen meters down a passage. She wasn't doing a very good job of guarding. She couldn't help peering worriedly over her shoulder at the new Pat Adcock. The woman looked really terrible. Extreme fatigue, yes; that figured. Marks of pain and stress on her face, why not? She'd obviously been through a tough time; but there was something else that was nagging at Patrice while her new copy was doing her best to answer questions. And there were lots of questions. "Are there any others?" "Not anymore." "Do you mean the others are dead?" "Christ, yes! Can't you smell them? But listen, do you guys have anything to eat?"

Well, they didn't; Dopey had promised there would be all the food they wanted, once the terminal was working again, so why encumber themselves? (But Pat had observed he'd taken food for himself; probably that didn't count as an encumbrance.) He was fidgeting about, doing his best to ignore the petty human concerns. "Please," he begged in agitation. "It will be some time before the bearer can have the power on line, perhaps as much as an hour. Then all will be well, but now we are still in great danger. Be vigilant! We must not be stopped now, when we are so close— What?" Dannerman was saying something to him, pointing to the new Pat. "Oh, very well," Dopey said impatiently, and glanced at the two remaining Docs. Who at once moved toward the new Pat. . . .

Who shrieked "Keep them away from me!" and turned as though about to run, but Dannerman stopped her.

"It's all right," he soothed. "Honest! I just want you checked over. This one's done it for us before, with Martín and Rosaleen. He's a kind of medical specialist—"

"I know what kind of specialists they are!" But by then the one Doc had her firmly held and the other was gently tapping and probing with its smaller arms, just as they had done with Martín Delasquez. The new Pat whimpered softly throughout the examination, but she didn't resist. The procedure took only a few moments. Then the Docs released her and stepped back, once again motionless in that corpselike standby mode.

"This transcription appears to be well enough," Dopey announced. "There is a certain amount of malnutrition, yes, but that will be mended when we have the terminal going. Otherwise her condition is normal, apart from some exhaustion—allowing, of course, for the fact that she is pregnant."

One conversation stopper after another, Patrice thought; the creature was full of them. She backed away from her sentry post—not so far that she couldn't still see down the short corridor, far enough so that she could look their new recruit in the face. "Are you, uh, all right?" she asked.

The woman stared at her, backing away from Dopey and the Docs. "*He* says so," she said shortly. And then, "Well, I guess I am. More or less." She was looking from Pat to Patrice; it seemed a time for introductions.

"I'm Patrice; this is Pat. There was another one—well," Patrice said, firmly closing that topic, "there was another one, but she died. What should we call you?"

The newcomer opened her eyes wide at that, but she answered civilly enough. "The others just called me Pat, mostly, because there was usually only one of us alive at a time. But Rosaleen said I was Pat Five, if that helps."

Dannerman swore. "Pat *Five?* They had that many of you?"

"They had at least that many of me," she corrected. "I don't guarantee the count. But you can call me Five if you want to. What's happening?" And when they had done their best to fill her in she scowled at the Dopey. "You mean the best we can hope for is to stay alive with the bird and the brutes in this wreckage—forever?"

The Dopey craned his neck to peer at her over his plume. "Wreckage? But it will not remain wreckage, Dr. Adcock Five. Once the Horch problem is eliminated we will build it all up again, better than ever, you will see. That will be a job for the bearers, that is what they are good at."

"They seem to be pretty handy gadgets to have around," Dannerman remarked, causing Patrice to give him a sharp look.

What was the matter with the man? Was he losing his mind . . . or thinking about something he didn't want to discuss? She wondered which.

"Oh, yes, highly intelligent," Dopey was agreeing. "Unfortunately their people foolishly declined to cooperate with the Beloved Leaders. They resisted quite violently, in fact. Ultimately it was necessary to dispatch most of their race directly to the eschaton. These specimens have been preserved; they are quite tractable now, since they were amended to remove their violent natures. Of course, they are no longer capable of acting on their own very much, but they are very good at following orders." Dopey's mind didn't seem to be on what he was saying; he was twisting in all directions to peer down the various approaches. "You've all got your weapons ready? We could be attacked at any time."

Patrice exhaled softly. *Amended,* she repeated to herself. *Quite tractable.*

She looked around at the others to see if they were thinking what she was. She couldn't tell. Dannerman had gone off to talk to Martín and Rosaleen, the others simply looked grim. Whether it was because, like herself, they were considering the possibility that the Beloved Leaders might have some similar plans for the human race she did not know.

"Damn," Pat said ruefully. "You know, I was almost getting to like the little shit."

Pat Five looked at her curiously. "For God's sake, why?"

Lamely, "Well . . . he brought us food. And other things. We would have starved without him."

Pat Five said in disgust, "Oh, Pat, what's the matter with you? You don't really understand what kind of people they are, do you? Tell me something. When you see the supermarket fish clerk checking the pumps in the lobster tank, do you think she does it because she wants the lobsters to be happy?" She glared at Pat, then abruptly added, "Why didn't you ever ask me how I got pregnant?"

Uncomfortably, "I did wonder, I mean about the implants."

"Right, the implants," said Pat Five, nodding. "The implants made a real problem for the damn birds. When they found out about them they just took the things right out, and, honey, that was not fun. Not for me, even though I was the lucky one; I survived the operation. Dan Three told me that the first two of us they tried didn't. Of course, they didn't bother with anesthesia. . . . And then they killed Dan, too. I think it was something about studying how the human body reacted to pain; he was screaming so loud I bet he could be heard all over the compound."

Patrice shuddered, but there was something else she wanted to know. As delicately as possible, she began, "Who was the—ah—the—?"

"The father?" Pat Five shrugged morosely. "Rosaleen thought it was Jimmy, one of the Jimmys, but I don't know. I'm not sure I ever met the gent." She glanced casually at the surviving Jimmy, who was standing suddenly thunderstruck. "All I know for sure is they had sperm they'd collected—I don't know whose—and so they did it to me by artificial insemination, you see. Looked like they just didn't want us to have any fun at all."

"Hey!" said Jimmy Lin, finding his voice at last. "I mean—hey!"

Pat Five scowled at him. "What are you getting excited about? I'm not going to ask for child support."

"It isn't that," he protested. "I just—you know—I mean, I feel sort of responsible if it was my, uh, sperm—"

Pat Five looked at him thoughtfully, then softened. "Well, don't worry about it. Listen, I think being pregnant had its advantage. I'm pretty sure that's why they kept me alive when the Horch started shooting and the birds terminated all the others.

They'd gone to a lot of trouble to knock me up; I guess they didn't want to waste all that work." She glanced at Dopey, nervously making his rounds of the guard posts. "There were two of those goddam birds arguing about it in the examining room," she said, nodding toward the shattered partitions at the far end of their space, "while a couple of the goons held me down. I was sure I'd had it. But then the birds walked off and the goons just dropped me and went away. And I've been here alone ever since."

Patrice couldn't stand still another minute. Pat Five's tale of horrors was more than she could handle. She moved toward the broken partitions. "Over here?" she asked. "Is that where they were doing it?"

"Don't go wandering away from your post!" Jimmy Lin ordered, and Pat Five chimed in:

"I wouldn't go there at all if I were you—"

But that came too late. Patrice had reached the partitions and peered through them. She couldn't see clearly in the minimal light that filtered in from outside, but that, Patrice thought, the contents of her stomach trying to rise up through her throat, was a good thing. There were bodies there. A Dannerman. A Jimmy Lin. Another of those half-absorbed corpses, caught incompletely flushed away when the power died, that was facedown but, she thought, probably had been another Jimmy Lin. The stench of decay was awful. She retreated to the others, holding her hand over her face.

Pat Five laughed—not unkindly. "I warned you," she said. "I've been living with that for days. The birds said it was all right, you know; they just sent them on early to the eschaton."

"So they told you about the eschaton?" Pat asked.

"That Tipler business, sure. They were asking a lot of questions about it just before they terminated the guys— Is something the matter?"

Pat and Patrice were exchanging glances. "You remembered the name!" Pat cried.

"Of course I remembered the name. Frank Tipler. Tulane University. He wrote a book. I also remembered that old what's-his-face told us it was a lot of crap, since the Hubble Constant showed that the universe wasn't ever going to collapse again anyway."

"I've been wondering about that myself," Patrice said, and Pat put in:

"Dan says it doesn't matter if it's true. What matters is that the Horch and the Beloved Leaders act as if they believe it's true, and—"

She stopped there, blinking; they were all blinking, as suddenly the lights were on. And from across the space Dopey chortled: "We have the power! Now we can serve the Beloved Leaders again!"

CHAPTER FORTY

Patrice

The return of the lighting made things clearer but didn't make them better; the place was still a ruin. An eye-hurting flicker told Patrice that, in spite of damage, just beside her one of those magic mirror walls was trying to reconstitute itself near the "examining room": bright mirror surface leaping from floor to ceiling, then crackling and turning dark again, over and over. "Stand back, Patrice!" Rosaleen warned urgently, but there was no danger there; Patrice was already hastily backing away. At the tachyon terminal Dopey was babbling in excitement as a Doc was doing something to its controls. Patrice couldn't see what, exactly, but she couldn't even see the controls, for that matter. Whatever they were, they were invisible to her. But Dopey was in ecstasy—delight, certainly; fear, too. "This is our most dangerous time," he called, then, joyously: "See, here are some weapons! Take them! Be ready! The machines will surely detect this energy, and they—oh, hurry!" But he was talking to the Doc again, not to the humans, who were quick to seize the trombonelike things as the Doc lifted them out of the cavernous interior of the terminal, then closed the door for the next batch.

"What about our food?" Jimmy Lin demanded, hefting the weapon.

Dopey looked at him distractedly. "Please be careful with that, now there is power! Food? Of course we'll get food from your Starlab, as soon as we are prepared to deal with the Horch machines. First the weapons, then a few more fighters. I believe we should make more copies of you, Agent Dannerman, since it is

probable that there will be some losses. Also General Delasquez
and Commander Lin; I think it is best to copy the males first,
don't you? Since, as I understand it, all of you males have had
some weapons training, while the females have not. Or not very
much. But of course," he added hastily, turning away to urge
the Doc to greater speed, "if you wish we will copy more females
as well, as soon as we have finished destroying the Horch machines—"

"Shut up," Dannerman said, pointing one of the weapons at
Dopey. Who goggled at him uncomprehendingly.

"But I have asked you, Agent Dannerman, to be very careful
with that weapon! It could easily accidentally go off—"

"Not accidentally," Dannerman said.

Patrice had never seen the alien look so bewildered. He stared,
his plume agitatedly flickering, then turned to the nearest armed
human, which happened to be Martín Delasquez. "I order you
to shoot him," he said.

Martín glanced quizzically at Dannerman, then shifted his
weapon as well to cover Dopey. "No," he said. "Do what Dannerman says."

Dopey was wringing his little hands again. "But what— But
the Horch machines—"

Dannerman said, "It's simple. If you can get things from
Starlab, you can send things to Starlab. Like us."

"That is true, yes," Dopey said, uncomprehending but reasonable. "However—"

"So do it. Tell that thing to transmit us, right away."

"No, no!" Dopey cried in panic. "We must fight them here!
The Beloved Leaders would wish that!"

Rosaleen had been listening intently; now she took a hand.
"Dopey," she said soothingly, "you just haven't thought it
through. If we fight the machines here we might lose, don't you
see? What Dan means, if we go to Starlab we'll be safe. There's

only one terminal there; we can guard it day and night, until your Beloved Leaders get around to reestablishing the communication channel there. That's what you had in mind, isn't it, Dan? Wouldn't that work?"

Dannerman didn't bother to answer. Dopey looked bewildered. Then, pettishly, he said, "Yes, I suppose so, perhaps. But I absolutely forbid it. I—"

Dannerman put his fingers in the loops of the weapon. "Don't forbid," he said, the gun squarely pointing at Dopey. "You'll do it our way or you'll have failed your assignment because you're dead . . . and then what will you tell your bosses when your eschaton comes around?"

It wasn't that easy. Dopey hadn't stopped arguing. In fact, he never did stop his frantic arguing— or pleading—even after he had given in and allowed the Doc to start the transmissions. Dannerman had to singe a corner of the alien's plume with the weapon before he would go that far.

But it was happening.

They were going home! Patrice stared in wonder and unbelief as the first batch entered the chamber—Rosaleen and the two other Pats—and the door closed behind them. To take them *home*! Which meant that in a moment Patrice herself could go home! She could hardly believe it, could not take in the sudden change in her outlook—first a dreary and interminable existence in the ruins, then, in the blink of an eye, the sudden prospect of return to Starlab—to *Earth*—to her *life*! And it was all *happening*! The terminal door opened again and it was empty. "Now you!" Dannerman ordered, pointing to Jimmy Lin. "And take Dopey with you, but keep an eye on—"

He stopped, listening. Dopey squealed in terror, and then Patrice heard it, too: a heavy, rapid thudding, and the distant buzzing sound like a hive of bees. The Doc that had started the generator was running ponderously toward them—

And behind it, rapidly catching up, one of the spider-legged machines.

This time Patrice was ready. She had her gun in both hands, aiming it carefully. Whether she hit the thing or not she couldn't tell—both Martín and Jimmy Lin were firing at the same time, and she saw the pale beam from Dannerman's Beloved Leaders weapon wavering toward the thing as well. Someone did. The machine spun around crazily and burst into flame, just as the other had.

Dannerman didn't wait. "Do it, Lin!" he ordered. "You too, Dopey; there'll be more."

But Dopey was complaining, wringing his little hands. "I cannot function without the bearers!"

"Then take them, damn it! All but the one running the transmitter!" And as the alien started to object, simply picked him up and threw him inside. The two Docs followed stolidly, making a tight fit; but then the door closed and they were gone. As the door opened again, Dannerman looked around and saw Patrice standing there. "Now you," he ordered. "Martín, too. I'll hold them off—"

Patrice obeyed. . . .

But not Martín. He grunted, "Who elected you hero?" . . . and shoved Dannerman bodily inside, as the door closed.

All Patrice saw was a pale lavender flash that went right through her closed eyelids, and a sickening jolt. And then the door opened and they all fell in a heap out into the weightlessness of Starlab. "That son of a bitch Martín," Dannerman groaned. "We'll wait. Maybe he'll make it. . . ."

They did wait. For long minutes. But Martín didn't come.

CHAPTER FORTY-ONE

Patrice

Never had the stale air of Starlab smelled so much like home. Never had the queasiness of microgravity felt so dear. Patrice couldn't stop grinning—nor either of the other Pats, nor Jimmy Lin, nor even Rosaleen, arms crossed over her belly to hold in some unannounced pain. Only Dopey and Dannerman seemed immune. Dopey, held in the arms of one of the Docs, was babbling: "Please, you must keep a weapon drawn and pointed at the terminal, in case one of the Horch machines follows. Why are you not listening to me? But it is *urgent*!"

And, though Dannerman had his gun in his hand—his own gun, not one of the now useless energy weapons—he was indeed not listening. He was looking around the Starlab corridor as though trying to get his bearings. "Jimmy," he snapped. "Do you think you can find the astronaut return capsule? Go check it out. I want to know if it's still workable . . . and if you think you can fly it."

"Sure," Lin said, "if that's what you want. But wouldn't it be easier to radio for a rescue ship?"

"Do you want to hang around here? Just do it. Go." And as Lin went off Dopey was frantically demanding to know what was happening.

"But you can't just leave the terminal unguarded, Agent Dannerman! Have you not heard me? If one of those machines follows—"

"It won't," Dannerman said grimly. "Stand back." He took aim at the closed door of the terminal and fired the whole clip.

"Now, that was foolish of you, Dan," Rosaleen said gravely. "How did you know they wouldn't ricochet around and kill us all?"

"I didn't," Dannerman admitted. "I guess I didn't think. But it looks like it worked." The high-speed loads had gone right through the door, and from inside there was a crackling and a smell of something electrical burning. "But let's make sure," he said. "Where's that bar you conked Jimmy with?"

Dopey gazed in horror as Dannerman methodically began to smash at the portal. "No!" he screamed over the crash of metal. "You mustn't! We'll be cut off from the Beloved Leaders until they send another drone, perhaps for many, many years!"

"So I hope," Dannerman agreed. "In fact I'm counting on it. The longer the better. If it's long enough, just maybe—the next time you guys come around to visit us—we'll know how to handle you."

AFTER

Later . . . much later, and a very long distance away . . .

Dan Dannerman saw the pale lavender flash; the door of the tachyon terminal opened and he leaped triumphantly out, eager to join the others in the safety of Starlab.

Startlingly, the others weren't there.

Still more startlingly, he wasn't even in Starlab. He was in a place he'd never seen. A pair of the wheel-footed Horch machines were standing there, but they weren't shooting at him. Nor could he have fired back if they had; he had no gun in his hand. Behind him he heard the door cycle shut behind him, then open again. The disheveled figure of Dopey spilled out, catapulting into him. The little creature glared at him. Then, as he saw the quietly buzzing machines observing them, Dopey's plume turned woeful gray and he began to sob.

"What's happened?" Dannerman demanded. And, clutching at straws, "Did we die? Is this your damn eschaton?"

Dopey stared at him mournfully: "Eschaton? Oh, you are a great fool, Agent Dannerman! Of course we have not yet reached the eschaton. We simply have been copied once more . . . and now we are in the hands of the Horch."

AUTHOR'S NOTE

One of the questions that confront a science-fiction reader is to decide how much of the "science" in a story is real—i.e., is at the time of writing consensually agreed by a significant number of actual scientists—and how much is made up by the author. I don't personally make up much in my writing. I do, however, quite often make use of scientific ideas that have been put forth by some actual scientist but fall a long way short of being consensual. For example, I did not make up the faster-than-light "tachyons" I have used in this story (and in others) in order to provide a mechanism for getting my characters around this very large universe in reasonable travel times. They were originally proposed by Dr. Gerry Feinberg and others thirty or more years ago. Tachyons may or may not exist. There is no direct evidence that they do. Feinberg was able to show that they are not excluded by relativity theory; but they have never been detected. So the question remains open for scientists—but, in my view, such concepts are perfectly legitimate for writers like myself to borrow.

Which, I think, is also true of the concept which provides the central thesis of this story, the "Omega Point" or eschaton at which every person who has ever lived will, it is said, live again, and then go on doing so forever.

Much of what I know about the stranger scientific ideas that are floating around comes from the kindness of friends, who know what sort of thing interests me and are often good enough to send me copies of obscure papers from unlikely sources. The stimulus which led to the present story came from a paper by Dr. Frank Tipler, sent to me some years ago by Dr. Hans Moravec of the Robotics Institute at Carnegie-Mellon University. Tipler's paper, originally published in a journal devoted to religious questions, was quite tentative in tone. However, it appears that, having started thinking on the subject, Tipler began to feel that he was onto something really important. So in 1994 he published a book, *The Physics of Immortality*, expanding on the original notion and buttressing it with what he says are formal, scientific proofs that it is true. There are some differences between the arguments in the original paper and those in the book, however, and I should mention that in this novel I have preferred to follow those of the original paper.

Tipler's claimed scientific proofs take the form of quite abstruse arguments that are dense with equations and occupy 223 pages in his book. I am not qualified to pass judgment on the accuracy of his science, and the reviews of the book that I have seen in various scientific publications have been, to put it as impartially as possible, pretty uniformly unconvinced. Still, Tipler is a heavyweight scientist in his own right, and we all know that the history of science is full of pioneers who were at first scorned—but were ultimately shown to be correct.

So the question remains: Are we indeed all going to be reborn at some remote time eons in the future?

I don't know. If I had to bet, I must confess that I would be inclined to bet quite heavily against it . . . but it is certainly pretty to think so.

FREDERIK POHL

Palatine, Illinois
March 1995

TOR
BOOKS The Best in Science Fiction

MOTHER OF STORMS • John Barnes
From one of the hottest new names in SF: a shattering epic of global catastrophe, virtual reality, and human courage, in the manner of *Lucifer's Hammer*, *Neuromancer*, and *The Forge of God*.

BEYOND THE GATE • Dave Wolverton
The insectoid dronons threaten to enslave the human race in the sequel to *The Golden Queen*.

TROUBLE AND HER FRIENDS • Melissa Scott
Lambda Award-winning cyberpunk SF adventure that the *Philadelphia Inquirer* called "provocative, well-written and thoroughly entertaining."

THE GATHERING FLAME • Debra Doyle and James D. Macdonald
The Domina of Entibor obeys no law save her own.

WILDLIFE • James Patrick Kelly
"A brilliant evocation of future possibilities that establishes Kelly as a leading shaper of the genre."—*Booklist*

THE VOICES OF HEAVEN • Frederik Pohl
"A solid and engaging read from one of the genre's surest hands."—*Kirkus Reviews*

MOVING MARS • Greg Bear
The Nebula Award-winning novel of war between Earth and its colonists on Mars.

NEPTUNE CROSSING • Jeffrey A. Carver
"A roaring, cross-the-solar-system adventure of the first water."—*Jack McDevitt*

TOR
BOOKS The Best in Science Fiction

LIEGE-KILLER • Christopher Hinz
"*Liege-Killer* is a genuine page-turner, beautifully written and exciting from start to finish....Don't miss it."—*Locus*

HARVEST OF STARS • Poul Anderson
"A true masterpiece. An important work—not just of science fiction but of contemporary literature. Visionary and beautifully written, elegaic and transcendent, *Harvest of Stars* is the brightest star in Poul Anderson's constellation."
—Keith Ferrell, editor, *Omni*

FIREDANCE • Steven Barnes
SF adventure in 21st century California—by the co-author of *Beowulf's Children*.

ASH OCK • Christopher Hinz
"A well-handled science fiction thriller."—*Kirkus Reviews*

CALDÉ OF THE LONG SUN • Gene Wolfe
The third volume in the critically-acclaimed Book of the Long Sun.
"Dazzling."—*The New York Times*

OF TANGIBLE GHOSTS • L.E. Modesitt, Jr.
Ingenious alternate universe SF from the author of the *Recluce* fantasy series.

THE SHATTERED SPHERE • Roger MacBride Allen
The second book of the Hunted Earth continues the thrilling story that began in *The Ring of Charon*, a daringly original hard science fiction novel.

THE PRICE OF THE STARS • Debra Doyle and James D. Macdonald
Book One of the Mageworlds—the breakneck SF epic of the most brawling family in the human galaxy!